SAVING

FRIAR LAURENCE

LOVE, DEATH, AND REDEMPTION IN THE TWENTY-FIRST CENTURY

A SHAKESPEAREAN NOVEL

ARTHUR LaFRANCE

COPYRIGHT AND DISCLAIMER

BOOKS AND MAJOR ARTICLES
BY ARTHUR B. LAFRANCE

BOOKS

Law of the Poor, West Publishing, 1973

Welfare Law: Structure and Entitlement, West Publishing, 1979

Criminal Procedure: Trial and Sentencing, Anderson Publishing,1994

Bioethics: Healthcare, Human Rights and The Law, LexisNexis, 2006

ARTICLES

Federal Litigation for the Poor, Arizona State Law Journal, 1972

Criminal Defense Systems for the Poor, Notre Dame Law Review, 1974

Civil Commitment: The Judicial Role, Journal of Law and Psychiatry, 1998

Child Custody and Relocation: A Constitutional Perspective, Journal of Family Law, 1996

Healthcare Reform in The United States: The Role of The States, Seattle Journal of Social Justice, 2007

Animal Experimentation, Animal Law Review, 2008

DEDICATION

FATHER VALERIAN LAFRANCE, O.P.

Saving Friar Laurence is written with due attention to Friar Laurence's talents and failings, both great and deplorable, as reflected in Shakespeare's *Romeo and Juliet*. Throughout, the author envisioned the huge intellectual, spiritual and physical presence, as well as the warmth of personality, of his uncle, Father Valerian LaFrance, O.P., as providing the framework for the figure of Friar Laurence in this book. Both he and Friar Laurence are distinctive individuals, and over time I have come to love each. The careers of both are distinguished and, in the end, of great benefit to humanity. For that, I dedicate this book to them.

"I have fond memories of your uncle. He was such an interesting character, and I will always remember him. You have my permission to publish the drawing, as my gift."

Ken Fallin, New York, NY

PREFACE

Central to *Saving Friar Laurence* is a Faustian bargain, trading Friar Laurence's soul for immortality ...

Doctor Faustus, Christopher Marlowe (1593)
My heart so hardened I cannot repent,
scarce can I name salvation, faith or heaven,
but fearful echoes thunders in my ears:
"Faustus, thou art damned!"
Scene 7, line 20

Was this the face that launched 1000 ships
And burnt the topless towers of ileum?
Sweet Helen, make me immortal with a kiss.
Her lips suck forth my soul. See where it flies!
Scene 13, line 90

Ah, my God, I would weep, but the devil draws in my tears.
Gush forth blood instead of tears, yea, life and soul.
Oh, he stays my time!
I would lift up my hands, but see, they hold them, they hold them.
Scene 14, line 28

Faust (Part II), Johan Wolfgang von Goethe (1830)
Horrible phantoms! Thus, you still conspire ...
Demons, I know, are hard to exorcise,
the spirit-bond is loathe to separate:
but though the creeping power of care be great,
this power I will never recognize!
Scene 20, line 11487

He who strives on and lives to strive

can earn redemption still,

and now that love itself looks down ...

is welcome to this place.

Scene 23, line 11936

Merchant of Venice, William Shakespeare (1596)

The quality of mercy is not strained:

It blesseth him that gives and him that takes ...

It is enthroned in the hearts of kings,

it is an attribute to God himself ...

Therefore, Jew,

tho justice be thy plea, consider this:

that in the course of justice none of us

should see salvation. We do pray for mercy,

and that same prayer doth teach us all to render

the deeds of mercy.

Act 4, scene 1, line 180

TABLE OF CONTENTS

INTRODUCTION

In the last decade of the 1500s, William Shakespeare wrote his great romance, the play *Romeo and Juliet*, but he styled it a tragedie because of the multiple deaths, including the two teenage lovers themselves, caused by the character Friar Laurence. At the very end, the Prince promised some would be pardoned, and some would be punished. Yet, for over 400 years, Friar Laurence was neither pardoned nor punished but condemned to repeat his crimes every time the play is performed. His victims' pain is his pain as well, a world without end.

Saving Friar Laurence is the story of how Friar Laurence became entrapped in this endless cycle of wrongdoing and how he then fought to escape. It is the account of how in the 21st-century an opportunity to end the killing and to do penance arose and of how good people—a young public defender, an ancient Abbott, a loving pediatric nurse, a brilliant drama professor—strive to help Friar Laurence to defeat the evil forces which entrapped him centuries ago. Those forces—an evil prosecutor and Chief Justice, a crazed Aryan supremacist—gather to protect the ancient bargain and bar Friar Laurence from redemption. In the climactic scenes, these forces clash in violent hatred.

As in all Shakespearean drama, some will live, and some will die, there will be romance and heartbreak. Action moves from courts to theater stage, and there is drama enough in both. Along the way, both settings, with all of their flaws, are accurately portrayed, and we meet memorable characters: the magical Dominican Abbot, workaday prosecutors Jack Riley, Slo Mo Levy, Kathleen Chung, the Dragon Lady. Equally memorable from the defense team, D Data, the doughnut-addicted IT computer whiz, and Ron Hoffer, the Nazi defense investigator. Most memorable are Jo, the gifted public defender secretary/paralegal, and Dorothy Arlow, and the love she shares with Friar Laurence.

And, of course, there is the man himself, traveling from the 1400s in Verona, through the 1600s in London, to 2019 in New Haven Connecticut. In itself an Odyssey of epic proportions.

But as is often the case with Shakespeare, the story begins in a modest place, in a routine conversation between Francis Collins, a public defender in New Haven, Connecticut, and the narrator of this tale, and his paralegal and secretary, Jo. It is the end of a long week, late Friday, and Collins simply wants to get to the neighborhood pub for a well-deserved, hard-earned beer, with the other defense attorneys and prosecutors. To drink as lawyers do ...

But Jo bars his way, for there is one last client to be seen this late Friday afternoon ...

CHAPTER ONE
ATTORNEY COLLINS
MEETS FRIAR LAURENCE

It is Friday afternoon, around 5:00, and I am seriously thirsty. Mid-May, but uncommonly warm in Connecticut. The sun is beating in through the grime on my third floor, hundred-year-old City Hall window, facing the New Haven Green, heating the back of my neck. I face the door of my law office and call out to Jo.

"Raise the drawbridge, I'm going into the Village to drink the women and waste the booze, or perhaps vicey versy."

I begin my move to the door, onto the roof, down the fire escape, across the streets below, to the tables down at Morrie's ... no, not the one they sing about, the other one, where we defenders meet prosecutors and drink as lawyers should, as Shakespeare said, into the weekend, oblivion and beyond.

"Not so fast, you silver-tongued devil, there is yet one more client to see before you tilt froth, so to speak," replies my trusty secretary, paralegal, and partner in defending crime, Jo.

And we might as well get this out of the way immediately: she is bright, beautiful, a classy dresser and terrific law person, with endless legs, who made it clear when interviewed that she would not sleep with me, ever, a proposition I never propositioned because, well, first, she is really, really good at managing me and my practice, and secondly, if you are counting, her husband is really, really, really big. A former lineman on the Calvin Hill nationally ranked football team at Yale. Not that that matters, I being married to Meg, MD, researcher at Yale New Haven Hospital, who has told me she is capable of surgery which, in case I fooled around, would assure it did not become a habit.

Okay. Here it comes, you were waiting for this, so I say it—

"Say it ain't so, Jo," which I have said a million times, and add, "It is risky business to stand between a man and his brew."

To which she replies—

"I really, truly think you are going to want to wait around for this client, I really, really do," as she steps into my office from the corridor, all the walls being Home Depot plywood panel partitions subdividing the abandoned third floor of the abandoned wing of the City Hall, which itself should have been abandoned long, long ago, into flimsy cubicles. Mine at least has a genuine wall, with a nonfunctioning fireplace. I know. I tried it. The malfunctioning part. Big mistake. Story for another time ... back to beer.

I look at my calendar on my computer and cell phone and see no appointment, no name, nothing, nada.

"A walk-in, right? Not in custody, right? Police aren't pounding up the stairs in hot pursuit, right? Not rounding up the usual suspects?" And before Jo can say, "right" or worse yet "wrong," I continue, "I hear there will be a Monday this coming week. Set this walk-in guy up with an appointment for late afternoon. I'm outta here. There's a PBR waiting with my name on it somewhere in America, specifically, four blocks hence."

Undeterred, Jo says, "Sit." Whenever Jo says, which she does now, with controlled urgency and perfect precision, sort of—

"Sit."

—then, well, I sit and ask the obvious, "What's so special? Has OJ taken a wrong turn? Has the president been impeached? Has he offered to commute the sentences of any of my killers? What's so special about this dude?"

"Well," says she, "four things. First, he's White (note here to the reader, no racist editorializing intended, simply a demographic observation, our clientele tended to be the other color, as did one-third of New Haven). Second, he's dressed in a robe and sandals, sort of LGBTQI drag meets Joan of Arc, but more like a monk. Further, my Liege (when Jo gets on a roll, I know Jo is getting to the good part), on the application form he listed as residence, Verona (now she's got me, being of Sicilian descent, I know where Verona is or was, and it is not near Wooster Square, the Italian section of town, and we've never gotten any of those). And, oh yeah, fourthly, he says he's a Catholic priest. How do you like them apples?"

I hate it when Jo is really, really good at this sort of thing. It usually means I can't do what I want to do, which here and now is start drinking, maybe a Rolling Rock, or several of them. So, says I, "Okay. As we say, you have piqued my interest, but to really peak it, and keep me dry, why can't this wait until Monday? Eh? Answer me that. What's the good Father done and why can't it wait until Monday?"

"The charge, he says, is murder," is the rejoinder. Well, not easily deceived, because I have done more than a few of those, I quickly point out that if this were true, he'd be in our swell new 100-year-old commodious jail, without bail, not sitting in our ratty, crappy waiting room, because we are in one of the forty or so American States that have the death penalty and bail is not granted in capital cases where "the proof is evident and the presumption great," which it always is, otherwise our clients would opt to be banished to, say, Bridgeport or Mongolia or Mantua.

3

Now Jo plays her trump card:

"As to the innocence versus presumption stuff, the good Father opts for innocent. He says there are two so-called victims, a young boy, and a thirteen-year-old girl. He secretly married them so the young boy would not kill himself, but the girl's parents scheduled her to marry a village idiot, so our future client got her a drug that made her appear dead, which both the parents and the young boy believed, so he killed the idiot and himself, and when the thirteen-year-old girl came out of her drug-induced coma, she did likewise. Killed herself, that is."

Jo paused, as anyone would, having unburdened herself of such a sentence and adds, "And he says that none of this has happened yet. But it did a long time ago, and it will again. And he has defenses."

So, I quickly jump on the obvious, and say, "The guy is nuts."

Jo, recovering, notes swiftly, "That is the one defense he hasn't mentioned."

My shoulders slump, I begin to sweat. "Defenses? He thinks he has defenses? Did he attend law school up the road? Did he sleep through the lecture on criminal law?

Don't answer," say I, "Those were rhetorical questions.

"Well, try this, tell him I said that if he is about to commit a crime, we are ethically, professionally, and a dozen other ways bound to turn him in and also warn the victims. There's a California case on that, I think, a shrink didn't warn a girlfriend, who got offed by the nutcase boyfriend he was counseling. So, tell him to give us the victim's name, and you will text, email, and tweet the victim a warning, heading off the homicide. No harm, no foul. Slick. Easiest murder case I ever won."

4

I rise from my chair, heading for Morrie's, but my beer is not meant to be, for Jo tries this:

"Them, he hasn't killed them. A boy and a girl. And there's no way to warn them, they can't be reached by Internet or text or smoke signals or any other means. I asked for their addresses. He says their families are here, but he's afraid to contact the kids."

"So, we contact the families, they'll know how to reach them. You get to do the honors. What are their names?"

A funny smile is playing across Jo's face; I have seen it many times; I used to think it was a shit-eating grin (I don't know why it's called that, but it is only one of life's many mysteries), but that isn't fair and I have come to recognize that it's really a "gotcha" smile, as in, well, "gotcha" and she says—

"Montague, the boy's family is Montague, as in the Montague Fiat/Ferrari dealership in Hamden," and she pauses, for me to say—

"Right. Oh sure. I see. That would mean the girl's family is Capulet, as in Capulet's Funeral Parlor and Final Resting Home over in West Haven. Right?"

"Right."

And I get this next part right because, before Yale Law School, I attended Yale Drama School—

"And that would make our client's name ... Father Laurence? Yes?" I pause, look up at the ceiling, and say softly, "And I am Francis Collins, who was Shakespeare's lawyer." Shit. Damn. Fuck the beer. "Show the man of the cloth in ... call it benefit of clergy"

To which Jo, smiling, says, "Gotcha."

Jo, with a grin, showed the priestly client into my office, saying "Francis, let me introduce Friar Laurence, of the Dominican Order; Friar Laurence, this is Attorney Francis Collins, of the Public

5

Defender Order," and smiling broadly, she added, "Let me leave you two distinguished gentlemen to sort this out, but before I begin my weekend regimen, let me present Friar Laurence's rendition of the standard application form, on which" smiling yet further, "I might point out three nonstandard entries."

Jo pauses while I skim the application form. We are a state agency attached to the judicial department, to provide free legal services for those who cannot afford an attorney. Every state has such an office, as a result of the Gideon decision in the 1960s by the Supreme Court. Not only was it a good decision, but it was also a decent movie. There is now a right to counsel in every felony case and any misdemeanor where the defendant might go to jail if convicted.

I had started law school without a clue as to what I wanted to do, was intrigued by the trial work forensics program at Yale Law, went to work doing trial work for a corporate law firm, and volunteering for federal court criminal appointments. I did well, and it soon became apparent that my hobby was more interesting than my vocation, although the long-range financial prospects were not nearly as heartening.

Fortunately, Meg, my bride, was also interested in public service within her field, research medicine, and between the two of us, we managed to pay the rent. And happily, share bed, breakfast, kids, and politics.

So, I have reviewed thousands of applications for a court-appointed attorney, and they are mostly no-brainers. They are all poor. When people can afford to hire a private attorney, most of them do so, under the mistaken idea that privately retained attorneys are better. In fact, those of us who specialize in indigent defense become truly adept at the ins and outs of a broad range of criminal law, trial

6

practice, and the personality and quirks of judges and juries. Our major handicap is too damn many cases.

Friar Laurence has made a good choice, and being a man of the cloth, his estate planning probably includes a vow of poverty. Hence, he qualifies. However, he must be a resident, and the criminal activity must be in the state of Connecticut. And his application is interesting, a distinct departure from the norm:

FINANCIAL ELIGIBILITY

Income-ten pounds per annum; last source of income-alms and churchly support; last place and nature of employment-Verona and Oxford, England, as Friar, Order of St. Dominic, Holy Roman Catholic Church, ordained in the Year of Our Lord, 1589;

Assets-None

ADDRESS AND CONTACTS

Place of birth, Verona, Italy, 1564;

No living relatives

Residences: Dominican Order, St. Peter's Church, Verona, Italy, and Monasteries of the Order in varying principalities throughout Italy, most notably Verona, Padua and Mantua, and Community of Friars, Oxford, and London, England, and currently, St. Dominic's Abbey, on The Green, New Haven, Connecticut, c/o The Office of the Abbot, Friar Dominic. (since last week);

CRIMINAL CHARGES

Homicide(s), conspiracy to commit same, stalking underage children, facilitating felonies concerning same (underage marriage, bigamy, kidnapping), interference with parental rights, failure to register as a sex offender.

So, I regarded Friar Laurence. He was in a Friar Tuck-like robe with hood, wearing Birkenstocks or Tevas. He was tall, even sitting

7

down, with a largish nose, brown hair with a bowl cut, huge hands, and not sweating. That was interesting, because I was. Sweating. It being a hot Friday afternoon and all, and there was no AC in the abandoned wing, third floor of City Hall. And Friar Laurence was smiling, not a huge grin, but, well, bemused.

I waited, paused, and refrained from saying, "Is this all bullshit or what?" Not the best entree to attorney-client relations, but would have conveyed some of the reality that he and I were jointly bemused about. By. With.

Instead, I said, "This is a first for me, and let me say, I welcome it. The routine can get, shall we say, really routine."

He responded with a warm grin and an amazingly deep voice, "Son, it is what it is. And verily, more to the point, I am what I am ... as impossible as that seems."

"Well, you know, that may be enough, because we provide free legal service for indigents in criminal cases. Until this very moment, we have never had to be concerned with whether they are alive ... which you can't be, born in the same year, I note, as William Shakespeare," here channeling my inner Shakespeare 101 through 415, having been a Lit major at Yale, and taking everything I could on the Bard, man and boy, and then getting through the second year of an MFA at the Drama School, again on the Bard (enough with the Bard) before discovering there was no way to make a living at it, and getting kicked out and then going to law school.

Apologies for the long biographical aside.

I continue, "Rather than rely on the text in the application, I'll rely on the obvious: You are here, you are breathing and speaking and occupying space, you appear to be who you claim to be, and that's enough for me. If we go on farther, I have an investigator and a researcher who can double-check these very sophisticated observations.

"Son, says Friar Laurence, "I sit here before you; am I not real enough? If you held a mirror under my capacious nose, would it make mist? If you tickled me, would I not laugh? Cut me, would I not bleed? Do not worry about the improbabilities, nay impossibilities, of our situation. It's a mystery. Go with it. If Whitman could find a universe in a blade of grass and God in a grain of sand and then there's something about a mustard seed and lilies of the field ..."

"Okay, okay." I break in, "I mean you're good. You are here and as real as you seem. Although why you aren't sweating raises some questions in my mind. But then that leaves questions of how you got here, only a week ago, and why here in particular," gesturing to my Home Depot-framed cubicle, "as opposed to the offices of all those white-shoe corporate attorneys across the street who have recently discovered the deep pockets and moral rewards of securities fraud, RICO and government abuse.

"Why me, to get specific, my good padre? All I want is a cold brew. I mean, how did you get here from your time, to this crappy office in New Haven, and why?"

"I honestly cannot answer that, and it puzzles me," says Friar Laurence. "But I am not alone. For example, you are the direct descendant of Shakespeare's lawyer, Francis Collins, whether you know it or not. Check it out: $49 and Ancestry.com will prove me right.

"Then mix in your esteemed senior District Attorney ... what's his name, Edmund Coke, Sr., potentially a direct descendant of Sir Edward Coke, a genuinely obsessed prosecutor in Shakespeare's time, driven to draw and quarter criminals, especially Catholic priests

9

(fortunately, mostly Jesuits); stir in a bit of a Chief Justice, John Popham, also with an antecedent back in my day ... I could go on, but you get the picture: everything old is new again. Here, it ..."

"Look," I interject, "all this proves nothing, and even if true it's just random chance, a bunch of Old English law types ... why wouldn't they end up being here, as Anglican relics? Connecticut Yankees settled this place back in the 1600s, which, I note, is your era."

Undeterred, he says, "What about the Capulets and the Montagues? Back in the day, I arranged the events which killed their children. Now, in your time, their descendants are running a funeral home and an automobile dealership, right here in New Haven.

"And they have kids. Go ahead, guess their names."

With that, Friar Laurence leaned forward across my desk, pressing his hands together under his chin, making a tent or church steeple of them, and added, "As we say, the plot thickens. We don't simply have a sprinkling of Englishmen descended from Shakespeare's time; stirred into the plot, or pot, are the characters from one of Shakespeare's most famous plays.

"And then add me, the most infamous character therefrom. I am here in person. And there may be others—Coke and Popham, perhaps."

Friar Laurence paused, sat back in my office chair, resting his arms on the chair arms, turning the palms of his hands up and looking at them, saying, profoundly troubled, "All of these personalities, and the relations they represent, are gathering here like the flotsam in an eddy, or the iron pyrites attracted to a magnet. I do not say that alone adds up to anything. By itself, it may be only a mildly interesting oddity.

"But I do say that what is doing the gathering and attracting, the eddy or the magnet, the unknown force, does amount to something. And more importantly, the thing creating it must add up to something.

"Else, why is this happening? Why has it not happened previously in the 425 years since Shakespeare wrote the play, *Romeo and Juliet*? There must be more and it is that which has drawn me here. In my 400-year quest to stop doing evil, to start doing good, to redeem myself, to restore my soul, never before has this staging occurred.

"And added to the cast of characters, or whatever this is, we have you as an English major at one of America's great universities, with one of America's great drama schools, a direct descendant of Shakespeare's attorney, Francis Collins. Now, for the first time, it seems the crimes committed so long ago will be filtered through the criminal process. Perhaps at long last, I can obtain judgement, an end."

I sat and listened to this deeply troubled man. All those centuries ago, he had entered the Order to do good, and in all the centuries since, he had done evil. And, he said, in all that time, he had sought to redeem his soul. I looked at him, and it was compelling. What was emerging here and now was genuine; only the questions and answers remained uncertain.

And so, I turned to the kinds of questions I usually ask. And again, these were hardly ordinary. "Friar Laurence, usually when I see somebody it is after arrest and arraignment and bail, or while they are in custody in jail, in any event, always after-the-fact. Crimes have been committed; they are charged. In this case, right now, with you, neither is true.

"What then, is it that you want from me as an attorney?

11

"Let me add, as you perhaps know, that in our century, in this country for over 200 years, what you say to an attorney is privileged and cannot be used against you. Moreover, I cannot be compelled to disclose what you say. And so, let me ask, what are the crimes, and why have they not yet been charged and what is it you want of me?"

"I don't really need to tell you, Francis, may I call you Francis?" Friar Laurence responded, "The crimes I am involved in. You studied them when you studied the play, *Romeo and Juliet*. My criminal record was aptly written by Shakespeare, aptly related by me to the Prince in Act Five, Scene 3, of *Romeo and Juliet*.

"Let me begin at the beginning," Friar Laurence began ...

"No," says I, "let's begin at Act Five, Scene 3, line 229 of *Romeo and Juliet*, where you confess all to the Prince at the end, and he refuses to pass judgment on you, saying only some will be pardoned and some will be punished."

CHAPTER TWO
THE FRIAR'S TALE
(ROMEO & JULIET, ACT V, SC 3, L 229)

Friar Laurence leaned back in his chair, playing with the ballpoint pen he had used to fill out the APPLICATION/INDIGENCY form. He seemed upset and tried to compose himself as he recalled the events that led to the deaths of Juliet Capulet, Romeo Montague, and County Paris all those centuries ago. Finally, he dodged the issue by saying—

"What do you call this?"

"Which, this?"

"This thing I used instead of a quill and ink."

"It's a ballpoint pen."

"Amazing. Can I keep it?"

"You can keep all dozen if you will only get on with your story ...."

"Shall I begin at the beginning?"

"How about the middle? Where things get interesting ..."

And then Friar Laurence sat up, placed his hands on the edge of my desk, began softly, but firmly, "I will be brief, for the time I may have left is not as long as a tedious tale. And I note you have a yen to yon pub ...

"I was the greatest, able to do least, yet most suspected of a direful murder, and here sitteth I, both to impeach and purge myself, condemned and myself excused."

A bit impatient, I interjected in what I hoped was an appropriately Elizabethan manner, "Then sayeth thou at once what thou dost knoweth." Hearing what I had just said, I immediately regretted it, for as a longtime student of Shakespeare, I knew intimately the speech which Friar Laurence had delivered in Verona and was now revisiting.

"No, not 'knoweth,'" corrected the good Friar, adding, "perhaps this will move faster if you do not mimic or mock my accent, and I try to speak in your grating mid-American, 21st-century twanging delivery. So, let me get on with my story, much as I told the Prince when the events themselves unfolded some 400 years ago.

"Romeo was husband to Juliet, and she was Romeo's faithful wife. Both died, loving each other to death, at their own hands."

I interjected, again, a more moderate tone this time and with less sarcasm, just for clarification, that while they had died "at their own hands," it was because of events Friar Laurence had set in motion. He agreed and went on.

"I married them, and their stol'n marriage day was Tybalt's doomsday, whose untimely death at the hands of Romeo caused the Prince to banish Romeo to Mantua, Juliet and Tybalt being of the familia Capulet, much favored by the Prince, over Romeo's family, the Montagues. Juliet went into mourning, but for Romeo, not Tybalt, deceiving her parents, whom I had also deceived by secretly marrying Romeo and Juliet."

"So," I commented, "there is a third death, as I recall, that would be Tybalt, at the hands of Romeo. But I am unclear as to how that hooks up with you ..."

"Pay attention!" said Friar Laurence, under great stress. "I said, I had married Romeo and Juliet secretly. I kept this from the parents and Prince. Do you follow?" I nodded, somewhat abashed. He continued, "While Juliet was still pining for Romeo, the Prince, to remove that siege of grief, would have had me marry her perforce to Paris, a wealthy gentleman from the County."

14

"Hmmm," I interjected, "That would be bigamy ... a felony, a serious crime, and so now we have the felony murder doctrine at play. If their ultimate deaths are somehow connected to the illegal marriage and deception of the parents, even if you did not intend or foresee their deaths, it is still murder because it was caused during a felony. Like burning a building down, not knowing someone is inside. Of course, you kept from her parents the fact that Juliet, underage, had married Romeo."

"Then comes Juliet to me," Laurence continues, "and with wild looks bid me devise some means to rid her from this second marriage, or there in my cell, she would kill herself."

As he paused, I jumped in, "Cell, you say. Were you already under criminal judgment?"

"No, a cell was my room in the abbey, far too small to accommodate more than myself. And please try to pay attention, count on your fingers. And toes, if necessary," said the good Friar, somewhat miffed, and then continued. "You might note here, what I next did was due to her importuning me, to keep her from killing herself, and so it was an act of charity, in defense of others, namely, Juliet."

"So, I gave her—so tutored by my art—a sleeping potion, which so took effect as I intended, for it wrought on her the form of death. Meantime, I writ to Romeo that he should hither come at this dire night to help take her from her borrowed grave, being the time the potion's force should cease. The parents would think her dead; Romeo would find her alive and take her abroad. In the end, all would be well. There is, however, many a slip twixt cup and lip."

Sitting in my office, as the late afternoon shadows lengthened, it was as though the events themselves were unfolding before me. And

15

now, it seemed I had never before heard this speech or seen the play, although there had been multiple occasions. I could feel the mournful sadness mount in the lives of multiple people, as events moved with deadly certainty.

I said, amazed, aghast, "How could you possibly think this could work? You were going to make the Prince and Juliet's folks think she was dead, but Romeo would take her away alive after the funeral, from her tomb? And when they came back the next morning, week, month, whatever, the tomb would be empty? My God, what then?"

I went on, thinking all of this through, "And now you are adding kidnapping to bigamy and, BTW, if Romeo and Juliet had, as we say, consummated this marriage, which was void apparently for lack of parental consent, it would be statutory rape. So, either of those, if your albeit well-intended scheme went south and she died from the poison, would provide the felony for felony murder."

"You know," said Friar Laurence, "Your bedside manner could use some fine-tuning, Francis. I was doing this because I loved the children, and they loved each other, and I was only trying to do good. How could I see that it would go so badly? Because it did go south, as you say.

"He which bore my letter to Romeo, saying Juliet was alive, Friar John, a fellow Dominican, was stayed by accident, and returned my letter, undelivered. He had stopped to help another brother and was in turn, stopped by officials thinking the two had been in a home corrupted with the plague. In a recurring cycle, the plague would sweep through Verona and kill 1/10 or 1/20 of the population.

"Friar John returned the letter to me on the day Romeo, if he had received it, would have met me, and we would have gone to Juliet's tomb as she revived."

16

"Let me guess," I jumped in, stunned by the bizarre inanity of this. "Going back, Romeo would have encountered County Paris, whether Juliet was alive or not, and had to kill him. He had already killed Tybalt. He had lied to the parents. Was this a guy you should have cared so much about?"

I pause. I see that the Friar is becoming quite upset, possibly murderously miffed by my free-associating with his life and deaths. He rises from his chair, looming large in the late afternoon sun, reaching for the largest rosary I have ever seen, leaning toward me, and I remember that this guy could be a serial killer, I invite him, with apologies, to sit and continue. "Please," say I, "continue."

"I will, but first, let me observe that as an English major, I would think you would have a better recall of what happened exactly and pretending otherwise now does not help either of us. You might instead perhaps be more mindful of my efforts to save the lives of these children, not end them."

"Good point," say I, adding, however, "I didn't pay much attention to the romances in Grad School, I was more into comedies and tragedies," and then, pausing to check myself, "of course, Shakespeare called this a Tragedie, didn't he? Anyway, I left in the middle of my third year, when the leading Shakespeare prof rejected my doctoral proposal." I'm not quite sure why I said that and feeling embarrassed, I said, "As to your efforts to save the children, duly noted. Pray, continue," which Friar Laurence did.

"At the prefixed hour of her waking, came I to take Juliet, appearing dead from the potion I had administered, from her kindred Tybalt's vault, meaning to keep her closely at my cell till I conveniently could send for Romeo."

(I, here, kept wisely to myself, the preposterous thought, that it might be years before Romeo would come, during which interim, the parents, Prince, and a lynching mob of villagers might storm the countryside, seeking the monster who had stolen Juliet's body from Tybalt's vault, the village people bearing torches into the night seeking a dead bride, crying "It's alive. It's alive ..." You can see why I kept this thought to myself).

Friar Laurence continues, "But when I came, some minute ere the time of her awakening, here untimely lay the noble County Paris slain by Romeo, and the true Romeo, by his own hand, dead. Juliet awakes, and I entreat her to come forth and bear this work of heaven with patience, since having now become rid of two husbands, County Paris and Romeo, she was free to seek improvement of them."

I could hardly comprehend this, but restrained myself; was he telling her to look on the bright side of things, she could now troll on Facebook or Match.com, Craigslist even, while surrounded by the still shuddering corpses of her husbands? Was he? I dared not ask.

Friar Laurence went on, "But then a noise did scare me from the tomb, and Juliet, too desperate, would not go with me. But as it seems, did violence upon herself in grief over Romeo's death, by kissing his dead lips which still bore the poison he had purchased when he mistakenly heard Juliet was dead and which he took believing her, mistakenly, dead. All this I know, and to the marriage, her nurse was privy. Confessing all of this to the Prince, I added that if aught in this miscarried by my fault, let my old life be sacrificed some hour before its time, unto the rigors of severest law.

"And I added to the deaths of Romeo and Juliet, that of the County Paris. Romeo's man had brought his master news of Juliet's death and then in post he had come from Mantua and gone to the tomb, and

Count Paris had come to strew Juliet's grave with flowers, when anon came one with light to ope the tomb and Paris drew on him, being Romeo, who slew Paris before killing himself. So, my machinations had led to the death of at least three.

"The Prince was there at the end and read a letter from Balthasar, Romeo's man." Then, the Prince said, "This letter doth make good the Friar's words, their course of love, the tidings of her death; and here he writes that he did buy a poison of a poor 'pothecary and therewithal came to the vault to die, and lie with Juliet."

"Go on," I said to Friar Laurence, who was struggling.

He continued, "The Prince then spoke to me, 'We still have known thee for a holy man' and called Capulet and Montague, to 'see what a scourge is laid upon your hate, that heaven finds means to kill your joys with love. And I, for winking at your discords, too, have lost a brace of kinsmen. All are punished.'"

"As to me," said Friar Laurence, "the Prince repeated, 'We still have known thee for a holy man. Go hence to have more talk of these sad things. Some shall be pardoned and some punished; for never was a story of more woe than this of Juliet and her Romeo.'"

The sun was almost gone now, dust motes drifted golden in the early evening, the long shadow of death hung heavy. The Friar's head was in his hands, bent over his knees as he sat in my office chair. "Tell me again what happened to Juliet," I said, why I do not know since I know it all by heart.

"She took the poison cup from her husband's hand, found it empty, kissed his lips for the poison there, as she said, 'To make me die with a restorative,' her last words were, 'Thy lips are warm.'"

Friar Laurence was deeply disturbed by his narration and added softly, "I loved them, you know. I genuinely tried to save them."

19

I let some time pass, then I said, "Perhaps if you had done the right things, to them and the parents and the Prince and County Paris, they would have lived. Everything you did was taking all of you farther in the wrong direction—more pain, more suffering. Especially on your part."

Then I looked hard at Friar Laurence and realized for the first time, what it was that he was seeking and why he was there in New Haven, and I said, "It must be that way for you every time you go through the play knowing how it will end, every time, and yet still doing what you do, is it like the first time? All the pain and sorrow?"

His voice came softly from a distance in the gathering darkness of my office. "Yes. Every time ... is the first time."

And looking as if for the first time, into his eyes and it seemed his soul, my hands on my edge of the desk, his on his side, the two of us locked together in deep sadness, a moment frozen in time, I said, "It seems to me by now you have long ago paid the price for the wrongs you did.

"But I don't remember what happened to you. Were you ever tried? Was judgment ever passed? Were you pardoned or punished? After all, the Prince said some would be pardoned and some punished ..."

Friar Laurence looked up, the gathering shadows darkening the deep hollows of his face, and he stared across my desk to say, "No. There has never been a judgment. All these centuries, I have waited, unable to pass judgment on myself, to make amends, seek forgiveness, wanting an ending, but judgment has never come. I am in that place between life and death, neither alive nor dead, neither fiction nor real, unable to find an ending.

20

"The closest I can think to describe to you is life on your death row here in America, where prisoners await the death penalty year after year, decade after decade, punishment is withheld and that in itself is the worst punishment. But they at least know an ending, death, awaits them. A pardon may even be possible. I see that on your television and in your newspapers.

"But my punishment is worse. This is my punishment." And at the word "this," he sat upright, raising his hands, spreading his arms, as if to encompass the world.

"I cannot make restitution, seek forgiveness, do penance. It is a life without end when what I most need and seek is just that, an end. There is no surcease of my sorrow. That is my punishment. It is the worst kind of immortality.

"My crime and punishment are immortality.

"Do you see?" Friar Laurence asked.

I did, but I didn't. How could I?

Was he saying he wanted death? That would be the only righteous punishment for his crimes. As a defense attorney, I knew I could prevent that, possibly even get him off, whatever the charge. I had had murder cases with death penalties and defeated every one.

But did he want to die?

I had been looking down, and now I looked up. In the deepening gloom in my office, I looked directly into the eyes of Friar Laurence, and it seemed that they were the eyes of a different man. I had seen such eyes before, whose were they? And it came to me, they were the eyes of Abraham Lincoln, after the death of his son Will, in every photograph, deeply rimmed, deeply lined, deeply burdened with ineffable sadness.

After a long pause, I said, "Perhaps, if nothing else, you and I are in a place that deals in endings and judgments, if not justice. Our courts, I, myself, deal in finality. We render judgment. Is that why you are here after all these centuries?

"Do you seek justice?"

"An ending or judgment, perhaps, yes," said Father Laurence, "but not justice. It is said only the Angels seek justice; the rest of us cry mercy."

It was hard to see where to go with that or how to respond. So, I said what I know, "As yet, I hope, you have committed no crimes in my time, and the crimes in yours are beyond our jurisdiction. So, we are here now with respect to crimes uncommitted. Lawyers deal with such things. Is that why you are here?"

Friar Laurence said, "I do not know. If that is necessary for an ending, for this quest, then so be it." Great, I thought, future crimes by a man from the past in my present ...

So, I did what all experienced trial lawyers do when baffled, I sought a continuance. I rose, we reached across the desk, I took the enormous hand of Friar Laurence in my own, and then, for reasons I still do not understand, put my other hand on the back of his, and with his hand in my two hands, said, "I will see you here at eight on Monday. We will get this thing sorted out. Trust me. Try to stay out of trouble until then."

And then I added, "I need a drink."

We rode the tiny elevator to the ground floor and went our separate ways into what was now an early Friday evening. I left Friar Laurence to his memories and his quest, while I slowly walked the three blocks away from the Green to Morrie's Irish Pub.

I reflected on how my prejudices were changing toward Friar Laurence, whom I had always thought utterly despicable. Now, I felt deep sympathy and sadness. Truly, as he said, he loved those children. But he had tried to play God. And like Icarus, he had flown too close to the sun. Some, the Prince had said, would be pardoned, some punished.

I defended a client once who told me if convicted of murder, he did not want to fight the death penalty and spend his life in prison. He wanted me to offer no opposition at sentencing, so he would get death. I told him I could not do that ethically. I didn't know then, I don't know now, whether that was right. Maybe it was playing God.

Enough. Like Friar Laurence, I needed a place to lay this burden down. Unlike the good priest, I had such a place, Morrie's Irish pub. At the corner of two of New Haven's major downtown streets, down a flight of well-worn concrete steps, through swinging doors with brass handles, into a crowded bar, where everybody knows your name.

Think, Cheers.

It is truly and wisely written, by someone, who knows, that "malt does more than Milton can, to justify God's ways to man. Ale, man, ale's the stuff to drink ..." So. Morrie's Irish Pub, on a Friday evening.

Houseman, I think. I think it was A.E. Houseman.

It is much later, as you can tell from the chapter heading, and the scene shifts to Morrie's, named whimsically, in an Irish way, after both the owner, Morris O'Brien, and Morey's, the place that has tables at Yale, which used to be exclusive to third generation Yalies, but now can be accessed by anyone who can make mist on a mirror and has an equally viable credit card (no debit cards, please). And so, the Ivies change ... eighty years ago, Harvard kept out Jews, and now it is the Asians who are suing. "Can they do that, Frank?" asks District Attorney Ed Coke, short for Edmund, the Old Lion of The Bar, himself an Old Blue, who is sitting opposite me and is definitely no kin to Morrie.

To which I reply, "What, keep them out? Or sue? How should I know? Let's stay on topic." (I'm still trying to figure out what to do with the good Friar.) They only make up twenty per cent of the entering Harvard class and on test scores alone could make up 110%, at Yale, 100 ...

If the preceding sentence seems a bit disjunctive, and it feels as though you're coming in on the middle of a conversation, well, welcome to the tables down at Morrie's, in the third round ...

"So back to that," says Edmund, who hates being called by his full name and who will be prosecuting Friar Laurence if ever there is a prosecution, and who now knows why I was late to Morrie's watering hole, where his preferred drink is anything English that is not Irish whiskey or scotch or Kentucky bourbon, "back to that. You're telling me you just spent two hours with a white guy in drag who may yet be a killer, or possibly less interesting, a stalker of kids, based on past history. What? A pedophile? I hate pedophiles ... and hasn't been charged by me or anyone else yet and wants you to advise on defenses not yet triggered because ... because ..." long, drunken pause ...

Prosecutor Ed continues, answering his own question, "Maybe he wants to die, and is it ethical, you want to know? Speaking of which, shouldn't we not be talking about this? Attorney client privilege, or the Fifth Amendment or some such? Should I move on to the fourth round?"

"You were a little slow picking up on that," says I, "doubtless owing to the five shot glasses arrayed before you, so you are already ahead of that fourth round. As a result of which tomorrow you won't remember this conversation, so I am not worried about your using my statements against the good Friar, but anyway, I have yet to quote him here and haven't signed on as his attorney, so anything I say cannot be used against him and so the privileges are still in play, maybe, and are not compromised or waived or abandoned or whatever. But jumping ahead, suppose we plead out, say to manslaughter and time served, I mean, the guy's four hundred years old."

Ed sprays Bass Ale, into which he has been dropping shot glasses of whiskey as depth charges, onto hard drinkers to his left and right. "Okay," says he, "400 years. Of course, and a double homicide. Frankie me lad," dipping into his bad simulation of an Irish brogue. "I know you're not serious, but let's play along, and the real issue is only whether to go for the death penalty or not. So, tell me how he says he's going to do the deed."

"Deeds." I reply, "There are a boy and a girl and he marries them, both under age and contrary to parents' wishes, to each other, and her

25

father and the good Friar are later going to marry her to a country bumpkin, while the first guy has fled to another country, where he has been banished (we pronounce that banish.ed, Ed) for killing someone's cousin, but the Friar will get him a note to come back and flee with her after she wakes up from a coma induced by drugs the Friar concocts to make her father think she's dead, but the boy never gets the note, hears she's dead, buys illegal poison from a pauper pharmacist, comes back and kills the bumpkin and then, on seeing her look really, really, Godawful dead, he kills himself and she, upon waking up, joins the club. Dead Characters Club, that is. Jesus, I can't believe I just said all that!"

While I pause for breath, this having been one helluva tedious and long sentence even with punctuation, and take a long pull on my PBR, other lawyers around the round table begin pounding the table and chanting "Hang Friar Fuck, hang Friar Fuck," to the great entertainment of multiple bemused onlookers, most of the Catholic persuasion.

Ed recovers from apparent stupefaction and states the obvious (to drunken trial attorneys on a Friday evening) "That's not just two homicides. You mixed in kidnapping, bigamy, cousin extinction and a few other felonies I can only guess. It's felony murder and we call it murder one, of the capital variety."

A defense attorney jumps up and says, "Come on Ed! Hell, it just sounds like attempted child abuse that went bad. Break it down to a misdemeanor and the Friar walks."

"No way," says Ed, "The bastard dies. And I don't think hanging is sufficient, I'm going for drawing and quartering. Here's to my great, great, great, grandfather: death."

This brings the entire defense Bar to the bar, and one says, "Come on, at worst, negligent manslaughter, how could he foresee they would kill themselves? ... probation."

Another says, "Hey, they killed themselves; they committed a crime themselves. Assumption of risk!"

Following which a fourth or fifth (who's counting?) shouts, "Assault with a dead weapon! It's not even a crime."

And then another says, "Even if they were dead, it's a mistake of fact, not guilty!"

The first lawyer, slowly recovering and focusing on the prospect that this might actually become a case, says, "Wait a minute, how come the kid didn't get the note and save the girl? I mean the Friar actually tried to prevent the deaths and used a reasonable method, so at most it's negligent homicide."

At this, after a long silence, I intervene and say, "It was plague." Like pandemic. It went through London every five to ten years; 2000 people would die in a week."

"What?

"The messenger, who was a brother of Friar Laurence's Order, couldn't get through because of quarantine due to the plague," says I, "you know, shit happens."

"No shit," says Ed.

"This means," shouts the very first defense attorney, working his way back into the fun and games, "impossibility. Friar Fuck couldn't commit the murder because he was prevented by forces beyond his control."

Another adds, rising out of the beer before him, "Plague?"

"Today they have shots for that." Says a third, also rising to the occasion.

"Shots. Did someone say shots? Who's buying?" pointing at me.

I turn to Ed, "So what do you think of this? Not your average traffic court dustup."

Ed, being a prosecutor to the core, says, "It's so crazy some part's gotta be true, somehow. Francis, me lad, I sincerely hope you and I get this case. I like the detail, especially the drawing and quartering part." And with that Ed rises slowly and lurches, one unsteady foot after another, out of Morrie's dark, oak paneled, turn of the last century, leaded glass window bar and up the stairs to street level, think CHEERS, into the early evening twilight, dragging a long shadow into the weekend.

One of the newer defense attorneys turns to me and says, "I don't think I would want to try a case against anyone who likes drawing and quartering. What's his name?"

"Coke," says I, "Edmund Coke. Four hundred years ago, there was an ancestor, Edward Coke, he really did have people drawn and quartered and beheaded. At one point, a visitor to London reported there were some fifty heads mounted on London Bridge. He prosecuted anyone who was anybody, legends, like Sir Walter Raleigh. He led the prosecution in the Guy Fawkes Case ..."

"I thought that was like Halloween" he said.

No," I replied, "But close. It was a Catholic conspiracy to blow up Parliament and everyone else, by thirty-four barrels of gunpowder in the basement. The Fifth of November, 1605, when James was King. Jesuits were involved. The Pope had declared a fatwah on Elizabeth. If you want to read rabid, vicious, exorbitant summing up by a prosecutor, there are some pretty good books on Coke's cases."

"Well," says he, "Here's to genetics and Sir Edmund of Coke."

"Amen to that brother," says I, thinking religious and racial prejudice have their own way of surviving centuries. Have I spoken too freely here? What got into me?

CHAPTER FOUR

DOES THE PAST FEAR THE PRESENT?
OR THE REVERSE?

After leaving Friar Laurence, as noted earlier, I went to Morrie's Pub to hang out on the typical Friday evening with my cronies from the criminal bar, perhaps sharing more than I should have about my most recent interview and potential client. It is not unusual for attorneys to share war stories, and what plays at Morrie's stays at Morrie's, usually. But this was not within the realm of the usual.

Somehow, I have become involved with Friar Laurence, a pivotal figure in the death of Romeo and Juliet in the play by Shakespeare of the same name, which means this client may be fictional, although he seems real enough. He may also be dead, or at least should be, since the play was written somewhere around 1595, about 400 years ago.

All of this tends to kill a normally robust interest in a good round of stout. These were not normal times.

So, I went home, at around 9:30 or 10:00 PM, further tucking in my two children, Earl Warren and Ruth Bader (why not? Feel free to name your kids after dead aunts and uncles, we prefer to name them after our heroes, living and dead, and anyway, we refer to them as The Chief and RBG, respectively) under the covers, they having already been read to and slipped under the covers by their mother, Meg.

We swapped new developments from the world of medical research at Yale New Haven Hospital and the universe of criminal defense, now vastly expanded by the vistas Friar Laurence opened. In both of these worlds, we have professional limitations on privileged communications and trade secrets, personalities and factoids, still, we married each other for all sorts of interesting reasons, physical and intellectual, and these continue to guide us despite professional limitations which have, well, shall I say, their own limitations?

As a person, one of Meg's most captivating features are energy and enthusiasm, plus a transcendent intellect and a loving embrace for all things human. There are no ends to the possibilities she can consider. In Meg's world, pursuing the improbable and discovering the unknown are workaday quotidian pursuits, not far different from my fictional Friar reaching into reality in entertaining ways.

Consider, she said, Santa Claus defended by John Payne, in Miracle on Something or Other Street, or the fictional movie star who leaps from the silver screen in *The Purple Rose of Cairo* at the behest of Woody Allen, or all those people in *Midnight in Paris*, again at Mr. Allen's behest ... These were people, crossing parallel universes. Why not?

Meg needed to pause to take a deep breath before addressing aging. Father Laurence's extreme age was not unknown in the natural world; extreme cold slowed metabolic processes for simple organisms over millennia, and cryogenics was developing the potential that even, she said, Ted Williams might live forever, or be revived after death. And she knew of medical researchers in a number of universities who were exploring the processes and meaning of aging itself, with a view toward putting a stop to it.

It may be, she said, that in Father Laurence, we are not dealing with a super old person who has traveled in time without aging at all. Her endless curiosity had led her to read Einstein and the commentators, some fiction writers, who have dealt with the possibilities of time travel. HG Wells for one, the *Time Travelers Wife* for another, that movie where the father and the son communicate across decades through amateur radio, *Frequency*, and the other movie where Denzel Washington is able through time to track and influence prior events. Meg is not strong on remembering titles, but she is keen about any theory which entertains the possibility of Father Laurence traveling 400 years to our time and place.

None of this, she conceded, could precisely account for Friar Laurence popping up in our particular time and place, but it all pointed in that direction, within the realm of human imagination. And then she added, that as normal human beings late into Friday night, being real people with real needs, we might turn from fiction to facts and from senility to sex, turn off the lights, and pursue our own personal fantasies, and that, boys and girls, ladies and gentlemen ... that is what we did—followed by sleep.

Sleep has its bad points. At a symphony or play or a Little League ball game on Saturday, I am apt to get an elbow in the ribs. A voice says, "Come back, big boy. Trial waits until Monday." It is Meg.

But at 4:00 on a Saturday morning, it was Father Laurence prodding me, accompanied by a cluster of interesting folks from Shakespeare's fiction and Shakespeare's time: Sir Edmund Coke, Chief Judge John Popham, who ordered the guilty drawn and quartered with alarming abandon, Dr. John Hall (Shakespeare's son-in-law), Simon Forman (a creepy physician/astrologist), a prince (well, not just any prince, but The Prince) and at least one Capulet and one Montague. And Francis Collins, Shakespeare's lawyer. Not that they were all here, but many descendants certainly were, too many to be dismissed as insignificant, too few to ignore the question: How?

The how question was baffling. But the question of why is more important and interesting than the question of how. There is something about our place and time and its people which draws

Father Laurence. This New Haven, its context: the Capulets and the Montagues are here (can it be, is it possible, that they have children and that their children are named Romeo and Juliet?), the descendant of Shakespeare's lawyer (as noted previously, I am that person, Francis Collins) is here, a latter-day Shakespeare major at a local university, and then too, are those occupying the roles of chief judge and prosecutor which have, it seems, ancestors in Shakespeare's time.

And who knows. Perhaps, like Friar Laurence, some other old-timers are gathering here and now, as yet unknown to thee and me. Especially, me.

There must be something uniquely present in today's New Haven, an impending event or development, drawing on characters from the past. The city itself dates from the mid-1600s, as the cemetery on Grove Street behind the Law School attests, with its headstones of skull and crossbones. At the same time, it is a place in ferment, the population having gone from 70% white in 1970 to approximately 30% today, accommodating growth in African-Americans to 35% and in Hispanics to roughly 15%. All of this has impacted on the percentage of poor, the quality of public education, the incredible variety of cuisine, the melting pot, and the polarities of ethnic cultures.

One consequence, in today's politics, has been the growth and extremity of white supremacists and archconservatives. At the same time, Italian-American and Irish Catholics, along, paradoxically, with Jewish synagogues, continue a stable religious vitality. It is an interesting, complex brew of change and tradition and contention.

This element of change may be what is drawing people here, something having to do with a play written 400 years ago and set in a time and place 200 years earlier. What happened in those times that may affect what is happening here today? What happened then is, a play was written, *Romeo and Juliet*, along with other plays, and people in the play died. How could that affect our time, for that matter, how could Friar Laurence?

Or try the reverse; what is happening here that could affect the earlier time? Is Friar Laurence here now, not to affect our world, but to change his? Back then? And people from then are gathering to oppose Friar Laurence? Perhaps. In England, Shakespeare's time, writing the play in 1596. Or yet earlier, the time the play is set, Verona Italy in the 1400s. Perhaps people back then are concerned that our time and place, this City on Long Island Sound, may impact events or solutions to problems set in place in Shakespeare's time.

Was something done then that we may undo? Something those people cannot risk losing? Does the gathering of people here today have as its purpose solving problems or opposing their solution?

And here, my penchant for mixing movies and reality kicks in. Could we be playing out *Ghostbusters*, and is Friar Laurence the Key Master? The *Matrix* and someone, who knows, is Keanu Reeves. Good Lord, insomnia is a dangerous thing ... back to reality, this reality, please.

Given all of this, I am doing at 4:00 in the morning what any experienced trial attorney does. He or she considers all of the potential possibilities and personalities and filters them through a criminal trial framework. Any trial requires witnesses for the prosecution and witnesses for the defense, aligned around a theory on either side.

The most essential part of all of this is a tight, concise theory of the case. It is the lodestar; it is the gyroscope; it is the compass point that guides counsel from beginning to end. It must be stated within ten words to a spouse, colleague, anyone who will listen. And that theory of the case guides counsel at every point, from initial questions to jurors and opening statements, through cross-examination and direct examination and on to closing arguments and instructions by the judge.

A trial is a minefield and a maze, but the message is simple: the theory of the case, repeated enough times so that the jury soon begins to recognize it and remember it well enough so that they say to themselves, of course, that's what this is all about.

At 4:00 on a Saturday morning, I found myself thinking about the theories Ed Coke, prosecutor extraordinaire, might pursue against Friar Laurence and what my responses, humble and deferential, yet ultimately triumphant, might be. And all of this in a case not yet filed, an arrest not yet made, a client not yet accepted ...

What crimes might Coke charge? What harm will he seek to prevent? If Friar Laurence killed before, will he kill again? Conspire, again? Aid or abet illegal sex by underage minors—interfere with parental rights? With nothing else, Prosecutor Coke may weave his theory of the case out of such materials.

Sleep, Shakespeare wrote, ravels up the tattered sleeve of care. But caring too much reverses the process and so at 6:00 morning, on what promised to be a brilliant spring Saturday, I moved toward the kitchen and the coffee maker, no longer Joe DiMaggio's Mr. Coffee or an ecologically disastrous capsule maker but a simple French press, hoping that fatigue would not make the process of grinding and filtering too complex and spill the whole damned thing ...

CHAPTER FIVE

MEET THE ABBOT

HE READS MINDS AND HAS A WAY WITH TIME

It is Saturday morning, 9:00 AM, after a sleepless night, time to spend half a day closing out last week's cases and preparing for next week's. Friar Laurence falls into both categories: he made the cut on Friday afternoon, last night, and he may be coming up on Monday, depending upon what the prosecutor chooses to do with crimes as yet uncommitted (that is, in our time).

This is not the usual question I deal with on a Saturday morning. More often, I close cases, noting outcome and whether appeals should be taken, and make notations or brief memoranda as to what pleadings or motions should be filed or are to be heard in the upcoming week, and most importantly, what hearings are scheduled, either for sentencing or trial or pretrial motions, such as suppression of evidence.

Those are accompanied by directions to my indefatigable investigator, Ron Hoffer, to find witnesses and arrange for their presence, first for interviewing and then for appearing in court. The research on appeals and motions is for D. Data, American Greek with an unpronounceable name, think George Stephanopoulos, thrice over, a former high tech start-up king, now bored third-year law student at, where else, Yale. And all of this is coordinated with flair and efficiency and follow-up by Jo, about whom, more earlier and later.

All of this has to be efficient and routine and quick, both my Saturday morning processing and then my weekly work, since my office disposes of somewhere around 600 cases a year, opened, handled, closed, a total of 12 a week or nearly three a day, opened, handled, prepared and presented, with negotiations, interviews, hearings, sometimes trials, conferences, research, conclusion, sentencing and, sometimes appeal. Nobody has ever said it was easy, sane, or just. It isn't any of those things. And it doesn't pay well.

And on a Saturday morning, that work is competing with time commitments to Meg and the kids for a hike up Sleeping Giant State Park, or a trip to the Peabody Museum to see ancient bones, or a drive to the Bronx Zoo or possibly a game at the Yale Bowl or tennis on the clay courts. These are important and weighty duties, prompting me to move quickly through my case review and preparation on a Saturday morning, helped by the familiarity of what I'm doing as routine; most of it I have done hundreds of times before, and most of it offers little opportunity for innovation or need for reflection.

However, today is a bit different: there is Friar Laurence. I push Meg and the kids back to 1:30 and go in search of the good Friar. We need to talk. On his application form, he noted his residence as being long ago and far away, but he also noted last night he would be in residence at the Dominican Abbey on the Green in the center of New Haven.

The Green is a large square open space comprised of two city blocks, divided by Temple Street, some 16 acres, dating back a couple hundred years, to a time when sheep and cattle grazed on common land, replaced when pedestrian footpaths developed, with a takeover by local residents playing bocce and selling drugs, and Yale students playing ultimate Frisbee and passing between town and gown on their way to pizza, coffee, and bagels. And drugs. And homeless people with their lives in shopping carts.

On the perimeter are stores and hotels to the south, university buildings to the north and west, City Hall on the east, and an occasional church or three. These may be in the middle, Protestant, with white clapboard or brick walls with high elaborate steeples, on the north, or Catholic, with heavy 19th-century brick and Romanesque trimmings, and similar steeples, one of the latter being blessed last night with the presence of Friar Laurence. That would be the Dominican Abbey at St. Dominic's Cathedral near St. Mary's parish church. All of this is landscaped by maple, oaks, and elm trees.

It is a brief walk from my office in the City Hall on one side of the Green to the Abbey and its heavy wooden door, with lead glass windows, stone framework, and a hand-beaten, iron handle. I stand before the church of my forbears. I bang the bronze knocker. The door opens.

Framed in the doorway in the noontime sun, against a darkened interior, is a diminutive man with a fringe of white hair, wearing Kris Kringle (or John Lennon) glasses on his nose, a Dominican robe identical to Father Laurence's, and the same kind of footgear, and peering up at me, although I am not very tall. He says, "Francis Collins. I have been expecting you. I am Friar Dominic, the Abbot." I silently reflect; I'm not quite sure how he knows my name or has been expecting me. He continues, "I will explain. Please enter." Again, I silently reflect, how did he know what I was thinking? He bounces his eyebrows and says, "I said, enter."

I do not bounce my eyebrows in return. Having been told to enter, I do so.

The interior is what you would expect. Stone walkways around a courtyard with a fountain in the center and a statue that looks strangely like St. Francis feeding the birds, but that cannot be. (Well,

38

why not? What did St. Dominic feed? Oops, careful, the Abbot probably heard that, so to speak.) We cross that and enter a building with stately windows of leaded glass, portraying biblical scenes, with the names of donors, heavy wooden furniture, office doors off to one side, a large door leading to a chapel on the other. We find a door that says Abbot's Office and enter. We sit.

The Abbot says, "Perhaps you are wondering how I knew you would be here?" No shit, think I. The Abbot's eyebrows bounce again, this time higher. There are hazards to reading minds; it appears. I wonder if I can think crudely enough to blow the brows off his forehead.

"Father Laurence said you were his attorney or would be. I have worked with many good attorneys, and I know you first start with gathering the facts, beginning with your client. And I knew he gave this address. And so, I assumed you would come here to meet with him. There is also, as you perhaps know, a certain family resemblance to your Collins ancestors.

I try not to reflect on what he had just said, yet I am intrigued that he would know of a family resemblance, going back 400 years, when I could not get beyond one or two earlier generations. This also suggested unusual preparation for an as-yet unscheduled meeting, when I had not committed to representing Friar Laurence, hardly an average client.

Friar Dominic continued, "I know that Friar Laurence will not be an average client, as a matter of understatement, being perhaps 400 years old and perhaps having killed children in another world, and possibly also being fictional."

Well, thinks I, you got that right.

"And so," the Abbot continued, "I thought we should meet, and I might help by saying we here at the Abbey have had occasion to provide sanctuary for many such travelers over the years. They come to us to stay for a while, and then they move on, having achieved whatever it was they came for. In many instances, they do not know their purpose in being here. But it always has something to do with their prior life, setting things right, concluding unfinished business, frequently doing what they should have done in their own time but occasionally doing things which are now, for the first time, possible for them."

As we sat there, and the afternoon wore on, the light shifted, and it seemed the room became larger and while it was still adequately illuminated, outlines seem to blur a bit. The outside noises of traffic and passersby drifted away. I could barely hear the bells of nearby churches toll. I wondered whether it was because I had skipped lunch.

"No," the Abbot said, "lunch has nothing to do with it. When dealing with these searchers, their very presence impacts our time's usual bounds, indeed, reality. Things become in a state of flux. We provide a home and context, so these travelers, these seekers, like Friar Laurence, survive in our chaotic, crazed time, but their very existence here disturbs the normal fabric of our time. You are experiencing that now."

"Well," I responded, "it seems you are describing the world of Dan Brown in *The Da Vinci Code*. But I don't resemble Tom Hanks, and my world is insistent on humdrum routine. I need to talk with Friar Laurence about the terms of representing him, any crimes, or wrongdoing I need to know about, so there are no surprises if Coke files charges on Monday. Potential witnesses who might be helpful.

These are the usual beginnings of the criminal process, none of which may apply here since Friar Laurence is neither humdrum nor routine.

"Still, I have to work with what I have.

"And what I have is a family that deserves my attention. Would you ask Father Laurence to come by my office early Monday morning, say about 7:30 AM? I am assuming, of course, he is not here right now. And I am afraid I have taken too much of your time already. My wife and children are doubtless wondering where I have been the last three hours."

"I'm afraid you have not listened carefully," said the Abbot Dominic, leaning forward across his desk, his eyes now twinkling behind his John Lennon glasses, "as I have said, with these travelers, the usual parameters of our world are in flux, at least as they apply to their quest to accommodate what is needed. And so, our time together is a part of that. What is needed is for you to spend time with Father Laurence, and at the same time, accommodate your good wife and children. So, look at your watch, do you have time to do both?"

"Well, I am sure I don't," I said, but I looked at my watch as instructed and noted that although we had spent a good hour or two together, my Timex still read 12:15, the time I had arrived at the Abbey. As John Cameron Swayze used to say, it takes a licking, but it keeps on ticking, which was, of course, before the era of digital watches, which perhaps was the good Abbot's point. Time had stood still.

"No way," says I.

The Abbot, now smiling, and seeing that I am beginning to understand, responds, "Way."

I was beginning to like him.

He continued, "I should add one other consideration. I do not pretend to understand what Father Laurence is about, but there is a paradox: What is going to happen was determined long ago, but for it to happen in our time, it must accommodate the needs and limitations of our time and our lives and respond to the unique properties of our moment in time. What has brought him here has been a long time coming."

As he said this, I adjusted my Timex marathon watch, thinking I need a Fitbit, and shook it. It began to move. I responded, "So, let's assume I buy into this; does this mean the fix is in? If there is a trial, it will be a farce, the whole thing rigged? Are you saying that Friar Laurence is here for having killed children centuries ago—which cannot be altered—to play a role decided centuries ago—which cannot be undone? Anything I do is charade?"

"Ah," said the Abbot, "I see you are quick, and you see the paradox. The answer is simple; things are not rigged. Indeed, with these Seekers, their very point in coming is to resolve the things as yet unresolved. The basic elements of the universe stay in place. There is still a difference between good and evil; there are still choices people make, guilt and innocence remain, judgment and justice must be served.

"But a unique set of circumstances is gathering here. An opportunity is presented. But no more than that.

"It was determined long ago that for Seekers who travel, our rules and limits must remain in force. And yet we accommodate needs of such as Father Laurence, whose unknown task is so important that only he may undertake it. The outcome has not been decided, only that it shall be decided, and it shall be here."

And here the Abbot leaned forward across his desk toward me, although I did not recall sitting down, and said softly but firmly, "In Father Laurence's case it seems, he has been brought from a fictional realm to our own for that resolution, which I must accept could not be found in his own time and place. But this does not mean he is or has been fictional and is a stranger to our realm. Indeed, he may, in fact, be a stranger in the fictional world Shakespeare created, and our reality may, in fact, also be his.

With that, the Abbot leaned back and bounced his silver-white eyebrows. Twice. "We, of course, do not know who or what brought him," he added.

Curiouser and curiouser, I thought, wish I had known that at 4:00 this morning.

"Look," I said, standing and spreading my arms wide open in a way which, upon reflection, I am embarrassed to say must have resembled our Savior on the Cross, "I believe you know what you're talking about, but please believe that I do not. What I do know is, I am simply a Legal Aid lawyer, and cosmic justice is not my specialty. My specialty is the day-to-day stuff in Connecticut courts.

"The principles and procedures I work with are clear. Friar Laurence, in some fashion, must accommodate them. As his attorney, I will do the best to get the best outcome possible, and I do not believe that has been predetermined. For my part, the most I would claim is I am as good a lawyer in my field as there is in Connecticut. And I hate to lose."

Rising, Friar Dominic, the Abbot, raised his hand as though in blessing and said, "I am sure that is more than enough, and I am equally certain that you will not lose. Although, I do not know what losing and winning may be in this context. You should go now to your family."

Then, he added, "In your weekend with your family, could you possibly attend tomorrow morning's mass at 10:00? I'm not inquiring as to your present religious affiliation or even your religious faith. But it might be a good way to help you get oriented and to help Father Laurence as well. This may take an hour tomorrow morning, and I cannot promise to compress that time, as I have been able to do this afternoon."

"Does this mean he is conducting the Mass?" I asked, quickly thinking to myself, "Of course it does, Dummy." And equally quickly added, "Yes. Of course. And I think we would all love that. See you in church," and I started for the door, wishing I hadn't added that last part.

As I tugged the door to the Abbot's office open, the noontime sun flooded in through the hallway, blinding me momentarily, and I heard a sound behind me. As I turned, a shaft of light shone warmly on the desk and spot where the Abbot had been. He was gone.

As I moved from his office door, through the corridor and out into the street, it occurred to me that the Abbot had managed to leave his office although I occupied the only exit door. You could do worse than have such a man on your side.

I looked at my watch. It read 12:30, and although it was digital, I thought I could hear it ticking, as I went out to the New Haven Green, in the bright sunshine and sharp golden green of a warm Spring day, and saw the crisp outlines of the shadows and the colors of our world, with ample time for me to spend an ample day with Meg and the kids.

The steeples, elm trees, and lilacs all stood strong and clear on this bright spring day.

All was good.

CHAPTER SIX

NOT YOUR AVERAGE MASS

It is now Sunday morning; an average spring day is building, green grass and blue sky and white and pink dogwood with light purple lilacs and with the beginning of buds on the apple trees. The fragrance of Connecticut in the spring is like none other I have ever experienced. Mixed with and enhancing all of this is the heavy aroma of maple syrup at IHOP, where I tell my team that we are off to St. Dominic's as soon as we finish our waffles and pancakes.

"So, eat up," I say.

Ruth responds, mouth full and dripping, "And that will take like, FOREVER," uptick emphasis on the third syllable of "forever!"

Earl, with the measured sagacity "Well, counsel, shouldn't we have gone to confession?" following which he returns to his bacon.

"Huh," I offer, "I would really like to know what sins you have to confess ... and as for 'forever,' eternity is the stock in trade of the Church."

Before I could go on, mercifully, Meg creates forward movement by saying, "Your dad has taken on a big case, and he may need the help of the Pope. You know who he is, right?" To which both kids respond, "Whoa. Big-time! Heavy-duty ..."

We pile into the 25-year-old Volvo DL 240 wagon, and a few blocks and minutes later are parked behind St. Dominic's. We have been here before, occasionally, for average masses. But this is not your average mass.

For one thing, it is being celebrated by, who else, Friar Laurence. The Dominicans are a preaching order, in contrast to the Franciscans and the Jesuits, who specialize in feeding birds and running universities, and other lesser Orders. So, it is not surprising that a traveling Friar might pinch-hit in the pulpit, particularly when we learn, in a strange almost weird paradox, that we are about to hear Friar Laurence address the international crisis of child abuse in the Catholic Church.

For all sorts of reasons, the topic is timely, particularly in light of the movie *Spotlight*'s popularity and the media coverage of firings and prosecutions of rogue priests and occasional cardinals, many for misdeeds decades old.

The sanctuary is full.

Father Laurence's condemnation of the Church's misdeeds is unequivocal and compelling and moving, as he puts a human face on a tragedy which most certainly has touched many of the men in the audience who once were boys, and many of the women in the audience who were and still are their mothers. He condemns those who did nothing or, worse, covered up the scandal and moved the predators to unsuspecting parishes. He is particularly unforgiving of the failure of higher-ups to deal openly and firmly with what he calls "a cancer at our core."

He indicts Bishops and Cardinals, but not the Big Guy. He calls for reforms in training and counseling of older priests and more open socialization of younger priests.

Meg leans over and says, "Let's hear him condemn celibacy of priests."

"What's celibacy?" asks Ruth.

"They can't marry women," Meg replies.

"Eeeeuuuwww," is the response.

"Well, I don't mean they marry each other," Meg adds. "O?"

47

Friar Laurence concludes by saying he does not criticize his fellow priests lightly. "We are all a product, including me, to a very real degree of the constraints and pressures and temptations of priesthood. We can all of us, including me, do grave harm. In the far-off past, I engaged in conduct leading to such harm, and I seek daily forgiveness. I pray to avoid the dangers into which all priests and others who undertake God's work may fall.

"We are all of us, sinners, everyone here. While the sins of priests, especially those who were sexual predators, are especially heinous because of our special privileges and responsibilities, it is the misdeeds of those responsible for the priests, which seem most unforgivable. Yet we believe that all sins, even theirs, may be forgiven in time.

"Perhaps. Let us hope so. For my part, I fervently hope it is true. For me, for you, for all God's children. When Jesus said, 'Suffer the little children to come unto me;' He surely did not mean for them to suffer."

The paradox that the Monk in the pulpit was responsible, long ago and far away, for the waywardness and ultimate deaths of two young teenagers escapes most in the congregation, but most certainly not two, the Abbot and the prosecutor, Edmund Coke, as we shall see. Coke, particularly, seems riveted by Friar Laurence's dramatic and impassioned delivery.

Communion is celebrated, the censers and bells perform their magic, the kids love it. We pass down the center aisle, under the heavy dark oak choir loft, and the brilliant reds and blues of the Rose window above it, out to the steps of St. Dominic's, where the parishioners are meeting and greeting the preacher and the Abbot. The mood is muted and somber, but Friar Laurence has won their

48

hearts and receives many commendations on his delivery and sentiments.

He must truly have been something back in the day, whenever that was ... and wherever.

I shake his hand, saying, "Well done." He asks if we can stay so he might greet my family; I pause and then assent. We are pressed from behind, and so I move to the Abbot and say, softly, "Interesting choice of a traveling preacher, especially for that subject."

He nods, I think sadly, and says, "In our Order the pulpit is available to those with insight and experience and the gift of preaching, all of which Friar Laurence has in abundance." I nod and move on.

All of which makes this not your average mass. Then, too, there is this. As we stand aside and are joined by Friar Laurence in the atrium of the Cathedral, next to a fountain where the sounds of birds and water splashing are mixed, I find myself for the first time introducing a client to my family. An older and wiser attorney once told me that we public defenders do not belong to country clubs, and we don't bring our clients home.

But here we are, and I introduce Meg and Ruth and the Chief to Friar Laurence. He extends his huge hand to each and bends down to meet them, and each, in turn, greets him with appropriate politeness, doing their mother proud. He says a few kind words to them about me and about the kind of work I do, saying that he and I are both engaged in the Lord's work. Something about the poor shall inherit the Earth. He asks about their schoolwork and how proud they must be of their mother.

At this point, since I see the Abbot coming over as well as some other individuals, I gather my brood and say it's been a pleasure to

49

see a professional at work, and I would look for him tomorrow morning at my office at 7:30 AM. He agrees, and as we are about to turn, I hear a voice pierce the air, pronouncing my name, saying, "Francis, my lad, perhaps we might have a word with the good Father and you before your fine lady and children spirit you away ..." Oops.

It is a command, not an inquiry. It is the voice of Edmund Coke, prosecutor extraordinaire, and this is the third thing which makes this not your average mass. I ask Meg to take the kids and wait in the car, saying this won't take long. I get a sympathetic grimace from Meg, and they leave.

Edmund asks if I have agreed to represent Friar Laurence. I respond in the affirmative if Friar Laurence is agreeable, and the Friar nods assent. That, as they say in law, constitutes a contract. I ask whether any conversation could wait until tomorrow ...

Coke agrees but says, "I have been puzzled by a number of aspects of this matter as I learned about it Friday night at Morrie's, and then there is this morning's paper," which he seems to be holding under his arm. Turning to Friar Laurence, Coke says, "If I understand matters correctly, you're seeking representation as to crimes not yet committed and charges not yet filed, all relating to conduct some 400 years ago and 10,000 miles away, very possibly in a wholly fictional world. Is that a fair summary, Father?"

I do my lawyerly thing and quickly say, "Don't answer that question."

But Friar Laurence is too quick for me, and raising his hands before him and turning his palms up toward the heavens, says, "I would say that is fair. I can certainly understand why it would be perplexing for you. Would you like some help?"

50

Again, I do my lawyer thing and say, "Please, puhleeeeze, don't do this!"

But Ed Coke knows what he is about and knows his man and says, "Absolutely I would like some help. Isn't that why we are all here at St. Dominic's? Although I must say," he adds, "this is hardly your average mass."

To which I add, "Amen to that, brother."

As to that, Father Laurence says quickly, and with no slight irony, "Francis, I believe that's my line, not yours.

With that, Father Laurence turns to Edmund Coke, looking down on him although Coke is well over six feet tall, and says, in a deep, modulated bass voice, "Edmund. May I call you Edmund?"

Coke, able to think of no other response says, "Absolutely."

"Edmund it is, then," Father Laurence continues, "If I may be so bold, it seems to me you are distracted, perhaps even confounded, by irrelevancies. You are diverted by time and space, age and distance, the differences in realities, yours and fictional, and so on. These are all very interesting, I quite agree. They bother me fully as much as they bother you, even though it is I who bring all of these perplexities into your life and that of Francis.

"But suppose you were unaware of all these sideshows. What would you see? A somewhat over the hill, yet larger-than-life, Dominican monk. If you prick me, I bleed; in the sunlight, I cast a shadow; at night my weight presses down the mattress on the cot in the Abbey; my voice reached, and I hope moved, hundreds this morning. My fear that I may commit harm is assuredly real, as witness my consulting Mr. Collins. I am real, and the other parts about me which don't seem to add up frankly don't seem to me very important.

Friar Laurence continued, while I considered having a stroke or seizure, "I am not sure why I am here. I know I have done harm in the past. I am afraid I could do it here again. It is a paradox, but we both, you and I, have a job to do: find out why I am here and keep me from hurting people again."

By this time, Friar Laurence had placed his hand on Coke's shoulder and had drawn him close. It was as though Coke was mesmerized. Suddenly he shook himself, and with an upsweep of his hand, forced Laurence's arm away and stepped back. The monk was much larger, but the prosecutor was quick, and with his movement, he distanced himself, nearly tripping over a low wall containing the fountain behind him.

I grabbed Friar Laurence by the elbow and began turning him back toward the Abbey, away from Coke. But Coke spoke, saying, "Wait, Francis. I agree with Friar Laurence." Turning toward him, Coke said, "Whatever you are and whoever, you pose a real danger. I do not believe that you killed two teenagers 400 years ago or that you have traveled here from Shakespeare's fictional world. However, I do believe, which is even more frightening, that you hold those beliefs and that you are here to act on them."

Turning to me, Coke said, angrily, "I don't suppose you have seen this, have you, Francis? It's *Romeo and Juliet*, déjà vu all over again." With that, he held up the entertainment section of the New Haven Register Sunday morning edition, the paper he had under his arm, with a lead article and photographs on a radical reworking of *Romeo and Juliet*, in rehearsal at the Yale Drama School, my almost alma mater before the Law School.

He threw it at my feet, and as I stooped and skimmed it, Coke turned to Friar Laurence, pointing his finger up at the monk's face, and said, "But you knew all about this, didn't you? You knew that *Romeo and Juliet* was in rehearsal here, with a possibility of off-Broadway later, as a musical and in two weeks' time opening for a week's run here in New Haven. That's why you're here."

And then he added, emphatically, "Because the kids are here."

With that, I say, "Oh come on, Ed. even if Friar Laurence somehow is from out of town or even another country, why would a student production bring him all the way here?"

"Because," he replies, losing it now, "Because there is a pattern here."

He continued, "The two roles are played by two kids from Hillhouse High, where they are national caliber vocalists and have starred in *West Side Story*," here pausing for breath, "and because they are children of two longtime New Haven Italian families, the Montagues, and the Capulets." Coke grabs the paper from my hands, and turns to Friar Laurence, and reads from the lead column by local pundit, Thomas Doyle:

What are the odds? The children of the local Ferrari dealer and funeral home have starring roles, with the same names as the characters in Shakespeare's play, Romeo Montague and Juliet Capulet. Synchronicity, if that is what this is, means the Director's name would be Burbage, and around the landscape, maybe, there would be other descendants, say, a Chief Judge Popham, or a Chief Prosecutor Coke, or even a public defender, Francis Collins, all from Shakespeare's time ...

And guess what, folks, there is. Are. Whatever.

That is, they are here. Now Burbage and supporting cast, in a revolutionary reworking of Shakespeare's classic. All we need now, to pick names at random from Romeo and Juliet, would be a Mercutio, say, not hard with our Italian population. Or even a Nurse, no name necessary. Think we could find one at Yale New Haven Hospital? And how about a Monk from out of town? I bet there's one right now at the Abbey on the Green, where probably there is also a Brother John ...

I pause, thinking well, what he doesn't know is I have a monk from out of town at the Abbey and a nurse, a first for me, Dorothy Arlow, whose case is scheduled for Tuesday, and I look up to see Coke and Friar Laurence are frozen, immobile. Coke continues, "Doyle's article concludes:"

I don't know what's going on, dear hearts; call it synchronicity or serendipity or just good cosmic karma. I am almost tempted to say something's rotten in the state of Denmark, but I would be mixing my ... metaphors, plays, something.

Anyway. See this production; the kids are gonna be phenomenal.

With that, I stood there, glancing from the paper to Friar Laurence's face, and beheld shock and bewilderment, and on Coke's face, anger, and deep concern. Friar Laurence spoke very slowly, saying, "I did not know any of this. I find it frightening, but in a way, it brings things into focus. It may, in part, be why I have been drawn here. It concerns me, Mr. Coke, fully as much as you."

Before he could say another word, I said to Coke, "Do you know anything more about this? Is it the same play, the same story? Is it different?"

And with this, the final factor which made this mass not just your average mass, revealed itself. Coke looked from Laurence to me, paused, and said, in the voice I had heard him use summing up to dozens of juries, "It is the same old, same old Shakespeare. But there are two differences, and that is why I am here and why I think your client is here.

"The kids are high school seniors here in New Haven at Hillhouse High School, and so talented they have been taking courses at the Yale Drama school. I think your client knows that and that their names are Montague and Capulet. Those were the families in Shakespeare's play, and I believe your client intends to repeat that history and inflict serious bodily harm on these youngsters.

"There is one other difference. Professor Burbage has done what he calls," and here Coke read from the article, "a radical, historic, reworking of the play. Never before done in the history of *Romeo and Juliet.*

"I don't know what it is, but I think your client does and is here to stop it. And hurt these kids. And I intend to stop him. Even if I have to stop Burbage."

Coke stormed off, saying over his shoulder, "You will hear from my office tomorrow morning, Francis. Have your priest ready," startling parishioners who turned and stared.

Friar Laurence was disturbed, saying, "That is a troubled man."

"Yes, I said, "and so am I. I think we would be better served in the future if you wouldn't confess openly to future crimes to the County Prosecutor, with a dozen witnesses standing by, especially while I am saying not to. It just might hurt my reputation. See you tomorrow morning."

The Abbot stood next to Friar Laurence, the shadows lengthening around them as the afternoon cooled, and shadows settled on the elms on the New Haven Green, and deep concern settled on the Abbot's face.

CHAPTER SEVEN

MONDAY, MONDAY ...

It is Monday morning, and, as you can imagine, we had a lot to talk about, after Sunday's not very average mass, on the way home to Hamden, only a few miles from the New Haven Green and Saint Dominic's Cathedral. In that short space of time, I impressed upon Earl and Ruth that what they had seen and heard was confidential, private, remarkable, and not to be discussed at school, or anywhere. In the phonetic impatience of youth, each said, the single word "Dad," dragging the vowel endlessly up, across and then down so that the word spoke volumes. Specifically, it meant that as the children of a lawyer dad, they were appalled that I would think it was necessary to tell them what they already knew in their DNA.

Upon arriving at home, Meg said, "The kids got it right; this is heavy. It's a little like *To Kill a Mockingbird* meets *Lincoln in the Bardo*, only you may be representing John Wilkes Booth."

"Thanks, I needed that," was my response. She kissed me; we had dinner, watched PBS, and went to bed.

This morning Meg was off early to her job, solving cancer and other inconsequential matters at Yale New Haven Hospital, but left coffee for me and breakfast for the kids on the counter. Going out the door, she said, "Keep me posted. This is not going to be your ordinary Monday morning/Saturday night drunk and disorderly arraignment court." And with that, she was launched.

Stay tuned, New England Journal of Medicine, JAMA, and Lancet ...

My turn to get the kids to school. On time, on target, we were out the door, and after dropping kids, I headed into the morning 7:30

rush hour traffic to downtown New Haven. While passing through Spring Glen and Whitneyville, I reflected on where we were with Friar Laurence's case. Upon arriving at home last night, I had shifted from trying to make sense of the improbabilities surrounding the man and the case to the more immediate and familiar approach of trying to figure out what the prosecutor, Edmund Coke, might and could do.

If Coke intended to prosecute crimes back in England or Italy, our courts would have no geographic jurisdiction. Plus, trying to apply our present-day laws would encounter a small stumbling block known as the prohibition on ex post facto laws, meaning you can't punish an act under laws passed after it. If Coke decided to try Friar Laurence under law as it existed in 1600, procedurally, it wouldn't work either. There was no right to counsel back then. Juries of your peers would be hard to select, the right to confront and present witnesses for the defense, all guaranteed in our time, didn't exist, as Sir Walter Raleigh found out. And coerced confessions were standard. And then, of course, there were differences in sentencing for crimes, like beheading and drawing and quartering and other such quaint customs. Our 8th Amendment has something about banning cruel and unusual punishments, unusual in our times, that is.

No, it seemed to me, Friar Laurence could only be prosecuted, if at all, for crimes committed this decade, in this town, in this state of Connecticut, USofA. So far, these added up to nada, zippo, zero, zed. But that was not the end of it. My good friend and fellow member of the bar, Edmund Coke, knew, as did I, that there are ways of prosecuting people to prevent them from committing future crimes, interceding in advance to prevent them from hurting other people. That is the purpose of the crimes like attempt, conspiracy, harassment, menacing, stalking, or possessing tools for arson or burglary, or why not think big—insurrection. All of these are ways of dealing with people who have only begun to plan or talk about or perhaps even barely think about doing something criminal.

The problem with all of these is, in our jurisprudence, we do not punish mere thought or intent. And so, a man following a woman down the street on a soft summer afternoon may be engaged in totally innocent behavior, unless she is white, and he is black and it is a small town in the deep South of the United States, and it is the early 1950s. (True case.) So, some overt act or some other evidence is required to punish future crimes; otherwise, 100 million Americans owning firearms could be punished for attempted hold up of a liquor store or a hobby gardener could be arrested for buying bags of fertilizer, although he had no plans to blow up a federal court building. So, charging a conspiracy, say to rob a bank or shoot a President or defraud consumers or fix prices, requires conduct evidencing criminal intent, a substantial step.

So far, it seemed to me, Coke had neither intent nor steps to show stalking or intent to harm on the part of Friar Laurence involving the local high school teenage actors, Romeo and Juliet of New Haven, Connecticut.

Is Edmund Coke thinking along these lines? Doesn't he have enough on his plate with drive-by shootings, drug dealings, garden-variety rapes, and murders? Will he prosecute an over the hill monk on gossamer evidence that consists of character, coincidence, and circumstance?

Does he really want to deal with the paradox here, of prosecuting a man from the past for future crimes?

As always, I pull myself back to the present with the help of a following driver with a heavy hand on his car horn, and proceed down

Whitney Avenue past the Peabody Museum and School of Management toward the Green and City Hall and the State criminal courts, parking behind our ancient, decrepit City Hall and my dilapidated wing. There, on the third floor, Jo, my trusty administrator, and paralegal and stalwart confederate awaits with a text at 7:45 in the morning. It is, of course, from Edmund Coke, who has been ruminating along the same lines and considerations as I adumbrated above (well, reckoned up, I suppose) (for those of us who are frustrated as I am by AutoCorrect, the word adumbrated was rendered as adam braided ...).

Coke's text read as follows:

Francis Collins, Esq.

Office of the Public Defender

Please present your client, Friar Laurence, recently of London and Verona, at 10:00 AM arraignment court, for arrest and the setting of bail on charges of failure to register as a sex offender under Connecticut's Megan law, stalking, and conspiracy with an unnamed co-conspirator. We understand Friar Laurence resides at the Dominican Abby on Church Street, New Haven, and we have deferred arrest there for reasons of sanctuary and privacy. However, if you and your client fail to appear, as herein directed, a bench warrant will issue to be executed by noon today. As a matter of courtesy, the probable cause affidavit for the arrest makes no reference to your indiscreet disclosures of Friday last.

Please be advised that we will request bail be denied, and we will request an immediate competency hearing, seeking indeterminate commitment of the defendant, as he has demonstrated delusions as to his own time and place, and identity.

Very truly,

Edmund Coke,

County Attorney for New Haven County

The chief prosecutor had gone through much of the same analysis as I, but with one difference: he believed he could prove that Friar Laurence in our day and time had already committed or was about to commit crimes subject to our jurisdiction.

As I was reviewing and digesting this, Jo poked her head around the corner of my office to announce the arrival of Friar Laurence himself. He entered and sat in the very same chair he'd occupied Friday, but now under different circumstances. We talked.

I explained that he was being accorded elite courtesies. Ordinarily, he would have been picked up and arrested, then booked, and then held and presented in court with the usual Monday morning crowd: hookers, pushers, drunks, thugs, bruisers, and, rarely, if ever, a man of the cloth. Avoiding that was good.

What was not so good was Coke's intent to move for an immediate hearing to get denial of bail and to have Friar Laurence declared incompetent. If successful, he would be denied trial and would be institutionalized for an indeterminate time, perhaps forever. At the use of the word "forever," Friar Laurence smiled and commented that being placed somewhere forever might be a better existence than his present state, in which he drifted for centuries from place to place.

He asked a few questions about the charges, which I answered by saying that stalking was a relatively recent crime, and registering as a sex offender stemmed from the death of a girl named Meagan, I think in New Jersey, killed by a man some twenty or thirty years ago, who had prior sex convictions. Registration is now required in most states.

Friar Laurence pointed out that each of the charges involved an intent on his part to do harm by failing to register or by stalking or by agreeing with someone to commit murder. I agreed although the intent was somewhat different in each instance. He then asked if he did not know how he got here or why he came or what he was to do, how then could he be convicted of having intent? My response was that Coke did not believe him and would try to persuade a judge or jury not to believe him. And circumstantial evidence would seem to support Coke's position.

What then, about failing to register as a sex offender, when he had never been convicted of a sex crime in this country, and his prior conduct was centuries ago. Good points, I acknowledged, but Coke would probably say Laurence had arranged for underage teenagers to have sex and marry illegally, and that might be enough. True, a long time ago, but the reach back in Meagan's law has no limit.

Friar Laurence was beginning to wear a seriously worried frown. "Scary, the way you lawyers think," he said, "and even more scary that you can work out Coke's reasoning and make it sound plausible. I would rather you work out plausible defenses to crimes not yet committed!"

To which I replied, "That's why you pay me the big bucks, so there are no surprises, and we develop defenses. It helps that I have studied Mr. Coke's twisted pattern of thinking for many years. Not to worry ..."

Focusing on the immediate, it seemed to me the most urgent issue was the bail hearing. Usually, defendants are released simply on a promise to appear, called a "recognizance," and sometimes accompanied by a small amount of cash in a more serious case. In around half of the states, bail could be denied in capital cases, "where the proof is evident, and the presumption is great." Denial, I said to Friar Laurence, is almost automatic in a homicide case. Defendants

61

facing the death penalty are likely to flee, it is thought. People are released pending charges when they have community ties and will appear on time.

But, once again, Friar Laurence asked the key question: how could he qualify for bail if he did not know how he got here or that he would assuredly stay? And then he pressed the reverse, for the same reasons, how could any amount of bail be adequate for him, indeed any form of restraint?

Even if he promised to appear as ordered, even if he were held in the most solitary of jail cells, one day, he might simply be gone, as he had appeared, without warning.

"Point well taken," I said, "but perhaps not our strongest argument for getting bail." A conundrum.

With that, we were out the door; Jo handing me seven other files as we went. These were appearances and pleas worked out during the previous weeks, some for clients I would be meeting the first time that morning in the holding room adjoining the criminal courtroom. The noise, the smell, and the body heat would be intolerable. So, with the lack of time and consultation between attorney and client, the only thing which saved this process of justice from being, as they say, a mockery of justice, was that cases were usually routine and had standard dispositions on pleas of guilty, which the client had been brought to see as a kind of fairness.

Or at least survival.

Until the next time.

I explained this to Friar Laurence as we walked along. He inquired as to what his plea should be, and I said that it was too early in the process to know, but for today the plea would be not guilty. He said he did not see how it could be otherwise. He had no intent to harm anybody and did not know in the most fundamental way why he was in this place in our time. But then he added, "I am very much afraid that I may harm someone in some way."

"That may be true," I stated flatly, "but let's let that be our little secret."

As we stopped at the traffic light opposite the courthouse, I looked hard at Friar Laurence for the first time that morning. He was no longer in a robe and sandals, instead, in jeans and a tan corduroy jacket, with a dark green turtleneck and desert boots, an outfit from a decade or two earlier, but certainly from our century. Well, the last one anyway. A large wooden crucifix hung on a woven chain on his chest. He did not look as pale and fatigued as he had on Friday, and in fact, had a modest tan, a trim haircut, and was wearing a Fitbit watch (!) I said, "Looks like you're getting with the program."

"Well," said he, "the Abbot has some experience in helping people like me to adjust. He and I spent some time Saturday and yesterday with Roku binging on Netflix and Amazon prime. I think my favorites are *Schitt's Creek, Midsomer Murders, Bosch, Boston Legal,* and *Fleabag.* She got four Emmys, you know," he said, turning toward me. "I enjoyed the *Da Vinci Code* a lot. We also watched some movies on criminal trials; I especially liked *My Cousin Vinny, The Verdict, To Kill a Mockingbird,* and *Justice for All.* Too, *Lincoln Lawyer.* In another life, I think I would like to be you."

I let that pass. I'm thinking, that's a lot of binging.

He reached for the door handle on the weather-beaten, grimy door into the filthy, noisome, stench-filled corridor of the New Haven District Court. We pushed our way through the crowd as described above toward Arraignment Court, the docket being heard in the cavernous General Criminal Court Room, on the first floor. If a case comes to trial, weeks later, it is upstairs in a smaller, less smelly court on the third floor. As we dumped our personal belongings and my attaché case on the conveyor belt and passed through Security, I asked one of the assistant sheriffs which judge was sitting in arraignment court.

"Your worst nightmare, Francis," came the response. "The good news is, Friday is only four days away. It is the anointed Chief Justice Popham himself, whom I have never seen handle arraignment court, but you can be sure that law and order will prevail, which is not necessarily good for your side of the aisle." And with that, having cleared me and my briefcase and my client, he called "next."

"Oh, fuck," I replied and pushed on, catching up with Friar Laurence, who breezed through security with nothing to show since everything he had was plastic, or well, wood. "You seem to know what you're doing," I said.

Friar Laurence replied, "Well, I also watched some airport movies; I especially liked *Airplane*. Also, that one where Tom Hanks can't get out. The Abbot said he was preparing me for court by "streaming" on the Internet. What is the Internet?"

"I will explain that to you later," I said, "after you have explained God's infinite mercy and why Joseph didn't get pissed when his wife got knocked up. Right now, I'm a bit perplexed as to why the Chief Justice of the state court system on a Monday morning is handling nickel dime cases in Arraignment Court."

With that, we entered through swinging doors into that very same court room. And the aforementioned ambiance intensified by a factor of ten.

CHAPTER EIGHT
AND NOW, LOWER COURT
MEET HIGHER JUDGE, POPHAM

Monday at 10:00 AM, was the time appointed by the district attorney, Edmund Coke, for us to appear on charges of stalking, failure to register as a sex offender, and conspiracy to commit murder. (Murder?)

It is now the appointed hour, and the courtroom is full. The business at hand is arraignment, the entry of pleas. The most expeditious is "guilty." Cases are called at random, with private attorneys jockeying to get their cases called first, to move onto other business back at their offices. Today, it's mostly "not guilty," followed by a continuance. Move the sludge down the pipeline. There's always next week.

Friar Laurence looks around the audience of some 200 people and says, without condemnation, "These look like the ordinary Saturday night crowd raising hell in downtown London, or Verona, on the morning after. Or perhaps two mornings after." I cannot disagree. Almost all of these people are here on misdemeanor charges related to drinking, gambling, prostitution, dealing in drugs. In the latter case, most of them are consumers, not pushers, and most certainly not wholesalers. Most couldn't post bail. Later this morning, those out on bail will appear; the difference is palpable.

Criminal court is not a cross-section of the community. It is a demographic dredge off the murky bottom of society. Occasionally the middle-class wanders in, perhaps by mistake, or as a witness, or a professional. Sometimes they are relatives. The black and Hispanic populations of New Haven are overrepresented, the Italian-

Americans, who tend to dominate much of New Haven culture, are underrepresented, having moved largely to East Haven, West Haven, and North Haven, where they represent half of the population. Rarely present are the Jewish population of New Haven, long a significant percentage, but now located in suburban communities although they have left a number of synagogues and two yeshivas.

Sometimes people in the audience are there to see what criminal court is all about, as with the Civics class from Hillhouse High. I see Joe Thomas, the Civics teacher, my high school debate coach, shepherding some fifteen or so of his students, some of whom were at St Dominic's yesterday. I recognize one wearing Nazi garb, tan shirt, and pants, all spit and polish, a hank of black hair across his forehead, a smudge of black mustache under his nose, a wannabe Adolph Hitler look alike. I give Mr. Thomas a thumbs up, and he tosses me a small wave. I nod quizzically toward the Hitler knockoff, and Mr. Thomas shrugs as if to say, "It takes all kinds." So much for democracy and Aryan supremacy.

There are a much smaller number of down at the heel private attorneys, trolling for clients, hustling those hapless targets who appear to have money. The private attorneys make their approach, get the basic facts of prior record, of activity on the evening in question, of cash liquidity and within minutes of conversation with the DA, who is equally eager to get rid of the file, arrange the best off the rack deal money can buy. The newly acquired client can walk out the door, case closed. The private attorney's notes are on the back of an envelope.

All of this is done in a crowded, noisome, overheated, humid, ancient, smelly courtroom with peeling paint and high, sagging ceiling. The walls and floor are dingy; the windows are streaked; those who have been in custody since Saturday night are in a holding tank directly off the court room and can be seen and smelled through a crowded barred window. It is a scene out of Dickens, any number of French or Russian novelists, a Kafka scene out of *The Trial*, ironic, because 90% of cases will never go to trial. We are there to ensure that. So is the judge.

I sit Father Laurence in the front row while I locate my seven files, a low number for any Monday morning, arranged by Jo, who understands that Friar Laurence's case will take time and energy away from what might have been an additional five or so clients. I talk individually with my standard issue clients and explain that I have reviewed our investigator's file, and if they are interested in pleading guilty, which seems suggested by the police report in the file, we can dispose of this case this morning, on the usual favorable elements: reduction to a misdemeanor or civil infraction, and community service or treatment or possibly a fine or even probation. But no jail time.

Regardless of the crime, especially if the client has a prior conviction, this is a pretty good deal. Within minutes I am ready to speak to an assistant DA. I am always careful to say, even when it is not indicated, that we are prepared to try the case for someone who wants to plead not guilty. I add that I enjoy trials, and it is the client's choice.

Either way, pleading guilty or not guilty, even in a mobbed court, people are arraigned individually. They are advised of their rights and may defer plea, but the judge is favorably disposed toward anyone who wishes to dispose of his or her case this morning. I am always reminded of Mama Morton from *Chicago*, offering reciprocity. If the plea is guilty, the judge inquires as to whether the defendant did it, is

67

pleading freely, what are the facts, what is the prosecutor's recommendation, all understood? Okay. Done. Next case.

Justice may be blind, but she always stands for the individual, always. In all the trading and bargaining, one deal is never in play: we never trade one client for another. We never go for a lesser deal on A for a better deal on B. Never.

I live for cases that are not routine, that do not flow like grain through the goose of justice. I live for the unusual cases where perhaps justice is at risk, or a good fight to be fought, cases like Friar Laurence's. Which we reach close to noon. "STATE VS FRIAR VALERIAN LAURENCE, NUMBER 22639-19," intones the clerk. With that, Friar Laurence, who has been sitting in the front row, all this time, rises and comes forward, standing next to me. The courtroom goes quiet; not often Friars get brought before the Bar. He is large, dressed upscale, jeans, corduroy jacket—at least for this venue. And for those looking closely, well, not too closely, he has a large crucifix on a woven rope around his neck and comes through the gate in the bar with assurance and stands next to me.

We are at a long wooden table, bearing multiple scars, carved names, and cigarette burns (yes, in a courtroom—don't ask), opposite the clerk who has just called the case and on the same side as the district attorney, Edmund Coke, who is on my left. The judge, who today is Chief Justice John Popham, notes all of the above about Friar Laurence then reacts with heightened interest to the charges being read by the clerk because these are felonies—failure to register as a sex offender, stalking, conspiracy to commit murder—and they are accompanied by a request for a competency hearing and the denial of bail. The fact that this will require a hearing with witnesses is not lost on the judge, nor is the imminence of lunch, which awaits him if he can but vault over the impediments before him.

"Gentlemen," says the Chief, leaning forward so that the dim light in the courtroom shades his eyes, "would someone please tell me what the hell this case is doing here?"

With this, Friar Laurence moves closer to me, leans down, and whispers in my ear, "I think I know this man."

With this, I think, oops.

And with this, Popham sits up straight, slaps his hand on the bench before him, saying, "Does the defendant wish to address the court? I asked someone to explain what the Hell this case is doing here, and the defendant said something. What was it?"

To this, I begin to respond that it was nothing, but before I can say this, Popham says, "I think not, Mr. Collins. I think it was something. I would like to hear what the defendant has to say this case is about and what it is doing here."

And with this, we are off to the races. In court appearances where only formal entries are involved, like a plea or setting bail or imposition of a sentence, the defendant should say nothing. Absolutely nothing. Usually, if he says anything, there is a negative result. District Attorney Coke, standing to my immediate left, begins to choke, trying to stifle laughter. This upsets Popham even more, causing him to ask Mr. Coke whether it is he, not Father Laurence, who is the defendant here. And by the way, what seems so funny. It is now my turn to stifle laughter and draw the judge's attention and irritation. During which Father Laurence leans down toward me and asks whether Justice Popham is John Popham and, since Father Laurence is huge, his huge stage whisper carries across the table, up

69

the bench, and to the attention of the judge, who is indeed, Chief Justice John Popham.

He looks at Friar Laurence and says, "Sir, you believe you know me. I can assure you we do not travel in the same social circles, in view of your religious vocation and the charges against you. Moreover, I can assure you it is pure happenstance that we meet at all, since handling a Mickey Mouse docket such as this comes my way only by the mishap that Presiding Judge Jay Johnston was this morning struck by a bus while crossing Chapel Street. Jaywalking, I might add." This brings a certain amount of merriment back into the picture, accompanied by a minor ripple of laughter.

Turning to Edmund Coke, the Chief Justice says, "What are we doing here?"

Coke mutters under his breath, "I thought you'd never ask." And then, more loudly, "The defendant is here to have a criminal complaint served upon him, which I do hereby effect by handing this warrant to him and instructing the bailiff to take him into custody."

The smallish bailiff moved toward Friar Laurence, but Chief Justice Popham, never one to give up control of his courtroom, intervenes by saying, "Simple service is sufficient for now, Mr. Coke. Let us turn to custody after we have resolved the issue of bail. These are felony charges that ordinarily require a substantial amount of cash as a down payment on a professional bond. Why is that not sufficient?"

"We request the court to deny bail. The most serious charge involves homicide, sufficient in itself to deny bail. But in addition, we have charged stalking and failure to register as a sex offender, both felonies involving itinerant and unstable misconduct. And all of this is consistent with the defendant's character, which involves no known residence and traveling great distances for the purposes of doing harm.

"We believe that Friar Laurence has come to New Haven for the specific purpose of effecting the deaths of two teenagers who are in high school here, members of established New Haven families with businesses here, and presently in rehearsal for a musical production of *Romeo and Juliet* at the Yale School of Drama, preparatory to off-Broadway this summer. The show has drawn widespread attention because the Director, Professor Burbage of the Yale Drama School, has done a radical revision of the play, challenging centuries of tradition, he says, and we believe Friar Laurence has come here to oppose Professor Burbage's efforts and inflict harm on the two young actors.

"In light of this, this case would seem wholly appropriate for the denial of bail, on the grounds of imminent danger to others and improbability that Friar Laurence will appear for trial. Additionally, competence is at issue because Friar Laurence claims he has traveled through space and time from 400 years ago, where he was a fictional character in the play *Romeo and Juliet*, in which his character kills the young lovers. Obviously, the man is a nutcase."

Before I could say a word, Justice Popham leaned forward and said, "Mr. Collins, don't bother with your usual pitch for bail. Let me ask a few questions of both you and Mr. Coke.

"First, has Friar Laurence ever been convicted of a crime involving sexual misconduct or children or anything at all, anywhere?"

I could hear Edmund Coke beginning to choke, and so I stepped forward to help him, by saying, "No. Never. Nowhere. No how."

Perhaps improvidently, I added, turning to Coke, but saying it too loudly, so that Justice Popham heard me, "Ballgame!"

Popham jumped on that and said, "Well, Mr. Collins. This may be a game to you, but it is not to me. Be careful, you're walking a thin line. Hearing no contradiction from Mr. Coke, I sense that there is little likelihood Friar Laurence will be convicted of failing to register as a sex offender; though he may well be a pedophile but there has been no adjudication of that fact. However, I might note that for your benefit Mr. Coke, our statute on registering does not require conviction if equivalent evidence of misconduct is established.

"Turning to the stalking charge, Mr. Coke, is there anything in the file to suggest Friar Laurence has had any contact with these two children or that he has attempted to have any?"

To this, Edmund sputtered and then said, "This case only arose on Friday, and we have not yet had time to conduct a thorough investigation. We would ask the court's indulgence, while we interview the two teenagers and other witnesses who might shed light on the answer to your question ..."

Prompting the Chief Justice to interrupt abruptly, saying, "Mr. Coke, I take it the answer to my question is no. I might add, Mr. Coke, that your ancestor, Edward, to whom you bear a striking resemblance, also had difficulty with brevity. We will not pursue this now since it may only lead to another lengthy circumlocution on your part, when we are all trying to get to lunch.

"And so, I turn to my third question, Mr. Coke, since at present there seems little evidence of imminence of danger or harm, why should we fear that Friar Laurence has conspired to commit murder? Do you have statements or evidence, weapons, or secret meetings with confederates? Anything at all?"

My good friend to my left, now reconsidering his choice of vocations, responds, "Yesterday afternoon, after a mass at St. Dominic's at which he presided, Friar Laurence, in response to my question, answered that he has traveled 400 years and thousands of miles, as a result of causing the deaths of two teenagers in the Shakespeare play, *Romeo and Juliet*, and fears that he has been transported to our time possibly to repeat the crime. During a sermon in the mass, he said he fears he has done harm and prays daily not to repeat. Taking all of that at face value, we believe there is probable cause to fear he will make an attempt on the lives of the young teenagers in the play at the Drama School."

I have been stunned by the cogency and force of Coke's success at weaving a net of genuine plausibility out of circumstantial evidence, so I am prepared for the Chief Justice to lend credence to Coke's presentation. He has a long-established reputation himself as a law-and-order trial judge and before that as a prosecutor. His opinions on the appellate bench have been far to the right and punitive in the extreme. It is hard to tell which of us, Edmund Coke or I, is more dumbfounded and startled, indeed amazed, by what comes next.

The Chief leans forward and says, "Mr. Coke, are you keeping me from lunch because of the absurd rantings of a senile Dominican priest, which at most might support your request for a competency hearing, but hardly a denial of bail? Or are you telling me that you credit those rantings and believe he is a killer from another time and place?"

Coke is about to say, "Aw, what the Hell, just pick one," but—

Popham cuts him off and says, "Choose carefully; you can't have it both ways. I intend to dispose of this quickly and will hear witnesses after lunch. I am not pleased with the delay created by counsel and

73

this defendant. As for you, Mr. Collins, please practice brevity; your ancestor, to whom you bear a striking resemblance, had the same deficiency as Mr. Coke's.

Court adjourned until 2:00 PM."

With that, Chief Justice John Popham rises, as do the counsel and audience and officials with him, all standing while Popham exits, stage left.

With that, Friar Laurence turns to me and asks, "Was this what you were told as we came in would be your worst nightmare"?

To which I replied, "In a sense. It meant we would not have the regular judge sitting, who moves cases like lightning and with minimum friction. Instead, we got a rookie and a mess."

Friar Laurence is puzzled, saying, "The Chief Justice is a rookie?"

"Yes," I reply, "in the sense of not being able to move business in the routine against the background of common understandings and practices."

"So," Friar Laurence says, "It is not usual for a Chief Justice to sit on arraignment court?"

At this, Edmund Coke guffaws, "No, Friar Laurence, his being here is no more ordinary than the Pope taking over your local Abby. Ordinarily, judges claw their way up to the appellate bench to avoid precisely this kind of duty. But here he is, so it appears the cosmos is giving us the full Monty, for which thank you very much." And with that, Coke, battered and beaten, leaves to prepare for the hearing at 2:00 PM.

As he passes me, I say, "I thought you did a great job, Ed. Popham loved it."

Without turning, but bending as if to pick up a document, Coke replies, "Up yours, Francis," and strides out of the courtroom.

And now, as I turn Friar Laurence toward the back of the emptying courtroom, I say, "And I have a question for you. Why did you say you thought you had met this man before? I am quite certain that Chief Justice Popham and I have both spent our entire careers in the courtrooms of Connecticut."

Here, Friar Laurence drew himself to his full, towering height, scanned the now empty, echoing courtroom, and paused, intoning, "Francis. That's my point. This is not your 21st-century Chief Justice."

He continued, "Today's Chief Justice John Popham is, I'm quite certain, the same John Popham who presided in the Gunpowder Conspiracy in 1604, where he convicted Guy Fawkes. He also tried the Jesuit, Southwell, and ordered him hung, drawn and quartered. He was a law-and-order judge for the Crown, convicting Mary, Queen of Scots, and Sir Walter Raleigh. In numerous cases, he worked with District Attorney Coke's ancestor. Now he is here."

I am sure I looked incredulous. But Laurence drove his point home, "How else would Popham know that you and Coke resemble your ancestors. Do you have a drawing or painting of the original Francis Collins?"

"No," I replied, "his only claim to fame was handling Shakespeare's minor business litigation and drafting his will. There is no likeness of him anywhere." Stunned by all this, I added, "Well. We have descendants of Elizabethan progenitors all over this case. Why bring on another original, actual traveler, like you? I won't even bother to ask how this is done or by whom."

To this, Friar Laurence replied, "I would have said to help today's Edmund Coke prosecute me. Popham worked with Edward Coke on the cases I mentioned; their politics were identical. Together, today, they could certainly put me away for a long time."

I added, "The ancestor, Edward Coke, prosecuted Walter Raleigh, an absolute legend, with such mean, nasty, vicious language, he would be held in contempt today.

"But wait," I reflected, "as they say at 3:00 in the morning, there's more: yesterday's Coke turned soft. Back in the day, As Chief Justice of the Court of Common Pleas, he cut back the Star Chamber; he declared the King was subject to law; that laws of Parliament were void if contrary to common reason. He was kicked upstairs to the King's Bench and finally dismissed for narrowing the meaning of treason. He was forced off the bench, and in Parliament got the Petition of Rights passed against Charles; together with the Magna Charta, the two are England's Constitution."

"And so," continued Friar Laurence, "perhaps there is a danger that today's Coke won't be tough enough, may have some soft spots like his ancestor. Yesterday's Popham was a straight law-and-order, right-wing, hang 'em and cut 'em Chief Justice. He never changed. And he is here today, the real thing, not a mere descendant like Coke or you, forgive me, Francis, to put me away."

"But his rulings today were all wrong," I said, "it is as though he passed through Alice's looking glass. Every ruling he has made so far favors the defense. Well, that is no crazier than anything else in this case," I said. "It would seem someone wants to keep you on the street and at liberty. Whoever sent you, sent him. Why? Go figure ..."

We stood to leave the courtroom, this shop of curiosities, with Friar Laurence adding one more bit to the puzzle. And it was this, "All of these cases where Popham and Coke worked together, plus the prosecution of a Jesuit, Father Garnet, all were in support of the protestant church of Shakespeare's time, all were part of that anti-

Catholic frenzy. And, as you may have noticed, we Dominicans are a Roman Catholic Order.

And with that, we went out into the bright sunshine of the New Haven Green, strolled across to Louis' Lunch on Crown Street, highly recommended by the Whiffenpoofs, where they claim to have invented the hamburger, no ketchup or mayonnaise or relish. It's Louis' way or the highway.

Issues of competency could wait an hour or two.

CHAPTER NINE

LUNCH AT THE PLACE WHERE LOUIS DWELLS
AND COKE IS HOISTED ON HIS OWN PETARD

Over lunch, Friar Laurence and I discuss the two remaining stages before he enters his not guilty plea: bail, and competency. I tell him we will take him over to the bail officer and have an intake done, which involves standard forms and questions that he will blow off the charts since he will tell the truth: he is 400 years old, last residence was Verona via London, his only local connection is the Dominican Abbey, and he has no family or employment or connections, other than the Abbot and the Order and me. Oh yeah, and he's not sure how he got here or when he might be gone ...

Would you hire this man to babysit your kids? To park your car? If not, he is not a good bet for bail.

As for competence, there are two kinds. One applies only in criminal cases, whether a person is competent to stand trial: can he assist in his own defense, does he understand the charges, can he communicate with counsel? No problemo, it would seem. Laurence is a bright guy, highly educated, and so far, at least, looking to me for guidance. He can stand trial, sure.

The other kind of competence is broader and, for Friar Laurence, problematic: a person is competent if able to care for himself and not a danger to self and others. The good Friar seems iffy on this kind of competence, given his lack of home and income and lack of comprehension of how he got here and where he is going, his open statement that he is afraid he will hurt somebody, plus his prior history of, well, killing kids ...

Friar Laurence takes umbrage at this last phrasing, saying, "I hope you can come up with a better phrasing to what seems to me an excessively unkind way of summarizing my position, which was to help the kids deal with unreasonable parents and tribal animosities and getting married."

We have been joined by Friar Dominic, the Abbot. He volunteers to testify on Friar Laurence's behalf on both bail and competence. He has now been with Friar Laurence for a week. He can attest to his normalcy and reliability within that time frame.

There is another thing, Abbot Dominic adds, he is considering having Father Laurence hear confessions ... At this, I burst out saying, "Holy shit! Are you kidding me?"

Both men of the cloth exchange glances and the Abbot continues, "We are shorthanded. Father Laurence has extensive experience. The exchanges are anonymous. As you may remember from your youth, Francis, it's a very cut and dried process. A little like that plea bargaining you were doing. Quick. Standard packages, especially for teenagers."

Here the good Abbot looks at me closely, as though reading my mind, once again bounces his eyebrows and adds, "You know, you were boring, Francis." (And here, again, the Abbot seems to have access to my mind, even decades ago. Huh. What did I confess back then?)

I reconsider my initial reaction quickly, saying, "Oh, what the hell. This will fit right in with everything else about this case. I would be delighted to put you on the stand. Especially since I don't have any other witnesses and probably can't call Friar Laurence."

This gives the Abbot yet another opening. "Perhaps I could suggest one other character witness, Francis," pausing now for effect, my appreciation for the magical Abbot keeps growing, "and that would be the District Attorney himself." He pauses, with a grin, for my reaction. And he gets it.

"Oh, swell! Edmund Coke, descendant of that distinguished prosecutor Edward Coke, is now going to be called as a witness against his own case, as a character witness for what he believes to be a crazed killer.

"What, exactly, do you think my brilliant cross-examination could extract from my worthy opponent, the chief district attorney, one Edmund Coke?"

Abbot Dominic, never one to be flustered by heavy sarcasm or unprepared for insightful commentary, replies, "The usual."

At this, I snort, "At long last, something usual about this case, I simply ask the prosecutor if he attended mass, who delivered the sermon and what was it about, did he or anyone else leave in the middle or did he stay and does he remember what was said? And what exactly was that?" I am thinking, it's a pretty damn good twist, isn't it?

To which the Abbot, bouncing his eyebrows as usual, responds, "You got that right, Francis. Can you go with it?"

"Well, there isn't much choice, but I think it might work. Sure, that makes two witnesses, sort of."

"So that's two witnesses," says Friar Laurence, "and I could be the third despite your statement earlier that I cannot testify. You didn't say why, but I assume it's so I don't incriminate myself or say something I contradict later. Is that right?"

"That's a pretty good summary," I say.

"Despite that," Friar Laurence continues, "My streaming of selected criminal cases on the Internet tells me this is a pretty good turnout of witnesses for a competency or bail hearing, on such short notice. And the prosecution will be trying to show that I am incompetent, which might well help with our diminished capacity defense at trial."

"Huh," says I, somewhat dazzled by the neat twist Friar Laurence has put on this question of testifying, and I say, "I am somewhat dazzled by your Internet expertise."

Friar Laurence continues, "And isn't there something in the rules of evidence or procedure to the effect that statements during an examination for psychological or psychiatric purposes cannot be used to prove the defendant is guilty, just the psychiatrist's conclusions? Plus, without me, Coke has no case, so he would probably stipulate not to use the hearing evidence later at trial. How do you like them beans?"

I pause and reflect on the colloquialism, trying to hide the fact that I am dazzled (I think I mentioned that above), then I recall that I cannot hide anything from Abbot Dominic, and so I say, "Time to go. How did you like them pizzas? New Haven claims to make the best pizzas in the world."

To this, Father Laurence responds quickly, "That is the one thing I shall miss most if I ever return to my own time. There are no pizzas in England or Italy in my time. In fact, there is no Italy! So, I will miss them and CNN and *Saturday Night Live* and *Comedy Central*. I doubt I can get Internet coverage to extend to the 1600s."

The Abbot leans close to me and says, sotto voce, "Shall we tell him about roaming? Do you think roaming is a possibility?"

"I checked it out," says Father Laurence, "I couldn't afford it on my cell phone plan. It might drive me into poverty ..."

The two clerics elbow each other laughing, and one says, "Perhaps our clerical sense of humor might get us an appearance on SNL."

Not likely, I think to myself. The Abbot bounces his eyebrows at me ...

I look at my two lunch companions and say, "We need to hurry. We have used far more than the hour we had to be back by 2:00 PM."

"Look at your watch," says the Abbot, "I think we have plenty of time to get back, set up the bail intake, and settle down before the Chief Justice levels his guns." The Abbot is correct, somehow less than 30 minutes have passed ... Very strange, until I recall ...

We quickly walk the six blocks to court, open the outside door, and wait on tired benches in the crowded hallway for 15 minutes while Friar Laurence does his interview with the bail intake officer. When they return to the corridor, the bail officer, Miriam Anderson, with whom I have had extensive dealings, shakes Friar Laurence's hand and says, "I consider this to have been a privilege, Friar Laurence. Yours is the most interesting, possibly bizarre, interview I have ever conducted. Good luck. We do not often get itinerant monks, especially those from London, or was it Verona? Italy, right? And you have yet to commit your crimes, or maybe you did them 400 years ago ... I think I will stick around. I want to see how this plays out."

Then, crossing the crowded entryway, we enter through the swinging doors to what is no longer the arraignment court but Courtroom Number One. As we enter, the clerk is calling the case of State versus Friar Laurence, Edmund Coke is at counsel table with a detective beside him, and seeing us, waves broadly for us to join him, which we do, Friar Laurence and I at counsel table, the Abbot in the first row immediately behind us.

CHIEF JUSTICE POPHAM

"Mr. Collins. How nice of you to join us. I note with pleasure that Friar Laurence is still with us, a fact somewhat inconvenient for Mr. Coke. Let the record note that we will treat as a single matter the two issues of denial of bail and determination of competence, in a consolidated hearing, given the shortness of time and the absence of objection by counsel.

"Do you have any objection to going forward, Mr. Collins? Mr. Coke?"

MR. COLLINS

"None, Your Honor. Friar Laurence is intrigued by the possibility that my esteemed colleague Mr. Coke will attempt to pull a rabbit out of a hat and would like to see it done. I assured him that Mr. Coke does it all the time. Beyond that, if we get that far, I will offer three witnesses, Friar Laurence himself, his superior, Abbot Dominic who is the administrator of St. Dominic's Abby here at the Cathedral, and a third, perhaps a bit of a surprise witness, a player to be named later."

CHIEF JUSTICE POPHAM

"Name our mystery guest now."

MR. COLLINS

"The player to be named later is the prosecutor himself, Edmund Coke."

MR. COKE

"Not on your life!"

CHIEF JUSTICE POPHAM

"I will be the one to rule on Mr. Collins' life if and when we get that far; in the meantime, the ball as they say, is now in your court, Mister Coke. You have the burden of proof and persuasion; do you have either in hand?"

MR. COKE

"I do, in the person of Detective Seamus O'Connor, of New Haven's finest. I now call him to the stand."

O'Connor comes forward from the audience section, through the gate in the railing which separates the courtroom area from the audience area, and stands to take the oath as administered by the clerk. He sits. This ritual is effected perfunctorily, and I reflect that with either of my cleric witnesses, it might be a bit more complex, but we shall wait and see. In the meantime, Detective O'Connor is, as one might expect, very Irish, heavyset with a full head of wavy silver hair over a florid face which has been warmly and well served for decades at Morrie's watering hole, call Central Casting for Brian Dennehy ...

Coke's interrogation begins quickly, by formula, and moves swiftly to the point. Which is, that the good Detective O'Connor is a longtime congregant of St. Dominic's, was there on Sunday when Father Laurence delivered the sermon, and was nearby, well within earshot, as Chief District Attorney Coke later confronted Father Laurence, so Seamus O'Connor is able to testify as to who said what. Namely, Father Laurence believes he is several hundred years old, from a place thousands of miles away, does not know how he got here but fears that he will commit harm, having said as much during the sermon in the sanctuary.

Ballgame.

MR. COKE

"Do you have any questions of this witness, Your Honor?"

CHIEF JUSTICE POPHAM

"If I did, I am perfectly capable of asking without an invitation. The important point is whether Mr. Collins has any questions or is dumbfounded and bedazzled by the brilliance of your footwork here."

MR. COLLINS

"Officer, you say you are a communicant of St. Dominic's, and were there yesterday when Friar Laurence conducted mass?"

OFFICER O'CONNOR

"Yes."

Q. "Did you stay for his entire sermon?"

A. "Yes."

Q. "Do you recall what he said?"

A. "Absolutely."

Q. "And what was that?"

MR. COKE

"Objection."

CHIEF JUSTICE POPHAM

"On what grounds?"

MR. COKE

"Relevancy, materiality, and competence."

CHIEF JUSTICE POPHAM

"You have been watching way too much Perry Mason, Mr. Coke, and need to update not only your objections but also your taste in viewing. I think where Mr. Collins is going is to turn your witness into his witness by having the officer testify that the Friar's sermon was a thoughtful, well-constructed and searching condemnation of child abuse and the church's failure to deal properly with that epidemic. And if that is not where he is going, then I recommend, Mr. Collins, that you go there directly. Proceed. Oh, and by the way, objection overruled."

I stand there, wondering how the Chief Justice knew the contents of Friar Laurence's sermon of yesterday. A question for another time. I turn and look at the Abbot, receiving the customary eyebrow bounce. I turn back to Seamus O'Connor and inquire of this archetypal Son of the Sod what Friar Laurence said.

A. "He said essentially that the Catholic Church in recent decades has been consumed by thousands of instances, worldwide, of adults complaining that they were subjected to abuse while children by priests in parishes across the United States, Ireland, the United Kingdom, and other places as well. Moreover, this misconduct was compounded by cover-ups by church administrators and punitive retaliation against those who complained. Offending priests were moved from parish to parish with no corrective action and no discipline. This violated the church's contract with God and parishioners alike and was a corporate sin crying out for resolution."

Q. "Was there more?"

A. "Yes, Friar Laurence spoke at length about the vulnerability of young children, Christ's invitation and insistence that the little children be suffered to come unto him, and, in view of all this, the actions necessary to repair the wounds to Christ's children and his church."

Q. "Without extending this too much further, as to the content of the sermon, can you tell us whether Friar Laurence expressed his own personal or professional view of this offensive pattern of misconduct?"

A. "Yes, he was appalled and moved to tears, and many in the audience were moved to tears, as was I, and said he felt physically and morally repelled."

MR. COKE

"Oh, sweet mother of God!"

Looking to my right, I observed that Friar Laurence was hunched forward over counsel table, his hands spread out in a fanning pattern, and he was staring at them. There were tears in his eyes. I paused, for effect, and then turned to officer O'Connor.

Q. "Let me try coming at the sermon from a slightly different approach. I am going to assume that as a regular communicant at St. Dominic's and elsewhere, you have probably heard dozens and perhaps hundreds of sermons. Did you recall all of them afterward with the clarity and detail that you have shown here with respect to Friar Laurence's sermon of yesterday or is this unusual?"

MR. COKE

"Objection!"

CHIEF JUSTICE POPHAM

"Overruled."

A. "It is most unusual."

Q. "Was this because of the content, or the mode of delivery, or both.?"

MR. COKE

"Objection!"

CHIEF JUSTICE POPHAM

"Overruled."

A. "Both, but particularly Friar Laurence's powerful delivery. We were all moved."

Q. "Was it among the best sermons you have ever heard?"

A. "Yes, absolutely."

Q. "The product of a fully competent mind?"

MR. COKE

"Objection!"

Q. "No mumbling, no stumbling, and no bumbling over words or ideas?"

MR. COKE

"I would like a ruling on my objections."

CHIEF JUSTICE POPHAM

"No, you wouldn't, they are all overruled. You may continue, but finish up, please, Mr. Collins."

Q. "Officer O'Connor, any question in your mind as to Friar Laurence's competence?"

MR. COKE

"Obj... oh, the Hell with it!"

A. "None whatsoever."

Q. "Let me shift ground from whether Friar Laurence seemed competent in his delivery to whether his words indicated he is morally destitute and may pose a danger to others. Were his words, Officer, the words of a man bereft of morality, posing a danger to others, particularly children?"

A. "Absolutely not."

MR. COKE

"Objection! Objection! Calls for opinion, beyond the scope of direct, total speculation, and, and ..."

CHIEF JUSTICE POPHAM

"Before you throw in 'irrelevant, incompetent, and immaterial,' let me simply say, Mr. Coke, that your objection is overruled, I will take Officer O'Rourke's testimony for what it is worth, which I would say is considerable, and, unless counsel have further questions, excuse the witness with the thanks of the Court."

MR. COLLINS

"With the permission of the Court, I do have two or three more questions."

CHIEF JUSTICE POPHAM

"Be brief."

MR. COLLINS

"Officer O'Rourke, your testimony earlier about what Father Laurence said of where he is from, and of the danger he is afraid he poses, did that come before or after the sermon?"

A. "After."

Q. "Did it change your opinion as to the competence and moral fibre of Father Laurence?"

CHIEF JUSTICE POPHAM

"With only one or two more questions to go, we would all be well served by avoiding or drawing objections."

A. "No."

Q. "Why not?"

A. "Because it is clear that Friar Laurence does not plan to do harm, does not seek to do harm, and is frightened by the very prospect."

I looked to my right; Friar Laurence was nodding vigorously. I turned to look at the Abbot sitting behind me, receiving his signature eyebrow bounce. With that, I turned back to the Chief Justice and said, "No further questions."

"Good choice," said the Chief.

"We will stand in brief recess," the bailiff intoned, "all rise," and with that, Chief Justice John Popham exited, stage left.

I turned to Edmund Coke and said, "Ed, I really think that went well. I really, really, really hope you have more witnesses."

During the brief recess, I huddle with the Abbot and the Friar, and the first question I have is, "Friar Laurence, you believe that this Chief Justice Popham is the same law-and-order, string 'em up judge who had defendants halved and quartered in your time. Yes?" He nods. I continue," That hardly explains why he is kicking the prosecutor around and making rulings favorable to us. Any thoughts?"

The answer comes wrapped in whimsy, "Perhaps he is experiencing jet lag from excessive travel?"

Before I can respond, the Abbot interjects, "Perhaps, rather, he is trying to create an appearance of even-handedness, before he rules favorably to the prosecution." But then he adds, "Perhaps he intends to keep Friar Laurence at liberty in the community, with the thought that my good Brother will engage in misconduct, assuring conviction on the pending charges. He may be of the view that if you give a man enough rope, he will hang himself."

We reassemble at the counsel table, and I note that for a midafternoon in criminal court, there is an unusually large audience assembled. The Chief Justice enters from the chamber's door, rises to the bench, the bailiff intones "all rise."

Coke says, "Your Honor, as our next witness, we wish to call Miriam Anderson, the chief bail officer." And we are off to the races.

Like everything else in this case, Ms. Anderson's appearance as a witness is unusual. Ordinarily, the bail officer makes her decision to release or sets terms in her office. Rarely does the bail officer testify.

Ms. Anderson is sworn, Coke asks whether she interviewed the defendant, for how long, and whether she spoke with other people concerning his competency and his likelihood of flight. I interpose a hearsay objection as to any reference to what the "other people" said. Coke responds somewhat acidly, that "Mr. Collins objection is not only ill-timed, since I have asked no questions, but it is also without foundation since Ms. Anderson would testify as to what they said only as the basis of her conclusion, not for the content or truth of what they said." The Chief Justice overrules my objection, telling Coke to get on with it, which he does by asking what they said. Objection. Overruled, again.

And the Chief turns to Ms. Anderson and says, "Please tell us what you learned in your investigation and what your conclusion was, and please expedite this if possible."

"First, of course, Your Honor, I interviewed Friar Laurence. We have a standard form that covers education, employment, residence, family, and other ties to the community. None of them applies to Friar Laurence. To be precise, his 'community,' if he has one, is some 5000 miles away in England and Italy. Our budget would not cover long distance calls to confirm his associations with the Dominican order and the churches there. There is one other problem, but I will simply pass it by, to the effect that Friar Laurence says that until a week or so ago, he was living not only in another place but another time, either the 1400s in Verona or the 1600s in London, in either event, cell phone service and long-distance calling would not be available."

Here, Ms. Anderson looked up at the Chief Justice and added, "Maybe this is obvious. But they would not have been invented. Am I clear?" The Chief nodded, Mr. Coke nodded, the Abbot, the Friar and

I nodded, and the audience began tittering, perhaps laughing, maybe a guffaw or two.

Here, Coke cut to the chase, saying, "That being true, I assume you recommend he be held with no bail, since the charges here are at the felony level, including homicide and there is no way to guarantee Friar Laurence will appear for trial. Correct?" Here, Coke turned partially toward me, obscuring his face from the Chief Justice, and with his typical SEG, said, "Ballgame."

I had already prepared for this and was turning to tell Friar Laurence not to lose control over being locked up when I heard Ms. Anderson say, "Not quite so, Mr. Coke. In such cases, where nobody has resources or ties or places in the community, there is the paradox: he or she has nothing to keep her here, but, at the same time, no place to go and no way to get there. We call this the ne exeat, (meaning no exit), paradox."

Well, thought I, "I haven't heard this before," and without thinking, said as much.

"You and I are in the same position," said Popham, "Ms. Anderson, if it has a Latin name, in law, that means there is a form or format for dealing with it. In such cases, what do you do? I must say I would be inclined to lock the defendant up."

"What we do, Your Honor, is consider two other factors. First, is there a place for the defendant to stay such that he is likely to remain for trial? Here, there is, since I talked with the Abbot of St. Dominic's Abby, Father Dominic, who is at counsel table. He assures me that Friar Laurence has been a stable, dependable member of the clerical community here for well over a week and fits a pattern with which Father Dominic is familiar, of longtime members staying as a matter of routine for as long as need be.

"I asked Father Dominic, and he replied that based upon conversation and observation, he could attest that Friar Laurence appears to be a long-established member of the Dominican Order. The second factor is a motive: talking with Friar Laurence and sitting here and listening to Officer O'Rourke's testimony, it is clear that Friar Laurence espouses deeply held values and believes he has come here in pursuit of validation of them in his life."

Here, Coke, clearly losing it, slams his note pad on the counsel table and enters an objection, asking that the testimony about the ne exeat paradox be stricken, as based on speculation and hearsay, particularly as to the reference to Father Dominic. The Chief leans forward from the bench, with an expression on his face approximating an unaccustomed smile, and said, "Again, Mr. Coke, it appears that you have hoisted yourself on your own petard, first officer O'Rourke, and now Ms. Anderson, being your own witnesses, have done your case considerable harm. As to speculation, predicting what any person's conduct will be is inherently speculative. As to the summary of Friar Dominic's comments, I note that he is here in court, and if you choose, you may call him to cross-examine him as to whether he made the statements. Before you do so, as one old courtroom lawyer to another, let me say, I suspect that his position will not be favorable to you, and you may want to consider moving on."

With that, Coke turned again to Ms. Anderson and said that he wished to move on from the bail question to the question of competence.

In her professional and official capacity, was she required to assess the competence of people before releasing them on bail? The answer was affirmative. And had she done so in many cases? Again, affirmative. Then Coke summarized portions of Ms. Anderson's testimony, to the effect that Friar Laurence had said his home was either London or Verona and in either instance some 4 to 600 years ago, was that correct? Once more, an affirmative response. With that, Mr. Coke asked the critical question, pointing to the obvious and the absurd, "Do you believe that to be true?" I sensed Friar Laurence leaning forward intensely, waiting for the answer.

Here I rose and objected; Ms. Anderson's personal opinion did not matter. Coke responded that the Chief had allowed speculation, why not professional opinion, bearing on competence, since it is part of the process? Popham leaned forward, sustained my objection, and suggested to Mr. Coke that the proper question might be whether, in her professional opinion, given her training and experience, was it likely that Friar Laurence was speaking the truth.?

Coke thanked the Chief, turned to Ms. Anderson, and posed the question, and her response was, "No. Of course not. If he is from another time and place, he would long ago have been dead. Which he clearly is not. It's not my opinion; it's simply a matter of fact."

"And so, Ms. Anderson," Coke leaned forward, pointing his finger at her and shaking it, "this means you propose to turn loose into the community a man who is either blatantly lying or plainly crazy. Is that not so?" I rose to object, but before I could utter the words or state the grounds, the Chief overruled me, saying that Mr. Coke would be permitted to cross-examine his own witness, who should answer the question.

I tried to think of another objection but could not and sat down.

Ms. Anderson paused, Coke repeated his question; she responded that she had heard it the first time and had thought long about this matter, her answer was as follows: Bail officers deal at great length and frequency with mentally disturbed individuals. Whether clinically insane or not, their competence to stand trial or care for themselves may be at issue. We assess that.

"Friar Laurence is rational, stable, and has a place to live, and has been observed there for well over a week. In the short time he says he has been here, he has absorbed an enormous amount of information as to time and place and circumstance. He is not crazy; and in my judgment, he is competent to aid and assist counsel in this proceeding, the test of competence."

Coke quickly interjected, "And so this must mean that he is ..."

"Lying?" Ms. Johnson interjected, "Friar Laurence clearly understands that he presents himself as an impossibility, as being from elsewhere and from another time, and he also clearly understands that he worsens an already impossible posture by saying he does not know how he got here or why. No person would intentionally concoct such a lie since no one would believe it, including himself. But Friar Laurence does.

"So, we come back to the question, is he mentally incompetent or insane? Someone holding these beliefs might well be insane but would not understand the improbability of the expressed beliefs. In competency hearings, when the defendants say they hear voices, they believe that they hear real voices. When somebody believes that he or she is the King of Ethiopia or the Queen of Greece, they believe it is true. They do not believe it improbable or irrational. Friar Laurence holds his beliefs but understands that, even to himself, they seem incredible and irrational.

"One remaining factor tips the balance, namely his belief that he is here for a purpose, that he has been brought here to resolve an issue in his life and to do good, as penance for prior mishaps. Whatever those were, the belief itself speaks volumes for the man, as does officer O'Rourke's earlier testimony concerning Sunday's sermon and the Church's pattern of misconduct. It was a remarkable sermon and the fact that the Abbot invited him to deliver it is ample evidence of the Abbot's respect for Friar Laurence.

"In my judgment, he is not lying, and he is capable of functioning well in our time and place. His belief that he is from another time or place does not counter that, though it is logically inconsistent.

"Mr. Coke, I am sorry as can be that I cannot tie this up in a neat package; my recommendation is that Friar Laurence be released on his own recognizance, restricted to residence at the Dominican Abby, in the custody of the Abbot, Father Dominic, who will assure that Father Laurence will appear as ordered and when ordered by this Court."

"Ms. Anderson," Coke began, "you referenced 'mishaps' earlier in Friar Laurence's life. Did he tell you what they were?" The answer was negative. "Do you know whether they involved children, teenagers say?"

Answer, "No."

"Would your recommendation of release change if you knew that the so-called 'mishaps' involved extended conduct leading ..."

And here I am out of my chair pounding the table, shouting, "Objection. Calls for speculation. Beyond the scope of direct! She has said she does not know!"

The Chief himself uses the gavel on the bench, responding sternly, "Sit down, Mr. Collins. Sit down! Presumably, Mr. Coke will connect up whatever he has in his folder. In any event, Ms. Anderson will not be speculating if given a hypothetical, she says, in her experience, it could have an impact. Sit down. Objection overruled"

Coke resumes his question, "Would it matter if the so-called "mishaps" involved extended conduct by Friar Laurence, deceiving the parents of one of the children, encouraging them to marry illegally and flee the country, and then take medications leading ultimately to their deaths?"

I'm so appalled I cannot object in time before the answer comes, "Yes. Definitely."

And now Coke goes for the kill, "Would it matter, further, if the two children, a boy and a girl, were in a play and that very play today is in rehearsal here in New Haven, and the young kids playing those roles, are from families identical to those of the boy and girl whom Friar Laurence killed?"

There was an objection out there somewhere, but I could not think of what it was or articulate it.

A preternatural stillness and chill settled in the courtroom; it seemed a mist floated high against the ceiling, obscuring the balcony and the tops of the ancient windows. I looked to my right; there were tears on Friar Laurence's face, and beyond him a shimmering next to the Abbot. It was as if time stood still and ghosts walked the antique aisles of the courtroom. I looked back at the witness. She gathered herself ...

Miriam Anderson leaned forward in the witness box, placing both hands on the rail, she spoke softly, in a whisper, "Are you saying that the roles of the children in this *Romeo and Juliet* play, in rehearsal here, are being acted by children of the New Haven families, the Capulets, and the Montagues? And that this Dominican monk, here today, was that same Friar Laurence, from Shakespeare's time?"

Hair stood up on the back of my neck; I felt goosebumps. I rose. Before I could stop him, before I could object, Coke asked, "Would it matter!?" *Would it?*

And Chief Justice Popham, simultaneously, said, "Sit down, Mr. Collins." There was a long-drawn-out hush, as though the very walls of the old courtroom sighed.

Miriam Anderson replied, "Yes. Yes. It would ... not be mere coincidence; it would suspend all normal probabilities ... it would break my heart."

"No further questions," from prosecutor Coke.

"Mr. Collins?" from Chief Justice Popham.

"Thank you, Your Honor," I replied, and turning to the witness, asked, "but that would be impossible, wouldn't it?"

Answer, slowly, from Ms. Anderson, "Yes."

As I paused to ask the follow-up question, which was whether she would agree then that her opinion would not change, the Abbot leaned across Friar Laurence to whisper urgently, "Don't ask that, Francis."

And I did not. "Nothing further, Your Honor."

Coke rose from his seat and addressed the court, saying, "I have two more witnesses, Friar Dominic, the Abbot at the Dominican Abby, who is sitting at counsel table with Mr. Collins, and the defendant himself, Friar Laurence, may it please the court."

Here Chief Justice Popham rocked back in his chair, clasped his long bony fingers behind his head in interlocked fashion, and responded, "It does not please the court, Mr. Coke. We have heard fully from your own witnesses as to the Abbot's positive view of Father Laurence. We have also heard sufficiently from Ms. Anderson as to Friar Laurence's mental state and position in the community. As to your last reference to a play being in rehearsal, a matter of coincidence seems unimportant, that matter is not in evidence and, even if it were, mere happenstance seems immaterial."

Before he could continue, Coke exploded, "Coincidence! We are not dealing here with happenstance!

"I intend to prove this so-called coincidence is the very reason Friar Laurence came to New Haven in the first place. It provides motive for the stalking charge, and the similarity in the circumstances supports the conspiracy charge as well, plus the failure to register as a sex offender."

Chief Popham drew a long breath, asked Coke if he was quite finished and would he please sit down, which Coke, regaining control, did.

Chief Justice Popham then rendered his decision with the following remarks. "This has been an unusually hurried and compressed hearing, addressing three different subjects at once. Usually, bail and competence are decided separately, although they involve similar issues. The third issue, the substance of the charges, is a matter to be resolved later. And so, Mr. Coke, you may return to the competence and bail subjects when you have more time to prepare adequately. My decision, today, is only preliminary, at best, very much so."

He continued, "Still, what we have heard from officer O'Rourke and Ms. Anderson has been thorough and thoughtful. These are experienced professionals. They have managed to fit highly unconventional facts into a conventional framework. The conclusion is clear; at this point, Friar Laurence is competent to stand trial and to be released into the community with the appropriate restrictions Ms. Anderson recommended.

"I will now add the further restriction of a restraining order, prohibiting Friar Laurence from having any contact with the children acting in the *Romeo and Juliet* production, or any contact otherwise with the production itself or indeed going anywhere near the high school they attend." Leaning forward, Popham looked directly at the Abbot and said, "Father Dominic, are you willing to assume the care and custody of Friar Laurence pending resolution of this matter?" The Abbot nodded in the affirmative. "Are you prepared to advise the court immediately upon suspicion of any violation or misconduct by Friar Laurence?" Again, the Abbot nodded in the affirmative.

The Chief then turned to the stenographer and said, "Let the record show that the Abbot responded in the affirmative and that I am treating his doing so as a commitment under oath, which I am certain you understand, is that correct, Friar Dominic?" A final nod in the affirmative.

"With this, Friar Laurence shall be released on his own recognizance, subject to such further evidence or hearings as Mr. Coke may pursue."

Chief Justice Popham rested his chin on the backs of his interlaced hands, resting his elbows on the bench, and added, "Frankly, Mr. Coke, I am as surprised by my ruling as you are. I have a long-standing reputation and commitment favoring the agencies of law-and order. Partly my decision favoring Friar Laurence is that you have moved too quickly, with insufficient evidence. Partly it is that the Supreme Court is in recess, permitting me to stay with this case and fast-track it and bring it to trial quickly, if possible, within two or three weeks."

With that, Popham hit the bench with his gavel, stated that court was adjourned, the bailiff intoned the customary "all rise," which we did, and the Chief Justice exited through the door behind the bench.

Edmund Coke turned to me and said, "Francis, me lad, the grand jury sits Wednesday. You can expect to hear from me Wednesday morning. You, of course, cannot attend, but the bailiff behind you has in hand a subpoena to serve, right here, right now, upon Friar Laurence and the Abbot, requiring them to appear and give testimony.

"I need hardly tell you they will require appropriate advice." And here he smiled, "As if that would help." And with that, Coke, with long strides, went down the center aisle and out the swinging doors.

I turned to the Abbot and Friar Laurence and said we should get together tomorrow afternoon to talk about what just transpired and to prepare them for the grand jury. Did they have any questions?

Friar Laurence spoke, saying, "Francis, I feel as though I have a story to tell, and you should've allowed me to bring the Chief around."

I was dumbfounded. The Abbot, who had been drinking from a water glass, began choking. "For one thing," I said, "There was no chance. He didn't want to hear from you. Every lawyer in the country would agree with what I'm going to say: by talking at this point you could only make your position worse. Say nothing to anybody, and I will see you tomorrow afternoon. In the meantime, you and the Abbot should go to the bail office and arrange release."

As I turn to leave, I pause and turn back to say, "You should understand that what we have witnessed is one of the strangest performances I could ever imagine. The Chief Justice sitting in arraignment court. A law-and-order judge releasing a potential killer on his own recognizance. The chief prosecutor trying to lock up a priest by turning an arraignment into a mini-trial on competence and absconding. An experienced bail officer coming to tears as she recommends release.

"Gentlemen, this is not my first rodeo, and I believed I had seen it all, but I have never seen anything like this. Maybe I've just never been to a real rodeo. But I truly believe we made a little history today."

The monks go off to the bail office, and I proceed down the center aisle, passing a few of the much-bemused onlookers, still, well, bemused, in their seats. As I walk out the swinging doors into the entryway beyond, the only people left are Joe Thomas and his high school civics students, who give me a small round of applause, again something I am not accustomed to, and the Hitler Youth look-alike, in his sharply pressed khakis, now with an SS button (!) on his collar, throws me a sharp salute.

Okay, I can live with that, but please, no straight arm Sig Heils, please.

I think I hear heels click.

I tip my imaginary hat to the assembled throng. Back to the office.

CHAPTER ELEVEN

MEET MR. D. DATA

It is now late afternoon, having wasted almost an entire working day on preliminary proceedings, which almost never happens (as with the pumped-up competency hearing) or usually consume less than five minutes (as with setting bail). My trusty comrade in arms, and crack secretary and paralegal, Jo, greets me at the office door as she is going home. She inquires of the day's festivities and comments, a bit brusquely, that this kind of performance will hardly pay the rent, the electricity, the computer research databases, the cell phone ... Here, I interrupt, to add, her exorbitant salary. "Amen, to that, brother," she adds. "Oh, and as to databases," Jo says, "Mr. D. Data himself is waiting for you in your inner sanctum."

This is good news. Mr. D. Data is a third-year law student at Yale, while working nights and weekends at his day job, as a techie geek team supervisor at Savant Services. Com., from which he retired as CEO and boy wizard owner and inventor, with enough stock to buy a second rank law school (say, Harvard), but instead he enrolled in Yale. Along with his fellow law students, Data has mastered the half dozen or so databases essential to today's law practice. What Mr. Data brings to the party, in addition, is mastery of obscure disassociated apps in the deep recesses of the Internet, and knowing the limitations and arcane potentials of such mainstream resources as Lexis, Westlaw, and the like. All of this is built on a Master's level base from Caltech and 15 years in the industry, enabling D. Data to boldly go where no geek has gone before. Just don't call him a geek.

Mr. Data's real name is impossibly Greek, making George Stephanopoulos or Constantin Papadopoulous look like one of the

Smith brothers, Mark or Trade, hence the abbreviation to Data, which in our office serves as both first and last name. I find Data sitting behind my desk, feet up on the computer keyboard, a gigantic Italian sub dripping olive oil and pasta sauce on his eternally soiled blue Oxford cloth, button-down shirt, which is taxed to the max to restrain his huge stomach.

We have developed an easy familiarity since he walked into my office during the first week of his first year as a 40-year-old student at Yale Law briefly stating his credentials and seeking to work in the kind of law where, as he put it, getting his hands dirty would not be an occupational hazard, but a testimony to justice. A little presumptuous thought I, but then I skimmed his one-page resume, a copy of which he handed me, shaking off a piece of pepperoni.

Summas everywhere and a Forbes lead as top tech CEO under 30. And a WSJ header when he retired. "You could write your own ticket on Wall Street," I said.

"Maybe," he replied, "but it wouldn't be covered in marinara sauce, or haven't you noticed my clothing? (I had). I don't think I quite fit the image.

I call him D. Data; he calls me C. Collins.

"Hey, C," says D. Data, "I understand we've got a live one who's 400 years old! Way to go! Anything for me in this? I'm getting tired of working on the impact of Connecticut having abolished the insanity defense." We had a case where we needed to know what the remaining alternatives or substitutes might be. This particular defendant killed his wife's paramour, Froggy Marciano, in plain sight one balmy Spring afternoon in front of the Friendly Bar and Grill, emptied a Glock into his chest in broad daylight. Went in, called him out. Froggy accepted, followed by his friends, as improbable as that seems, that Froggy would have friends. So, there were witnesses. So, self-defense is out. Froggy had been mocking our client, doing the double horns thing to John Dante, while also doing his wife. It drove Mr. Dante nuts.

D. Data had suggested insanity for three reasons: it's crazy to shoot your victim in broad daylight in front of his best friends; plus, Dante's wife is as homely as last week's salami sub, and who in his right mind would kill over that? And then, finally, alibi and self-defense are out of the question, since our guy was indubitably on the street, well-armed, in one of New Haven's seediest neighborhoods.

Problem is, while the charges were pending, the legislature pulled the insanity defense and offered no substitute. So, as indicated, we are trying to figure out what else there might be. And also considering finding a Latin phrase in the Constitution which says, Hey They Can't Do that After the Fact (whatever the fact is).

So, what we are seeking is a theory that when charges are pending, the State legislature cannot repeal the insanity defense, which we assert we want to assert and then we will argue repealing retroactive was unconstitutional, something about due process, especially since it's after the fact of our guy killing Froggy, we will add something about ex post facto there. Never mind, our defense is a loser. Never mind, we don't believe it. We claim it, get a judge to uphold the legislature, and argue error in denying our right to the defense. It sets up an appeal, and we have our bargaining chip.

And so, "Yes," I say, "D. Data, there are some things for you to do on the Friar Laurence case.

But first, you have to move your considerable bulk out of my chair, remove your feet from my desk, clean up the marinara sauce, and take a few notes. Here's what we're looking for. And here is why today's research potential is so significant ...

"Jo may have filled you in on the background. Our client, the good Friar, has a set of flimsy charges pending, chiefly stalking and perhaps conspiracy to commit murder, maybe failure to register as a sex offender—"When?" interjects Data—all linked to what he may have done to a couple of teenagers as Shakespeare's Friar Laurence in Verona 400 years ago, but it's present-day reality is based on the animus of our esteemed nemesis, D.A. Edmund Coke, and the fact that Shakespeare's play, *Romeo and Juliet*, is in rehearsal here in New Haven, where the parts are filled by a young girl from the New Haven Capulet family and a young boy from the New Haven Montague family. Prosecutor Coke puts these coincidences together with the fact that our client has appeared out of nowhere and was overheard to say Sunday that he is very much afraid he will do some harm here.

"We may reply to Coke that you cannot convict on coincidence, but he will rejoin that if it walks like a duck, talks like a duck, and has killed before, it's probably a killer duck. He believes the good Friar came here deliberately to do harm, and he is going to look for substance to connect them dots."

D. Data looks up from the iPad where he has been typing furiously and says, "So you want me to look for exactly what Coke's looking for?"

"Absolutely," I replied, "and do it in a way that leaves no tracks for Coke's researcher to capitalize on."

"Oh good," replies D. data, "I love it. A stealth operation. Do you want me to hack into their computer and rip off whatever they find?"

Of course, I do, but that would leave tracks inevitably, plus there is a small ethical question, and so I reply, "Only if you can get away with it."

"You never disappoint," replies D. Data, and then adds, "they'll try to do the same to us. Shall I let them and throw a few red herrings and false leads their way, with one or two inconsequential nuggets of truth?"

"Ah, yes," say I, "you never disappoint."

"So," D. Data says, "put me in the picture. What am I looking for?"

"Come at it two different ways, one as if our Friar is telling the truth and the other as if he isn't, and look for the circumstances which might confirm either one. Standard cross-examination investigation techniques. If he is telling the truth, then there is no plane ticket, no hotel receipt, and no credit card record to show the trail. If he is lying, of course, then those do exist.

Similarly, if he does not know why he is here or how he got here, then there are no similar incidents in his past or, indeed, anyone's past in any country anywhere. Contrarily, if there have been other Romeo and Juliet productions with our Friar or someone similar appearing, then that tells us something important, although I'm not sure what. Also, check to see if R&J has ever been revised like they apparently are doing at the Yale D School.

You see what I'm suggesting? Cast a broad net and see if our client is lying or, at a minimum, see whether this is not his first rodeo."

"Ah, yes," says D. data, "A defendant lying to his attorney. Will wonders never cease? Saints preserve us," with a slight Irish brogue, or is it WC Fields? "So, all I have to do is visit whatever records exist concerning the thousands of productions of the play, *Romeo and Juliet*, over the last 400 years in whatever communities or countries the productions took place. Would you like this before lunch today? (A little irony here.) Will tomorrow do?" (A little less here.)

With that, we begin to narrow the scope and highlight points of comparison. What makes this feasible, and not a needle in a haystack situation, although it certainly is that, is what is unique here is the combination of the roles being occupied by the scions of the original families. That can't happen very often in prior centuries, if at all.

Another distinguishing factor is the play being produced with a visitation by Friar Laurence outside the context of the play itself. Again, that is so improbable, in fact impossible, that it cannot have happened very often. In fact, never. What, never? Well, hardly ever. And, being noteworthy, let us hope someone took note. Especially if revised.

D. Data continues, "So let me work this and come up with other such concatenations and run them on the usual databases, plus the Library of Congress and their sister institutions in London and Paris. Also, the Folger in DC. You know all this. The actual search will be mechanical and relatively quick, even though it will go through thousands of documents. The trick is, in advance, to take lots of time constructing the query. We want red flags not red herrings. That's where the fun is. As I think about it, if I work all night, tomorrow noon might be realistic." He snapped his iPad shut and rose as if to go.

"Not so fast, you sly dog," I interjected. "There's another way of looking at this. What gets clients in trouble, whether they be presidents of the United States, a discontented husband like John Dante, or an itinerant Friar, is talking too much and making damaging admissions or inconsistent statements. So, let's take a look at social media and see if our client has made an appearance."

With this, D. Data burst out laughing. "C. Collins, only you would think a 400-year-old priest would be chatting on Facebook, tweeting on Twitter, and tubing on YouTube! Perhaps he is cruising on Timbr or Pinterest or doing personals on Craigslist. I can track all of those. It'll be fun. And while I'm at it, I can scroll through Instagram and Amazon, and the Chinese thing and see what he's shopping for." Demetrius, which is what the D in D. Data stands for, is clearly enjoying this.

So, he asks, "Anything else?"

"Well, yes, two unrelated things." Here, I pause. "One, see if you can get into the records of the Dominican order and go as far back as possible to see if there are any traces of Friar Laurence here or elsewhere or, as the Abbot has suggested, of other travelers or seekers of similar sort and what they were all about and what happened. Two, keep an eye out for any suggestion in any of these present-day searches for danger to Friar Laurence, any suggestion that mishaps may befall him or that anyone is out to get him."

"Huh," says D. Data, "you think someone may be stalking our stalker?"

"That," I reply, "would not be the strangest thing about this case, not nearly. Keep an eye out for it."

"Danger, Will Robinson, danger," says D. Data, and exits stage right, through my office door, leaving napkins, cups of white sauce, a crumpled garlic and clams white pizza box from Frank Pepe's Famous Pizzeria Napolitano, and a crushed PBR can scattered on my desk.

I sweep all of this into the wastebasket next to my desk, descend the two flights of stairs to my ancient Volvo, drive out Whitney Avenue toward Hamden, past the Whitneyville and Spring Glen

Congregational Churches, and the occasional Catholic edifice, and arrive in time for dinner.

Meg extends her arms and says, "Welcome."

The kids say "Daddy" in unison.

We sit, eat and I listen to how their days went. Just another day in the life of C. Collins, Esq., Ace Public Defender.

CHAPTER TWELVE

TUESDAY, SHIFTING GEARS

It is now Tuesday morning, and I have spent the drive into the New Haven Green reflecting on my search assignment to Mr. Data. It was at once, both too broad and too narrow. My Galaxy cell phone and it's Google app enable me to dictate memoranda while stuck in traffic and to transmit them via Bluetooth for editing prior to my arrival at the New Haven Green. Never mind that I have increased the risks I will never arrive, with the same fate for fellow travelers, exponentially. Or that it's illegal.

At least my Internet wizard will have my last will and testament.

MEMORANDUM TO FRIAR LAURENCE FILE, #1

TO: DATA, D.

TUESDAY MORNING

SUBJECT: *Romeo and Juliet*, Stage Productions

We have discussed researching Friar Laurence's travels, if any, over time, looking at performances of the play *Romeo and Juliet*. Check out newspapers, journals, books, memoirs, letters, looking for something similar to what we see or fear here. Prior to the 20th-century, any evidence of such travels would of necessity be in written form, reporting, reacting to, or recording our client's presence or some unusual occurrence such as an act of violence, especially on R&J. In the Yale D School, we understood only Macbeth's name could not be mentioned due to uncommon numbers of deaths in performances; maybe R&J is in second place. Look at Shapiro's books: *Shakespeare in America and Shakespeare in a Divided America*.

111

Since *Romeo and Juliet* is the most popular and frequently performed play in all of Shakespeare's canon, we should limit ourselves to the most significant venues and productions:

In England

1595-1610 Globe Theatre

1662 Lincoln's Inn Fields, William Davenant

1750-1800 Garrick's run

1679 and 1744 Little Theater and Theater Royal, Drury Lane, Otway, and David Garrick

1803 Covent Garden, John Philip Kemble,

1882 and 1884 Lyceum Theatre, Irving and Mary Anderson,

1935 New Theater, Olivier and Gielgud

1954 and 1974 Stratford Upon Avon, Glen Byam Shaw and Terry Hand production

1996-2020 any major university (you pick 'em)

In the States

1845 +/- Shakespeare Riots, NYC

1865 Lincoln Assassination

1900 et seq., any production in New York, Boston or Chicago, especially

1957 *West Side Story*, Jerome Robbins, Stephen Sondheim, Leonard Bernstein and

1960s Central Park, New York City, Shakespeare in the Park, Joseph Papp

1996-2020 any major university (you pick 'em)

I am not optimistic. If our man was in attendance, or in the environs, it would have been as part of a large audience, with no reason to stand out and every reason not to. And evidence that he was NOT there is almost as useful as any that he WAS. (Think it over.) Then again, perhaps, something significant will turn up. Especially helpful would be any program or playbill showing our Friar Laurence actually played a part.

FC

MEMORANDUM TO FRIAR LAURENCE FILE, #2

TO: DATA, D.

IN RE: ROMEO AND JULIET, FILM VERSIONS

TUESDAY MORNING

Data,

I would like you to do a similar search with respect to movies. As with the plays, I am not looking for him in the cast of actors. But unlike stage productions, film versions have only been around for the last 120 years. So, we are not limited to text records or reports, but there may be film, video, or photographic evidence that Friar Laurence was in the audience or in a crowd gathered for the location. I should think that is possible on opening night, especially with the more controversial films.

It may even be possible Friar Laurence appeared in the films as himself in the scenes which involve crowds, for example, the swordplay scenes or scenes where the Prince is addressing the warring factions. If so, he may be dressed in whatever garb the producer or director assigned to people in Verona or whatever the time/setting was. However, his physical stature is such that he is likely to stand out.

As a search tool, I would suggest facial recognition. You may use our standard client headshot of Friar Laurence, taken by Jo as a part of our initial protocol.

Unlike the stage productions, the number of films is limited, and I think manageable. IMDb estimates about 1300 films made of

Shakespeare plays; Wikipedia puts the number of full productions at about 250. Only about 30 of these are *Romeo and Juliet*. It should be feasible to use Netflix or Prime or one of half a dozen services to visit film libraries (Folger?). Stream and fast forward the film and use scanning software to look for Friar Laurence in the crowd scenes. Incidentally, as you scan these, they told us in the Drama School to pay attention to which are good drama and which are good film. Here are the best, let me know whether the distinction holds up:

1936 MGM, George Cukor

1968 Verona Productions, Franco Zeffirelli

1995 Twentieth Century Fox, Baz Luhrmann

I have no desired outcome. If Friar Laurence has never previously pursued filmings of *Romeo and Juliet*, that is okay. Or, if he has, we can also use that. What would be upsetting will only be if he has been connected and violence ensued, involving him. In that event, please print out from the film whatever images seem to involve our Friar Laurence. Look specially to see if our man, however briefly, has appeared in the role, itself

As I have mentioned previously, I would expect the opposing team may be undertaking similar research. It is important not to leave tracks for them to follow.

Treat this with top priority and secrecy, and keep me posted.

FC

MEMORANDUM TO FRIAR LAURENCE FILE, #3

TO: DATA, D.

IN RE: SOCIAL MEDIA

TUESDAY MORNING

This is the third and last memorandum of this morning to this file.

The present memorandum authorizes an Internet search of today's Social Media websites. Examples would be Facebook, Twitter, YouTube, Pinterest, and any other venues or websites, and relevant podcasts, which invite or support exchanges of personal views on contemporary issues or personalities. Obviously, any statements by or about Friar Laurence would be extremely useful, especially bearing on his purposes in being here. They could well be incriminating, supporting expanded criminal charges, or simply be sources of impeachment at trial.

So also, any statements by the Dominican Order, locally or elsewhere, recent or ancient, may be significant. Even if they do not bear directly on Friar Laurence, they may shed light on his claimed purpose and identity and on the Abbot's claim that he is simply one of many harmless "seekers" or "travelers."

And do a reverse search; instead of starting with Friar Laurence, search as well about the two teenage actors, who may be the cause or the victims of his presence in New Haven. See what they are posting on their Facebook pages or elsewhere, about loves, enemies, each other, the play, the cast ... and any dreams about a large man in a robe from far away?

And run a crosscheck to see what others are saying about them. It is especially important to learn whether anyone has developed a hatred toward them or is working on a vendetta. There may also be opposition to the play itself—it is very controversial. In 1845 or so, they killed 40 people in the New York City Shakespeare riots. As always, cover your tracks; these kids are very savvy, and verrry mean. I am hearing Janis Ian, or is it Celine Dion, in the back of my head, singing, "I learned the truth at seventeen ... it isn't all it seems at seventeen ..."

FC

I arrive at the parking lot behind City Hall, enter through the back door, wave to Big John in the Little Elevator, and sprint up the two flights of stairs. The stairs lead directly into the reception area where, at 8:00 AM, there are already several potential clients in attendance. They have clipboards with our intake sheets, providing all of the contact information and financial information required for public defender work. The clientele's demography is exactly the reverse of that prevailing in most of America, a product of the economic forces at work in this country.

Jo, sitting at her desk, directly in front of the small hallway that leads back to the inner offices, looks up, raises her eyebrows, gives two thumbs up and says, "Nice work on those memoranda. Did you kill anybody on your way in? Also, I'm beginning to think that you are spending more time on the Internet than I ever would have thought possible; you left out TikTok and Snapchat, though."

I reply, "That is soooo yesterday" and continue into my office. I have no idea what those are. Then I add, "And how about those lists? I did them from memory!"

"Doubtful. The Arlow file is on your desk," she calls over her shoulder to me, "and Mrs. Arlow will be in in half an hour. You're scheduled for trial at 10:30. The trial memo is on top of the file. Ron, our intrepid investigator, is on his way. D. Data called to tell you he's got the three memos and will start with #3, the social media one first; that'll be most fun. He's hoping Friar Laurence has been trolling for deviates ... that's a joke. And don't bother me for ten minutes; my nails are drying."

Although Friar Laurence has consumed my life over the past few days, office flow has continued with other, more routine cases. An

116

urban public defender office usually processes between 450 and 600 cases per year per attorney. If you figure 2000 working hours, that is a little more than three hours per case, for intake, interviewing, investigation, negotiation with the other side, research when (rarely) necessary, pretrial motions—most often to suppress evidence illegally obtained—and conferences with investigators, witnesses and clients, court appearances, and rarely, hardly ever, trial.

The rare trial is viewed as an anomaly since the system is set for high-volume disposition. Nobody has time for anything else, and so if the rare defendant has a tenable defense or claim of innocence (they are not the same), the prosecution will increase the attractiveness of the plea offer, with the paradox that the more innocent a defendant looks, the better the inducement to plead guilty.

I have never gotten over this; I hate having a defendant plead guilty while maintaining innocence ... for two reasons, at least. I love trials. More important, I don't like standing by with my client entering a plea of guilty when the judge asks, "Are you pleading because you are guilty" and the defendant, my client, lies by answering "yes." We are all of us, prosecuting attorney, defense attorney, judge and defendant, and possibly arresting officer, engaging in a charade, more appropriately, a fraud.

Today is one of those anomalies, a real live trial. Dorothy Arlow will go to trial on charges of breach of peace, disorderly conduct, resisting arrest, abusing and assaulting an officer, and assault with a dangerous weapon (something about throwing a butcher knife at her husband across a frozen parking lot one cold night in December, her defense being, in a generic sort of way, that her husband deserved it. Plus, at most, she breached the peace by yelling rather loudly, plus moreover, she works as a nurse at Yale New Haven Hospital in

117

pediatrics, supporting three kids (which is why her income is sufficiently low to qualify for public defender services); plus, she has a dick of a husband, who, if I may modify my previous statement, really deserved more than he got.

The sympathy factor is sufficiently high so that the prosecution offered to drop all charges in return for a plea to disorderly conduct, and a $25 fine, with the understanding that her record would be expunged in six months. Mrs. Arlow declined, and I am delighted.

The problem is that most judges do not want to interrupt their workflow for a trial, and so there may be a penalty for going to trial if she is convicted on even one of the minor charges. Moreover, to put the maximum pressure on the prosecution, I have claimed the case for a jury. This will slow flow even more, upping the ante for a straight-up dismissal. Jury trials take more time; there is a selection process before the jury is put in a box, and then, after all the witnesses testify, there is a set of written instructions read by the judge to the jury. And then, of course, they retire to deliberate, and that may add additional hours.

So, basically, we will tie up at least one prosecutor and one judge and a gaggle of good citizens for a day or more. Somebody has to pay for that. As I have explained to my client, she is the most likely candidate if convicted. But as I also explained, I love going to trial, I have a high percentage of winning those cases that do go to trial; and if she is convicted, I will find a way to file an appeal, giving the prosecution yet another chance simply to dismiss.

CHAPTER THIRTEEN
MEET DOROTHY ARLOW

What we will do in half an hour is review with Mrs. Arlow her testimony. There is a good argument for not putting a client on the stand as a witness if it can be avoided. At my level of the game, they tend not to be very articulate. They tend to be unattractive. They tend to lie. And they tend to be/seem guilty.

The strong point for Mrs. Arlow is that none of these is true of her; she is a most presentable medical professional, a pediatric nurse at Yale New Haven Hospital, caring for three children while coping with a deadbeat husband. With luck and careful selection, we will have a number of her peers in the jury box. The prosecution is forbidden constitutionally from discriminating against African-Americans as potential jurors, and while it is difficult to prove when that happens, it is an invaluable issue for appeal. That issue would be lost if we took the case to trial by a judge.

One other consideration is that with a rotating assignment of judges in criminal court, we can never be certain who we would get if the trial is before a judge, many of whom are hostile and vindictive. Of course, if we get one of those in a jury trial and lose, at sentencing, we'll have that same vindictive judge, doubly pissed ... especially if he or she thinks we put on perjured testimony via a lying defendant.

There are a number of text messages on my cell phone plus some pink slip notes from Jo arranged in order of urgency, with the top one being from Jack Reilly, who will be the prosecutor, saying that by 9:00 AM he will have withdrawn the offer to go with disorderly and a $25 fine and expungement in six months. He thinks I would be crazy to pass it up. I agree, but I have a client who wants to go to trial, and

I think we have a good case. I carefully put the pink note inside the cover of the Arlow file since later it may be important to have a record of who said what in plea bargaining.

I glance over the trial memorandum, prepared for the judge, covering the usual ground: list of witnesses, offer of proof, anticipated evidentiary issues, requests for instructions. Submitting this at the outset heads off surprise or ambush by the other side and gives me a heads-up as to how the judge will rule before I present my case. There is attached, separately, a summary outline of the opening and closing, in anticipation of what the evidence will show. This, of course, is for my file, not the judge.

Dorothy Arlow appears on time, dressed professionally but inexpensively. I like her as a person and love her as a witness; she is direct, measured, warm, and engaging. She would appeal to female and male jurors, alike, across racial and economic lines, a rare quality.

I pull out her statement and go over it with her, with the litany of questions we will follow. Essentially, she had come home from work around 6:00 PM in early December, parked her VW Bug in the parking lot behind the apartment, to find her husband prepared to leave immediately, the three kids having been left to themselves. She would have to get dinner; he would not be there. She asked where he was going; he said he had a meeting, she had asked, "What is her name and where?"

The exchange quickly deteriorated, with his making comments about Mrs. Arlow's frigidity and she responding with references to his drinking, drugs, and womanizing. The full exchanges were reflected in the statement and would be drawn out by using open-ended questions, such as, what did you say then, what did he say then, what did you do, what did he do? I have told her that if the F-bomb was used by her or him, she should be specific in placing and describing it. After 10 to 15 minutes of this, he said I've had enough of this shit and started to leave by the back door, where the Volkswagen was parked. She blocked the door; he ran out the front door and around the end of their unit to the car.

At this point, I will ask, who bought and paid for that car? Mrs. Arlow will say that she did and needs it to get back and forth to work and transport the kids. I will then resume the narrative with questioning as to what happened then? She will say that she ran to the kitchen, grabbed whatever she could from the drawer closest to the back door, ran outside, and saw police stopping her husband.

There was an exchange; they came toward her while he went toward the car. They said something to the effect of he has a right to take the car; she rejected that, ran around Officer Graziano, and threw the three items in her hands at her husband: one was a clay pot, which hit him, the second was a metal colander which bounced off the Volkswagen Beetle, and the third was a butcher knife (Oops! My oops ...) which sailed over his head and the car harmlessly, as far as she knows. It was never found; she thinks the lady across the parking lot hid it.

The butcher knife is a major factor. It was never found. If the prosecution cannot prove it, then we should not put Dorothy Arlow on the stand since she might fill that hole in their case. Subject to be discussed ...

We will then return to the narrative of what happened as she ran toward him, Officer Graziano tackled her, threw her on her back to the ground, and she said, "Get off me you, white, Guinea, motherfucker."

"What happened then?"

Graziano hit her in the face with his fist. That is the last thing she remembers until she woke up in the emergency room in handcuffs.

What emergency room? Yale New Haven Hospital. Where you work? Yes.

How badly were you injured? Broken nose, black eyes. Bruised lips. Could this have come about as a result of your falling on the frozen ground when Officer Graziano tackled you? No, I broke my fall with my hands and broke my wrist at the same time.

I called him the names when he grabbed me, and that is why and when he hit me. Are you certain? It may have been as I went down. Or when I was on the ground, I am not sure. Perhaps he was afraid you would throw him off you and kill your husband, so he needed to immobilize you?

"Are you serious? No! He outweighs me by at least 70 pounds ..."

The car and the police beating are important factors. Each provides a chance to shift the case from a trial of Dorothy Arlow to a trial of the husband and police officer. They hurt her. Put them on trial. Call it plan B.

I then reviewed with Mrs. Arlow the usual litany about how to behave as a witness. I would give her open-ended questions; she was to answer truthfully. With my questions or the district attorney's questions, if she did not remember, she should answer that she did not remember. Answer the DA's questions yes or no; let me, on redirect, give her a chance to explain. If she thought that she was being made to look bad or inconsistent, not to push back but maintain her composure, on redirect, I would cover the ground, and above all, she should not let Jack Reilly upset her.

Our witnesses would consist of Mrs. Arlow and Doctor Simon Forman, head of trauma, and the ER at Yale New Haven Hospital. He and I had talked for 10 to 15 minutes last week; he had done his internship and residency at Harlem General, he knew battered faces when he saw them, and this was one of the worst he had seen. The bruises and broken bones were not caused by a fall, and were consistent with a blow to the face from above with a good deal of force while Officer Graziano had her pinned to the ground. Moreover, Mrs. Arlow was outweighed by approximately 70 pounds.

Finally, I said that she, Mrs. Arlow, might not testify, we would decide that in the light of the State's witnesses. If they failed to make their case, or painted her favorably, or our expert carried our case sufficiently, there might be no need. If not needed, better not testify. She would be facing an expert professional prosecutor, which, as a witness, she was not qualified to do. Defendants, no matter how well-prepped, generally are not strong witnesses. We would come back to this.

She asked, and so I said it was likely the jury would come back not guilty on abusing and assaulting an officer or assault with a dangerous weapon but convict of disorderly conduct or breach of the peace. The maximum penalty would then be 30 days in jail, but most likely, if the judge had any heart or manhood, he would fine her $25, possibly suspended. I asked if she had the money with her, prepared to dig into my wallet, not a recommended practice for a defense attorney. She said she did.

With that, we left for the courthouse, my telling Jo to tell Ron to make sure the doctor knew we were on trial, and would let him know if it was going ahead, and would be looking for him about 2:00 PM and to let me know whether and when he could be there. The usual, said Jo.

As we passed Jo to go toward Big John and the Little Elevator, Jo checked out Mrs. Arlow, and then I heard her clear her throat, and I turned. "Nice," said Jo, and gave me two thumbs up.

The criminal courtroom at 10:00 in the morning is filled with usual demographic wreckage. The audience, as always, is a mixture of races, ethnicities, cases waiting to be called and cases waiting to be disposed, lawyers with business trying to get out, lawyers looking for business trying to get in, prosecutors calling cases and confirming deals across the counsel table as the case is being brought up, judges taking pleas and, all in all, simply a day at the races. But today, I have a racehorse.

State versus Dorothy Arlow is called. We come forward, and the prosecutor, Jack Reilly, announces, "Set for jury trial Your Honor at 10:30 today." The courtroom goes quiet; as mentioned earlier, this is an anomaly. Take note.

The judge is a younger, newer member of the bench, and he leans forward, saying with just the slightest odd accent, "Well, Mr. Reilly, this is interesting. How quickly can we get through the rest of the routine docket to get to this gold mine of advocacy?"

Reilly responds, "Well, Your Honor, if Mr. Collins and his client are still insisting on turning down the Offer of the Century, we should be ready to go and impanel a jury by 10:30."

The judge, Roderigo Lopez, leans forward, looking me straight in the eye across the distance of 20 feet, and says, "Deal of the Century, Mr. Collins? Does your client understand what was offered and what she is turning down?"

"Yes," I reply.

"What was the offer?" asks Lopez looking at Ms. Arlow.

Reilly replies, "Dismiss all but disorderly, $25 fine, recommended to you."

"Wow," says Lopez. "Mr. Collins?"

"Your Honor, Mrs. Arlow is innocent of disorderly, abusing and assaulting, resisting arrest, and felonious assault upon her husband with a thrown, phantom butcher knife which, if it ever existed, missed by a country mile. I have explained to her that on trial there is a good chance of acquittal, and at most, if convicted of the misdemeanors and one felony, despite her clean and spotless record as a longtime pediatric nurse at Yale New Haven Hospital, and the mother of three, and the unfortunate wife of an abusing, non-supporting deadbeat husband, she might face jail or even prison time. However, I have also explained to her that if a compassionate judge such as yourself were hearing the case and doing the sentencing, even if convicted, she would most likely face probation."

"Thank you," Mr. Collins," responds Judge Lopez, and turning to Dorothy Arlow, standing immediately to my right, he says, "You have heard Mr. Collins' eloquent if protracted response, Mrs. Arlow. He is a very fine attorney. Do you insist on going to trial despite Mr. Reilly's most attractive offer of a $25 fine recommendation on pleading guilty to disorderly conduct?"

"Yes, Your Honor," Arlow responds, "Mr. Collins has explained all of this, and even with the prospect of going to jail, I truly believe I am innocent and would like a chance to prove that."

Judge Roderigo Lopez wraps this all up with, "Well, Mrs. Arlow, you shall certainly have that chance and, I hope Mr. Collins has explained, that you do not have to prove anything. Indeed, you do not even have to testify, the burden of proving your guilt rests with the prosecution, and let me now turn to Mr. Reilly and ask, Mr. Reilly, are you prepared to go forward at 10:30?"

"Absolutely, this felon should not go free."

I mutter, "O, come on, Jack ...

"Oh, my," says Judge Roderigo Lopez, "the Deal of the Century is being replaced by the Trial of the Century. May I live to see many such days in this and other courtrooms before dementia and senility eclipse my career. Counselors, and Madame, let me thank you for this most welcome break from the humdrum tedium of criminal court. We will call the remainder of the docket and return to State versus Arlow at 10:30."

As we turn from the counsel table, Dorothy Arlow asks, clearly intrigued, "Who was that masked man?"

"I do not know. He is not what I expected, not very Hispanic, despite his name; he is not young, and I think quite experienced. He and I have never met at court or bar functions.

"Should I be worried?" she asks.

"Oh, I don't think so. I always favor smart judges and a smart jury. I like this fellow's style."

State versus Arlow is moved to the smaller Jury Trial Court on the third floor, away from the large, dingy, and depressing Criminal Court where we have been entering pleas. There are some amenities. There is a small jury room off to one side, where the jury retires when the judge hears matters not for their ears or where the jury deliberates their verdict after hearing all the evidence. Also, the wear and tear on the floor, the furniture, and the bench is much less. And the smell is better.

CHAPTER FOURTEEN
STATE V ARLOW
OPENING STATEMENTS

The trial begins by bringing in a group of 20 or 30 potential jurors, drawn at random from the large panel ("the venire") gathered for this term of court. The jurors are given a number in the order they were chosen. They stand, are sworn, and sit.

Judge Lopez tells them, as a panel, the charges that are pending, introduces counsel and the defendant, and asks them to name their witnesses. Judge Lopez gives some of the facts from the charges in the information, but very little. He addresses the entire panel and asks them if they know defendant or counsel, and questions as to prior knowledge of the facts of the case, of the potential witnesses, as to whether any of them have been involved in similar cases involving a family disturbance or police engagement, and whether there are obstacles which would prevent them from serving.

Some jurors raise their hands when Lopez asks particular questions. He will follow up and ask about their concerns. Do you know Mrs. Arlow from the hospital? Mr. Reilly has drafted your will? Did your husband beat the shit out of you? Or vice versa? Were you wrongfully arrested? Is your wife nine months pregnant, due any day? The judge will ask whether the witness nevertheless feels he or she could sit fairly and impartially in the case; if not, the judge will excuse and dismiss the potential juror.

Of the jurors who remain, Lopez has already found no "cause," but we can still use a discretionary challenge, known as "peremptory," meaning no particular reason need be given to exclude the juror. Peremptories are limited in number and precious, because there may be jurors whom we do not want for purely subjective reasons, based on information in the questionnaire, employment, age, gender, race, neighborhood, education, or just plain attitude. I have marked those I do not want, and Reilly has done the same.

We alternate who goes first with the questioning. Lopez is one of those few judges who permit lawyers to ask questions of jurors individually. I love it. The point is to acquaint them with my theory of the case (here, lack of intent, defense of property, self-defense), raise some of the facts of the case, or some of the "rules of the road"—burden of proof, presumption of innocence—and so forth. My questions are "softball questions," pointing the way to the right answer and asking that the juror agree, as a person of goodwill, to do the right thing. I want to win them over—easy questions, easy answers, easy friends.

"So, if Judge Lopez instructs you that the burden of proof is on the prosecution, and if you had a reasonable doubt, would you give my client the benefit of it? So, your verdict would be for not guilty? And if Judge Lopez instructs you that the jury, to convict, must be unanimous, and if you held a legitimate doubt, would you stick to your beliefs while listening fairly to the other jurors?"

All of these questions are not repeated for each potential juror, but of course, they all hear them because they are in the room, and the message that is delivered is that they should do the right thing. And vote for Dorothy Arlow.

It goes quickly. Out of the jury panel hearing, we exercise our challenges, alternating, so the jurors who will remain will not form an impression of who we liked and didn't like. And when we are done, the remaining jurors are sworn to the case. Judge Lopez instructs them on the basics before going to lunch, emphasizing they are to discuss the case with no one, absolutely no one. If they are approached, tell the judge.

With that, the clerk intones, "all rise," and we proceed into the bright sunshine of a fine spring day, the hurly-burly of people scurrying to and from work and lunch, the mixed fragrances of an ethnic smorgasbord of people and food, in downtown New Haven, Connecticut. We could do worse.

Dorothy Arlow and I leave the courtroom together and go to one of the food carts on the Green, I get a salami and rye, and she gets a fruit cup with yogurt; we sit with coffee and talk.

As the jury selection proceeded, before I challenged for cause or on peremptory grounds, I consulted with her. By prearrangement, if there was somebody she liked, the pencil on the table was vertical, pointing to the bench. If she felt someone should be excused, she turned the pencil parallel to the judge's bench. I had the ultimate veto.

Jury selection is the subject of much magic and mysticism. There are high priced psychologists who advise attorneys in high-priced cases. In major corporate litigation, there will be mock jury panels and beta testing of theories and population samples. At the lowest levels, lawyers may operate on prejudice: you always want the jury to be of the same background as your client, some say. But what if one of those people made something of themselves from that background and are hypercritical of those who did not? Or, in Dorothy Arlow's case, there is a domestic dispute, so perhaps we want women who have experienced that? But what if they did and kept control of themselves and judge her badly because she did not? And if she dresses stylishly or expensively, will that draw resentment or admiration?

We have a jury of twelve, three of whom are African American. There had been three others, excused for cause, so a pattern of discrimination did not appear. I would not have expected that Reilly would do racial profiling, setting up an issue for appeal under Batson versus Kentucky. Of the twelve, five are women. Reilly had attempted to exclude women, but the grounds didn't play out. Education and employment were favorable, and we agreed that it looked like a good group. My client thought that, on a personal basis, she would like to get to know many of the jurors—a good sign.

My preconceptions are two: one, I like jurors who seem to like me (hence, the individual questioning), two, I like smart people because I think, invariably, I develop a smart theory and delivery. There is a third criterion: if my client doesn't like a potential juror, we use a peremptory. She doesn't need to explain.

We review her testimony and the option again, if it should seem wise, simply to offer no testimony whatsoever. Possibly, the jury would dislike Reilly's witnesses. Maybe they would help our case. The emergency room doctor had checked in and would be there at 3:00 PM. If we chose, he could be our only witness. We would make that decision at that time.

With that, we go back to the third-floor courtroom, take our places at counsel table, and wait for opening statements. Judge Lopez has the clerk return the jurors to the box and makes the usual inquiries about whether they had spoken with anybody concerning the case or had been approached by anybody. He added that from here on out, they were also to avoid newspapers and television or radio of any kind. It could lead to a mistrial. SOP.

He then explained that the lawyers would make brief, and here he turned, looking at Reilly and me, emphasizing the word "brief," statements, following which witnesses would be called. And with that, he turned to Jack Reilly and—

JUDGE LOPEZ

"The floor is yours, Mr. Reilly."

MR. REILLY

"I want to thank the jurors for their service and emphasize that you will hear the evidence first and then the law from the judge afterward. Mr. Collins and I will present the case in anticipation of what the judge will say. His instructions will be based on the witnesses' testimony, which I expect would be as follows:

"The victim, Mr. Arlow, would testify Mrs. Arlow came home late, encountered Mr. Arlow, who had cared for the children all day, as was the arrangement, prepared to head out the door as soon as she arrived. Again, this was customary. She initiated an argument; angry words were exchanged, and he left to go to the car. Mrs. Arlow followed into the parking lot, yelling loudly, calling him names, and throwing objects at him. One of these was a butcher knife. (Oops, think I, mistake, Jack.) This had gone on long enough, and often enough, so that neighbors had called the police, who intervened. Officer Graziano will be called to testify that it was necessary to restrain Mrs. Arlow, who then assaulted Officer Graziano.

"Essentially it was a case of 'he said, she said,' in the sense that none of the neighbors witnessed the action in the parking lot. However, the weight of evidence would be on the prosecution's side, since Officer Graziano arrived while the events were unfolding and is an experienced New Haven police officer. And it was incontrovertible that Mrs. Arlow was pursuing the victim and threw objects at him.

"Mr. Collins might attempt to sway the members of the jury with sympathy for the defendant, who does have a nursing position at Yale

New Haven Hospital while raising three children, and is an attractive individual; still, the judge will instruct you that the case is to be decided not on sympathy but the facts. It was a simple, if sad, domestic dispute that got out of control. The evidence would show proof beyond a reasonable doubt of disorderly conduct, breach of peace, assault with a dangerous weapon, abusing an officer, and resisting arrest.

"I am confident that on all of the evidence, the jury will return a verdict of guilty. Thank you, and now you will hear from my esteemed colleague, Mr. Collins."

He turned back toward the counsel table, and as he passed, leaned over toward me and whispered, "That felt really good, Francis. I think maybe I'll apply for Opening of the Century." And he sat down, next to Graziano.

Reilly knew he had done an excellent job, cool, measured, professional, winning. It helped that he was tall, trim and athletic, with the deep-set eyes and the black wavy hair of an advocate who, depending upon who he had put in a jury box, could draw on either Irish or Italian-American lineage, and I had seen him do both to good effect. Here, I think, sometime during the trial, he would refer to his Italian grandparents.

What I had to do now was a similarly polished presentation, but with a little more passion, turning the heat up and pushing back. I rose to do exactly that.

JUDGE LOPEZ

"Mr. Collins?"

MR. COLLINS

"Ladies and gentlemen of the jury, Your Honor, it is always a pleasure to watch a craftsman at work, smooth, restrained, polished, but perhaps a little slick and quick. Mr. Reilly has a way of pulling together a skein of yarn, making it seem like a full sweater, when in fact, as my Italian-American grandmother (What? You thought I was Irish?) used to say, 'It is full of moth holes.'

"The charges are disorderly conduct, breach of peace, abusing an officer and resisting arrest, and assault with a dangerous weapon. Only the last is of serious moment, and I will say nothing now except, at the end of the case, there will have been no supporting evidence. So, you may dismiss that charge right now.

"Let us turn to disorderly conduct. Mr. Arlow, the so-called victim here, engaged in an argument with his wife. Mr. Reilly says Arlow will testify he was caring for the children all day and leaving as customary when Mrs. Arlow came home. What Mr. Reilly did not describe, and what either Mr. Arlow or Mrs. Arlow will describe, is the content of the exchange and the children's condition when Mrs. Arlow came home.

"Let us say that Mrs. Arlow, having just finished a hard day as a pediatric nurse, was tired and exhausted and understandably provoked by what she found when she came into the home. In the exchange which followed, in terms of disturbing the peace and disorderly conduct, you may well conclude that Mr. Arlow was as much at fault as Mrs. Arlow. So, an important part that Mr. Reilly left out is the misconduct on that occasion by the ne'er-do-well, frequently drunk, abusive Mr. Arlow."

MR. REILLY

"I object. Outside the scope. And irrelevant. Mr. Collins is engaging in character assassination."

JUDGE LOPEZ

"Please, Mr. Collins, you know the rules."

MR. COLLINS

"Yes, Your Honor, but Mr. Reilly has painted Mr. Arlow as a 'victim,' when, in reality, this hard-working public servant, the sole support of her three children and her ne'er-do-well husband, is, in fact, a victim of long-suffering duration. We think we should be allowed to prove that."

MR. REILLY

"He is still doing it, Your Honor."

JUDGE LOPEZ

"Mr. Collins, proceed with proper restraint."

MR. COLLINS

"And now, the police officer becomes involved. What Mr. Reilly left out, and what the evidence will show, is that the Arlows had one automobile, purchased by Dorothy, in her name, on which even today she is making payments, while, I might note, her husband has kept the car to this very day, this man who is the 'victim' here, still keeps the car which Mrs. Arlow needs to get to work and support her family then and now, and so it was that evening that she went to prevent him from stealing her automobile."

MR. REILLY

"Objection to the word 'stealing.'"

JUDGE LOPEZ

"The littlest artistry, if you please, Mr. Collins. Perhaps 'taken' or 'purloined?'"

MR COLLINS

"Thank you, Your Honor. I'll go with purloined. I studied for a Masters in Shakespeare at the Yale Drama School. Purloined it is. And the pursuit in the parking lot, the evidence will show, is in legitimate defense of property by Mrs. Arlow, in support of her family. As to the abusing and assault on the officer, again the summary from Mr. Reilly omitted the fact that the officer grabbed Mrs. Arlow, after she had thrown the articles in her hands, and threw her to the ground, as she went down, to save herself, she extended her left arm and what Mr. Reilly also left out is that at about this time, after the words, 'Stop it, you white Guinea motherfucker,'" I want to prepare the jury in advance, "The officer punched Mrs. Arlow, either, as she went down, or as she lay on her back, in the face."

I pause. I look over at Dorothy Arlow and see tears. I go to her, put my hand on her shoulder. I look at the jurors; I see they are similarly affected. I turn to look at Reilly and Graziano and say—

MR. COLLINS

"Mr. Reilly, would you please have Officer Graziano stand at this point?"

MR. REILLY

"Why?"

MR. COLLINS

"I think you know why."

JUDGE LOPEZ

"I think we all know why, Mr. Collins, and I think it is not only unusual but unnecessary. There is a considerable size disparity, which you may bring out in cross-examination. I would suggest that you conclude your opening statement as quickly as possible."

MR. COLLINS

"Oh, yes, I forgot, I guess Mr. Reilly did too, that as Dorothy Arlow lay unconscious on December 10, on the icy, frozen ground, just fifteen days before Christmas, Officer Graziano handcuffed her. Unconscious.

135

"Let me conclude; it is for you to decide, when you hear all of these facts, whether Mrs. Arlow abused Officer Graziano or assaulted him, an officer professionally trained in how to restrain people, an officer who outweighs Mrs. Arlow easily by 60 pounds. Or you may well conclude, setting aside the sympathy which I certainly hope you do feel for my client, that when all the testimony is in, the prosecution will have failed to come close to proving a crime beyond a reasonable doubt; indeed, you may be left with only one question, not guilt or innocence, but why was this chickenshit case ever brought to trial?!"

Reilly is on his feet, Lopez is leaning forward, I am turning toward Mrs. Arlow nodding and beyond her, in the first row of the audience, the faces of three middle-aged black women smiling amongst the crowd, and on the other side of the aisle, Father Laurence and Abbot Dominic smiling. It then occurs to me there is a voice behind me, that of Lopez, J., admonishing me—

JUDGE LOPEZ

"Mr. Collins, you've turned your back on this Court much too abruptly and inappropriately, as well as having used language wholly inappropriate to the court setting, and for both of these I now look to you for an immediate apology."

MR. COLLINS

"I do apologize, Judge. I meant no disrespect for you, or for that matter, Mr. Reilly or the members of the jury. It is simply that, at times I get worked up and respond with more passion than is perhaps appropriate. I do apologize."

JUDGE LOPEZ

"Apology accepted. There is no rebuttal, Mr. Reilly, with opening statements, and so the next stage will be for you to call your first witness, which you should do after a ten-minute recess. This court stands in recess until 2:15."

With that, he rises and exits through the door in the back of the courtroom.

I turn and say to Jack Reilly, "How did you like them beans?"

He replies, "This case just opened with the two Opening Statements of the Century, Frannie, (he knows I hate that and he is the only one who does it), and over his shoulder as he turns, "but you're going down," and claps me on the shoulder, heading for the men's room, followed by Graziano, who I think is of similar persuasion—that I am going down.

I sit beside Dorothy Arlow, asking, "Feeling better?"

To which she responds, "Yes, much." And then she turns to the three middle-age, attractively attired black women in the audience section, just on the other side of the rail, nods to them, and they smile back, then turns back to me and says, "Those are former girlfriends of my husband. While we have been married. I emphasize, 'former.'"

And then, pausing, Dorothy Arlow says, "I see you also have your cheering section; do you always travel with priests?"

I reply, "I find they bring me luck, especially with Catholic juries. But we may have made our own luck here." Dorothy Arlow and I stand, Friar Laurence and Abbot Dominic wave and leave the courtroom ahead of us.

"Who are they?" she asks.

I say, "They are Dominican Monks from the local Abbey, involved in another case."

She pauses, looks me directly in the eye, I notice for the first time we are of similar height, and says, "Let me know if you want me to help with any part of their case. Any part. Especially the tall, good looking one, with the dark eyes and huge hands. What is his name?" There is a far-off tone, is it wistful? in her voice.

I pause, wondering how she has taken in so much detail in a fraction of a moment, and then remember to reply, "Laurence. Friar Laurence."

"He looks a lot like Bond." she replies, "James Bond. I like that. A lot."

CHAPTER FIFTEEN
STATE V ARLOW
THE STATE'S CASE: A FEW GOOD MEN

Outside the court, waiting for Judge Lopez's clerk to call us back in, we are about to start hearing the State's case, which will doubtless consist of the pathetic victim, Mr. Arlow, who had been living on his wife's nursing paycheck, followed by sensitive Officer Graziano, testifying that there was an argument when he arrived, a scuffle with Mrs. Arlow, and naughty language hurled in his direction. The prosecution's case thus consists of two fragile American males, whose immaculate personae have been sullied by a pediatric nurse. I think Jack will have to dig deep on this one.

I have reviewed cross-examination approaches with Mrs. Arlow. The safest line always is to impeach a witness with a prior inconsistent statement. The second is to lead a witness into a statement or position that is absurdly preposterous. A third is accusing a witness in the form of a question, which the witness denies, but the jury hears it, setting up your rebuttal witnesses. And last, the most fun, and possibly the riskiest, is goading a witness into losing control, the very thing which had led him to punch Dorothy Arlow on that December 10th evening ... or me in this courtroom today.

But of course, there is always the option of no cross-examination at all. If your theory of the case has not been hurt, if the witness has destroyed himself, maybe actually helped you for any number of other reasons, there is often no need to ask a question. And, always, asking may open the door for the witness and opposing counsel to bring in evidence not otherwise admissible. Never, ever, open that door.

Frankly, we think our best witnesses may be the prosecution's witnesses.

While we were waiting outside the courtroom, we were also waiting for Ron Hoffer to produce, as if by magic, which he frequently does, our strongest witness, a medical expert. Ron steps up the staircase toward the courtroom door, directly toward us. Ron is committed to working on behalf of indigent defendants because it finally occurred to him after 20 years as a city police officer that he was tired of cops lying and that a man of principle belongs on our side. He looks at me before I can say anything, and he says, "Be of stout heart and true, mine Fuhrer," (he loves that line. He knows I think he is a Nazi at heart), "the US cavalry will come up those stairs in just a moment and you will know that moment when the staircase begins to shake."

Which it now does.

And the largest man I believe I have ever seen rises slowly, hugely, vertically, impossibly, YARD BY YARD, to dominate the entire horizon of the staircase and landing. Hoffer moves toward him, risks his hand in the man's hand, and says, "Welcome, Dr. mumble mumble mumble ..." and turns to me saying, "may I present Dr. Simon Forman, former Chief of Staff, Emergency Department, Harlem General Hospital, New York, New York?" I am thinking, absolutely you may, you can do anything you want with a man this huge, and step toward Dr. Forman and I say, "I cannot begin to tell you how huge a hole in our case you are going to fill." Dr. Forman looks down on me, a large smile illuminating his dark visage, a gold tooth gleaming in the very center (well, left-hand side of center), and says," I get that a lot," in a voice straight out of James Earl Jones, in *Field of Dreams*. Or maybe *Othello*.

140

Standing there, with only a minute or two before going back into the courtroom, I say to Dr. Forman, "Has Ron briefed you on the case? Essentially the police officer says my client, Mrs. Arlow, slipped on hard, icy pavement and broke her nose and battered her upper facial bone. Have you seen the x-rays?"

"Yes, I have," says Dr. Forman, "and I have seen slip and fall face plants, and this is not one. I have also seen slip and fall police face plants, which this emphatically is. I would say that Officer Graziano has a future as a bouncer or a brawler, but he is not a very smart liar if he thinks he can claim the lady's face was broken by anything other than his right cross to her jaw. And cheekbone. And nose. Possibly twice."

And with that, we enter the courtroom, Ron, Mrs. Arlow, and I, three abreast, drawn in the wake and shadow of Dr. Simon's form, stopping conversation on his way. He sits behind the counsel table, next to the three stunning African-American ladies, who immediately take full measure of his presence, all visibly friends of Dorothy Arlow, former friends of Mr. Arlow, and we all rise as Judge Lopez reenters to take evidence in the case of State versus Dorothy Arlow.

Judge Lopez says, "Call your first witness, Mr. Reilly."

"Thank you, Your Honor, State calls Billy Arlow to the stand." I look at Mr. Arlow hard, trying to size him up, but really trying to see how the jury would evaluate him. He is trim, good looking, a fine mustache, a gold chain, a sharp dark red sport coat, grey slacks, glossy shoes. No wedding ring, the women will notice that. The men may notice the clothes, too fine for an unemployed man depending on his wife for support. He seems too much at ease, hard to quantify that. A ladies' man, I think. I ask Mrs. Arlow.

"Do people like him?" I ask.

She whispers, "Yes, they do, especially women, for a while, I did, loved him. But I think there is a part people don't trust. He plays cards, but after a while, they tell him not to come back."

I see that. I think the jury will, too.

Reilly's questioning is quick, direct, and matter-of-fact. He establishes that Billy and Mrs. Arlow have been married for ten years, have three children, he is an out of work bartender, having lost his job over a "drug incident," he adds, "not my fault," and he is now the stay-at-home parent while his wife is off to work.

Reilly's questioning then proceeds as follows:

MR. REILLY

Q. "Do You own an automobile?"

MR. ARLOW

"Yes."

Q. "On the night in question, December 10 last, was there an incident concerning that automobile?"

A. "Yes."

Q. "Would you please describe, in your own words, what transpired?"

A. "At about six, Mrs. Arlow, the defendant, my wife, came home from work as a pediatric nurse at Yale New Haven Hospital and came in the door, immediately finding fault with the condition of the house, the condition of the children, the condition of me as well. Specifics? Kids grime, no dinner, the odor of booze, not the kids, on me.

"I responded that she might find the area more satisfactory if she spent more time cleaning the house and helping with the kids, making our home, into our home."

Q. "And what did she say to that?"

A. "She used language you would rather not have me repeat in front of the jury, and with that, I decided to leave."

Q. "Was it your custom or pattern to leave at about the time Mrs. Arlow got home?"

A. "Sometimes."

Q. "And where were you going?"

A. "To the Newhall Bar and Grill around the corner, to meet with friends."

Q. "What happened then?"

A. "She said, not with my car; you are not. I said it's our car, grabbed the keys, and went out the back door to the parking lot. As I proceeded toward the car, I heard the front door slam, I heard her call me a goddamned motherfucker, and I felt a bowl bounce off my head. I ran farther to the car, and a colander hit my feet, hitting the car. As I opened the car door, I heard a police officer telling my wife she could not interfere with a man taking his car. I heard her say it's my car, and I slammed the door behind me. As I pulled out of the lot, out of the corner of my eye, I saw the police officer fall, with my wife, to the ground. And that's all."

MR. REILLY

"No further questions."

JUDGE LOPEZ

"Your witness Mr. Collins."

MR. COLLINS

"Your Honor, I would like to take a moment to consult with my client."

JUDGE LOPEZ

"Only a moment, Mr. Collins."

I turned to Dorothy Arlow, sitting to my right, our heads close together, and said, "This is one of those times when all of my careful questions for cross-examination might be better unasked."

"Why?" She asked.

I replied, "Because the jury does not like him, and as a witness, he said nothing about the butcher knife, which is the basis for the felony charge. We do not want to give Reilly a chance to redirect to fill these omissions. Also, there's no evidence that your voice was at a high level, or loud, only that you used some bad language. That's not enough for disturbing the peace or disorderly conduct. Basically, his testimony has not hurt us. If I ask questions, Reilly might recognize what he has left out and use redirect to fill the missing links."

"Well, what about being fired for a drug incident?" Should you go after that?"

I laughed, "Oh, no. It's a trap. He laid it out there for me to get hammered on cross, or help him bring something in on redirect that he can't get in otherwise; I don't know what it is, but I smell a trap!"

"You guys are devious," she said, a slight touch of admiration in that, and then said, "sounds good to me. We could always call Billy back, yes?"

"Yes, but right now, the State's case is too short, too sweet. The jury's going to say, "Where's the beef?" They want more to convict.

MR. COLLINS

"The defense has no questions of this witness, Your Honor."

Lopez turns to Billy Arlow and says, "You may step down. Call your next witness Mr. Reilly."

Reilly stands and says, "The State calls Officer Anselmo Graziano." As he is being seated, Reilly turns to me and says, "I'll get you with this one, Houdini." The officer is sworn and drops his bulk into the witness chair.

Judge Lopez says, "Proceed."

Reilly has Graziano give his name, rank, years of service, whereabouts on the evening of December 10, what it was that brought him to the parking lot behind the building where the Arlows live, and what he found when he arrived on the scene.

MR. REILLY

"Please tell the jury what it was you found upon arrival."

OFFICER GRAZIANO

"The message from dispatch was simply that a couple was arguing in their apartment. I parked in front, heard voices in back, and walked around the end of the apartment complex. There I saw Mr. Arlow approaching a red Volkswagen Bug, one of the new ones, then the back door of an apartment flew open, and Mrs. Arlow came out with objects in her hands. It was dark. I could not see the faces of either of them or what she had in her hands. She ran toward Mr. Arlow."

Q. "What happened then?"

A. "He was very close to the automobile, turned, and was inside within a moment or two. She threw what appeared to be a bowl; it almost hit him, then what turned out later to be a colander, which hit the car, and then a long thin object, which may have been a butcher knife and sailed over the car. While this was happening, he had started the car and was backing out."

MR. COLLINS

"Objection to the words, 'which may have been a butcher knife,' speculation and opinion."

JUDGE LOPEZ

"Officer Graziano, how far were you from the defendant when she was throwing these objects?"

A. "About 20 feet."

Q. "And from Mr. Arlow?"

145

A. "About the same."

Q. "And what was the lighting, where was it coming from, was there direct lighting onto the parking lot?"

A. "There was none. There were lights over the back doors of the various apartments. They only illuminated the back stoop. There was no lighting over the car."

JUDGE LOPEZ

"Objection sustained. The jury will ignore Officer Graziano's speculation. Another time, Mr. Collins, you might ask for an opportunity for questions, such as those I just asked, in aid of an objection, before making the objection itself."

Q. "What did the defendant do after throwing the kitchen objects?"

A. "I had stepped between Mrs. Arlow and her husband. She told me to get out of the way that he's stealing my car. I said, if it belongs to the two of you, there's nothing I can do, and you have to go to court. She said that's bullshit, I pay for that car, I bought it, and he's not going to drive off to see his girlfriend in my fucking car. Get out of my fucking way. And she tried to get past."

Q. "Did she use those exact words? That was rather strong language wasn't it?"

A. "I have heard worse, and yes, those were her exact words. She was pretty pissed."

Q. "What happened next?"

A. "I stepped in front of her, blocked her way, as the car was leaving the parking lot. She tried to get at it, and I blocked her, and she pushed me back, causing me to stumble. I reached out, grabbed her shoulder to steady myself; she said something like, 'get your hands off me, you white Guinea motherfucker,' and spun away from me, slipping on the ice, falling flat on her face. I called an ambulance; she was taken to Yale New Haven Hospital."

Q. "Again, Officer Graziano, what did she say to you?"

A. "She called me a white Guinea motherfucker."

Q. "Thank you, Officer Graziano. Your witness, Mr. Collins."

Reilly turned away from the witness, going back to counsel table, and then leaned over, as he sat down, and said "Careful now, Francis. Luck is one thing; skill is another."

It does seem to me I have to go after this witness. Most people, including these jurors, have respect for police officers. Plus, New Haven being New Haven, three jury members have Italian surnames, and probably one or two others have Italian-American ancestors within a generation or two. Graziano had used a moderate well-spoken and careful manner in his presentation.

One way of shaking that is to bring up what he left out, making it seem he was deliberately trying to mislead or conceal important evidence from the jury. Another is to confront him with an even more credible witness, forecasting through my present questioning what we will hear later from Dr. Simon Forman, who I have sitting right behind me. And then there is always, calling Graziano names ...

So, first, what Graziano left out.

MR. COLLINS

"Well, Officer Graziano, it appears you were moderate, serving as a peacekeeper, simply trying to block Mrs. Arlow from possibly committing a crime. That correct or fair?"

OFFICER GRAZIANO

"It is both, and thank you."

Q. "When the defendant reached out, to steady herself, was Mrs. Arlow herself steady?"

A. "Yes."

Q. "So how much weight did you put on her, so she fell down?"

A. "Very little, I was just trying to stay up because of the ice. But I guess I leaned hard enough."

Q. "Hard enough to do what?"

A. "Well, she fell on her face and broke her nose and possibly her cheek. She was knocked unconscious."

Q. "Oh, you left that out of your direct testimony. You made it seem as though it was just a slip and fall. So, she was badly hurt? Even though you had not put much weight on her, you say?"

A. "Yeah, it's not just what I say, it's what happened. I was concerned enough that I called an ambulance. She didn't try to get up; I don't think she could."

Q. "So, she was unconscious, even though you say you pushed her very little?"

A. "Yes, I believe so. You know, I know you're trying to make it seem that I pushed her harder and knocked her down, but she just fell as I was reaching for her. So, I called for the ambulance and cuffed her."

Q. "Well, Officer Graziano, it does seem strange to me that if you didn't push her hard, you still knocked her unconscious, and stranger still, that if she was unconscious, you went ahead and handcuffed her. That's another thing you left out in your direct testimony. Doesn't that seem a little cruel? Or am I wrong?"

A. "I'm not trying to hide anything here. I cuffed her, right, that's standard department procedure."

Q. "But you left that out of your direct examination, didn't you? You failed to mention that after you knock this woman down, so hard that you knock her unconscious, you say, you nevertheless felt it necessary to handcuff her as she lay on the freezing December ground? Is that your testimony? Did you at least get her a blanket or something, maybe a jacket, from your squad car?"

A. "That's my testimony. If you don't restrain these people and something happens, they sue you. Look, it all happened pretty fast. The ambulance was there within a few minutes. I put the cuffs on quickly so that if she came to, she could not hurt herself or me."

Q. "So, you claim the cuffs were to protect you after you knock 'these people' unconscious? Is that your testimony?"

A. "I didn't knock anybody unconscious. You're twisting things. It was a domestic dispute; things got out of hand, that's all. And yeah, domestic disputes are about the most dangerous things police face."

Q. "Even more than a robbery or brawl or drug bust? Even when the so-called perpetrator, herself a petite professional woman, has been knocked out and is unarmed?"

MR. REILLY

"Objection, Your Honor, asked, and answered. Mr. Collins is badgering the witness."

JUDGE LOPEZ

"Sustained. Point made, Mr. Collins, move along."

MR. COLLINS

Q. "You say the ambulance got there quickly. When they had Mrs. Arlow in their care, did you remove the handcuffs then?"

A. "No, I instructed them that she was dangerous, and they were not to remove the cuffs until they were at the hospital."

Q. "Who had the keys to the cuffs?"

A. "I kept them."

Q. "Well, wasn't that out of your jurisdiction? Suppose they had needed to remove the cuffs to give treatment en route? Wasn't it really excessive from the outset to put on the handcuffs with no way to render assistance?"

MR. REILLY

"Same objection, Your Honor. You've already made your ruling, and Mr. Collins is flagrantly ignoring it."

JUDGE LOPEZ

"The witness may answer, but this is the last along this line of questioning. Mr. Collins."

A. "Look, I want to answer this. She had just attacked her husband; she had tried to knock me down and get at her car, I mean the car, she had called me foul and abusive words ..."

Q. "That's it, isn't it? She called you those words when you reached out and restrained her, she called you a white Guinea motherfucker, and you knocked her down and then either punched her in the face as she went down or when she was on the ground, isn't that how she became unconscious?"

MR. REILLY

"Objection! Badgering the witness."

JUDGE LOPEZ

"Overruled. The witness may answer."

A. "I don't appreciate your sarcasm, Mr. Collins. I followed standard procedure. These people can hurt you without warning."

Q. "These people? What do you mean, unconscious, badly beaten, PROFESSIONAL NURSES, whom you have knocked to the ground and broken their facial bones? Are these 'the people' you mean?"

A. "No ..."

Q. "Your fear was she might regain consciousness, get back out of the ambulance, and come at you with her bare hands? On an icy surface?"

A. "Worse things have been known to happen."

Q. "Oh, yes, I remember now, it was front-page news. 'Officer Assaulted by Unconscious Nurse, Fleeing Ambulance' was that it?"

A. "Again, I don't appreciate your sarcasm. Domestic disputes are totally unpredictable. Danger is unavoidable. When you get a call to tell you that you're going to a domestic brawl, these people are capable of anything."

Q. "Well, Officer Graziano, there it is again, 'these people.' Was there something different about 'these people' than other people? Let me raise a different line of questions, Officer Graziano, you've been on the force for ten years, Officer Graziano, you are trained in restraining subjects. Did you have pepper spray, mace, immobilizing materials, a baton, a gun, anything else with you to restrain an unconscious nurse?"

A. "I have all of those supplies, and more, in preparation for any eventuality. And I resent your suggestion that I would attempt to use them on an unconscious person."

Q. "But you did use them, didn't you? Cuffs on an unconscious nurse and mother of three? And I am trying to figure out why. Wasn't it simply anger on your part? As I say, Officer Graziano, now we're getting down to it; please stand up next to me?"

A. "Why?"

Q. "Just do it!"

A. "You can't talk to me like that."

Q. "Well, His Honor can, and so can the prosecutor, and I will ask both of them to instruct you to stand next to me before the jury."

JUDGE LOPEZ

"The witness will do as requested."

Q. "Is it fair to say, Officer Graziano, that you are three inches taller than I am, at over 200 pounds probably 30 pounds heavier, and with all of your training and supplies, is there any question in your mind but that you could easily restrain me and not work up a sweat? Put me down and immobilize me if necessary, without inflicting broken bones or unconsciousness?"

A. "None. You would be down and out. Nothing broken."

Q. "And, necessarily, Mrs. Arlow, weighing only 125 pounds, would go down easier; no need to inflict those injuries was there?"

A. "I would not hit a lady, there was no need for me to do so, and the cuffs were strictly preventative."

Q. "You would not hit a lady, you say. But you have in the past, haven't you? There have been complaints filed against you with the Department, yes?"

MR. REILLY

"Objection! Outside the record. Not relevant. No competent evidence. Motion to strike."

JUDGE LOPEZ

"Objection sustained; motion granted. Mr. Collins, move on. The jury will ignore those remarks."

Q. "You say Mrs. Arlow simply slipped and fell, knocking herself unconscious. Yes?"

A. "Yes."

Q. "Isn't it much more likely, Officer Graziano, that when Mrs. Arlow called you a white Guinea motherfucker, you were sorely provoked, grabbed at her, knocking her down, and then punched her in the face? Or did you punch her before so she then fell down already unconscious?"

A. "Absolutely not! I've heard it all before! Why should I be upset simply because a housewife loses her temper and wallows in gutter talk?"

Q. Well, Officer Graziano, it's usually the attorney who asks the questions, but since you asked, I would answer that you found the word Guinea to be a racist, ethnic slur, especially insulting to you as a proud Italian American. I would also answer; further, you found the reference to your race, 'white,' to be a racist insult by an African-American person. And you found the phrase 'motherfucker' simply to be, as you say, insulting."

A. "Yes, but ..."

Q. "The question calls for a yes or no answer, and you have just answered yes. Let's close with this."

"Officer Graziano, your claim is you did not inflict injuries on Dorothy Arlow; somehow, she just fell.

"Our position is her injuries could only have been made by a direct punch to the face and that you were angry and out of control.

"Now, we will have a doctor, Doctor Simon Forman, who will testify in a few moments, a professional, lifelong emergency room physician in Harlem and now on the faculty at Yale New Haven Hospital, who has examined the x-rays of Dorothy Arlow's face, and he will testify to this jury here in just a few minutes that the broken bones in Defendant's face, and the wounds to her body, are all consistent only with a fist to the face, blunt force trauma, and inconsistent with a flat facial fall onto the pavement. If he so testifies, do you have an explanation for this jury as to why you are right, and he is wrong?"

A. "Only that you can buy an expert and get them to say anything."

Q. "And that's it? He's lying, and you're telling the truth?"

A. "Yes, if that's what he says ..."

MR. COLLINS

"A moment to consult with my client, Your Honor?"

With a nod from Judge Lopez, I turn to counsel table, take a drink from a glass of water, and say to Dorothy Arlow, "Anything I left out?"

She shakes her head, "I can't think of anything."

"Well now, Dorothy, let's see if Reilly falls into the trap." She looks at me, questioningly. As I sit beside her, Reilly is out of his chair, and his first question to Graziano went directly into the trap.

MR. REILLY

"Officer Graziano, the terms that Mrs. Arlow used, motherfucker, Guinea, referring to you as white, they were all offensive, were they not?"

OFFICER GRAZIANO

"Yes."

Q. "Mr. Collins highlighted this to suggest they provoked you into punching Dorothy Arlow. Did you?"

A. "No."

Q. "Well then, tell the jury why it is these terms did not provoke you, though they were so intended."

A. "Because they are common street terms in certain parts of the city, commonly used by certain segments of our society, and we are trained to ignore them. In fact, with some of these people, it's joking around between themselves."

Q. "Thank you, no more questions."

MR. COLLINS

"I notice, Officer Graziano, that you said these are common street terms 'in certain parts of the city,' commonly used by 'certain segments of our society.' And in fact, with 'some of these people, it's joking around between themselves.' Here's my question Officer Graziano, are you referring to African-Americans? That they are somehow different from the rest of us? Isn't this racial prejudice?"

154

MR. REILLY

"Objection. This is outrageous, and Officer Graziano deserves an apology. I request the Court to admonish Mr. Collins to refrain from his own prejudiced, bigoted attacks on law enforcement officers, who deserve our wholehearted, unreserved respect for the difficult jobs they perform so well!"

JUDGE LOPEZ

"Objection sustained. No name-calling please, Mr. Collins."

MR. REILLY

"I request the Court to instruct Mr. Collins to apologize to the witness for his insulting name-calling."

JUDGE LOPEZ

"Oh, I don't think that is necessary. Officer Graziano has testified to his ability to ignore insults, and I am sure he has been called worse than Mr. Collins, even at his most creative, can conjure up. The witness is excused with the thanks of the Court."

MR. REILLY

"One more question, please, Your Honor?"

JUDGE LOPEZ

"Yes, counselor, one."

MR. REILLY

"Officer Graziano, Mr. Collins has tried mightily to claim you punched Dorothy Arlow, the Defendant, in anger, out of control, in the face that December evening. And he has established that you could easily take him down, breaking no bones, though he is some 40 pounds heavier than the Defendant. Given that disparity, if you had punched Dorothy Arlow in anger that night, would her face appear as it does here today, with attractive, regular features, no scars, and no sign of injury whatsoever?"

MR. REILLY

A. "She would still today show the evidence of those injuries. She doesn't because she got her injuries in a fall. You can't put Humpty Dumpty together again."

MR. COLLINS

"Objection! Calls for speculation. The witness is not a medical expert. In a few moments, Mr. Reilly can cross-examine our medical expert."

JUDGE LOPEZ

"Objection overruled. Testimony will stand. You may use your expert for rebuttal purposes, Mr. Collins."

MR COLLINS

"Well, then, I too have one more question of the good Officer, and that is, just now, who did you mean when you said, 'You can't put Humpty Dumpty together again?'"

A. "You know who I mean."

Q. "Yes. Yes, I do. And what you meant as well."

A. "What do you mean by that? You know ..."

MR. COLLINS

"I have nothing further of this witness, Your Honor."

JUDGE LOPEZ

"Mr. Reilly? The witness may step down. Thank you, Officer Graziano."

Graziano steps down, deliberately walks close to the counsel table where I'm sitting, and whispers, out of the hearing of the judge and jury, "Anytime, anyplace, you Mick son of a bitch." I restrain myself from calling him a white Guinea motherfucker. Something about my grandmother, I guess, or maybe Graziano's size.

Graziano leaves the courtroom, obviously pissed.

As I turn to Dorothy Arlow, smiling with some restraint, she asks, "What was the trap for Reilly.?"

I look over at Jack, who apparently has taken a course in lipreading, and says, "Yup. Gotcha on that one, Francis," and then turns toward the bench. I hear Reilly say to Judge Lopez, "The prosecution rests."

Judge Lopez responds, "This court stands in recess for 15 minutes. When we return, Mr. Collins, you will present your case. The two of you are in danger of actually finishing in time for me to instruct the jury before we break for the evening. Try not to compromise your hard-earned momentum and, as always, Mr. Collins, think carefully about whether you need to put on any evidence at all," and here, Lopez is looking directly at me. Lopez cautions the jury about discussing the case and exits the bench.

The clerk intones, "All rise."

I say to Dorothy Arlow, "Let's go to one of the attorney conference rooms on the third floor, meet with our investigator and talk about where he thinks we stand. That last comment by Judge Lopez was an indication that I may not need to put on testimony because, if I draw the correct inference, he thinks the jury has already made up its mind in our favor. I am not so sure."

Mrs. Arlow said, "If he's right, that's a good thing, but poor Doctor Forman will have wasted his time."

I reply, "Judges have been known to be wrong, that's why we have courts of appeals."

As we leave, Friar Laurence leans in and says, "Nice job on the cross, Francis." The Abbot nods in agreement.

The four of us proceed out the center aisle and Friar Laurence adds, "The Abbot has us streaming courtroom movies as part of my

20th-century immersion, Francis. Last night, we finished *A Few Good Men*. Reilly matches up well with Kevin Bacon and you, of course, with Tom Cruise. Of course," Friar Laurence adds, looking down upon me, "you are a lot taller than Cruise."

"And better looking," adds Dorothy Arlow, more for Friar Laurence's benefit than mine, I suspect.

I notice, as we pass, the three friends of Dorothy Arlow are smiling, and beyond them, Joe Thomas' high school class, with the Adolph look-alike, still dressed in the starched, light tan Hitler Youth outfit. Mr. Thomas nods to me, says, "Nice job,"

I say, "Thanks. What did your Hitler Youth think?"

"He's a white supremacist, a Proud Boy, and of course, believes in civil liberties for only Aryans. So that excludes your client and Graziano. So, you can see, he was conflicted by the good job you did on the bad cop." Then he shrugs.

And we are all out the swinging doors. Ron, meeting us outside the swinging doors, seeing Young Adolph, mutters, "Crypto Creepos."

Dorothy Arlow, Ron Hoffer, and I step into the hallway outside the courtroom, where I say, "This case has taken an interesting turn.

"The real question is, do we need you to testify, Dorothy? The jury already has a favorable picture of you: hard-working mother, professional in a sympathetic field, supporting a ne'er-do-well husband, the victim in a probable beating by a police officer. If we already have all that in place, do we need to call the defendant at all? Maybe we don't offer 'wife' as a witness, going with just the doctor."

Mrs. Arlow asks, "What is the problem with my testifying?"

Ron adds, "I have the same question. The jury always wants to hear from the defendant."

"Well," I say, "The risk is that as a witness, Mrs. Arlow might supply some of the missing elements, possibly referring to loud arguments or missing butcher knives, on cross-examination. On direct, she might come across as vindictive, or haughty, or nervous; it's always hard to predict. One thing is for sure; Reilly will bait her.

"Right now, I think the jury thinks very highly of you. We should not risk losing that, particularly when the only thing we need is to destroy Graziano, and for that, we have the doctor."

"You know," says Ron, "It's always hard for us in the middle of a trial to read the jury. How about your two priests? It might be interesting to see what they think. Get a lay perspective, non-lawyers."

"I agree," says Mrs. Arlow quickly, "would they sit in and talk with us?"

I walk over to the two priests and say, "It would be helpful, if you can, to give your impression of who is ahead on points, so to speak, at this point. Specifically, has Reilly gotten enough out of Mr. Arlow and Officer Graziano to make a sympathetic or even a winning case? Do I need to have Ms. Arlow testify? If you were on the jury right now, would you vote to acquit?"

Abbot Dominic goes first. And he says, "Quite simply, I found that there was not much sympathetic about either Mr. Arlow or Officer Graziano. If I were on the jury, I would want to find a way to vote against them. Also, looking at the State's case, I would be wondering why this was brought to a jury. So, I guess, maybe the jury right now would go not guilty. If your doctor witness destroys Graziano's testimony and essentially proves that he is a liar, I should think that would be enough. You do not need to have Mrs. Arlow testify, although I'm sure the jurors will want to hear from her."

Friar Laurence says, "I agree. For many of the same reasons. But I would add, I have been observing Mrs. Arlow closely as the testimony proceeded, and she has seemed a warm, intelligent, and attractive person, just sitting there. The jury would see that, even if she doesn't testify." At this, I notice he has Mrs. Arlow's undivided attention.

Mrs. Arlow says, "Thank you for those kind words."

Friar Laurence adds, "I have done a lot of theater in my time, and the Abbot and I have both preached to large audiences, and I think, simply as a matter of theater, you have this audience of twelve already on your side. As I understand this 21st-century system, with a felony among the charges, the State needs a unanimous verdict, which means, Francis, all you really need is one vote out of 12 to hang the jury."

I turn to Ron and ask what he thinks. A man of few words, he says, "We don't need her on the stand. We can only lose by opening her up to cross-examination."

I say, "I would ask the judge to instruct the jury that they are not to draw a negative inference from you not testifying, that every person has a right to choose to testify or not. Even professional actors can fumble their lines."

At this, Friar Laurence clears his throat, puts his hands on the table, and says, "Perhaps I could add something?"

"Please do," says Mrs. Arlow, before I can speak.

"Well, it is this. As I mentioned, I have some experience with the theater, both as an actor and a director. What Mr. Collins says is true. Being a professional nurse, a mother, and the other roles in your life involve high pressure and tension, but nothing prepares you for being a witness in a criminal case unless you are Marlene Dietrich."

I do a doubletake on that, look at the clock, thank everybody, and say to Mrs. Arlow, "We'll start with the doctor. When he is done, I will check with you; likely, we will not need to put you on the stand. Okay?"

"Okay," She says, and we all proceed back into the courtroom."

I notice Friar Laurence is walking alongside my client, with Mrs. Arlow turning, and looking up at him, and saying, "I particularly appreciated your comments. Thank you."

"You are most welcome," he replies.

As the jurors file in, they can see Friar Laurence place his hand on Dorothy Arlow's shoulder and stoop to whisper in her ear, an intimate endorsement for the Irish and Italian Catholics on the jury. With the priests returned to their seats in the audience section, near the middle-aged African American rooting section, we return to counsel table, and Judge Lopez says, "Mr. Collins, call your first witness."

With that, I call for Doctor Simon Forman to take the stand. Without too much religious or racial or ethnic profiling, the jury scans the audience section for the expected trim, Jewish, professional physician, balding with a Sigmund Freud beard perhaps, to rise from the audience section, so they are visibly amused and somewhat bemused when an absolutely huge African-American male steps forward, testing the gate in the bar as he approaches the witness chair, to stand before the clerk, be sworn, and seats himself in the very same witness chair, which was strained by Officer Graziano. I only hope that when Forman has finished his testimony, we can get him out of that chair. If we can't pry him out, perhaps that will be our plausible excuse to the jury for not calling Mrs. Arlow to the witness stand later.

The preliminaries go quickly.

MR COLLINS

"Dr. Forman, please state your place of employment"

DOCTOR FORMAN

"Yale New Haven hospital."

Q. "What is your position there?"

A. "I am an associate professor of trauma medicine. I am chief of the trauma department and directing physician for the emergency department."

Q. "Within the field of medicine, what was your training?"

A. "Columbia University Medical School, a residency in trauma medicine, in which I am board-certified, ten years as staff and then Chief of Staff at Harlem General Hospital. And then I accepted the appointment here at Yale in New Haven, which I just described."

Q. "Dr. Forman, please state any honors received or any publications you have authored ..."

MR. REILLY

"The State is ready to stipulate that Dr. Forman is eminently qualified in whatever field and for whatever purposes Mr. Collins chooses. Let me say, at this point, I am at something of a loss and I am sure the jury is as well, since the charges are against Mrs. Arlow for misconduct, not for anything requiring medical evaluation. And so, I reserve the right to object, at the appropriate time, that this is all collateral and irrelevant. But for now, we will agree that Dr. Forman is an eminently qualified physician in the field of trauma medicine."

MR. COLLINS

"We are delighted to accept the stipulation, and I would only respond that Dr. Forman will testify that the injuries suffered by Mrs. Arlow are sufficient by themselves to acquit her of any charges of misconduct as to Officer Graziano and that the officer's credibility as to the remaining charges affecting Mr. Arlow is most suspect."

Q. "Dr. Forman, were you here earlier to hear the testimony of Officer Graziano?"

A. "Yes, I was."

Q. "Do you recall his testimony concerning the physical encounter with the defendant, Dorothy Arlow?"

A. "Yes, I do."

Q. "I call your attention particularly to the part where he testified that she fell and landed on her face on the pavement, causing her to be rendered unconscious. Do you recall that testimony?"

A. "Yes, I do."

Q. "Now, Dr. Forman, were you the examining physician when Mrs. Arlow came to Yale New Haven's emergency room?"

A. "No, I was not."

Q. "Are you acquainted with Mrs. Arlow other than today in this courtroom?"

A. "Yes, I am."

Q. "In what capacity?"

MR REILLY

"Objection, relevance?"

MR. COLLINS

"Simply trying to establish a baseline as to whether the witness knew Mrs. Arlow's appearance prior to the encounter on December 10 and was able to view her appearance subsequently."

JUDGE LOPEZ

"Objection overruled, proceed."

MR. COLLINS

"You were acquainted with Mrs. Arlow? How?"

A. "Yes, she has been a mainstay of our pediatric nursing staff and has participated in my conducting rounds dealing with children who have experienced trauma."

Q. "Could you describe her appearance prior to the incident on December 10?"

A. "Yes, I would say that Mrs. Arlow's facial features were regular, her bone structure fine. Overall, an attractive woman, as she is here today, I might add."

MR. REILLY

"I want to object ... objection withdrawn. Oh, get on with it, Collins."

(Laughter)

MR. COLLINS

"Now, Dr. Forman, at my request, did you review the x-rays that were taken on December 10 of Mrs. Arlow after the ambulance brought her to the emergency room?"

A. "Yes, I did."

Q. "Could you please describe, in general terms, what the x-rays of her face and head revealed."

A. "Yes, well, in Harlem, particularly, I had multiple occasions to see x-rays of faces which had encountered fists in fighting situations, and what Mrs. Arlow's x-ray revealed was exactly that."

Q. "Could you explain?"

A. "Yes, her nose was broken and dislodged at the midline from what would be her left toward her right. There was a fracture to her cheekbone, again on her left side, and fascia and sinuses were crushed."

Q. "Indicating what?"

A. "That she had been struck by an assailant. The location and orientation of the trauma sequelae are consistent only with the specific trauma on the left side of the face and inconsistent with a person falling flatly on her face, where the injuries would be distributed in a more generalized manner."

Q. "I take it, Officer Graziano, using his right fist hitting Mrs. Arlow on her left cheek and continuing to push the nose off-center, breaking it, he would be the source of the trauma, not a fall onto the pavement?"

MR REILLY

"I object most strenuously, there is no evidence that this witness was present during the incident in question, and so cannot offer even the remotest speculation as to who delivered the blow causing the injuries, if, indeed, they were not caused by falling onto pavement.

165

The only testimony is to the effect that Officer Graziano not only did not inflict those injuries but vehemently protests he would never do so and would never need to do so. I object. If my brother Collins wants to pursue character assassination, he should put the only other witness from the scene on the stand, and have Mrs. Arlow testify in this proceeding on her behalf."

"We are all eagerly wondering what she would have to say."

MR. COLLINS

"And now I must object most vehemently. This is an underhanded and sneaky attack by Mr. Reilly, for which he should be ashamed, knowing full well that a defendant need not testify in her own behalf and is often best advised not to do so where, as here, the Prosecutor behaves as Mr. Reilly does. I request the court to instruct both Mr. Reilly and the jury that not only does Mrs. Arlow have a right not to testify but that Mr. Reilly has engaged in inappropriate negative commentary, just now, on her freedom to exercise that very right. I would ask the court to grant a mistrial if this trial were not going so well in Mrs. Arlow's favor. Instead, I object."

JUDGE LOPEZ

"Well, I was promised the Trial of the Century, and it appears that we are working hard at producing one. On the other hand, we are needlessly consuming time. Let me instruct the jury that Mrs. Arlow need not testify, that Mr. Reilly may not comment negatively on that, and I don't understand that he has done so presently, that his objection is well taken and sustained. The witness will refrain from speculating as to who delivered any blow to the face if such was the case. Gentlemen, thank you for the entertainment; let's stay on track. Back to you, Mr. Collins."

Q. "Was there further injury, other than to the nose?"

A. "Yes, As I have testified, fascia and sinuses were compressed, the bony structure around the left eye and the cheekbone on her left side were fractured and compressed, consistent with a fist by someone striking her face with great force."

Q. "Is it possible to form an opinion to a medical certainty as to the parties' relative positions when the blow was struck?"

A. "Yes."

Q. "Would you tell us, please?"

A. "Yes, well, Officer Graziano is significantly taller than Mrs. Arlow, so they were in all probability not standing since he would then have been hitting down on her. This was more of a blow coming in level with Mrs. Arlow's head. For that, it is most likely that Officer Graziano was above her as she lay on the ground. He would then have cuffed her."

Q. "Let me see, Dr. Forman, are you saying that after she fell to the ground, Officer Graziano stood over her, on the ground?"

MR. REILLY

"Objection; calls for a conclusion. Lack of foundation. Speculation ..."

JUDGE LOPEZ.

"Sustained as to the reference to Graziano, otherwise objection overruled, of course it calls for a conclusion, Mr. Reilly, which is why we have experts. Continue, Dr. Forman."

Q. "So, Dr. Forman, the fist would be coming down on Mrs. Arlow's face, in a direct line with the left side of the face?"

A. "Yes."

Q. "The back of her head would have been resting on the ground?"

A. "I assume so."

Q. "If a heavy blow is struck to the front, while the head is resting on an impenetrable background, what is the probable consequence?"

A. "Cerebral trauma. Concussion. Serious injury. As evidenced by the injuries I have already described, plus injuries reflected to the back of the head and the interior of the cranium."

Q. "Were there front and back x-rays taken of Mrs. Arlow's head on her admission to the emergency room on December 10?"

A. "Yes."

Q. "And did you review the entire set?"

A. "Yes."

Q. "And was there evidence of trauma to the face from a blow and resulting trauma to the back of the head on the exterior and the interior, specifically, on the brain?"

A. "Absolutely. The x-rays were taken within 45 minutes of the injuries, and swelling within the cranium was already developing. The injuries to the front of the face were easily visible, and extensive and longer lasting; the injuries to the back of the head were probably resolved within a few days."

Q. "So, my last question, Doctor Forman, were you here when Officer Graziano testified that Mrs. Arlow slipped and fell and landed on her face injuring herself, leading to transport to the emergency room?"

A. "Yes, I was."

Q. "Was he speaking the truth?"

MR. REILLY

"Objection, calls for an opinion outside the witness' expertise and a legal conclusion. Ultimate issue, to be decided by the jury."

JUDGE LOPEZ

"Objection overruled, I take it the question is whether Dr. Forman's findings are consistent with Officer Graziano's testimony, and your question is better phrased in that way, Mr. Collins."

Q. "Was he speaking the truth, Dr. Forman?"

MR. REILLY

"Same question, same objection, I request that you admonish Mr. Collins."

JUDGE LOPEZ

"And I do so, now. Objection sustained. When you are pointed in the proper direction, Mr. Collins, it seems whimsical, at best, even perverse, to persist in error. I repeat, the objection is sustained. Move on."

Q. "You've described extensive injuries and internal swelling; would these be associated with pain, and if so, how much?"

A. "Yes, the pain would be extensive, perhaps not at first because of shock. But then, within a few moments or minutes at the most, there would be extreme pain. Probably accompanied by a state of being unconscious. That would be a mercy."

Q. "In the x-rays, which have now been circulated to the jury, on which you have pointed out the fractures, I see there is a notation that the patient was handcuffed. Why would that be noted?"

A. "Well, perhaps because it would make it difficult to position the patient for treatment and x-rays ... perhaps because it would be most unusual. There would be absolutely no need to cuff an unconscious patient ..."

Q. "Can you think of any imaginable reason for Officer Graziano to cuff Mrs. Arlow?"

A. "None whatsoever. Certainly, no medical reason. Or custody, she was unconscious. Perhaps simple mean-spirited nastiness and abuse on the officer's part."

MR REILLY

"Objection. I might say the same about the doctor's testimony at this point; perhaps we should inquire as to how much he is being paid. And as well any personal relationship with the defendant. Motion to strike."

JUDGE LOPEZ

"Motion granted. Mr. Collins, unless there is anything further, let us assume you have concluded your direct examination, and it is now Mr. Reilly's turn to question the good doctor."

MR COLLINS

"Thank you, Dr. Forman. Your witness, Mr. Reilly."

Jack Reilly arises, obviously approaching the task before him with great care. There is nothing quite so formidable as an expert witness defending a sympathetic position.

In a sense, the best way to approach an expert is as if he or she is a witness to an event—like a car wreck. So, the basics apply. What was the witness' position to observe anything? What has the witness in fact observed? How much does the witness now recall? Does the witness seem to be overreaching in his or her testimony, given the limited basis for that testimony? And always, questions about reports, prior statements, things that should've been done but were not done, simple bias, all of that is fair game for cross-examination. Plus, prior relations with the subject individual, the defendant.

A frequent mistake is to assume the obvious. So, it is always best to start with basics. What is the witness' acquaintance with this case or this patient? How extensive has the examination or investigation been? Not what was done, but what was not done and should have been. If possible, get the witness to admit the limitations of his or her testimony. Save the combative questions to last ...

And so, Jack Reilly, begins with basics.

MR. REILLY

"Dr. Forman, were you the treating physician that night on duty in the emergency room when Mrs. Arlow came in?"

A. "No."

Q. "Did you see her then?"

A. "No."

Q. "So, you really cannot testify from first-hand medical observation as to her condition upon arrival? Is that true?"

A. "Yes."

Q. "Have you examined her since?"

A. "No."

MR. REILLY

"Motion to strike, this witness testified with no foundation for his observations or opinions. He never examined the patient. Everything he has to say is based on hearsay or photography. We require direct observation and testimony as a foundation."

MR. COLLINS

"His testimony has been based upon decades of experience and trauma medicine dealing with the kinds of injuries reflected in the x-rays, which he has evaluated. Also, relying on other physicians' treatment in a case is customary in medical practice, is it not, Dr. Forman?

A. "Yes."

JUDGE LOPEZ

"Objection overruled, and motion to strike denied, the jury may take the testimony for what it is worth."

MR. REILLY

"There were other physicians who saw her that evening, treated her in the emergency room, arranged for the radiology and x-ray examinations, and made the assessment of fracture and concussion, is that correct?"

A. "Yes, there were."

Q. "I note that the defense has called not a single one of them. I also note, Dr. Forman, that your testimony has been limited to what the x-ray pictures themselves showed. Is that correct? You have not yourself examined Mrs. Arlow's face or head, either that evening or subsequently, yes?"

A. "Yes."

Q. "Also, as to whether or not there was a concussion, would that be a diagnosis within your expertise, or would that be something for a brain specialist?"

A. "It could be either, but more likely the latter."

Q. "Which you are not, correct?"

A. "Yes."

Q. "You said that there was damage to the back of the head, and that could lead to a concussion within the head. Correct?"

A. "Yes."

Q. "But these x-rays that evening are all of the head's exterior. Would interior x-rays or MRI or CAT scans reveal the presence of a concussion within the head?"

A. "Yes."

Q. "Have you examined those pictures?"

A. "No."

Q. "Do you even know whether they were taken?"

A. "No."

Q. "So, your surmise that there was a concussion, and therefore that there had been blunt force trauma to the back of the head lying on the ground, was simply that, wasn't it, a surmise?"

A. "I suppose so."

Q. "I assume that there are extensive records concerning Mrs. Arlow's condition and treatment that evening and the following days. Have you consulted those?"

A. "I had intended to, but I have been on call and on service since 7:00 AM yesterday, some 30 hours without sleep."

Q. "Well, let me say I have always admired healthcare professionals for their dedication and ability to extend themselves to what seems to me beyond the limits of human capacity, but, in all fairness, wouldn't your testimony today be better informed if you had reviewed the records?"

A. "In all fairness, I must agree with you, Mr. Reilly."

Q. "And by all fairness, Dr. Forman, I mean fairness not to Mrs. Arlow but to Officer Graziano, whose performance you have challenged severely. It did seem that you were defending Mrs. Arlow strenuously, so let me ask how well do you know Mrs. Arlow, Dr. Forman?"

A. "I have worked with her for a number of years, consulting with her on children on the pediatric floor who had been subject to trauma. She has also on occasion rotated through the emergency room service, with particular attention to children."

Q. "And on such instances, have you had occasion to discuss the cases, observe her services, and become acquainted with her?"

A. "Yes."

Q. "Would this be true of many nurses?"

A. "Some."

Q. "But more so with Mrs. Arlow?"

A. "Yes."

Q. "So, is it possible that your appearance here today and your testimony are both influenced by your strong, personal and unusual professional relationship with Mrs. Arlow?"

A. "I suppose you could say that, to some degree, but I object to the words 'personal' and 'unusual.'"

Q. "And has your future relationship influenced or affected the way you delivered testimony and the conclusions you reached here today, on behalf of Mrs. Arlow?"

A. "No! And I resent the insinuation. Mrs. Arlow is a fine professional, and I respect her as such."

Q. "Well, I did not mean to imply any impropriety or anything by way of a personal relationship beyond the hospital setting, but it does seem to me that you should be concerned that after this trial if Mrs. Arlow is convicted, that would have a negative impact on your working relationship, and possibly the way others view you in the hospital, wouldn't you agree?"

A. "I absolutely disagree, and I have every confidence that this jury will acquit!"

MR. COLLINS

"Objection! Objection! This is character assassination!"

This, of course, is what Reilly wanted. "And you are here to see that that happens, aren't you," accuses Reilly, and "you've done your best to make sure that happens, haven't you?" Objection from me, question withdrawn from Reilly, who says "I have nothing further of this witness," having done a fine craftsman-like hatchet job on my witness.

"Anything further on redirect, Mr. Collins?" from Judge Lopez.

"Nothing further, Your Honor." Dr. Forman is excused by Judge Lopez, with the court's thanks, and appreciation for his appearance today, given his work schedule over the preceding 30 hours.

JUDGE LOPEZ

"Call your next witness, Mr. Collins."

MR. COLLINS

"May I have a moment?"

JUDGE LOPEZ

"Only a moment, we're getting close to 4:00 PM."

I turn to my client, thinking Forman has pretty much destroyed Graziano, but then Jack may have destroyed Forman, and I nevertheless suggest to Mrs. Arlow there is no need to call her to the stand. On balance, I think Dr. Forman has carried the day. This is a difficult moment for any client. She pauses, looking at me, and says, "What do you think?"

I say, "Let's put this puppy to rest."

She agrees.

MR. COLLINS

"Your Honor, my client and I are in agreement that the jury has now heard, really, all there is to be heard about this case and is fully in a position to decide it, and that if we end our case at this point, they should be able to get the case from you this afternoon. We would like that. And so, Mrs. Arlow, as is her right, on my advice, will decline to testify."

JUDGE LOPEZ

"Mr. Collins, I understand. Let me confirm that Mrs. Arlow is in full agreement with the decision not to testify. Is that your decision, Mrs. Arlow?"

DEFENDANT

"Yes, it is, thank you, Your Honor," in a clear and thoughtful voice.

JUDGE LOPEZ

"Let me say to the members of the jury that there are often times a decision in a case like this, where the facts are fairly straightforward and have been fully presented, there is no need to call additional witnesses, and constitutionally a defendant may choose to exercise her right not to testify. I trust the jury will understand this and that it is fully as much a decision by the attorney as by the client, and members of the jury are to draw no negative inference from Mrs. Arlow's decision not to testify. I will so instruct you again later.

"Mr. Reilly, do you have any further witnesses or testimony?"

MR. REILLY

"No, thank you, Your Honor."

JUDGE LOPEZ

"Members of the jury, yesterday and then during the recesses today, counsel have submitted requests for instructions on this case. These are rules which are intended to guide you in your decision as jurors. Those instructions are standardized in the state practice book. I will read them later, but first, we'll hear from the attorney for the State, Mr. Reilly, and then the defense attorney, Mr. Collins.

"One of the instructions that I am to give you later states that you should understand their arguments are just that; they are not to be taken as evidence. You are to decide this case on the evidence as it came in through the witnesses. The arguments of counsel are simply to help you understand the points of view of the two different sides and assist you in evaluating the evidence to reach your verdict.

"Mr. Reilly, you're up."

Closing arguments are prepared well before the trial begins. If counsel are carefully prepared, what takes place later in the courtroom itself is simply a replay of the preparation. However, there have been a number of developments which might not have been anticipated, for example, Mrs. Arlow has not testified; Dr. Forman's testimony was strong against the prosecution, but then seriously devalued by Reilly's cross-examination; and similarly, Officer Graziano's testimony was sorely challenged by my cross-examination. And the Phantom Butcher Knife vanished into the night on December 10.

So even the carefully prepared summations must be adjusted in the light of what developed in the courtroom. However, that may be, an attorney must start with a theory of his or her case, boil it down to ten words, and then advance it consistently at each stage of the trial, and finally, at last, in the closing arguments. The theory in the closing arguments should resonate with the jurors as something with which they have already become quite familiar.

Jack Reilly's theory of the case is simple: this is a domestic dispute gone bad. Simple but sad. Ten words; perfect. He takes the jurors through a checklist of the elements of the charges. There is little passion in his delivery, and there is no joy in this task, he could express outrage at the way Officer Graziano was treated, at the danger posed to the children by Mrs. Arlow's excess. But this is truly not the Great Case of the Century; it is only a sad, little, domestic brawl.

Justice here is a sad song, in a minor key, and Reilly soft-pedals it.

For my part, my job is easier. My theory of the case is reasonable doubt. I follow Reilly's list. Here, here, and here, the State has failed utterly to prove a central element. I end with the assault with a deadly weapon, the Phantom Butcher knife, which was never found.

Unlike Reilly, I throw in some indignation at the end: at the way Reilly slandered Doctor Simon Forman in court after 30 straight hours on duty at Yale New Haven Hospital; at the way Officer Graziano lied and punched Mrs. Arlow, and cuffed her unconscious; at the way Billy Arlow drove off into that bitter December night leaving the mother of his children unconscious on the frozen ground.

I ask for a verdict of not guilty on all counts.

A little indignation is good for the soul; like a thunderstorm, it freshens the air, it feels electric. As I turn, thanking the jury, I see Friar Laurence nod approvingly and, as I sit, Mrs. Arlow reaches over and places her hand on my forearm, saying thank you. Reilly offers no rebuttal. It is now all up to Judge Lopez.

The instructions are the usual; we learned a lot of them in high school Civics class from Joe Thomas: burden of proof, presumption of innocence, need for jurors to listen to each other, the necessity for unanimous verdict on a felony, and then instructions on each of the charges, an essential element in each is that the defendant have clear intent as to each. Those are references also to freedom of speech and defense of self and property. Judge Lopez instructs the jury to retire to consider their verdict and directs the bailiff to bring dinner to them in the jury room. In their absence, he tells counsel to stay close since he would anticipate a verdict at about 7:00 or 8:00 PM. He and they retire.

Reilly and Graziano leave the courtroom quickly, with my saying as they pass, "Nice job, Jack."

Graziano saying, "Fuck you."

As I turn to Dorothy Arlow, she says, "Thank you; I think you have done a wonderful job."

I feel the priestly presence of the Abbot and Friar Laurence leaning over the bar behind us to say, "We agree. And we would like to take counsel and client to an early dinner at the Abbey, in anticipation that the jury will not be out very long."

I look at Dorothy Arlow and see that she is smiling broadly, and say, "I think we would like that."

As we leave the courtroom, I note that I am alongside Abbot Dominic and that my client is gently escorted by Friar Laurence, through the swinging doors, down the stairs, and into the warm spring sunshine of a late afternoon on the New Haven Green.

A familiar voice and hand come up behind me, to say, "Nice job, cowboy. Save a little space for dessert at home ... we women have to take care of the children you men bless us with," and with that Meg, who tries to get to all my closings, and often rehearses them with me at home, wearing her doctor's white coat with stethoscope in pocket from Yale New Haven Hospital, turns to Dorothy Arlow and says, "Good luck, Dorothy. Francis here is the best lawyer I know. He was in pretty good form just now, I thought."

And she moves off toward Hamden, to RBG and Earl Warren, and home, as we proceed across the Green to the Dominican Abbey.

The Abbot says, "We will be serving a buffet dinner along about now. We can get a table in a corner by ourselves, our chef is from Verona and has a wonderful way with Italian seafood recipes. Friar Laurence can be our guide. Please."

Mrs. Arlow is pleased, as am I. It is a short walk through traffic, across both blocks of the Green, divided by Temple Street, and within minutes we are inside the Abbey, in cool quiet and tranquility that seem to stretch back ages. There is a murmur coming from the dining room, which is only half-full. We draw curious glances as we enter, and the Abbot lets the staff know he has guests.

We go through a short line, choose from a fine array of appetizers, entrées, and desserts, and are politely seated in a quiet corner surrounded by dark oak at an ancient table.

The meal is quickly consumed, although there is ample time for Friar Laurence to commend the Abbot on his choice of chefs. It has been decades, Friar Laurence says, perhaps longer, since he has tasted the foods of Northern Italy, and these are very good. He adds, they are not quite representative of the Verona region, which he regrets and misses. Still ...

Mrs. Arlow turns to Friar Laurence and asks the obvious question, "May I ask why you two gentlemen of the cloth are sitting through my very ordinary humdrum case, in which as far as I know you have no particular interest?"

"Well," responds the Abbot, "clearly it has great importance for you. However, our interest is not so much in this case as in your attorney, Mr. Collins.

"So," Mrs. Arlow says," basically, you're using me as a canary in the coal mine to see whether he measures up?" We all laugh at the comparison. She continues, "And does he?"

"Well, what do you think of how he did?" asks Friar Laurence.

Mrs. Arlow looks at me and then turns back to Friar Laurence and says, without reservation or hesitation, "I think he did very well. He always seemed to know what he was doing, and made sure I understood. I was afraid," and here there was a tremor in her voice, "when I couldn't afford to hire a lawyer that I wouldn't get the best. But I think I did. Win or lose. Thank you." And with that, she turned and gave me a quick kiss on the cheek.

Mrs. Arlow turns the question around. "If I may, I am curious as to how you gentlemen thought Mr. Collins did and what kind of case you have?"

Friar Laurence clears his throat, looks directly at Mrs. Arlow, and says, "I think Mr. Collins did very well. As to my case, I am not quite sure how to describe it. Neither the prosecutor nor the presiding judge seems to be very clear either. Right now, the best description would be that I am charged with stalking, with a plan to kill, two New Haven teenagers, who are playing the roles of Romeo and Juliet in a musical version of that play at the Yale Drama School."

Here, Mrs. Arlow gasps and interjects, "Stalking them! Frankly, I don't see you as doing that, but I can get you a good deal on a used butcher knife if that fits into your plan." There is light laughter all around. Despite this light touch at the end, Mrs. Arlow is concerned and somewhat upset and adds, "Oh, I don't mean to make light of this. How is it possible anyone would believe this of you?"

Friar Laurence resumes, "Somehow the fact that the teenagers are from the New Haven families of Montague and Capulet, and years ago I had associations with those families, and that I have come a great distance at this particular time connects me to those children back then and today." Friar Laurence paused, then continued, "It also doesn't help that I can't give a good explanation for how or why I am here."

Dorothy Arlow is following this with great intensity. "Have you spoken with the children; do they even know you're here?"

"No," says Friar Laurence, "and in fact, the judge in the case as a condition of bail has forbidden me to approach or have any contact with the children, not that I would.

"Frankly, my circumstances are such that I am simply at a loss as to what connection I might have with the children myself. But there are a number of other circumstances connected with the play, even ancestors going back to Shakespeare's time, which seem to have significance, for example, the chief justice is a man named Popham, who was chief justice back in Shakespeare's time, and it is he who seems to be riding herd on me. And at the risk of frightening you, some part of me may be from that time, and I think Popham is, too."

And here, Laurence laughed his big, booming laugh, breaking the tension of the moment, and said, "In a way, I think it is Popham who is stalking me." Mrs. Arlow is relieved by this, although still troubled. This is not your usual dinner time conversation in her household ...

Dorothy Arlow reflects and says, "Whatever brought you here has brought us together, even if only in passing, and I hope I may be involved in a positive way with whatever you are experiencing."

Here, the Abbot adds yet another "circumstance," which he mentions as one of many, creating what he calls an odd mosaic surrounding these teenagers and Friar Laurence. "Let me say, before I share this, that this constellation of circumstances relating to Friar Laurence and the *Romeo and Juliet* connection does not make a neat or even rational puzzle, but in total, it is most remarkable. For example, the prosecutor in Friar Laurence's case and the judge trying it both have roles and names similar to their predecessors in Shakespeare's time. So also, our Francis here is himself a Shakespeare authority of no small measure, as represented by his undergraduate and graduate studies at Yale and likely a descendant of Shakespeare's lawyer."

He continues, "I mention all this, only to lead up to this question, Francis, the judge here is Roderigo Lopez, does that ring a bell?"

I answer, "Yessssss, now that you mention it. Roderigo Lopez was a Portuguese Jew, who converted to Christianity, and served as Queen Elizabeth's physician. He was charged and convicted of attempting to assassinate her, prosecuted by Edward Coke, convicted falsely, and hung, drawn and quartered."

And then this, "Some commentators think this contributed to Shakespeare's Shylock and Christopher Marlowe's The Jew of Malta. A decade later, all the Marranos, as Lopez's people were then called, were run out of England."

And with that, the Abbot says, "Francis, me lad, you get an A in Elizabethan history, now, for an A+ in conspiracy theory. Who sentenced Lopez?"

"Well," say I, almost incredulous at what I'm about to say, "I do believe that the judge who sentenced Roderigo Lopez all those centuries ago was then Chief Justice Popham, but as part of a

Commission. Rodrigues may be here for vengeance, to keep Popham from harming Friar Laurence. Good heavens!"

And I say to Dorothy Arlow, "Our Chief Justice Popham seems to Friar Laurence to be the very man he remembers from his own time; indeed, Popham professed to see a family resemblance between my attorney ancestor and me from that long-past era."

With that, the Abbot turns to Dorothy Arlow, "What seems to be happening is a gathering of flotsam and jetsam from Shakespeare's time and that of Romeo and Juliet, much like an eddy or a magnet gathers up the material around it. It may form a pattern. It may not. But still, there is an eddy or a magnet and something is causing them. It is the thing behind them that is important, and who or what put them there.

Dorothy Arlow gives a nervous laugh, "Am I part of this?"

Without thinking, I say, and immediately wish I hadn't, "Well, in the play, there is a nurse, a very important role, no name, however in a way, she sells Juliet out." Dorothy Arlow clearly did not want to hear this.

The Abbot pauses and says, "Perhaps we should stop weaving this fantasy. Quite possibly, it is all paranoia. I think Mrs. Arlow is beginning to fear that Othello will be next." I laugh and say, "Not to worry. Simon Forman took his place."

The Abbot bounces his eyebrows and turns to Mrs. Arlow and says, "Don't even ask ... and above all, don't worry. Your attorney spent too much time in the stacks of Sterling Memorial Library's Shakespeare Collection and the Beinecke rare books cube."

After a brief pause, the Abbot continues, "But in that connection, Francis, didn't you research a thesis proposal to go on for a Doctorate in Fine Arts in the Drama School? What was it about?"

I wonder how in the world he knows about this, as he does many things, and I answer, perhaps too curtly, "Like everything else here, it was about *Romeo and Juliet*, it was never read, the proposal was turned down, and I left the Drama School in embarrassment and disappointment. For unrelated reasons. It rankles still to this day. I never talk about it."

The Abbot turns to Dorothy Arlow, saying, "So you see. Your lawyer was at the Drama School, the play is the play that's being performed there next week, so we add another piece to the puzzle. Or is it now becoming a brick for an edifice?"

There is a pause in the conversation, and I note that the time is moving toward 7:00 PM. It has been very quiet in the Abbey dining room, darkness is falling outside as the spring evening gathers, the door opens, and Ron Hoffer enters, seeing us, he approaches and says, "It looks like the jury is coming back and the judge wants you in the courtroom."

Mrs. Arlow appears startled, turning to me and saying, "Isn't that quick? Is that a good thing?"

I rise and say what any experienced attorney would say at this point, "There is no telling what a jury will do. But if they canceled out Officer Graziano's testimony, in part because of Dr. Forman, that leaves them with a simple domestic dispute. They can hardly favor Billy Arlow. Do remember, though, that my prediction was conviction on one of the minor charges. If we don't better the Offer of the Century, I will be terribly embarrassed."

With that, we rise and take our leave of the Abbot and the Friar, who wish us well, Friar Laurence and Mrs. Arlow exchanging hopes they will see each other again, and follow Ron quickly back across the Green to the courthouse, under the cool shadows of the elm trees,

185

entering by the front door and, with a nod toward Big John's Little Elevator, he having left at 6:00 PM, we mount the stairs, two at a time. The courtroom doors open, we proceed down the main aisle, the prosecution is already present, and Judge Lopez instructs the clerk to bring in the jury, which happens in a mere matter of minutes.

There is a bureaucratic ritual to the reception and pronouncement of a verdict, but it is enough to report the jury's foreperson, when asked on each charge, responded "guilty" as to the breach of peace charge and not guilty as to the rest. The judge asked whether counsel would like the jury polled, and we declined. The foreperson stated that the jury members wished to tell the court that they recommended a lenient sentence on the conviction of breach of peace. Judge Lopez thanked them and said the fine would be $25, suspended for six months, to be remitted and conviction expunged at that time if there were no further incidents involving Mrs. Arlow.

Judge Lopez then turned to Dorothy Arlow and said, "Mrs. Arlow, you have just heard the sentence; if I could, I would set aside the conviction, but it does seem to me, somewhere in this sad set of facts the jury could find a breach of peace. I do not want to detain you any longer, since I assume your services are needed at home where," and here he looked in the audience section directly at Billy Arlow, "I trust Mr. Arlow Is no longer present in the home."

"That is correct," responded Mrs. Arlow, "but Is there nothing you can do about the fact that he still has my car?" Here, Reilly and I look at each other as Judge Lopez leans forward from the bench
JUDGE LOPEZ
"Is that true, Mr. Arlow, and if so, tell me why."
A. "It is true, and the reason is, I'm sure you will appreciate, possession is nine points of the law."

JUDGE LOPEZ

"Ah, we have here a lawyer. One who elevates the law above common sense and mercy and justice. Is your wife still making payments on the car, Mr. Arlow?"

A. "Yes, Your Honor, since I have remained unemployed for months."

JUDGE LOPEZ

"Well, I think perhaps we can work a small adjustment here. Do you have the car keys with you, Mr. Arlow?"

A. "Yes."

JUDGE LOPEZ

"I am asking these two gentlemen, court bailiffs, to take you into custody overnight as a material witness in this case, in the event that there are any further motions in the morning. As part of the booking process, photos, printing, creation of a criminal record, and custody are standard and unavoidable. I will also instruct the bailiff and the sheriff to turn over the automobile car keys to Mrs. Arlow so that she can take possession for safekeeping of her vehicle. And, as you say, possession is nine points of the law."

A. "You can't do this. Can he, Mr. Reilly?"

JACK REILLY

"My view is that he can do anything he wants. Anyway, I'm not your lawyer. Possibly tomorrow morning, Mr. Collins' office may visit you at the jail and arrange counsel. Possibly the judge, in his discretion, might rescind holding you overnight if the keys to the car were turned over to Mrs. Arlow, to be kept by her until your divorce case is resolved, and to assure you won't leave the jurisdiction. But of course, Mr. Arlow, it is entirely up to you, either way, jail or not, it looks like she will end up with the car."

A. "Alright, here are the goddamned keys, right here on this table. You can pick them up if you want them. I'm outta here."

JUDGE LOPEZ

"Mr. Arlow, you have not been excused. I would suggest you ask the court for permission to leave."

A. "I do ask permission of the court to leave, I do apologize, and the keys which my wife now has, I will not seek again."

With that, the judge gestures toward the rear of the courtroom and Arlow stomps out.

Judge Lopez turns to Reilly and me and thanks us for enlivening the humdrum life of a baseline criminal court judge and for doing what he considers a fine job in presenting the case. He turns to Mrs. Arlow and says, "Mrs. Arlow, I do hope you appreciate that what these two gentlemen did is as fine a job as any member of the Bar could, and I congratulate you and them on the outcome." With that, he declares that the court will stand adjourned until tomorrow morning and departs the courtroom.

As Mrs. Arlow and I are about to leave, Reilly turns and says, "Wait just a second. I have one question, who were the three rather attractive African-American ladies sitting in the front row immediately behind you and Mrs. Arlow? Did they witness the brawl in the parking lot? If so, Francis, you failed to list them and advise me. Who were they?"

Dorothy Arlow begins to laugh.

"Well," I say, "you might say they were character witnesses against Mr. Arlow. If called, they would have testified that they had had affairs with Mr. Arlow."

"So," Reilly says, "just window dressing for the jury?"

"I don't know," Mrs. Arlow turns to me and asks, "Could we have called them to testify that he was a lousy fuck?"

"Only if it was true," Reilly laughs, "Was he?"

"You don't have to answer that," I quickly say.

"I never asked them," Mrs. Arlow says, "But I believe that is what they would have testified. What are old friends for? Or were you asking for my appraisal?"

Reilly and I shake hands; he exits saying, for my ears only, "I'm coming to have a higher regard for Mrs. Arlow. So, I think, is your client, Friar Laurence," Reilly says, looking significantly over my shoulder. I look in that direction, where I see them deeply in conversation.

With that, I gather up my papers, along with Mrs. Arlow, and she, Ron Hoffer, and I walk into the night. In front of the courthouse, I say that if she will come by my office in the morning, we will arrange payment of the fine, and we will discuss the future expunging of her record. She promises to come by in the morning, thanks me again, and gives me a big hug. With that, I head home.

Meg hugs me at the door. Having taken a break from her job to sit in the back of the courtroom and hear my closing, she says, "Nice closing, Slugger. Just the right amount of passion and brevity, there's a lot to be said for that at the end of the day. And keeping her off the stand? Gutsy move. Chalk up another one for the good guys."

With that, she gives me a salubrious, perhaps salacious wink and says, "Your dinner awaits your Majesty, along with your loyal subjects." Over beef Stroganoff and Dr Pepper, followed by apple cobbler, the kids cross-examine me, raise profound doubts about my trial strategy, performance, and my fundamental competence to do what I do, turn to their homework. We read more of *The Lord of the Rings*, and it is off to bed.

We say good night to them, turn off their lights, brush our teeth, and test out the proposition presented earlier, whether passion and brevity indeed have a lot to be said for them and us at the end of the day.

It is now Wednesday morning and Meg and I get the household launched. RBG and The Chief head for school, laptops in their backpacks, along with cell phones, and some other electronic gadgetry which will already be obsolete by the time I learn its identity. We all exchange "I love you, you too" and pivot toward the outside world.

Meg is off to the world of medicine and research wizardry, dropping the kids en route. I am off to the world of law, dictate a few memos in my ancient Volvo en route, park behind the ancient City Hall and decide to take advantage of Big John and his Ancient Elevator, if only to maintain good relations with the City Hall scene. We exchange greetings, talk about the Red Sox and the Yankees, he says, "I hear you scored big on New Haven's Finest yesterday. Cool." And I find myself released by the accordion like scissor doors onto the reception area of our public defender office. Which is also ancient.

The only non-ancient article, so far, besides Meg, the kids and myself, is Jo. Her back is to me, she has a million-dollar view of the New Haven Green, and cannot see me reflected in the monitor of her desktop computer, and yet she says, "Good morning, oh my Liege. Your traffic terror memos have been transcribed, edited for grammar and punctuation, filed in the appropriate files, copies are on the right side of your desk. On the other side, that would be the left, are the five client files on which you have appearances this morning at 10:00. The clients will be here at 9:00. Maybe. In ten minutes, at 8:00, Demetrius Data, our bodacious Greek Geek, will be in to discuss what he has found in his whirlwind tour of cyberspace, in the digital service of Friar Laurence."

"Please do not disturb me for the next 30 minutes. Dorothy Arlow and I are doing our nails together. And congratulations, I understand you skewered a deadbeat husband, slivered Officer Graziano, another one of New Haven's finest you have now alienated, entrapped Jack Reilly, skated over a thinly prepared expert witness and came away with a good result adding to your legendary status on the streets of Gotham. As I say, I will be unavailable for the next 30 minutes."

As always, I am stunned by Jo's opening salvos, and wonder if people really talk like this in the real world. I rebound and say, "Great," and as I am proceeding to my office, turn and say, "Wait. You are doing what with whom?"

Jo pivots in her chair, turns and looks at me as though I'm having an uncommonly obtuse and turgid morning, and says, "Your client. Nails. Arlow. Dorothy Arlow. As in Bond, James Bond. She's bringing the nails." And with that, she turns back to face the Green.

I thought they all came with nails installed. Live and learn.

Data enters my office, backpack slung over his shoulder, laptop in his hand, bag from Dunkin' Donuts in his other hand, all of which, including his considerable body, he drops into a chair directly opposite me, looks at me and says, "Okay, Boss, I did all the public records with the parameters you gave me and I got nuttin'. Nada. El Zippo, zero, zed ..."

Before he can continue, I interject, "Are you trying to say that you found nothing?"

With that, he bends over into the Dunkin' Donuts' bag, pulls out a cup of coffee for himself and for me, and says, "Well, I wouldn't say existentially that was the case, since you like coffee with two sugars

192

and two creams, and here they are. Plus, there are six donuts in the bag, but your medically trained bride would perform experiments on me if I let you eat more than five, so you get only one of the chocolate-centered, cream-filled, plus two French crullers and two jelly-filled. But, yeah, otherwise, right, not a thing, well, almost"

Then he paused, and added, "You know, every creature that ever had a pulse or made mist on a mirror shows up somewhere in a database in some form or other ... if he, she, or it existed. Or exists. In some fashion."

There is a pause, so I take my cue, and ask, "Does Friar Laurence exist? Existed?" I replied, adding, "He did yesterday."

"Prove it," comes Data's reply, "because I can't." He leans back and says, philosophically, which I hate, "His existence is like the tree that falls solo in the forest or the sound of one hand clapping or ..."

And here I jump in and say, "Let's focus on the three memos: plays, movies, Dominican Abbey.

"We're looking for appearances by our client, possibly associated with trouble."

"Right," Data says, "I was able to get into more databases than you could spit at. Over the centuries, there have been numerous brawls and battles around Shakespeare. In the early 1600s, for example, outside the Globe, in the streets, and then later, 1640s, when the theaters were shut down and then the New York City Shakespeare riots in the 1840s with 40 deaths."

"40 deaths?" Say I.

"Yes," Data replies, "But there was nothing particularly focused on *Romeo and Juliet*. There has come to be a body of literature about deaths associated with *Macbeth*, but again, nothing to point toward our man Laurence.

"I ran our client through history, and as far as I can tell, this is his first rodeo. And by that, I mean, even in London and Verona, there is not even a birth or death record, or in this country, no driver's license, draft card, birth or death record, school stuff, and needless to say, he has no credit cards, no checking accounts, no military record. If he flew to New Haven or came on a train or bus, I would have found something, but to be repetitive, nada.

"If someone set out to construct such an invisible, nonexistent profile, there would be electronic evidence of the attempt itself. There isn't. I would say, he cannot exist and never did. But clearly, he does. He does, in fact, cast a shadow."

And here Data leaned forward, setting aside a sugar jelly doughnut, and added conspiratorially, "Of course, we should check to see if his image will appear in a mirror.

Just kidding, just kidding."

"He is conducting a stunningly successful plan for hiding in plain sight, and is a very dangerous Friar indeed," I muse, and then add, "But he is real.

"And the Abbey records?" I query.

And now, D. data smiles at me and says, "Well, here, things got interesting."

Data slid a folder across the desk to me, and scanning it, it was clear that starting some 150 years ago, a number of non-resident travelers, mostly clergy, began appearing in New Haven, staying and then moving on, after a few months. In many instances, the places of origin were listed as unknown, as were the ultimate destinations. The religious Orders and affiliations were wide and varied, with a few more Dominican and Franciscan monks, and the reasons for coming to the Abbey were quite varied, but a pattern emerged of professional

194

or pastoral concerns, frequently listed as seeking "solace" or "forgiveness" or "peace." Why or from whom or how was not listed. With respect to each individual, there had been a referral source, but they were blacked out.

"In fact," said Data, "I wouldn't be surprised to learn that the Abbot knew we were coming, gathered the information, and actually prepared two copies, one for us and one for the prosecution. The Abbot is an interesting guy ..."

Then Data goes on, "Back to the man himself, our client. So ... I decided to do just the man himself not limited to the Abbey here in New Haven. I went back through the Dominican database, which has now been digitized, their records going back to the year of the Saint Himself, Dominic of Guzmán or Caleruega (you don't want to know).

"Quite a guy. Studied at Palencia, Spain, founded a religious community in Toulouse 1214, as a mendicant order, like the Franciscans. Basically, he believed they should all live in utter poverty, pretty much exhausted and killed himself by that ...

"Of course, they didn't know about Dunkin' Donuts back then ..."

Here, Data, exhausted by his all-nighter, by his prodigious memory, and by St. Dominic, referred to his notes, "They took up residence in the Roman Basilica of Santa Sabina around 1222, where the Master is today located, and then the Dominicans developed a Province with an Oratory in Oxford, England, where 12 friars landed in Dover in 1221. Now, this key ..."

I interrupted and said, "I hope this is going somewhere. I have a number of files which demand my presence in court in a little while, this century."

Unimpressed, Data continued, "Stick with me. The Dominicans have always had dozens of universities and colleges, more or less, including the Dominican House of worship, at Catholic University in Washington DC. And more priories than you could shake a stick at.

"Dominic himself was a pretty busy guy, a little too doctrinaire for my tastes; he fought against the Albigensian heresy and the Manichaean heresy and maybe was involved in the Inquisition. The Order believed in torture as a means to finding the truth," here Data looked up, "and people died. Lots of them."

My eyes were beginning to roll back into my head, and I was beginning to long for Data to leave, but to leave behind his dataghnuts (a little pun there).

Data picked up the pace, "My point here is, this has been an Order with great discipline and continuity for 800 years of compulsively detailed records, listing absolutely everybody, I mean, *everybody*, connected with the Order. I hacked into the DC, Toulouse, and the Italian databases. They made it possible for me to look for our guy, Friar Laurence."

Here, Data paused for dramatic effect and a doughnut.

I sit forward, hooked by the dramatic effect and the doughnut ...

"I found him," he mumbled through a full mouth. It came out, "ah fommmmim mmim."

Interpreting liberally, I asked, "You foooooom 'im?" And then wildly risking everything, "Him?"

He had me now, and he mumbled on "Nnnnnn, thnnnnnn, ah looooossssss'm."

Meaning (I decipher), "And then I lost him."

"Shit," said I, "a promise mumbled to the ear and crumbled to the heart."

Then I asked, "How?"

"I ran the simple query, "Valerian Laurence, 1450–1600, Verona, Italy," through the Dominican database in Santa Sabina. It showed him ordained in 1589, so he would've been born around 1564, and in 1591 he was detailed from Verona to the Oratory in Oxford, England, to what becomes Blackfriars Hall, so named because the Dominicans wear black caps and are the Black Friars. It's now part of Oxford University but still owned by the Dominicans today.

"But there is no entry showing he ever got there. And no entry back in Toulouse or Rome that he ever returned—he's like Charley on the MTA—except, of course, by us, here in New Haven.

"That's it, ballgame. Friar Laurence falls off the face of the earth. And then bounces back 400 years later." Silence. Another doughnut. "Ballgame."

"Well, not quite," I reply. "Oxford is not very far from Stratford on Avon and along about that time, early in his career, our man Shakespeare was writing romantic comedies, like *Two Gentlemen of Verona*, *Love's Labour's Lost*, *A Midsummer Night's Dream*, *The Taming of the Shrew*, *The Merchant of Venice*, called a romance, *Much Ado*, and *The Merry Wives*. He was one busy guy, no wonder he didn't go home on weekends. Or maybe that's why he wrote the plays, so he wouldn't have to go home. Who knows what was there? When he was home maybe she only gave him the second-best bed ...

"So, when Laurence was in Oxford, Shakespeare was into romance. You really don't reach the tragedies for a long time after that. Early on, there were a few Henries, a Richard the Third, and Titus Andronicus (which no one has ever explained) with *Romeo and Juliet*, a romance but called a tragedie, a one off, a standalone. The other genuine tragedies, say *Hamlet*, *Macbeth*, *Othello*, *Lear*, *Antony and Cleopatra*, are maybe a decade later."

197

All of this from memory. I'm trying to impress Data. Data says, "I'm impressed. Jesus! Why would you remember that shit?"

I go on, "You should be impressed; I majored in Shakespeare in English lit at Yale, and then did two years out of the three in the Master's program at the Drama School. I memorized it because I love it ..."

I go on, "Why did Shakespeare write R&J then, when he did, with our client in it, unless the good Friar, in fact, got to Oxford and met Will in Stratford or London? Or maybe the reverse? Some connection, somehow, is likely. And consider this: Shakespeare and Burbage had an interest in the first Blackfriars Theatre in a monastery near St. Paul's Cathedral. Laurence was a Black Friar; there weren't many Black Friars in London at that time. There had to be a hookup.

"Friar Laurence travels to Oxford, disappears from our world, appears next in Romeo and Juliet's world. Coincidence? Or did Shakespeare use him the way he used so many other sources? Scholars think Shakespeare got the Romeo and Juliet story from an Italian poem, translated by Arthur Brooke in 1562. Maybe he got it from Friar Laurence, or at least the priest part."

"So, we have been wondering how a fictional character Shakespeare created could assume flesh and blood humanity in our time. Maybe the answer is Shakespeare didn't create him; he existed. Somehow Shakespeare hijacked him into fiction, and he's here now ... Is he highjacked in the play every time the play is performed?

"But here he is outside the play, what's different this time?"

"You've got the two-thirds MF of the MFA in the Bard, not me. You tell me." says Data, and with that, heaved his bulk to a vertical position, finished a fourth donut from his bag of six doughnuts, and said, "I'm off to Corporate Tax and then Mergers and Acquisitions, four hours of soporific doldrums in the Yale Tower of Power. It wasn't a mere coincidence that they built Yale Law School on Wall Street. Please tell me you have something for me to run through my laptop during class."

"Yes, indeedy," I say, and here I pause, "you're going to love this one. This case is all about the local production of *Romeo and Juliet*, right? and the two high school kids who are cast in the name roles, coincidentally from families of the same names. I want you to frolic through social media and get the straight skinny on each of them, what they had to say about themselves, others, what others had to say about them, and, while you're at it, see if our client has made an appearance. He has adapted amazingly well to the folkways of our time; he's wearing a Fitbit. I would be amazed if he has not made an appearance on social media." Here, I pause, adding, "I hope he is not trolling tastelessly.

"See what you can turn up on the kids on Facebook, YouTube, Instagram, Twitter, Snapchat, TikTok, whatever ... you will know where to look. As for Friar Laurence, try those, but also, Match.Com, or whatever you cruising dudes are using these days. Oh, and add, Ancestry.com."

"That last is a joke, right?" Data shoots back.

"All righty," says Data, rising and dumping a mound of powdered sugar from his jeans on the floor. "Oh," he said, "I know you love this. I always like this part best, when I leave and toss you a tantalizing nugget or two to keep you awake nights."

I interject, "Oh no, Sweet Jesus, not again."

Data says, "Oh. Yes. Here it is. Bad news. Somebody's out to get Juliet."

And with that, Data twirls lightly, laughing, says, "You know, this is all going to fit in perfectly with Mergers and Acquisitions," and is gone.

I know from past experience not to follow Data, when he does this; he is quick and gone. It's like the old Tom Swift books, which I would read to Ruth Bader and Earl Warren, where a chapter ends with something like, "and then a shot rang out," or "there was a cry in the night," or, "a body fell to the floor." How can the kid sleep after that? How could I? It's pure Data.

Sometimes he does what he now does, which is to put his head back into the door, looking a whole lot like Colombo in the old detective television series, and says, "Oh, one other thing. When I slipped into the national criminal database, I discovered that New Haven's finest fingerprinted our client yesterday, in connection with the bail and restrictive order. The prints were sent off. You want to know the result?"

I try to think of some snappy responses, but they are all lame, and I simply say "Yes."

"Nada, el zippo, zero, once again," is the reply, "but," Data continues, "but the FBI tech not only reported that there was nothing in their files but added the notation that they could not read the prints sent from the New Haven PD, because they were too faint, which he said, usually means somebody tried to save money by adding alcohol to thin the ink before it was spread on the pad. The tech's note said, 'Reprint and thin no more.'"

An awestruck silence settles on the third floor.

"You are shitting me," I reply

"I couldn't make this stuff up," says Data.

"Yes, you could."

"Well, I could, but I didn't. Truth." And he is gone.

It is now 9:30. I scan the five files, review the cover memoranda, and refresh my recollection.

The first four are negotiated pleas, two drug sales to undercover agents, and two liquor store robberies. The latter are unusual, and it is especially unusual to have two in the same week. But my crack investigator, Ron Hoffer, has reviewed the prosecution's files, they having an "open file policy," and photocopied police statements and witness statements.

All four of the defendants are in custody, in lieu of bail, where I did an intake interview, including defense witnesses, who did not check out. When this was mentioned in a follow-up interview, each of the defendants was eager to learn whether a deal might be made. Ah, yes.

There is a standard calculus, involving principally four or five factors in plea negotiations. One, mentioned above, is whether there are witnesses, or evidence, for the defense to argue plausibly for a trial. None here. A second is a likely sentence on a guilty plea, and this turns on whether there was violence or a weapon, none in any of these cases. The third is whether the defendants have prior records, and amazingly, none in any of the four cases. The fourth factor is the gravity of the offense, since the facts vary widely in cases having the same label, for example, a liquor store robbery. Here, in both instances, the kids ran in, diverted the clerk's attention, and ran out with bottles of cheap whiskey and wine, all captured on videotape. A grab and go. The last factor consists of the need to incarcerate the defendant, considerations, such as youth, or whether a defendant has a job and supports a family, or whether the defendant cooperated, turning in other defendants.

Essentially, these four cases were easy. Nothing indicated that the defendants were dangerous or likely to repeat. Each case, felony level, lowered to misdemeanor level, supported by a prosecutor's recommendation of one year in jail, suspended, with one year of probation—standard stuff. Where there is a sentencing matrix, this is in the green box, for go.

Since this had been worked out over the past week, my appearance at 10:00 AM with these four files would take approximately 15 minutes. It was unthinkable that the judge, no matter how much of a hard ass, would reject the recommendation. No pre-sentence investigation was required since these were misdemeanors.

At 9:45, in the lock-up, I review each case with each of the defendants, who would go through the litany on entering a plea of guilty by uttering the word "guilty" himself, and responding "yes" when asked, "are you pleading of your own volition and because you are guilty," by the judge. Piece of cake.

At 10:00, I jockey for position as cases are called, remind the prosecutor de jour of the dispositions as indicated in the file. We go through the dance; sentences are entered, defendants are released back into the community. I receive thanks, and congratulations, return best wishes and tell them to stay in touch. But not too often. As I say, piece of cake.

That leaves the last file.

State v. Charles Whiting, a murder case, but today we are consuming only a small piece of the cake, a motion to suppress evidence. On the Friday evening before he was to get married, just before Christmas, Whiting went to a dry cleaner's establishment to pick up a brown sport coat and gray slacks for the wedding. The door was locked; he heard shots; he ran to his car and went home, and the next day, with alternative clothing, went to the church—on time.

There, he was met by New Haven's finest, taken into custody for having killed the dry cleaner guy the night before, and taken to his apartment in East Haven, some 15 miles away. No search warrant. The police did not ask for permission to search; the door was unlocked, they simply entered and tossed the apartment, taking possession of a red hooded sweatshirt, a white shirt, blue jeans, a Boston Red Sox baseball hat, and a scarf, all of which Whiting was required to wear at a lineup, where he was identified later on his wedding morning by the lady who lived over the dry-cleaning shop. She described a dark sweatshirt, jeans, a hat; it was dark, she was looking down, there had been shots. He was a small black man. She was scared.

Whiting denied the killing. As he said, he had every reason to show up for the wedding and none to kill the tailor. When he heard the shots, he ran to his car, drawing on years of experience in Afghanistan: run, don't walk, to the nearest exit. No weapon was found. No fruits of the robbery, if that's what it was, were found. Whiting said he hadn't called the police because he did not want to get involved because he has a record.

No other suspect or culprit was found. The upstairs lady testified that immediately upon the shots being fired, the door below burst open, and Whiting ran out.

A motion to suppress keeps otherwise compelling evidence out of the case. The defendant argues the evidence was obtained illegally and should be suppressed as "fruit of the poisonous tree." A search under the Fourth Amendment either has to be pursuant to a warrant, supported by a probable cause affidavit, or fit within one of the exceptions to the warrant requirement, for example, a search that is incident to an arrest or in hot pursuit. The State said that the search of Whiting's apartment was incident to his arrest at the church.

We filed a motion to suppress because there was no warrant, there were no exigent circumstances to justify not getting a warrant, there was time to get a warrant, even if one was not necessary for the arrest at the church, and the search of the apartment some 15 miles away, so it could not be said to be "incident" to the arrest. Chimel v. California. Slamdunk.

But it all depended upon how the testimony came in and how badly the officers wanted to convict Charles Whiting. After all, a shopkeeper had been killed. And there were no other suspects.

The judge sitting this morning is an old wheel horse Criminal Court Judge, Luke Stapleton. He was a prosecutor 30 years ago, has been on the bench since, brooks no nonsense from either prosecution or defense, and while he favors good police work, he becomes truly displeased with sloppy police work. That is a good thing. That's what we have here. It is said of Stapleton that, sober, he is the second-best trial judge in the county; the first best (forgive the grammar) being Luke Stapleton, drunk.

State v Whiting is called, the prosecutor again is my good friend Jack Reilly; he correctly identifies the procedural posture of the underlying issues.

JUDGE STAPLETON

Any chance of settling this, Mr. Collins?

MR. COLLINS

No, Your Honor. Mr. Whiting was on his way to his wedding. His fiancée is sitting in the audience section today. She is hoping she will not have to return her dress. Let me point her out, she's the one wearing a wedding dress."

MR. REILLY

Cheesy, even for Mr. Collins, Your Honor.

JUDGE STAPLETON

(laughing)

I disagree, Mr. Reilly. I think the lady provides proof positive Mr. Whiting had a motive to show up for his wedding and not jeopardize that by committing a murder the night before. But I do not mean to prejudge this matter. Thank you, Mr. Collins, for the graphics on behalf of the defense. We will do our best for your young man, young lady. Schedule this for 2:00.

I turn to Whiting at the counsel table, and I say, "keep your hopes up, Charles. I think we have a good shot at this and a good judge."

"I hope so," he says, "we lost a lot of money on the caterer and the wedding hall."

"I can't do much about that," I reply as the bailiff takes Whiting into the lockup, "but we can certainly get your sweatshirt and jeans back." At this, Whiting laughs and the cuffs are put on.

As I go to the fiancée in the audience section, I notice my favorite priest, and I say to Whiting's fiancé, "Motions to suppress and illegal searches are my stock in trade. I will be amazed if we lose this. If we win it, there is a good chance Reilly and I can make the murder charges go away. Hold onto your wedding dress."

The young lady, whose name is Michaela O'Brien, smiles, tears come to her eyes, she says, "We're counting on you. We are hoping you will be our best man." And she proceeds up the aisle, out the swinging doors, to the third-floor landing. It occurs to me she is looking somewhat more pregnant than I remember her from a couple of weeks ago.

I turn to the Abbot and Friar Laurence and say, "Good morning, perhaps we might get a quick lunch."

There is an Italian shop with a lunch counter and outside tables three blocks from the courthouse, just beyond the City Hall, where we place our orders, take the little flag outside with our number on it, and sit down, waiting for plates to come with the finest Italian cuisine this side of Verona and Boston's North End. It arrives in short order. As we eat quickly, I say, "I should update you on a couple of things."

The Abbot adds, "And perhaps we may do the same for you." There is an icy tone in his voice.

I describe the instructions I had given to Data, the briefing I had received from him this morning, and the implications for our case. In essence, as I reflect upon what I'm saying, we have conducted an extensive and invasive search, which could be viewed as a gross violation of privacy. I add that we usually make a background check, although not this extensive, to avoid any surprises or ambush.

The Abbot puts his utensils aside, pushes back from the table, his bald head gleaming under the noonday sun, and he says, "Friar Laurence and I understand what you've done. We appreciate that this is careful work, informing you and your clients of the dangers to fear, and it is reassuring to learn that you found none. At the same time, it is upsetting that you did not share with us in advance that you would be undertaking such searches. In particular, hacking into digitized files of the Abbey and the Order is a matter of considerable concern. We are not defendants here.

"We could easily have blocked Mr. Data's efforts. Instead, we prepared the report which your Mr. Data described. We have two copies, one you already have and one we want you to provide to the States Attorney, Mr. Coke."

I find myself considerably embarrassed, stammer a bit, and then say, "Well, I do stand corrected, and I apologize. Being careful with the client and the client's position is part of my job.

"For example, Mr. Data Focused on past events that are similar to the staging of the play here, *Romeo and Juliet*. He went as far through history with respect to theater performances and filming as possible. He found nothing that incriminates Friar Laurence. Indeed, he found nothing in those connections relating to you. He is an unusually gifted computer and Internet craftsman, indeed, detective. On his initiative, having covered the ground I assigned, he then went to see whether there is a record of Friar Laurence within the Dominican Order."

At this, Friar Laurence leaned forward and said, "I suspect all he found was a notation that a Friar Valerian Laurence was detailed to our Oxford community in the year 1591."

I answered, "Yes. Should he have found more?"

"No. There are no other records. Nor could or would either of us attempt to expand on the record.

Friar Laurence continued, "As I'm sure you know, this was about the time William Shakespeare was writing the play, *Romeo and Juliet*, in which that character Friar Laurence figures prominently."

And here, Friar Laurence leaned forward, holding his latte in his hands, and speaking softly to me, "So your Mr. Data found something significant, a real live human being, loosely connected to *Romeo and Juliet*, of some 400 years ago, and quite possibly connected with our time, where and when the very same *Romeo and Juliet* is in production, but significantly altered." And here our Friar Laurence, sitting in an Italian restaurant on the New Haven Green, on a spring day, far removed from that time and place of long ago, smiles widely, opens his hands, and leans back in his chair, his camel hair sport coat opening at the same time, and points to the sidewalk under the noonday sun, and says, "Do I not cast a shadow?"

All three of us laugh at the absurdity of our situation and its many dimensions.

"So be it," say I. "It would seem we have gone from dealing with a fictional character appearing in our world to a real figure from history, somehow being transported here by Shakespeare's vehicle, what else, a play. This leaves us with a different puzzle, but still a puzzle. As a lawyer, I do not need to solve the riddle, only to consider how to package it, before we hear more from Mr. Coke and his obsessive compulsion to throw you in jail.

"I hope you are staying within the bounds of the bail order. Let me ask, before I return to court, what you think of what you have seen of what I've been doing in my professional capacity?"

"We are very impressed with your work on behalf of your clients, very much so, and we are most pleased to have you representing Friar Laurence," says the Abbot.

"Thank you, then," I say, "and is there anything else that you want to share with me?"

"Well, I, for one, am most impressed with your Mr. Data's work," says the Abbot, "and we have ordered a dozen assorted Dunkin' Doughnuts delivered to your office tomorrow morning."

"In addition," Friar Laurence says, "you may be interested to learn that I have an invitation to dinner tonight at the home of Dorothy Arlow. I have accepted. The menu, she tells me so that I may feel at home, is entirely of Northern Italian cuisine.

"I believe you and your resident physician are invited."

CHAPTER NINETEEN

CHARLES AND MICHAELA

MATRIMONY, MURDER, AND MOTIONS TO SURPRESS

I returned to the criminal courtroom somewhat chastened and embarrassed, but, as always, intrigued by the wizardry of both D. Data, my Greek Geek, and Abbot Dominic, who always seems one step ahead and a considerable level above. It appears that our client, Friar Laurence, is a real person, as he has always appeared to be, but still attended by some interesting questions, such as, how did he get here and why?

I put all of this aside as I went through the swinging doors to confront more urgent and mundane questions, such as what cross-examination to undertake with the anticipated story from the officers who arrested my client, Charles Whiting, at the church on his wedding day, for a homicide committed the night before, and then took him some 15 miles to search his apartment. They seized clothing used in a lineup, and Whiting is charged with murder. So it goes.

As I entered, I saw my old Hillhouse civics instructor, Joe Thomas, with his Civics AP class in tow, spending another afternoon at the Francis Collins Follies.

I paused, said hello to Mr. Thomas, and asked why they were here; after all, I said, it is only a motion to suppress. The Hitler Youth Look-Alike started to speak, but Mr. Thomas cut him off, saying, "Francis Collins, let me present my prize Neo-Nazi student from Civics, Otto Schmidt. He believes in civil rights for Aryans." At this, Otto spoke, "I'm hoping to interview you for the *HillHouse Happenings*, where I will expose the harm so-called civil rights have done to our city, and you can justify driving half the whites out. As Mr. Thomas said, I am an ardent white supremacist. Interested? It's our weekly newspaper."

I needed more briefing on Schmidt's background, so I said, "Let me check back with Mr. Thomas, and we'll see if we can work it out. Right now, I have to go forth and defend your civil rights, and along the way, those of Charles Whiting, a person of color. And his bride-to-be. You do believe in the Fourth Amendment, right?"

As I moved toward the courtroom, the Aryan white supremacist snaps back, "Sure, for those who have something worthwhile."

Down the center aisle, through the swinging gate, to the counsel table, a well-trod path.

Whiting was already at counsel table, with the handcuffs and legcuffs removed, he being a homicidal maniac, albeit with delusions of marital bliss. I sat next to him and said, "watch this."

"Showtime," he said, looking for all the world like an African prince or the head of a small nation in West Africa, hair closely cropped, Gold rimmed eyeglasses, somewhat below average height, and a little pudgy. This may or may not fit the profile of such folks, I have never met them, but you get the idea.

Jack Reilly was calling his first witness to the stand.

MR. REILLY

"Officer, please state your name and how you became involved with Mr. Whiting."

A. "My name is Vincente Donatelli; I've been with the New Haven police force for 20 years and was on night patrol with my partner John Robinson. Dispatch said there had been a break-in at a tailor shop, late Friday night, January 14, we went there, visited the tailor shop, talked with the lady upstairs, Mildred Watson, examined the shop and found clothing in disarray, the cash drawer was empty, but one particular receipt was on the floor, pertaining to clothing which had been tailored and cleaned for one Charles Whiting. That clothing was nowhere to be found."

Q. "Anything else?"

A. "Oh, yeah, there was a body lying behind the counter, belonging to the owner, Mr. James Fox, identified by Mrs. Watson. He had been shot three times, was lying in a pool of blood, and was dead by the time we arrived. There was no need to call for an ambulance; we arranged for the crime scene unit to be dispatched and, upon their arrival, turned the scene over to them."

Q. "Back to the receipt, what did it reveal, and what did you do?"

A. "The records indicated an address, which we staked out that Friday evening into the early hours of Saturday morning, when we saw a vehicle pull up at the Whiting residence, and a man whom we later identified as Charles Whiting, sitting right here in the courtroom today, get out of the car and go into the residence. Rather than arrest him based upon the description given, we decided to wait to see what he would do, possibly leading to evidence of some kind. Instead, a few hours later, he led us to St. Patrick's church in East Haven."

Q. "What did you do there?"

A. "There, Whiting was intercepted, arrested, taken back to his home some 12 to 15 miles away. Whiting himself was searched, revealing a set of keys to his apartment, which was then searched. The search led to the clothing used in the identification lineup at about 11:30 Saturday morning. We brought in the lady upstairs, Mrs. Watson; she picked out Mr. Whiting as the person who fled the previous night from the tailor shop downstairs. We did not find the clothes that Mr. Whiting had left to be dry cleaned."

Q. "Has that clothing been located?"

A. "No."

Q. "Was the shop examined for fingerprints or other evidence as to the intruder or killer?"

A. "There were random sets of fingerprints, none belonging to the defendant, and there was a video camera, but the unit was old and had not been turned on."

Q. "After you took the defendant into custody at St. Patrick's, was he interrogated?"

A. "Yes, we took him downtown, booked him for murder, my partner and I took him to the interrogation room, and we were joined by Detective Brown, who advised him of his rights under Miranda."

Q. "Did you also advise him as to why he was in custody?"

A." Yes, we told him it was for the shooting and death of the shop owner, Mr. Fox."

Q. "What, if anything, did he have to say?"

A. "The entire exchange was brief and recorded, and I have a copy with me, and one has already been provided to Mr. Collins, Mr. Whiting's attorney. Some of Mr. Whiting's language was a bit strong, so perhaps you would prefer that I not read it aloud?"

MR. COLLINS

"Oh, Judge Stapleton, Your Honor, we very much want the testimony and the confession, such as it is, read into the record. And we will stipulate that my client was properly warned under Miranda. I don't think there is any language that you haven't heard before."

JUDGE STAPLETON

"With that stipulation, it is always best to have evidence entered into the record fully, and so, officer, please read the statement as you heard it on that day."

OFFICER DONATELLI

"Yes, sir. Mr. Whiting's statement was as follows:

"'So, you have me here for shooting and killing Mr. Fox. I have been taking my business to him for years. I was picking up dry cleaning and tailoring on that Friday night because I was getting married today, as you assholes well realize. Why the fuck I would shoot somebody who has my clothing for a wedding the night before a wedding, my wedding, I might add, is just sure as shit beyond me. Can you think of a single goddamned reason?'"

OFFICER DONATELLI

"Should I keep going, Judge Stapleton? It's pretty much more of the same. A copy is on file, and Mr. Collins already has it."

JUDGE STAPLETON

"Oh yes, read the whole thing. I don't want to be the only person kept in the dark. So far, Mr. Whiting is arguing his case rather well."

OFFICER DONATELLI

"Well, sir, here's the rest of it:

"'I went there to get my clothing, the place was locked up, I heard three shots, and I left. I assumed the lady upstairs would call the cops, no need for me to do that, and I had a different suit of clothes for the wedding this morning, as you fucking well know. I did two tours of duty in Afghanistan, and I remember perfectly well a couple of survival rules. One is you never use three shots when you only need one. Another is when you hear more than one, get the hell out of there.

"'You assholes told me you're going to put me in a lineup. I want you to know I object and I will resist during any lineup, and I want to see a lawyer, now, before the lineup. One thing for sure, you better not pull cops out of the station or off the desk to put in that line up with me, they're all going to be at least five-foot-nine and weightlifters, so I will stand out in any lineup.

"'I want to see a lawyer, now, and the only other thing I got to say is you're a bunch of sons of bitches to bust up a wedding with the only woman I have ever loved. I hope you rot in hell.'"

MR. REILLY

Q. "Did Mr. Whiting sign the statement?"

A. "He did not. He was offered a pen, but he threw it at me. As I guess you can figure out, he was pretty upset."

Q. "The lineup which you have described took place after interrogation, and did you provide an attorney for Mr. Whiting?"

A. "No. He said he could not afford one and the public defender's office has a policy of not attending lineups. So, we proceeded without an attorney for Mr. Whiting."

Q. "Please describe the lineup."

A. "Yes, sir, there were four other males in addition to Mr. Whiting, all African-American as he is, dressed in sport coats and slacks as he had for his wedding, and of about the same age, late 30s, and complexion. Since he is rather short, the others were somewhat taller, but only by a few inches."

Q. "And would you describe Mrs. Watson's statements upon viewing the lineup?"

A. "Yes. She was in the viewing room, and through a one-way glass quickly picked out Mr. Whiting as the man she saw run from the shop after the shots rang out."

Q. "Was there any doubt in her mind?"

A. "No. She said that she had seen Mr. Whiting come into the shop on other occasions and recognized him on Friday night as clearly as she did Saturday morning in the police station."

MR. REILLY

"That's all we have of this witness, Your Honor."

JUDGE STAPLETON

"Your witness, Mr. Collins."

MR. COLLINS

"We have no questions of officer Donatelli, except I hope that if and when he ever marries, he behaves better than he did on the morning of Mr. Whiting's wedding."

At this point, a sharp elbow lodged itself in my ribs, coming from the personage to my right, and I hear him say, "What the fuck? Nail the bastard."

To which I whispered, "He hasn't hurt us. If I ask questions probing for a weakness, I may shine a light into a corner where I do not want Reilly to go."

"I hope you know what you're doing," said Whiting.

"Me, too."

At this point, Judge Stapleton leans forward, "I hope you know what you're doing, Mr. Collins." I am beginning to think that they know something that I don't know.

Reilly calls his second witness, Officer Robinson. Robinson essentially repeats what Donatelli said. And then Reilly takes him to the lineup situation, asks whether he had attended, whether Mrs. Watson had attended, whether she was in the booth with the one-way glass so she could see the people in the lineup, and whether she picked out a person from the lineup, as to all of these questions, he answered, "Yes."

Reilly then asked a rather important question, "And is that person sitting here today in this courtroom?"

Before Officer Robinson could respond, I rose and said, "Objection."

Judge Stapleton leaned forward, asking, "On what grounds?"

To that, I responded, "It's hearsay. Mrs. Watson is not on the stand. Only she can testify as to the truth of what she said." That, of course, is not the point, but I am hoping Reilly makes the point for me.

Which he does, saying, "It's not offered for the truth of the matter, but only to support the evidence for probable cause to search." Thus, linking the identification to the search. If the search goes down, so does the identification.

Excellent. If not, later I can challenge the identification on grounds of accuracy, since Mrs. Watson is a septuagenarian with eyeglasses the thickness of a Fresnel lens.

Judge Stapleton rules, "Objection overruled. The witness may answer for those limited purposes."

Robinson's answer is, "Yes, she picked out the defendant."

Now, I object again, and move that the answer be stricken, to which Reilly moans and says, "Oh come on!" (I'm thinking, that's pretty elegant), but as to which Judge Stapleton invites me to state my grounds.

I do, as follows, "Irrelevant. Events after the search cannot be used to strengthen the probable cause of the search. And in any event, the issue here is not whether there was probable cause, but there was a failure to get a warrant when there was plenty of time, and the search goes beyond the limits of searches incident to arrest, under Chimel v. California."

Before Judge Stapleton can rule, I hear, from behind me, in the audience section, "Cool. Way to go!" Later I will identify that is coming from Otto Schmidt, our Nazi clone android, but for right now I am waiting for Judge Stapleton to say, well, "Cool. Way to go!" which he does, but not in those exact words, after a few moments, in my favor.

Robinson's testimony as to what Watson said stays out. At a later time, if she is as a witness at trial, we will then move to suppress her testimony on the grounds that the lineup was unduly suggestive. So, we live to fight another day if we lose this day. But right now, we're looking pretty good. In fact, "I agree with that kid," says Charles Whiting.

"Prosecution rests," says Jack Reilly.

The rules on the motion to suppress are not clear, but it does seem that constitutional policy favors using a warrant, and if the prosecution is arguing for an exception, say, that the search was incident to an arrest, so a warrant was not needed, the burden of proof and persuasion both rest on the prosecution. You want an exception? Prove it.

I have explained to Mr. Whiting all of this previously, and I ask now for a moment from Judge Stapleton to repeat it, which he gives. I turn to Mr. Whiting, and I say, "Seems to me they haven't made their case, and there is little advantage to putting you on the stand. I know you would like to testify, but the outrageous facts of this case are already before the judge and favor your innocence, which doesn't matter on the search and seizure issue anyway. The only thing you can do if you testify is screw up, and right now, we're way ahead."

"Thanks for the vote of confidence," says Whiting, "but I am going to trust you on this one."

I stand and say to Judge Stapleton, "We do not intend to call any witnesses, Your Honor. And based on the state's testimony, we ask that the motion to suppress be granted and the seized clothing and the lineup identification be excluded from the case."

Judge Stapleton turns to Jack Reilly and says, "Mr. Reilly, any words of wisdom from you?"

Reilly rises, knowing full well that his officers screwed up badly, and says, "Your Honor, Mr. Collins has missed the point. My officers went to the scene on a Friday night; evidence pointed toward the defendant; they went immediately to his home and staked it out, staying on the case until they could catch him at the church. There was no time to file an application for warrant, would have been no judges—as I'm sure you appreciate—late on a Friday evening or into a Saturday morning available to issue a warrant, and once they had Mr. Whiting in custody, the exception they were pursuing was not incident to an arrest; instead, they did not need to get a warrant because they were in hot pursuit of a suspect."

Here I interjected, guffawing and exclaiming, "My God, they could hardly be in hot pursuit when they had him in cuffs in the squad car."

Judge Stapleton interjects, "Try to restrain yourself, Mr. Collins."

"Continue, Mr. Reilly," says Stapleton, which Reilly does, saying, "I wish to add, I hope without interruption, that in addition to hot pursuit there were exigent circumstances, namely the evidence in Mr. Whiting's apartment might be taken or destroyed by a co-confederate."

As to which, I say, "The only candidate in evidence would be the fiancée, sitting here in court today, wearing what she was wearing on, as we say, the day in question."

"Still," Reilly adds, "things happen." And she was left standing at the altar. Come on, Jack!

Judge Stapleton stares at Reilly for a moment, then—

JUDGE STAPLETON

"Nice recovery Mr. Reilly.

"Gentlemen, I will take all of this under consideration, and let me say, to the lady in the audience section in the wedding dress, do not despair. You may want to take that dress to a dry cleaner soon to get a few of those wrinkles out; just be careful who you choose as a cleaner.

"Gentlemen, well played. I'll have my ruling at your offices by this afternoon.

"In the meantime, Mr. Reilly, do you think it is necessary to keep Mr. Whiting in custody?"

MR. REILLY

"Well, this is a major felony, a homicide, but I suppose if he would show up for a wedding the morning after he killed somebody, he will likely show up in this court."

JUDGE STAPLETON

"Mr. Collins, how much bail could Mr. Whiting post?"

I turn to Whiting and ask, "How much?"

To which Whiting says, "My fiancée's father owns an automobile dealership. If I put down $10,000, will that do it?"

MR. COLLINS

"My client's fiancée's father owns an automobile dealership and could post $10,000 cash as security for a $100,000 recognizance, which we think should be sufficient. He is a longtime resident of the New Haven area, and while he has one prior conviction, it stemmed from a barroom brawl. He fights bigger than he looks."

JUDGE STAPLETON

"Any objection Mr. Reilly?"

MR. REILLY

"None, Your Honor."

JUDGE STAPLETON

"So be it. $100,000 bond, $10,000 surety—professional surety or family surety acceptable."

With that, Judge Lucas Stapleton, old wheel horse that he is, having shown us a few uncommon moves, rose, the courtroom rising with him, saying, "15 minutes recess," and exited stage left.

Jack says to me, "Looks like we both get back to the office a little early. Maybe you should take that book off the shelf, the one on cross-examination, so maybe you could do some someday, Frank."

"Call me Francis, Jonathan," I say, and with that, I turn to my client.

He asks, "What now?"

I respond, "You wait here, I'll call your father-in-law, or perhaps your fiancée is already doing that," since I note a white wedding gown is rapidly exiting the courtroom through the swinging doors, hopefully not getting hung up, "the bail officer, Miriam Anderson, will do the paperwork and you will go home this afternoon or early this evening. Give your fiancée a hug for me; she won the bail issue by simply being here."

Whiting pauses and then says, "Well, as I recall, it was your idea. Now I can see why."

Charles Whiting rises, still, the short, rotund West African Prime Minister figure that he is, gives me a hug, and says, "Thanks."

I say, "Don't thank me, give my ace office administrator thanks and maybe a big bouquet of roses, but no hug, she's the one who thought up the wedding gown maneuver." The bailiff comes and takes him away.

With that, I exit the courtroom, pausing to say to Joe Thomas and his dozen AP Civics students, "Well folks, I hope that was worthwhile."

Our Hitler simulacrum jumps in and says, "Nice lawyering. To make it totally worthwhile, though, you need to upgrade your clientele. Totally." There is a groan, in unison, from the rest of the class. And I think as I go back out through the doors, down the staircase, and into the late afternoon spring sunshine of the New Haven Green, that as afternoons go, this one was worthwhile. Totally.

Now let's see what awaits back at the office. Totally.

Up the stairs, two at a time, breathing hard as I enter the reception area, Jo at her computer, as always, facing away from me, says, rapid-fire, "Coke has moved the grand jury hearing to 10:00 tomorrow morning; I left a text message on Friar Laurence's iPhone, to be here at 9:00; your old Professor, one Burbage, at your old Yale Drama School, called to say that he's doing a Director's Overview for the public on his radically different production of *Romeo and Juliet* and wants you to be there, about 4:30; I said you would since you have a light day tomorrow, just a grand jury ..."

Jo pauses while I react to the message from Burbage, saying, "Did the son of a bitch say why he wants me there?"

Jo continues as if I had not interrupted her, to say, "And how did the wedding party go?" With that, she turned around and looked at me, with a smile on her face, a little smug, still, always a dazzling event.

"Take a bow," says I, "Your suggestion of having Michaela in full regalia (the rhyme is mine) paid off, and we should get a message from Judge Stapleton on a ruling before five. If we win, that's probably the ballgame, but either way ..."

221

"Yes," I know," Jo says; "call the DA's office, try to get the case scheduled for the middle of next week."

"But wait, there's more," Jo adds, and now I see why she has pivoted to look me squarely in the face as she says this, "Dorothy Arlow would like you and the doctor, that's the way she put it, to join her and Friar Laurence and the Abbot for Northern Italian tonight, around 7:30. I told her you would be delighted. I also added you would bring two good bottles of Italian varietal, none of that Thunderbird or Ripple swill that our clients drink. Okay?"

"Okay," say I, "if you copied the invite to Meg at the Med school, and she can set the kids up for a late dinner to follow the Arlow affair."

"Of course," Jo says, "she has already taken care of all of that. I got the address to her, and she will meet you at Dorothy Arlow's place. And ..."

"And," say I, "what?" thinking, it's hard to keep up with Jo, especially since it is my life she is organizing.

"Well," Jo continues, "you will remember from early this morning, in the deep, distant past, that I was doing my nails with Dorothy Arlow, a half-hour extravaganza which, incidentally, you are now free to admire." With that, she holds out her hands and advances her toes through open-toe flats, and they are, indeed, dazzling.

I say, "Dazzling. How in the world do you ...?"

She interjects, "Sausage. Do you want to know what goes into sausage or how it's made?"

"No, I don't."

"Good, keep it that way."

But, Jo continues, "Dinner should be an interesting affair; I will need a full report in the morning. I have kept your morning schedule light to accommodate, let me repeat, a full report."

222

And with that, Jo pivots in her office chair, returns to the desk with the two monitors and the full view across the rooftops of the ancient wings of the City Hall, and goes back to work, her work, my work. I think ... I don't know quite what I think ... My life is full of beautiful women. That's what I think.

I have 15 minutes to make it to the Drama school.

CHAPTER TWENTY

THE GREAT BURBAGE OVERVIEW

OF SHAKESPEARE AND BELSKY (WHO? BELSKY ...)

It is out the door, across the Green, dodging bocce players, ultimate frisbee players, occasional drunks, stray drug dealers, joggers with strollers, joggers without, homeless people with shopping carts ... a block or two and then to the semi-Gothic, Romanesque, Renaissance, whatever, architecture of Green Hall, housing the Iseman Theater, sort of a flexible, open space theater in the round where performances are conducted for small audiences, capacity 200 or so. Across the lobby, through the swinging doors, and into a small space, with a small audience present. Of the four theaters used by the D school, this was my favorite.

I spent two years in the study of acting and have many fond memories of the productions where I was chiefly cast as stage furniture. My talent seemed to peak as the aforementioned stage furniture. It occurred to me that I would never be able to join the company of such famous Yale graduates as Angela Bassett, Patricia Clarkson, Francis McDormand, Chris Noth, Jill Eikenberry, Paul Giamatti, on and on. They were at first a challenge. But as reality dawned, they became a caution.

And so, I switched to playwriting and tried reworking one of Shakespeare's plays, engaging in a death struggle with the department chair, Richard Burbage. My genius was no match for his ego. My proposal was shelved, without a hearing, as was I. I switched to the Law School, a few blocks away, loved forensics, mock trial, moot court, negotiation. I drew heavily on the Drama School basics.

I won prizes. I can only wonder why Burbage issued me an explicit invite, almost command, to this Director's Overview tonight.

I walk down the center aisle of the Iseman theater, seating distributed in a semicircle equally on either side, with aisles at the ends of those sections. I find a large group of what I take to be present-day drama students, plus undergrad students, high schoolers, who I take to be Romeo, Juliet, and surprisingly, the high school Hitler, Otto Schmidt. More surprising, he is placing his right arm around Juliet's shoulder. My quick take is, she is as repulsed as I am. Romeo is a good-looking guy, sitting on her other side.

There is a brief, interesting, unexpected moment when one of the drama students, an average height, dour, thin fellow, a bit of a fop with a wispy beard, dressed in camo pants and shirt, army boots, in his late 20s, strides over quickly and with a proprietary move, removes Hitler's arm from Juliet. As he did so, Romeo had been reaching across from the other side to do the same thing. The D student looked at him and said, with quiet contempt, "I've got this."

Romeo, showing no respect for his elders, replied, "You wish." Camo Guy returns to his seat four rows behind Juliet. So, I think, there is still drama at the Drama school.

The Drama student to my left looks at me briefly and decides to put me in the picture. "The Camo guy is Tommy Belsky, Shakespeare purest, Aryan crazy, a white supremacist, and yesterday's news in Juliet's romantic life; to her right, of course, Romeo. A perfect triangle ... It gets better. Belsky is cast as County Paris, to be killed by Romeo. The plot, as we say in the D School, thickens. I, by the way, am cast as Friar Laurence because of my charismatic resemblance to Woody Allen. I arrange for each of these three to die."

I say, "Thanks," thinking there could hardly be a greater difference between this stage Friar Laurence and my client Friar Laurence, from the real world, as I have come to think of it. I add, "You can't tell the players without a program."

"Well, no problem. And, as we say in the D school, it's Showtime. Tada," and he gestures toward center stage.

There now stands, in a single spot lit center stage, otherwise dark, behind a rostrum, a tall, ascetic looking, skeletal gentleman in his early 60s, wearing tan corduroy slacks, a black turtleneck jersey, a frayed gray tweed jacket with patches on the elbows, and a long, dark blue scarf, thrown once around his neck. He is also wearing, most importantly, a sense of self-importance. All of this calculated to convey Richard Burbage's perfect casting of the perfect, tenured Shakespearean professor, occupying the only endowed chair in the department. He raps on the rostrum, and the small audience settles in for a perfect Burbage performance.

I think, perfect. Smug prick.

He begins his best Laurence Olivier delivery.

"Welcome to tonight's Director's Overview of our upcoming performance of Romeo and Juliet. I have made a special effort to invite a number of you past associates of the D School because I anticipate this will be a truly historical performance and production.

"In a few more minutes, I will say a few words about myself, by way of introduction, but let me now say that in this audience, there is one person I want to single out for particular recognition. Francis Collins is with us, having some two decades ago been a stellar drama student with enormous potential," and here I am looking around to see where this legendary figure is, knowing full well that this is typical Burbage bullshit, but I am unclear why, when he continues, "which he took in a different direction, turning in a remarkable record at Yale Law School and now as a public defender here in New Haven. Both of these achievements prompt me to introduce Francis now, despite what Shakespeare, you will all recall, said about killing all the lawyers."

With that, Burbage gestures to me, imperiously indicating I should rise, giving me the opportunity to reply, by saying, "I'm flattered by this recognition. I know Professor Burbage recalls equally well the low stature of dramatists and theater professionals during the time of Shakespeare, and it would seem the only reason he did not advocate killing them was that he was one himself. Thank you for this welcome, Professor Burbage, I am eager to learn how you go about, what? Improving (really?) Shakespeare's play?"

Burbage pauses for a moment, decides to let me get away with that, and then adds this, "Some of my 'improvement,' as you say, I owe to you, Frances, hence your invite tonight," and then returns to his line of patter, "I know you all understand I enjoy a national reputation for playing creatively with scenes, settings, characters, dialogue, cutting out and occasionally adding on. It's not that I think Shakespeare was anything less than a brilliant genius; it is that I think Shakespeare is so transcendent that he is deserving of my very best efforts.

Burbage continues, now channeling his best, raspy Richard Burton, or is it Olivier, "All of the great directors brought themselves, their very best selves, as homage to Shakespeare. I am one of those, akin to Garrick, whose radical revision of one of Shakespeare's plays (that would be *Romeo and Juliet*) in the 1700s replaced Shakespeare's original version for 50 years, 450 performances. *Hamlet, Macbeth, Antony and Cleopatra*, all of these were powerfully shaped by the visions of people like Johnson and Dryden. Shakespeare has been performed as Mafia, Wild Western, even ethnic street gang musicals.

"With all due modesty, I believe I have the same great vision and responsibility as my predecessors, and I would add to that the benefit of centuries of perspective and learning. If we build better and see farther, it is because we stand on the shoulders of giants. And owe them nothing less than what they left us. I intend to do exactly that," he pauses, looking at the familiar faces in the audience, "with all due modesty, of course."

Ah, yes, yes, Richard Burbage, with all due modesty. Very modest. Of course.

Burbage speaks to us, in his carefully manicured and modulated baritone, now intertwining echoes of Laurence Olivier and Richard Burton, saying, "We are staging one of Shakespeare's most popular and problematic plays, it combines both transcendent language and romance, and wonderfully warm characters, on the one hand, and on the other, institutionalized hatred and rampant falsehood and tragic death. If you cast about in your memories, what you most retain is the love story. If pressed, and if you pay close attention, as I know all of you do, you can recapture the secondary theme of falsehood and death, but almost as an afterthought. It is as though Friar Laurence and his bungling, homicidal manipulations, were woven into the play, as an afterthought, by external forces unknown to derail the main thrust of the play for purposes undisclosed."

From farther back in the theater, on the other side of the central aisle from me, comes a muttered objection, "Oh come on! Shakespeare wrote the play himself ... External forces! What crap." I look around; it seems the interruption is coming from Belsky, the Aryan Camo guy.

But it is only a momentary distraction, and Burbage continues, assuming an anguished tone, "A director is thus immediately confronted, in this play, with the ethical dilemma: is his obligation to the author or the audience or the muse of his own genius? If it is to the audience, clearly, the director must deliver a romance in *Romeo and Juliet*. It is what the audience expects. It is what the audience deserves." And here, Burbage gestures broadly to the half empty theater, bowing in obeisance to the thousands of absent patrons who stretch back into the drifting mists of past centuries. "We owe them more than a performance; we owe them the truth."

Then he smiles, a bit patronizingly, conspiratorially, and says, "However, many would argue; indeed, the prevailing view is, that absolute fidelity to the words of the author is the minimum required. In our century, this is known as a Bardolatry: treating every word as though it came from on high and is etched in stone. This view," Burbage continues, "slavish worship of the words attributed to the Bard, is a clear break from the view and tradition honored in the previous three centuries, as I pointed out earlier. Great directors have sought their own way. Insisting that they—and today, I—cannot do so would be textually and morally wrong."

Burbage draws upon his undeniable theatrical resources and reserves, rolling out a thunderous voice, he speaks as though the theater is full and thousands hang upon his every word, to say, "Shakespeare invited, anticipated, desperately, I say desperately, needed, the collaboration of the genius of later times. We cannot even know with certainty what he wrote."

And here, as Burbage paused to let this heresy sink in, a rebuttal came from Camo guy, Belsky, standing in the center aisle and challenging Burbage, "His words and his plays have all been written and preserved, not just for an age but for all time. These are the words of Ben Johnson. Reworking or rewriting them is corruption. Denying Shakespeare is naked sacrilege, apostasy!"

While I am thinking Belsky has an unusually rich, if fanatic, vocabulary, Burbage pounds the rostrum before him and continues, "Good heavens, thank heavens, for Mr. Belsky." Burbage engages in a fabricated, seemingly contented chuckle. "If you didn't exist, I would have to invent you."

Burbage holds high his right hand, raising his first integer, and says, "First, the best source of Shakespeare's writing is the First Folio, but it was cobbled together by a couple of Shakespeare's partners from quartos, cast-off scripts, actor's notes, and occasional false publications; fully half of the plays which we now accept as holy writ were never published in Shakespeare's time! How can we say these words are Shakespeare's words?"

He continues, now holding up two fingers, "Secondly, perhaps most importantly, the First Folio was published in 1623, seven years after Shakespeare's death, and so had absolutely no participation or approval by the man himself. Ben Johnson, at the time, considered Shakespeare's equal or superior, had the wisdom and foresight to publish his own folio, so no one can harbor doubts as to his works. There is no such guarantee with Shakespeare.

Thirdly, now holding up three fingers, Burbage steps out from behind the rostrum and says, "Let me proceed now as quickly as I can, moving from a micro to a macro perspective," and here Burbage pauses to share the grand sweep of his intellect, "it is possible to look at a number of Shakespeare's plays and easily see that major components clash incongruously with other major elements. Falstaff is a wonderful figure, but how does he fit in? Shylock is undoubtedly a brilliant creation, but he is a burden to the rest of the play. In *Romeo and Juliet*, Mercutio and the nurse are dazzling, so much so, that it is said Shakespeare found it necessary to kill off Mercutio before Mercutio killed off the play.

"How shall we account for such incongruities? They are not all of a piece. But they are there, and we are looking at the offending piece in *Romeo and Juliet*: Friar Laurence and his misdeeds." And here, Burbage pounded the rostrum, "Friar Laurence's scheming and bungling are simply intolerable."

The brilliance of the delivery and the mighty ego of the man are compelling. At center from the very outset is his anguish at the burden he feels laid upon him to choose between fidelity to the audience and fidelity to the author. Clearly, the former has won. But that leaves the whole question of what to do with *Romeo and Juliet* when one is cast adrift by the author? Easy, give the audience what it wants. Or what the director wants it to want ...

That is what Burbage turns to now. "At this point in his career, Shakespeare was mostly writing histories and romances, with perhaps one notable exception, *Titus Andronicus*. About that, the less said, the better. So, the play, *Romeo and Juliet*, a tragedy, doesn't fit chronologically. Moreover, as a tragedy, it differs from the other tragedies later written by Shakespeare—*Othello, Lear, Macbeth, Hamlet*—whose major characters were all royalty and power-crazed and hugely flawed, and motivated at least in part by madness. And so, death in those plays is almost inevitable and appropriate as the endpoint.

"Here we are left with this double incongruity: *Romeo and Juliet* is not like the other plays Shakespeare was writing then, and not like the tragedies he wrote later. It is simply wrong that Romeo and Juliet should die in a heart-rending, almost accidental sequence.

"Moreover, it is preposterous that they should die through the bungling of characters who do not even belong in the play, Friar John, failing to deliver a message! An apothecary violating his code of ethics! Friar Laurence failing to get to the tomb in time! This is not methodology. These are instances of random madness, satire." Burbage declares.

"Without question, the ending is wrong. It makes no sense for Shakespeare, and it makes no sense for the audience. And so, despite Mr. Belsky's obsessive compulsion to see death wrongly delivered," Burbage continues, "this play cries out for a different ending. My, I should say OUR, production will deliver that. The structure and the characters remain the same, but fidelity to the play as a romance requires a major change in outcome."

And now Burbage positions himself well in front of the rostrum, at the edge of the lights on the stage, stretches his arms as if delivering a benediction and declares, "In our rendition, nobody dies in the Fifth Act ... Love will triumph. Truly this is right, and the only question is why it has taken 400 years for a director to say so. It may be that justice delayed is justice denied, yet it is still justice." Burbage's voice thunders and echoes across the theater and decades. "We will not be the last to deliver Romeo and Juliet to their deaths. We shall be the very first to give them life." I am thinking, only God and Burbage would have egos big enough to undertake such a task and deliver such a line. Yet, the hair is standing up on the back of my neck. This is great Vintage Burbage.

The audience, particularly the cast, is stunned. It occurs to me that the rehearsals of the play have not yet embraced the final Act. The cast has been playing and rehearsing *Romeo and Juliet* as traditionally attributed to Shakespeare. The outcome in the final scene is a sequence of deaths, County Paris, Romeo, Juliet. Now, each of them, we hear for the first time, will survive in the final scene. The earlier deaths of Mercutio and Tybalt need not necessarily be reversed. Those scenes have been rehearsed; they may have to be redone or not.

But the cast is now learning that when they proceed to rehearse the final scenes, Romeo finds Juliet alive, and she embraces a living Romeo! Even County Paris survives. Sure, there are minor details, but let the Prince deal with those. That's what Princes are for. Cool.

Happiness reigns, music up, riding into the sunset are Romeo, Juliet, County Paris, maybe Friar Laurence. Curtain down, footlights up. Curtain call for the cast. Huzzahs for the Director.

Applause. Modest cheering. Wonderment for all of us sitting in awe at this Director's Overview.

But not necessarily from those who must play out the revised play. Certainly, some of the cast are not applauding. In the main, their reaction is summed up first by the magical phrase, "Holy shit!" This from the actor who would play Friar Laurence.

"Oh my God," this from a thin, colorless grad student to my left, who perhaps is Tybalt or Mercutio.

This is followed by "Geddowdaheah!" from a large buxom woman, who I hope has been cast as The Nurse.

And from a tall, princely-looking figure, who presumably would play the Prince, saying, "Who will be pardoned and who will be punished?" Emphases on the last syllable ...

I would not say pandemonium has broken out, or that chaos reigns, or that all hell has broken loose, but Burbage is only ten days away from opening night, and he may be facing the prospect of mutiny. Or absurdity. And if this is not enough, in short order, from the actor who would play County Paris, Belsky, now sitting behind Juliet, in the fourth row directly before Burbage comes, "Are you out of your fuckin, mind?"

Belsky. at the top of his lungs, "This is fucking nuts."

Instead of being taken aback, Burbage smiles and seems delighted. For one thing, this seems to affirm the centrality of his self-importance. Or is it the importance of his self-centrality? For another, it underlines the freshness of his approach and its sheer audacity. On the other hand, the drama student playing Friar Laurence, sitting to my left, speaks to me again, saying, "What this means is that our rehearsal schedule is totally fucked." I look at him and think, "WWWAD, What Would Woody Allen do?"

Burbage stands tall amid bedlam, raises his arms out straight, palms down, pressing his hands and the audience down, and achieves, amazingly, something approaching calm. He manipulates his voice again, this time to a chatting mode, soothing, and says, "I know it is a new idea, and getting adjusted may take a bit of time. It may seem like radical surgery, but it will take minimal reworking. What is radical is the concept and the outcome."

At this, Belsky says, "Right. You're just turning the entire world upside down. That's all." He turns to the other people in the theater and says, "Is this nutso or what? I say we all walk. We can do this play as we rehearsed it; we don't need this third-rate asshole director to lead us into disaster." Belsky has now moved to the center aisle, addressing the audience, turning his back on Burbage, posing a serious challenge that Burbage will lose them.

Burbage, now considerably miffed, turns to him and says, "Belsky, sit down," and confidently says to the audience, "Doing this is easy. We could arrange for Friar John to deliver his message, or Romeo could never buy the poison. Friar Laurence could get to the tomb ahead of Romeo, Juliet could wake up before Romeo arrives ... The possibilities are easy; all we need is one small change, a small tweaking of the script. Romeo would embrace Juliet, and with the assistance of Friar Laurence, go off to Mantua, as they clearly should have," delivered straight out to the center of the audience, straight from Burbage's heart. His lips to God's ears.

He now looks directly at the center of the audience, raises his right hand in a gesture of workmanlike simplicity, and says, "A small twist of the plot, a bit of tinkering here, a turn of the screw there, and the whole thing would be different, and," and Burbage pounds the podium with his fist, "IT WOULD BE SO RIGHT." And here, Burbage has us in the palm of his hand, as a director and actor and a powerful demagogue, saying, "It would all be so easy and so simple. Then we would have a romance, as we should have, not a half-assed, error-driven tragedy by fuck up.

"Agreed?"

And here he opens his arms widely toward the 40 or so of us and says, again, "Agreed? Does anyone disagree?" It is almost like the wedding scene from *The Graduate*. Does anybody object to this marriage? Let them speak now or forever hold their peace. Or is it piece? Where is Dustin Hoffman when you really need him?

But instead of Hoffman, a voice centered in semidarkness, crying in the desert, Belsky again calls out, "Fuck, yeah. I disagree. Why save

Romeo? He killed Tybalt. He killed County Paris. He seduced an underage teenaged girl. He whimpered like a gutless cretin when facing banishment. He sniveled his way into duping Friar Laurence into breaking his vows. The play is right as rain; Romeo deserves death."

I am dumbfounded, I thought everybody loved Romeo, I mean, who wouldn't? This whole clash between Belsky and Burbage is great theater, and there is more. I mean, there's a movie here. Quick. Call Central Casting. Get me ... Morgan Freeman for Burbage and Hoffman for Belsky ... possibly James Woods.

Belsky moves down the center aisle, looking down on Burbage; he is angry and forceful in his military camo gear, his foppishness seems gone, as he continues, "The mob mentality of the Capulets and the Montagues had pretty much died away, and this clown, Romeo, had lined up what everybody agrees was a terrific chick in Rosalind, and all of a sudden, at a party he shouldn't have attended, he starts the chaos up all over again, sets them all back at war, all because of a crush on a girl who's not even legal. On a one-night stand!"

And now Belsky leaves the aisle, steps up onto the stage next to Burbage, and says, "You may be right, Professor Burbage, that this isn't a tragedy like those other plays, *Hamlet, Othello*, whatever, I mean all those guys started off heroes, but Romeo from the get-go is just a whimpering, immature, self-absorbed dick. The reason the play is a tragedy is that it holds out the possibility Juliet might marry Romeo. That would be a genuine tragedy. The only one with backbone is Juliet, and Romeo causes her death. Shakespeare got it right, and you got it wrong; it sure as Hell makes sense that Romeo shouldn't live. Romeo must die."

I am amazed by the passion and force of Belsky's rant, but I see that Burbage is only amused, responding with a patronizing tone, "Ladies and gentlemen, again, please greet and meet Tommy Belsky, who has a minor part in our production and a major problem in the world of white rage. Lest you think you hear erudition and high-flying analysis from the young man, let me point out that he stands for Aryan supremacy and confuses that with Shakespeare's excellence. He deserves sympathy since he plays County Paris and is the last of the characters to be slain by Romeo on his way to the tomb.

So, he does naturally have feelings against Romeo. But his passion, let us be clear, is personal, not principled."

Then I think of that little scene at the beginning, where Belsky takes Schmidt's arm off Juliet and Romeo stakes out his turf. I am hoping Burbage won't go there, praying that he won't, oh please don't, but then he does. OMG.

Burbage now looks directly at Belsky, across the electric space between them, and asks, "Is it possible, Mr. Belsky, isn't it more than just possible, that you have some self-interest in this, that you seek personal revenge on Romeo? In real life, I mean, I understand that you lost Juliet—lost her to Romeo, the young man sitting over here on my left. Is it Shakespeare who wants him dead, or you?

"And your pretense of admiration for Juliet? After she kicked you to the curb? Come on! That's rank hypocrisy! You want her dead, too. As dead as Romeo. Vengeance, Mr. Belsky, is a dish best served cold. Not this overheated sophomoric crap."

Belsky is stunned by this, left speechless by what, at best, is a foul blow in an uneven fight.

The fellow sitting next to me in the dark leans over and says, "That's the only thing Burbage got right. Belsky's been dating Juliet, and she dumped him last night for Romeo. That works, doesn't it?" And I am thinking, holy shit, yeah, that works. And I say, thank you, Friar Laurence.

Burbage continues, smugly thinking to minimize the carnage he has just created, and says, "Surely, Mr. Belsky, even you cannot oppose the justice in a happy ending."

Surprise. Belsky can. Belsky, still standing, jumped in and said, "And even you can't pretend that's what you pretend you're doing. The happy ending is already there, it is Shakespeare's, and it is justice for Juliet, Juliet's parents, County Paris, the Prince, even for Romeo, yes even for Romeo, justice is Romeo's death." And Belsky repeated himself, "Romeo must die."

There is fury and huge anger in Belsky's voice, and Juliet and Romeo move quickly away from him. Burbage responds quietly and patiently. "And Juliet, should she die too? After all, she deceived County Paris and her parents and rejected the plain advice of her nurse; should she die also? And the parents, who began the bloodletting of the generations; should they die?"

"I am not going to answer that because Shakespeare already has," retorts Belsky. "You are playing fast and loose with one of the great plays and minds of all time. There is Shakespeare on the one hand, unquestionable greatness, and there you are on the other you, a third-rate loser trying to elevate yourself by gutting a play that has stood for centuries."

I am flabbergasted at the aggressive, articulate attack maintained by Belsky, and I am filled with admiration for Burbage's equanimity. At the same time, I have admiration as well for Belsky's tenacity. The other people in the audience, some cast members, some drama

238

students, a few faculty, even those who applauded earlier, are now subdued, intimidated, and heading for the doors.

So, Burbage returns to what he claims is his main point, addressing all of us in the dimly lit Iseman Theater, "Regardless, I would be interested in any of your views on the three options I laid out. Could you please email or text me about them? And thank you for your interest. We have to wind up now."

The audience begins to file out, a couple of the grad students murmuring, "Only Burbage would have the balls to do a lobotomy on Shakespeare."

The response being, "That's not balls, that's chutzpah."

Another saying, "I think it's great!" The response, "Suckup." The last comment was, "I'd say that kid Belsky is toast. You don't fuck with an ego like Burbage's."

I am thinking back to my own time when I got kicked out of D School and thinking that the kid got that right; when loud voices attract my attention, Belsky and Burbage are at it again, this time Burbage losing it and saying, "Look, I've had it with you. I don't know how your Nazi supremacist friends can stand you, but I can't, and I don't have to." He turns to walk away, and Belsky reaches to grab him.

Romeo jumps up onto the stage from his chair, grabbing Belsky, yelling, "Don't," as Juliet steps between the two.

Burbage seeing what almost happened, says, "You're done, kid. Get your punk ass out of this theater and my play. I can recast Paris in a heartbeat, and almost anyone off the street could do it better than you. You're done."

Belsky stands, shaken, and says to Juliet, "Come on, Julie, let's get out of here."

Juliet, frozen to the spot, clearly horrified at the prospect, says, "No. I've got a ride with Romeo. And I don't think I want to see you again. Ever."

Romeo puts his arm around Juliet, turns to Belsky, and says, "You need help, man. You are seriously fucked. Totally."

With this, Belsky, ten years older than the high school student, can do no better than "Eat shit and die," and, followed by Otto Schmidt, the Hillhouse Hitler look-alike, stomps out the door closest to the stage.

Burbage speaks again before anyone else has had a chance to leave and calls out, "Wait, hold on just a minute. Let's do this. This, of course, has been simply a pleasant tete a tete (and I am thinking if this is a tete a tete, what the hell is WWW III gonna look like?) of my Director's play on the play." He smiles at his little pun, continuing, "In two days, I propose that we have a real Director's Walk-Through with the cast performing 'Burbage's Damage,' let's call it," giving the second word a bit of a French twist, "limited to Act Five. Friday.

"Here in this theater, you will see my thinking at work. That will leave us an entire week before the dress rehearsal and opening-night. I will have my revised Act Five scripts in your boxes by tomorrow morning. We will make history.

"So, on Friday, at 7:30, we will do Act V, as amended, a complete walk-through with costumes, and folks, I need you to provide a real live audience! That would be you who are right here, right now, plus an invitee or two or so for each of you, plus," and here he does a Ta-Da! "the families of our Romeo and Juliet, our high school thespians, the Montagues and the Capulets.

"Oh, and lest I forget, I particularly want the family of the young man playing Friar Laurence. I have big plans for him, and his family will want to hear about them. He is central to whatever device I use to change the play from Tragedy to Romance." And here I take a hard look, for the first time, at my Friar Laurence's alter ego ... thin, short, colorless, truly a Woody Allen knockoff, an improbable contrast to the man I am representing.

He says, "Is he shitting me? I am supposed to come to my own death?"

Burbage closes out his invitation with, "Tell those you bring, we are about to make history, Romeo and Juliet, The Romance. 7:30 PM Friday. Right here in the Iseman Theater."

Now I know, beyond any peradventure of a doubt, that all the world's a stage ...

CHAPTER TWENTY-ONE
DINNER AT DOROTHY'S

I leave the Yale Drama School in my ancient yet trusty Volvo 240 DL station wagon.

Once it was an upper middle-class vehicle and probably took young kids to prep school and then hauled them off to Yale or other such places. Now it has 250,000 miles, dents and rust where you wouldn't think they were possible, an unstoppable engine, and an embarrassing appearance protecting it from robbery and burglary by any of my self-respecting clients. It's a junker, but it's *my* junker.

I drive from the campus in the center of town, west and north, through the Dixwell Avenue section to well-preserved Section 8 housing. As I park, I am still reeling from and reflecting on the events which have just transpired. The "tragedie" is being ousted from *Romeo and Juliet,* and romance will prevail. The drama has been shifted from the world of the stage to the D School world of outrage and rebellion by one of the bit players, Belsky, and he has himself been removed from the scene, no tragedie there. It would appear he has also been removed from the life of the young lady playing Juliet, who is now in love with the young man playing Romeo. All of which, according to the Director, is as Shakespeare probably wrote the play before it was hijacked by unknown forces and events.

If nothing else, my life has been filled with coincidences of late. Another arises as Meg arrives to park next to my Volvo in her spiffy, ecologically sensitive Prius V. As she alights from her Hybrid, I note that she has a spring bouquet in one hand and a bag with what I take to be two bottles of wine in the other. This she hands to me and says, "You are now the perfect guest; a bottle of Amarone from Valpolicella and one of Soave from Monteforte, a couple of decent northern Italian wines. Which way?"

I, of course, have become intimately familiar with the geography of this place (but not northern Italy) during our court proceedings and opt to go in the front door, afraid I might stumble over the Phantom Butcher Knife in the back parking lot. Would I have any ethical obligations? Is it needed for tonight's tossed salad? Is there blood? Out, out, damned spot ...

I ring the doorbell, and Dorothy Arlow opens the screen door, dressed as a hard-working pediatric nurse, to welcome her attorney and medical research colleague. "Please come in." We do.

It feels good. There is a fine aroma of Italian cooking in the air, two priests are seated in the living room, three bright-looking kids being entertained by parlor tricks provided by the Abbot (who else?), and a sofa for Meg and me. Meg says, "Sit," which I do, and then says, "Can I help?" Dorothy Arlow accepts, and the two repair to the kitchen, just large enough for two skilled professionals to work medical miracles and talk shop. I help with the parlor tricks by playing dummy.

In 15 minutes, there is a knock at the door, Dorothy Arlow calls; "Will one of you get that please?" Friar Laurence does. A young teenage girl stands on the stoop, as the door opens, looks up at the doorman and calls through Friar Laurence to Dorothy Arlow, "Mrs. Arlow, it's me, Leticia, when do you want the kids back ... if ever?" (This last directed at the three girls.)

"The usual, 4:00 AM."

Leticia again, "I'm afraid we're doing drugs at our place starting at one ... They'll have to bring their own." (This last directed at the priests.)

"Oh. Okay. How about 9:30? It's a school night."

"Okay. All right if they get second helpings for dinner? They're always whining that you don't feed them enough."

"That's fine, so long as they bring back food for our guests, they don't allow takeout at the nunnery, you know." With that, Leticia gathers the three girls, with a practiced hand, walks them out the front door, calling over her shoulder as she goes, "Nunnery? Priests live in a nunnery?" And the door closes.

Friar Laurence sits opposite me, and he asks, "Hard day at the office?" I quickly recap the tour in the courtroom and then mention that the high point came a few blocks away at the Drama School, where Professor Burbage had done his Directorial Overview. I do not get a chance to finish because at this point, Meg comes in with a tray of cheeses, olives, and bread slices.

This effectively distracts Friar Laurence, who inhales deeply, and says "I feel as though I have been transported to the open shopping markets of Verona ..." He turns to the Abbot and me and says, "These are northern Italian cheeses, which I would not have thought one could find here in New Haven, even in Wooster Square. We have over 2000 cheeses, Provolone, Romano, and Ricotta are not hard to find, But Dorothy has outdone herself. These are cheeses from the North, Tabor is from Trieste, Sargnon is from the Piedmont, and this I think is Buernkase from the South Tyrol. And this one, I think, is from Lombardi, maybe it is Bagoss, named after one of your football players, I think, Lombardi."

The Abbot and I look stunned; in my case, grated Parmesan cheese is the full extent of my knowledge—from the Northern Kraft Region of Safeway. But then, that goes with spaghetti and meatballs and pizza. I'm not sure what region of Italy those are from. I became acquainted with them at Pepe's Pizzeria Napolitana and Yorkside Pizza here in New Haven.

That being precisely the correct moment, Meg returns with the two bottles of wine, saying to me that my choice of wines had met with the approval of our hostess, I could proceed to open them. As I reach for my Swiss Army knife in my back pocket, Dorothy Arlow returns with a somewhat more elegant but complicated-looking unit.

While I approach this complex machine, I glance at Dorothy, noting that sometime over the last few minutes, she has managed a complete wardrobe overhaul, with skirt, blouse, and jewelry of sufficient simplicity and style to win a man's heart. Not just any man, but one who has traveled much of the world and appreciates good taste. And an attractive woman. A man like Friar Laurence.

I master the wine unit, opening the two bottles with a flair, which takes a while, and the interim is filled with the Abbot and Friar Laurence reporting on their day spent visiting old Mystic Seaport, a reconstruction of, well, what else? an old Seaport at Mystic Connecticut, which I associate, since I'm getting hungry, with the movie Mystic Pizza, by which time, I find I can begin pouring the wine.

Friar Laurence refrains from commenting on the wine selection; perhaps he does not want to offend me, perhaps he's more of a cheese guy, perhaps he's thirsty ... I know he is drinking seriously, and the two bottles of wine vanish uno momento. Meg's choices couldn't have been too bad. Fortunately, the Abbot, never without magical charm, has produced three more, a Sangiovese and a Chianti and something, he says, from the Veneto region, wherever that is.

I open these, and they are transported to the table. Dorothy Arlow asks for the Abbot to sit at the head, and dinner is ready to be served.

245

I become lost in the meal presented. There is a large wooden serving bowl, filled with greens of varying sorts, no bottles of Kraft salad dressings alongside, a large steaming, casserole or stew bowl, with a ladle, filled with a fish stew, with pungent aroma, two long loaves of crusty bread, no olive oil, soft butter nearby. There are, as well, salt and pepper shakers and empty basic wine glasses, waiting for the Abbot's bottles of wine.

Dorothy Arlow asks whether either of our distinguished guests would care to say grace; I assume she does not mean me, a view shared by everyone else. Friar Laurence nods imperceptibly to the Abbot, who then proceeds with the litany I had grown up with, "Bless us O Lord and these thy gifts which we are about to receive from thy bounty through Christ our Lord, amen." We join in the amen, and Friar Laurence serves the Italian seafood stew for each of us as we pass our bowls.

Having grown up in an ethnically mixed neighborhood, I had eaten Italian cuisine and was accustomed to the heavy pasta and the tomato-based sauce, olive oil and garlic, served by my friends' mothers, from New Haven to South Boston to the neighborhoods of the Godfather. This was different; there was no pasta. The main dish was what I was familiar with as Cioppino, an Italian fisherman's stew, some tomato paste, but mostly fish stock laced liberally with clams, mussels, shrimp, and firm-fleshed fish such as halibut or salmon. This was different. It looked great, it tasted great, but it was a bit puzzling.

The Abbot, mentioned almost in passing, that I seem a bit puzzled and asked our hostess whether this was Cioppino or something a bit more northern.

At which point, Friar Laurence suggested, "Possibly Cacciucco? I grew up with that."

Dorothy Arlow smiled, saying, "I was hoping for that, but the New York Times cookbook and Martha Stewart couldn't quite give me all the guidance I needed. I hope I came close. I cooked it last night in the slow cooker; I hope it's not overdone."

Friar Laurence gave his booming laugh and said, "Even my mother could not find fault with this. Thank you. Thank you. Thank you."

The green salad went quickly, assisted by a side dish of polenta e fasoi. And again, Friar Laurence commented that he had grown up with that dish, and it was perfect. Our hostess bowed, blushed a bit and said, "Well, I will accept the compliment, but I must attribute this one to Blue Apron;" and seeing the puzzlement on both priests' faces, added, "a box comes twice a week by UPS, and it keeps me from having children who believe leftover pizza and PB&Js are the only main courses in American homes."

The conversation had been light and engaging, with Meg and Dorothy filling the rest of us in on how the hospital was doing, how research fit with service, how the mission was changing over the years, how the ethnic changes and racial shifts of New Haven had impacted not only the hospital and medical center but also the University's research program. It was all very interesting, and it was impressive to see the two women finding so much in common.

It was also fascinating to me to see how much Friar Laurence was smitten with Dorothy Arlow.

And then dinner was done except for dessert. Again, the two medical marvels disappeared into the kitchen while we cleared the table of dishes, and when we all returned to the table, there were five white plates with a kind of pudding or custard turned upside down from a mold, each with berries on top. They smelled strongly of vanilla. Dorothy Arlow sat quietly, the rest of us sat amazed, they were, well, exquisite, and Friar Laurence spoke, overwhelmed, and said, "Panna cotta ... my mother made it with hazelnuts. Almost nobody else did. This is wonderful. How could you possibly have known?"

Indeed.

When done, we moved from the table to our prior seating arrangement, and Dorothy Arlow said, "Perhaps all of you know this; if so, forgive me for asking, but I wonder if Friar Laurence could tell me a bit about how he got here? Perhaps even his purpose in being here in New Haven at this time. I do understand that you have a history with Romeo and Juliet (and I think, history? Well, maybe. But maybe no future ... I notice The Abbot, noticing me), and the play is being performed by two high school students from the families in the play itself. Are you somehow caught up in that?"

Suddenly it seemed I was hearing the thunder of silence, thinking the lady had a way of asking the key question, wondering as well what the Abbot was thinking as he looked at me and bounced his eyebrows, and I felt Meg hitting me in the ribs with her elbow. I had been getting that a lot lately. "Close your mouth," she whispered.

More silence. Dorothy Arlow said, "Well forgive me but ..."

And then Friar Laurence held up his hand and said, "No. Nothing to forgive. You have been wonderful to have us in your home and to go to great lengths to make special efforts to make me welcome. My hesitation is that I can't answer much of the question because I don't know the answer.

"I can only say that I am not sure how I got here. A week or two ago, I woke up in a strange place, this has happened to me often over my very, very long lifetime. I came to meet this wonderful gentleman sitting to my right, Brother Dominic, a Friar of the Dominican Order, and the head of our abbey here in New Haven, located on the Green.

"I remembered full well who I am and who I was, a Friar of the same order, an order of preachers, hence our degree, so to speak, is indicated by the initials O.P. I apologized for dropping in on him uninvited; he laughed, he said 'We get that a lot. You people are seekers, completing your life or your life's work or making amends for prior misdeeds in order to complete your life. You are seekers and searchers. Most of humanity,' he said, 'in lesser degree, shares the same plight.

"'But you are not just seekers … You are brought here for special purposes, even if you do not know why.' And here Brother Dominic had paused and asked me then, 'Do you know why?' But I didn't. I think, though, I am getting closer."

Friar Laurence looked around the room and said, "I think I am beginning to know why."

I looked at Meg. Dorothy Arlow and Meg looked at the Abbot, who said, "I think I speak for all of us, I hope including Mrs. Arlow, when I say, please go on."

With this, Friar Laurence said, "In the play, my misdeeds are well known. I performed a marriage without parental consent on underage minors, deceiving the parents, leading to the deaths directly or indirectly of County Paris, Romeo, Juliet, and possibly others. These figures live in a fictional world, but within it, they are real, and their pain and suffering is also real, for them and me.

249

"My real world is yours, not theirs, but I am a figure in their world, and so, every time the play is performed, I repeat my misdeeds. Over and over and over again, I experience the pain and anguish of inflicting their pain and anguish, and my punishment is that I have no end. I know I will do it again.

"They die, but I do not. I never do ... I cannot even enter purgatory. The dead may there expiate for their sins and move on. But I cannot. I have not died, I cannot atone ...

"I do not know how well each of you knows the play, but I'm certain that my fine attorney Francis Collins, having studied for a Masters in Fine Arts in Shakespeare Studies at the Yale Drama School, recalls full well, that at the very end of the play I confess my misconduct and I am met, essentially, by disdain, by the Prince, who says he will deal with Friar Laurence later.

"But he never does. Within that world, he is responsible for delivering God's judgment, and he does not do that! And so, I live through all this time, centuries, performance after performance after performance, in pain and anguish."

Again silence. What Friar Laurence has said is impossible, yet it is real. It seems the world has gone very cold and very quiet. Can I see my breath, hanging as fog, in this room now without walls?

The Abbot breaks the silence and says, "I assume Friar Laurence and I are the only practicing Catholics in the room at this time, although I do seem to recall, Francis, you were once a communicant in your youth. So, let me say that what we have just heard from Friar Laurence is what I might expect to hear in the confessional. That is, it is a description and an acknowledgment of conduct which offends the laws of the church and of God. Not only is it a description, but it is a declaration by Friar Laurence that he owns this conduct and repents of it.

"Is that a fair summary, Friar Laurence?"

"Yes," Friar Laurence acknowledged, "very much so."

"Then permit me," the Abbot continued, "to impose my role a bit farther by asking the indulgence of each of you here to treat what you have just heard in the strictest confidence. That also is a part of the confessional. If we do this, then as a member of the clergy, I can perform my role as I would within the confessional." I, of course, am wondering what his role is, having made my last confession when I was 12, which involved beating up three truly obnoxious punks who lived down the street, I hasten to add, with the able assistance of my older sister. I wondered then, and do still, where is the sin in that?

With all our assent, I am also wondering what comes next. "With that, you are probably wondering what comes next," the Abbot says, "and it is for me to ask, as I would in the closet confessional, whether the communicant, here Friar Laurence, not only acknowledges his responsibility but also asks forgiveness from our Lord.

"So, let me turn to Friar Laurence and at this point ask whether he does so?"

I see a lifting of Friar Laurence's grim aspect, as though a warm light had begun to play across him, as he says, "Yes, those are my sins or many of them, and I certainly repent of them, and I would dearly love forgiveness, though I think it is too much to ask."

And here the Abbot says to those of us who are non-Catholics, "It is sometimes thought that there is a kind of magic at play here, with the confessional, as though I can confer forgiveness, but I cannot. That is for God and God alone." He continued, "The confessional is simply a way of helping Friar Laurence to seek forgiveness, to repent, and to make amends.

"It is sometimes thought that participating in communion during a mass following confession is again a kind of magic in that it washes sins away. But only God's forgiveness does that. The magic in communion is the transformation of the bread and the wine, in an act of remembrance of Christ's sacrifice and what He said in the Upper Room to his Apostles.

"So, for Friar Laurence to be successful and free of the sin and pain he has carried for all these centuries, and to find release, he must make amends. His sacrifice must be proportional, more than equal to the harm he has done, indeed, outweigh it if possible. It would seem his sacrifice must be for Romeo and Juliet, but how and when and in what way only he can learn. Only then can he earn forgiveness and an end to his pain.

"But before there can be an ending, there must be a beginning."

CHAPTER TWENTY-TWO

THE PUB AT DEPTFORD

MEET WILL, KIT, AND THE ORIGINAL BURBAGE

The Abbot goes on, "We know that Friar Laurence at about the time Shakespeare was writing *Romeo and Juliet* was sent from Verona to our Dominican community in Oxford England, and we inferred they met, that is, he and William Shakespeare. But we do not know. And there is no record of his arriving or returning, but perhaps now we will hear ..."

Friar Laurence says, "Yes, if you like, I will tell you. It may take a while."

And the Abbot speaks, "As you know, I have a certain facility with time, so however long this may take, we have the time needed, the babysitters, the Uber drivers, the keepers at the Abbey, all will wait. Time is now ours. Or, more accurately, yours, Friar Laurence."

Friar Laurence goes on. "My story is short, foolish, in its own way, tragic. I was sent from the Black Friars community in Verona to our community in Oxford. Shortly after arrival, the Abbot there asked me to go from Oxford to London and meet with two businessmen named Shakespeare and Burbage. They had an acting company, and they wanted to buy or rent our unused Cathedral. I was to get their terms but not negotiate the deal.

"It was three days travel, and I was tired when we met on May 19, 1593. Shakespeare, Burbage, and I went to dinner, at a pub in Deptford, on a ford on the Ravensbourne, a small river with a bridge, now a part of Southeast London. It was an old inn, low ceiling, overheated, stained with the smoke of fireplaces and tobacco, reeking with the stench of the open sewer just outside. It was dark, even during the day, and people kept coming and going. We ate and drank for several hours until I could barely see or speak. I was a novice at all this, and they kept refilling my drink, mead, ale, whiskey.

"Looking back, I think this was deliberate ... planned in advance for what happened next.

"I was a young kid barely out of my divinity studies. I was dazzled. Shakespeare and I and Christopher Marlowe, who joined us later, were born in the same year, 1564, But they were cosmopolitan, with sophistication beyond my comprehension. They were famous, full of gossip and tales. And without the inhibitions and conventions I had grown up with.

"They had a theater company which performed before Queen Elizabeth, and later became the leading force in London theater, the King's Men, under King James. They produced plays, and Shakespeare had appeared in several and had written several, mostly comedies. This was all new to me. Friends of theirs would come by, slapping me on the back, saying how lucky I was to be spending time with such great men, and any friend of Will's was a friend of theirs.

"As I mentioned, we were joined later by a man introduced as one of the great playwrights of the time, Christopher Marlowe and three of his friends. They had all been drinking and hung around us for a while before Marlowe dismissed the friends, saying he would see them tomorrow, the 20th. He sat and joined us, and we continued drinking. Marlowe and Shakespeare were colleagues, competitors, good friends. He and Shakespeare and Burbage talked about staging plays, plagiarizing other people's work, hiring and firing actors, old theaters torn down and new ones built, politics with the City of London, the plague, all dizzying and exciting and way over my head, most of it I didn't understand. They kept filling my glass after glass after glass.

"It was as though today, Francis, we went over to Morrie's and sat at a table with Leonard Bernstein or Andrew Lloyd Weber, and Tom Hanks and Tom Cruise and Brad Pitt joined us. And everybody knew your name." I nodded, acknowledging that I would be overwhelmed by such company.

"Shakespeare, of course, looked like the famous printed image of him. Marlowe was different. In all the centuries since, only one image of him has survived, and it is dubious. He looks slight, with a wispy beard, a dandy, a fop, arrogant, cold. And evil. That is how he looked that night.

"The evening went on, with loud merriment, singing and group camaraderie." Here Friar Laurence paused, "I didn't know Marlowe then, I didn't know how evil he could be, but you must know of him, Francis, you studied Shakespeare's time."

Laurence seemed to want a break from the power of the memories he was recalling, draining him even as he told his narrative. He paused, and I picked up a piece of what I knew. I said, "Yes. Marlowe at that time was, if anything, a greater poet, for that is what they called playwrights then, than Shakespeare. By the time Marlowe was 29, he had written four plays that endure today, *Tamarlane, Edward II, The Jew of Malta* and, of course, in 1593, about the time you met him, *Faustus*, who sold his soul to Mephistopheles, later made into an opera by Gounod and rewritten by Goethe, in 1830 or so, in a huge two-part epic."

Here, another elbow. "Ouch. Am I going on too long?" A nod from Meg, wielder of the omnipresent, omnipotent elbow.

I concluded, "Well, more to the point, he was a drunkard, a brawler, an atheist, a debauched homosexual, had killed at least one man, run out of the Netherlands, jailed for all of this. At that time, he was under arrest for blasphemy. I am not surprised you were overwhelmed by his debauchery. But he was brilliant ... Shakespeare and he frequently traded lines and ideas. Centuries later, some people argued that Marlowe wrote most of Shakespeare's plays, but, of course, that was nonsense. He died that year, in fact, the next day at Eleanor Bull's Inn, and Shakespeare kept writing for another ten or fifteen years."

Dorothy Arlow, I noticed, had changed places on the couch with Abbot Dominic and was now seated next to Friar Laurence. She had brought him a large mug of tea. Friar Laurence continued, "I could sense he was evil; the force of his personality was overpowering. The pub itself was dark, but he seemed darker still, almost an entire area unto himself, even when he got up from the table, and when he returned, he walked in darkness. A force ..."

Here Friar Laurence shrugged and shook his shoulders, clasped his hands, and walked around the coffee table. He stood in the door to the kitchen and continued ...

"In conversation, it was as though Shakespeare and Burbage were in debt to Marlowe and got out of his way to give him a clear avenue for going after me. He taunted me for my religious beliefs, poverty vocation, celibacy, religious practices, and what he called my false modesty. He said our vows of poverty and chastity were simple hypocrisy; we had the wealth of the Church and the nunneries. We were posers in a charade.

"We argued and disputed about the divinity of Christ and the place of Mary Magdalene; he ridiculed all the teachings of the Church.

It went on for hours, the pub emptied, but the innkeeper kept bringing us grog, well beyond closing hour, as if primed to do so.

"I had been trained thoroughly in forensics and hermeneutics, but for the first time, I found someone more than my equal, someone who had gone to Oxford University, who challenged every one of my assumptions, someone, who would write one of the great plays of all time, as you say, Francis.

"And he brought it up, that play, Dr. Faustus. He was working on it at that time, a brilliant scientist who made a pact with the devil and sold his soul for 24 years of knowledge and debauchery. Faustus never again did anything worthwhile and was taken by the devil, despite repenting and recanting; I know something about that now. Yes, yes, I do."

Here Friar Laurence sat down, having pulled a kitchen chair into the living room, and leaned forward as if talking to someone in the center of the room, that someone being himself, and he being, for the moment, in a terrible role reversal, Christopher Marlowe.

"'Would you sell your soul, Friar Laurence, Order of the Preachers?' Marlowe taunted me. 'What would you take for it?' Marlowe mocked me.

"I was confused, I answered, 'Nothing. My soul is immortal.'

"'Ah, but isn't that the exact point?' asked Marlowe, 'for you will most certainly die, as all we mortals must.'

"But my soul will live on, I replied, after my death.

"Marlowe was quick to the point, 'Which means you have already sold your soul to God! What's the point of that? Why not to the devil? To deliver your soul to God, you must die. The devil would give you immortality.'"

Friar Laurence abandoned the role and addressed those of us in the room, saying, "I was stunned. I had never considered the paradox; my soul would receive immortality, but not I; I must die so my soul would live. Why not the reverse? And that was Marlowe's point. It was as though I were on the cross, and his words were nails driven into the hands and feet of my beliefs. I could feel the blood flowing from the wounds.

"'Why should you care about your soul, or for that matter God, if only your soul, not you, will be immortal?' Marlowe jabbed at my heart.

"Marlowe laughed at me.

"'What kind of a God is that? Sounds like a deal made with the devil!'

"Marlowe and Shakespeare and Burbage laughed long and hard at this dark humor, for surely I guessed then, and I know now, that Marlowe was there at the behest of the devil. They laughed then; the pub echoed, and I can hear the echoes here, now." As could I.

We sat in Dorothy Arlow's living room, in a modest home in a modest neighborhood in New Haven, Connecticut, a community stretching back toward those very years, the late 1500s when Marlowe bludgeoned Friar Laurence into mind-numbing surrender. It seemed the walls stretched away from us, leaving us met as on a darkling plain, swept with confused alarms of struggle and flight, as we witnessed this terrible struggle, as Friar Laurence bent forward and rested his hands on the coffee table, and reached back four terrible centuries to that awful evening in that awful pub in Deptford, England, May 29, 1593 ...

After a long pause, Friar Laurence raised his hands as if in supplication and continued, "And so it went, I cannot recall it all now, and I'm not sure how much I understood then.

"Marlowe said one thing which has remained clear for centuries since, and it was, 'If I could give you right now, immortality, would you take it? Imagine the good you could do. If your soul already has it, why not claim your immortality for yourself? Isn't it yours?'"

"What about Burbage and Shakespeare," asked Dorothy, leaning forward and taking Friar Laurence's hand, "While Marlowe was hammering and tormenting you, what were they doing?"

"I don't know," said Friar Laurence, "I have a dim picture that Shakespeare was taking notes, almost as though he were writing a scene for a play or a draft for a script. Burbage was simply looking at me, his face grim and somehow, ineffably, unutterably sad. I had a feeling they were all playing scripted parts, scripted well in advance, and perhaps played before.

"Finally, we were alone in the pub, and I felt beaten, bewildered and lost, sick at heart, I cried, 'Yes, I will give up my soul, but you must first tell me how. How can I relinquish my soul and acquire immortality?

"Suddenly, I remember Shakespeare's head came up, wildly alert. The space between him and Marlowe was electric.

"Marlowe said to me, 'Will, our friend Shakespeare, sitting right here, is about to finish the finest romance of all time, *Romeo and Juliet*, it will be immortal, and you could be in it, as the priest you are.'

"Marlowe leaned over me, and he said, 'It would mean you would be immortal, not your soul. In that world, there will be no end and no end of you. Do you want me to do it?

"'Do you? DO YOU? Say it, and it is yours.'

"And I asked, can you do it?

"Marlowe's answer, 'Absolutely.'

"Then, I replied, do it.

"Marlowe turned to Shakespeare, who put down the foolscap and quill he had been using and held his hands in front of himself, turning the palms up, as if to say 'here we are, at last.'

"Marlowe said, 'Will, I owe you some lines for what you wrote in my Faustus, how soon will your *Romeo and Juliet* be done?'

"Shakespeare replied, 'It is only partly written now; I have others; there is time.'

"'Is there a priest?' Marlowe asked.

"Shakespeare answered, 'Kit, of course, there is a priest, it is a romance, a priest must marry the young lovers. I have just now begun notes for the part. Here, take them. You write the part, and we will put our young Friar Laurence in *Romeo and Juliet*.'

"Ever since ..." Friar Laurence looked at each of us, in turn as he said this, "Ever since, despite intoxication and hours of bullying, and the passage of centuries, I have remembered with utter clarity, that it was Shakespeare who said, 'Here, take them. You write the part ...' not Kit Marlowe who asked for the notes. It was as though they had rehearsed the exchange in advance and were now playing it out on the canvas and stage of my life, and Shakespeare, as always, had the lead.

"Marlowe turned to me and said, 'If I can put you in Shakespeare's play and promise you immortality, would you abandon your soul?'

"I replied, "I have already said yes, what more do you want?

"'Nothing,' said Marlowe, as he rose, but I could swear now I heard him say, dimly, as if to someone not in the room, 'Only your soul. Only that.'

"Marlowe turned to Shakespeare and said, 'Sweet William, tonight, I will take up to my room at Eleanor Bull's Inn whatever you have of the script for *Romeo and Juliet*, and by noon tomorrow, I will give you Friar Laurence. I don't care how much longer you take after that,' and with that, Marlowe lurched out of the pub. I was unsteady myself, but as he left, I could swear there was the odor of sulfur, I heard the clicking of hooves.

"I recall that I then turned to Shakespeare and Burbage and saw utter sadness in Burbage's face, but a kind of relief and happiness in Shakespeare's face. I wondered at this, and said to the two of them, 'Can he do this? Can he arrange immortality for a man?' The two of them looked at each other, and Shakespeare spoke.

"'In 1616,' said Shakespeare, '20 years from now, I will die, and two of our fellow actors and business partners, Hennings and Condell, will collect and publish 34 of my plays in a Folio in 1623. It will become the second most prized book in the English language, after the King James Bible, and neither of these is written yet. Immortality. How do I know this?

"'Ask the man who just left.'

"He went on, 'In that Folio, the greatest writer of our time, Ben Johnson, will write that I was not a figure for our age, but for all time. How did that happen, how was it arranged? How will it happen that I will write plays over the next 15 years which will be immortal? And how do I know this?'

"And here Shakespeare leaned forward, looking deeply into my face, I felt, into my soul, and said, again, 'Ask the man who just left.'

"I started to speak, but Shakespeare held up his hand and said, 'Be quiet. You ask, how will you achieve immortality? Ask instead, how have I?'

"'William Shakespeare, of Stratford-upon-Avon, comes from an undistinguished, unsophisticated, unlearned community, an unlikely starting point for greatness. Moreover, I have meager education, little to none of the library I need, I have traveled nowhere, my learning is embarrassingly meager, my knowledge of Greek and Latin is pathetic, my association with the wealthy and royalty is virtually nonexistent.

"'Yet from this night forward, my career will change, and I will write the great dramas of all time, plays I do not yet know, *Hamlet*, *Macbeth*, *Othello*, *Lear*. Histories about kings and queens, dramas about the same. I will create characters of wild imaginings, Ariel, Caliban, witches of *Macbeth*, ghosts of *Hamlet*, the characters of *A Midsummer Night's Dream*, Falstaff. I will plumb the depths of madness and depravity, such that *Titus Andronicus* will seem a tea party.

"'The plays in my later life will seem unconnected with those which I have already written, good as they were, and they will outstrip the works of all of my contemporaries and the hundreds who will follow. Later generations will ask, how could such a man produce such work?

"'You now know the answer. Ask the man who just left here.

"'You ask, can Marlowe arrange immortality in exchange for your soul? The answer is, he has done it for me, and he has done it for himself; he pledged to deliver two human souls, and he has done so, yours and mine. I get immortality for my work; you get it through my work. His work is done.'"

Friar Laurence continued, concluded, by saying, "By the time Shakespeare was done his paean to Marlowe, there were tears in Burbage's eyes.

"He looked at us and said, 'You have both, the two of you, made pacts with the Devil.' Burbage stood in that empty, stinking, soot-stained cesspool of a pub in that woe begotten town and yelled, at the top of his lungs, 'What will it gain you? WHAT WILL IT GAIN YOU?' He turned to leave and wrenched open the door on its hammered iron hinges and cried to us, 'What shall it profit a man if he gains the whole world but loses his soul?'

"As Burbage stomped out of the pub, and before slamming the oak door behind him, he cried back, 'I regret being here, my part in this. I am so sorry. I pity all of us.' I pray there will come a time I can roll it all back. But I fear it will never happen. And we were left, Shakespeare and I, after the door closed, with the twin stenches of sulfur and of human excrement from the open running sewer outside that door. And I left with terror in my heart."

Friar Laurence concluded by saying, "I cannot go on, Dorothy. I am sorry to conclude our evening this way. But this is my story; this is 'The Friar's Tale.' I traded for immortality to do good, but any pact with the devil can lead only to evil."

And he sat with both hands on his knees, staring into the vast distance in this small living room, in the small home, in a small, undistinguished neighborhood of New Haven, Connecticut. And Abbot Dominic said, "Amen." And there were tears in the room.

After a short pause, before anyone else could say anything, I completed the narrative, at least as I thought it to be, by saying, "The next day, after returning the rewritten script, Marlowe rejoined his three friends in Eleanor Bull's Inn, and spent the day with them and several women drinking. He was dead by that evening on the 20th, stabbed by the man named Frizer, whom he had earlier tried to stab while being held by the other two men, and who was later pardoned for the killing. Marlowe had been a spy, and they killed him."

Friar Laurence picked it up and said, "I never returned to the Oxford Abbey, but went to Verona, only earlier, in the 1400s, the setting of *Romeo and Juliet*, which is why there is no trace in the Dominican Order computers or records of my arriving in Oxford or returning to Verona. And the world which had seemed so various, so beautiful, so new, since then has had neither joy, nor love, nor light, nor peace, nor help for pain."

And here he stopped, exhausted, slumped on the couch, next to Dorothy Arlow. No one spoke.

We had been many hours in Dorothy Arlow's living room. A chill had come into the air, and it seemed all the lights had gone dark. I reached for Meg's hand; it was cold as ice, and there were tears on her cheeks. I heard Dorothy Arlow sob, and I heard her ask, "You never saw beforehand the part you were to play?"

"No," replied Friar Laurence, "He never promised I could do good, and I should have known good cannot come from evil. One should not bargain with one's soul. I have been paying the price ever since. Faustus had Mephistopheles. I had Christopher Marlowe. And Shakespeare."

"Is there no way back?" Asked Dorothy Arlow, turning to the Abbot. "Can he regain his soul? Can he redeem himself?"

The Abbot himself was deeply troubled, as indeed am I now as I recite this tale, and the Abbot replied, "There is a God, we teach, and I believe, and that God would not give us souls to lose. We cannot sell our immortal souls, there is punishment for trying to abandon such a rare and marvelous gift, but that punishment, for Friar Laurence, may be coming to an end. That may be why we're here."

The Abbot went on, "In Marlowe's Faustus, the scientist is drawn off to Hell, but in Goethe's rendering, angels help Faustus to heaven, saying, 'He who strives on and lives to strive, can earn redemption still.'" The Abbot continued, "And Goethe wrote: 'Only the Love beyond Time ... Can loose the subtle bond.' It is my hope that that very same Love has brought Friar Laurence here. There were evil forces at play in that ancient Pub, and they are being challenged here today in the 21st-century.

"There is to be a radically different production of *Romeo and Juliet*, and that may be the vehicle and the occasion for setting you free from the terrible bargain made centuries ago. It is no coincidence that all of those figures from that time so long ago are gathering here in New Haven, and they are part of the closing of this tragedy."

Dorothy Arlow then spoke, "When I was a child growing up on a farm in Maryland, it was a farm my great-grandparents held after slavery and passed through the generations to my parents, every spring, swallows would come back to make their mud nests in the same eaves and porch posts as in prior years. We welcomed them. When the chicks were ready to fly, there would be a gathering of dozens of swallows on nearby power lines and tree branches. That gathering, I believe, was as necessary for those young birds to take flight as the gathering we are experiencing here in New Haven is for you. This is now such a gathering. I truly believe this is your moment."

With that, I stood, as did the Abbot and Meg, saying, "Before we go, I should mention that at the Drama School this afternoon, the Director, Burbage, said he is doing a major change with the play so that Romeo and Juliet do not die. He said a minor tweak, for example, the Friar's message does get through to Romeo, or he intercepts Romeo at the tomb in time to avoid the deaths there, or the apothecary does not provide the poison, any of these would make it possible for the romance in fact to have a romantic ending.

"Burbage said he has always felt that death and tragedie were wrongly inserted into the play. This is Friar Laurence's opportunity to undo the devil's bargain from so long ago. And Burbage's. He was in the pub at Deptford, regretting this bargain. He is here now to help undo it.

"On Friday," I continued, "Burbage is going to have a limited, public Director's Walk-Through of just Act V, testing out his changes. I think we should all be there. It will be Friar Laurence's chance to assure no more deaths and gain redemption. With Burbage's help."

Here, Friar Laurence interjected, "But if their lives are saved by someone other than me, say Burbage, my chance for redemption is gone."

I laughed, and probably should not have, saying, "From what I saw today, Burbage is going to need plenty of help. The forces working for your salvation, Dorothy here, the Abbot, Burbage, myself, Meg, are being met by a formidable opposition, Belsky, Popham, Coke, perhaps even Otto Shmidt. Others. Your opportunity will be there. Believe me, Burbage will most assuredly need your help."

Meg said, "Tomorrow is another day. Things will work out. In the name of love, let us be true to one another. For right now, I want to thank Mrs. Arlow for her very generous hospitality and a truly wonderful meal. I wish we had more time to spend with your kids, and I hope that time will come. Perhaps they could meet our kids. I hope your three children appreciate what a wonderful mother they have."

With that, Meg and I turned to leave, and as we opened the door to step outside, finding that the sun had barely set and it was early evening, I heard, behind me, Dorothy say to Friar Laurence, "I would be delighted if you could stay longer. Father Dominic, I will be happy to give Friar Laurence a ride back to the Abbey."

To that, the Abbot responded, "We will look for him at matins tomorrow morning; the side door of the Abbey is always unlocked, and thank you very much for a wonderful evening. You are truly a person of remarkable compassion. Good night."

At this, Meg turned, stepped past the Abbot exiting, said something to Dorothy, and returned with Friar Laurence to Mrs. Arlow's home. As the door closed behind them, I drove off in the Volvo to make sure our starving children had had enough to eat, done their homework, and then to read to them about Frodo, from Lord of the Rings, for bedtime.

I noted that, once again, the Abbot had worked his magic with time. A fine dinner, which had begun at 7:30 and had included drunken carousing at an ancient pub, and which had run for hours, was now ended at only 9:00. Yes, the Abbot does have a way with time.

Later, at home, when Meg arrived, I asked what she had said to Dorothy Arlow, and she replied, "I said, be gentle, he is an old man, 400 years old."

"And ...?" queried I.

"Oh," she answered, "all that pent-up lust? I have some of my own."

"Tell me about it," I said.

"I will," Meg said, "Later. First, I have to get Dorothy's kids from the car. This will be their first sleepover. I think somehow this had been planned. Their stuff was all ready to go."

I asked, "Should I alert RBG and The Chief."

Meg's response was, "I called; they think it's neat."

CHAPTER TWENTY-THREE
WHY IS FRIAR LAURENCE
IN JAIL THIS MORNING?

It is now Thursday morning, and the usual ballet takes place in the Collins residence, all hell breaking loose between 6:45 and 7:30. Meg and I are considerably hung over, and still astounded by the events of the day before, the reworking of a 400-year-old play and the rebirth of a 400-year-old man. Also, the wine we brought had been well augmented and leaves now, at least in my head, a monumental, foggy residue of hangover. Add to this the immediate reality of what to do on the morning after a sleepover the night before, with three young girls who need to be off to school along with RBG and the Chief.

The kids, RBG and the Chief are somewhat baffled by our torpor, unaccustomed somnambulance, and general floundering. Nevertheless, they step up nicely, showers arranged, clothing magically produced, breakfast on the table, lunches packed, kids launched out the door well-equipped for a rainy day, and we lurch and stumble to our respective vehicles, with Meg taking the Arlow girls to their school, somewhere ... over there ...

En route to downtown New Haven, I call Meg and say, "And you, what is your agenda for the day?" She responds, "Solve most of the world's medical problems and map an ambitious future, including uses for several orphan drugs, so that they will no longer be orphaned, by noon, and have a five-martini lunch, then deliver a lecture on CRSPR. And you?"

I respond, "Nothing quite so ambitious, I intend simply to loose upon the world you have elegantly saved a gigantic swarm of depraved and disgusting criminals, Guatemalan drug runners, all of whom I have saved from their just desserts, and all of whom will join you for the five-martini lunch. Where are you going to go?"

"The Café at the kid's hospital in the new wing at Yale New Haven."

"Oh good, my depraved criminals are all pedophiles and will fit right in. Any reading on how the sleepover went?"

Her response, "Thumbs up all around. RBG says we need a third kid. I told her we would rent one of Arlow's girls."

I arrive, as always, at the parking lot at the back of the City Hall, from which I ascend with elegance, delivered by Big John and his Little Elevator.

I step out of the scissors/accordion door and am greeted by Jo, relying on extrasensory perception and unerring intuition, facing the other way with her million-dollar view of the Green, as she says, "The four Drug Executive folders from the Guatemalan Drug Bust are on the left side of your desk, for arraignment at 10:00. Ron, our wonder dog investigator, will bring in the usual suspects by 9:30. The judge's clerk called over with the ruling on the Whiting Motion to Suppress, granted, but the venerable Judge Stapleton denied your motion to dismiss. I called Whiting and told him, he is delighted, and expressed the hope you will invite him and his fiancée to the *Romeo and Juliet* Walk-Through mentioned in this morning's *Register* article (I am wondering, what article in the *Register*?)."

Jo goes on, unimpeded, "The article in the *Register* reports that Burbage is going to have a dry run Director's Walk-Through tomorrow at 7:00 PM on the revised Act V of Romeo and Juliet, where they live happily ever and anon, which he has 'ravaged and savaged' according to a cast member he kicked out, and that Burbage has invited all of the Montagues and Capulets plus anybody else that the cast and you, Francis Collins, specifically named, would like to invite; which should certainly include me, but not my husband, who told me in no uncertain terms that he would rather be found in the proverbial ditch with the proverbial insects than go to anything having to do with Shakespeare, a view I do not share.

"Our man D. Data will be in to discuss with you his findings with respect to Ms. Juliet, who is, he says, 'in grave danger' (I think, is there any other kind? Thank you, Jack Nicholson) as he indicated previously; and finally, our favorite client, Friar Laurence, used his one call from the city jail to ask that you get him out. (Out? Friar Laurence is in? How do these things happen?) Oh, and yes, the District Attorney, one (I love it when she does this) Edmund Coke, through a clerk in his office, called to say that he will be presiding at the monthly grand jury to consider a number of cases this morning at 11:30, and as previously indicated, he will be summoning our two favorite priests, do you want to appear with them?"

Here, Jo inhales, drawing the first breath since she began her delivery/panegyric back in the Pleistocene age, when I stepped off Little John's Big Elevator (wait, Jo has me dizzy, it's Big John's Little Elevator, that's it.) continues, "How was the dinner?"

I am not sure where to begin. But I begin with the obvious, "Great food, heavy conversation about Friar Laurence, he spent the night, we took the kids ... WHY IS FRIAR LAURENCE IN JAIL?"

"I can answer that," says D. Data as he steps off Big John's Little Elevator, which in gratitude and reciprocity bounces up approximately two feet with a huge sigh before settling and then sinking two floors below. It is always a miracle to me how John and Data and three bags of Dunkin' Donuts can all fit on the same

271

elevator, but they do; it must be that they are all three squishy, and I am thankful.

"Suppose you and your little friends join me in my office, and we will try to do justice to our justice system, as I am wont to say," I say, and turn, leading the way. Data follows, leaving a trail of powdered sugar in case he needs to return on a dark and stormy night.

We sit. I trust my genetically gifted high adrenaline, high functioning metabolism to get me through two of Data's doughnuts while he does four, and I ask, "Well?"

Data says, "Apparently, our Friar confronted a couple of high school kids, including a Hitler look-alike, marvelously named Otto Schmidt, plus a Drama grad student, I believe the Drama student is one, Tommy Belsky, at Hillhouse high school this morning and thrashed them. Security called the New Haven police, who had an alert that Friar Laurence was to keep away from the high school, and so they took him in. Further deponent knoweth not. All of this by benefit of our local right-wing talk radio host, who apparently has a relationship with Belsky."

I take time to utter a groan, being intimately familiar with these Aryan purists.

Data then continues from his previous assignment by saying, "I found very little on Friar Laurence in social media. However, the good Friar has been doing a lot of shopping online at places like Amazon, REI, and Crate & Barrel (Crate & Barrel?), and other trendy sites. Friar Laurence's name did appear interestingly in a number of high school blogs, in commentary on the coincidence between his name and that of the priest in *Romeo and Juliet*, as well as a few comments by the previously mentioned Hitler Look-Alike, Otto Schmidt, Aryan member of Joe Thomas' AP Civics class, who saw Laurence well represented by a certain public defender, who, in passing, it is said, had not sold his soul to the liberal/radical Deep State.

"So much for Friar Laurence on the Internet, but," Data goes on, "there were internet flashes not relating to the good Friar, pursued by Belsky, bearing upon the young lady, Juliet Capulet, who has the leading role in the local play." Data continued, "Over the past couple of weeks, a darker string has developed. It appears that Belsky had been romancing Juliet, a relationship she has recently ended. This event has appeared not only on Belsky and Juliet's Facebook pages but also Belsky's survivalist and Aryan purity websites, the connection being that he favors returning New Haven to the purity of a few decades ago, and she and Romeo are unfit, being of Mediterranean, namely Italian, extraction. When Belsky says 'pure,' he really means it.

Data was familiar with the details from today's article in the *Register*. As a good researcher, he laid five photocopies on my desk. "Here," he said, "I take it, Belsky, as we have learned to know and love him, lost it and tossed it, at least to the extent of getting himself tossed out of the play and out of Juliet's love life. As I just mentioned, Belsky had already ripped her in his other life, that is, other than being Juliet's boyfriend, as an American Nazi Survivalist creepoid, she being a rich snotty, Italian-American bitch. Ah yes, love, unrequited."

Ron Hoffer had joined us, and at this point said, "My few remaining friends on the Force tell me that Belsky has participated in a number of survivalist's 'sweep exercises,' living 'off the land' as they say, chiefly by stealing food and other goods from service stations and small groceries. They have also traced several guns and excessive amounts of ammunition to him. I checked them out—automatics and one Glock."

And while I am thinking, I do not want to know how Ron has identified Belsky's guns, I ask, "Has either of you found anything reflecting imminent plans?"

Ron responds, "Nothing specific." He pauses and says, "It's happened right here in Connecticut, you may recall, without warning, other than the kinds of things we have found, which they found later." Data interjects. "Sandy Hook, Elementary, Newtown, 28 dead, Bushmaster and Glock, December 14, 2012. Since then, on average, one per week, nationwide. I'm good at statistics."

I'm thinking, "Good" isn't quite the word for it, maybe "scary."

Ron continues, "I deny raiding Belsky's home, but I have raided his purchase and reading sites, and the literature he purchases fully supports the picture that I just described. I can raid his car if you like, since I no longer need a warrant, not being a police officer any longer. I would like that, a stroll down Memory Lane. No weapons, of course."

I lean back in my chair, hold up both hands, and think, that way lies disaster, and decline.

"Here's the thing," Data continued, "and my most serious finding. Over the last week, Belsky's blog and Facebook page have begun to focus on Burbage. Burbage has stayed with the two teenage high schoolers, who are Italian, not Aryan, and who Belsky thinks, to quote him, they represent 'all that's wrong with American hypocrisy, the two of them are rich Wops, and he's the son (meaning Belsky) of a marginal Polish plumber.'

"Most recently, this morning, he posted that he and his cadre have decided sacrifices must be made, even if they are on their part, that is, Belsky, Schmidt, and the third guy. He didn't say what "sacrifices" means, but at this level, it's possible they're talking death.

"Put it all together, and he thinks Romeo should die. And here it gets interesting; he means Romeo the teenage boy actor and Romeo the teenage theater figure. Both Romeos must die."

I say to the two of them, "Well done." And hoping against hope, "anything more?"

Ron responded, "Well, boss, I come to you with the very latest of the Greatest Hits of Tommy Belsky. Here it is. As of 8:15 this morning, Belsky, Schmidt, and one of their Camo friends decided to drop out of sight or, as they say, "go into deep cover" to advance their weapons training and to work on what they call a national strategy. This was on Belsky's Facebook page. They did not say anything beyond this, but the timing is such that I believe they will act either against tomorrow's dry run Walk-Through on Act V or on next week's performance of the play, totally revamped."

"Tomorrow seems a bit soon," I say. "Can they get their act together, forgive the pun?"

Data responded by saying, "Yes, it seems too soon, too fast, too much. On the other hand, they have been feeding their anger and paranoia for weeks, possibly months. Also, taking out Romeo and Burbage tomorrow night would make sense to Belsky since it might mean that in next week's final version of the play, Act V would revert to the original manuscript, God's truth, as Belsky sees it. Maybe he would even get a chance to die as County Paris before Romeo dies. Perverse justice."

Ron adds, "Organized is not a concept these punks have ever met, let alone mastered. All they need is a semiautomatic or automatic, some shades, heavy raincoats, and a dozen clips in the pocket. They don't even need an exit strategy, other than suicide by cop. Almost enough to make me want to go back on the job. To think they would wait until they get organized, well ..."

Ron continues, "I know this is far-fetched and highly unlikely, but I bet the families and police in Newtown, the day before Sandy Hook, would have moved heaven and earth for the kind of information we have right now. There might be 28 people still alive there."

I begin thinking about the Guatemalan Bust case on my desk coming up soon and say, "Okay, Data, download as much of this from the Internet as possible, assemble the materials in logical headings if they exist, and get three copies to me by 11:00 AM in the grand jury room. Arrange with outline headings, showing the progression we have just discussed. I will turn copies over to my favorite prosecutor, Edmund Coke, and his investigator, Seamus O'Connor. (Here, Ron Hoffer groans.) Also, Data, get copies to the parents of Romeo and Juliet as well.

"These folks are all going to wonder how this connects up with my client and what I do for a living—makes me wonder, too."

Data rises, shakes the customary sugary residue into his customary space on my floor, and with ponderous elegance and grace, disappears into the waiting room toward Big John's Little ... But first, he does one of his magical 180-degree pirouettes, putting his head back into my office and saying, "What about a copy to Belsky's parents? And Schmidt's? How about the principal of Hillhouse?"

"Yes, definitely." said I. And then, I add, "Especially Belsky's parents, if he ever had any, and if they were human."

Ron adds, "In which case, if they are human, they may favor suicide by cop."

As my final assignment, I turn to Ron and say, "Our favorite clergyman is in the slammer at the city jail, to be presented sometime this morning, probably at 10:00 AM with our Guatemalans. See if you can hunt him down, he may still be there or he may be in the lockup at the courthouse. Get a brief statement regarding what happened and tell him we will look for him when he's brought up into the courtroom. And Ron? Notify the Abbot, but I bet he already knows."

Ron gives me a partial salute, says he knows all, and is out the door.

I call to Jo, who comes into my office, where she hands me a file, saying, "Here's this morning's article from the *Register*. It's surprisingly long, but to the reporter's credit, she picks up on Burbage's view that history will be made right here in River City. There are quotes from the Capulet and Montague parents, saying how pleased they are that at long last, the play may have a happy ending, and they hope to have a large number of their families at tomorrow's walk-through. They think it will be wonderful for their children."

Yeah, right, I think, if they survive.

I note Jo prominently displays the fingernails she did yesterday with Dorothy Arlow. She never does this. The early morning sun is playing across the diamonds; I pause and then reach for the exact right note, saying, "Dazzling, simply dazzling."

Jo's smile lights up the room and the immediate neighborhood out to the Green, and she asks, "Did you notice Dorothy's?"

I reply, "Absolutely. But nothing could compare with yours."

Jo ratchets up dazzling by a factor of ten and says, "You know you got pretty good lines for a middle-aged, white suburban dude."

And with that, she pivots and swings out of my office. "You come too. No wedding dress," I say.

"Thank you, Francis Collins, JD.," comes the reply. Then, a pregnant pause, and somehow, absolutely, I know something else is coming, something special, worthwhile, wholesome. And it does.

Jo adds, "They did it."

I ask, "Who? What? Whereof speaketh thou?"

Comes the reply, "Them. They. Last night, or maybe early this morning, maybe several times."

"They.

"Did.

"It."

With that, I pick up my cell phone, and call the jail, to find out where Friar Laurence is held and on what cause. I am thinking: What if Dorothy Arlow was under 16? I answer myself: That would be crazy. So is everything else about this case ...

The phone rings through. The ancient jailer answers the ancient phone at the ancient jail, and being old friends with my father, and recognizing my voice immediately without my asking, simply says, "Your priest is on the bus to the lockup, to be presented at 10:00 AM arraignments. Did you know he's got a grand jury appearance at 11:00?"

I say, "Good to know. What's the charge?"

The answer, "Assault with a Deadly Weapon. It appears he attacked two victims named Belsky and Schmidt, plus a third kid, who were hassling a girl student, and hammered them. With his crucifix. I'm not shitting you."

With that, I say, "Mickey, you're an American treasure. By the way, what was bail?"

"None," Mickey adds, "interesting, him being a man of the cloth and all, you know what I mean?"

"Well," I say, "it's a different world from when you and I went to Sunday school, Mickey."

He replies, "You can say that again," which I decline to do.

And then he goes on, "By the way, your priest should have been a pickpocket."

"What do you mean?" I ask.

"The desk sergeant says he tried to print The Good Friar for the second time, and again, it didn't take. No prints."

"Well," I say, "tell him The Friar's lawyer had one thing to say to that."

"What's that?" Mickey asks.

"Tell him I said, reprint and thin no more."

"Huh, that's a very priestly thing to thay," says Mickey, and then he hangth up.

And with that, I descend quickly to street level, sprint at a good pace across the Green to the criminal court, ascend to the second floor for the General Criminal Session, and there I find Ron with the four Guatemalans. They are medium height, medium complexion, well-dressed, and give the sense of being physically powerful, making handguns unnecessary. They are part of the international narcotics traffic stream, in which they've played mid-level executive roles.

Ron and I have the good fortune to associate with these gentlemen only because they were picked up when they had no money. There, of course, will be money, so I am simply a way station along their journey through the American justice system. My function is to make sure they say nothing, they do nothing to jeopardize their liberty, or most especially, the liberty of the people at the next level or two up, and that no judge, of reasonable persuasion, unloads anger and outrage on them.

So, this is a stroll in the park, and a window onto another world, to mix my metaphors. Piece de gateau.

Ron and I explained to these four businessmen, he speaking Spanish, that we will appear in court, the charge has to do with conspiracy to transport huge amounts of narcotics in interstate, maybe international, commerce. We will enter pro forma not guilty pleas; they will say absolutely nothing. And here, Ron hammers the word "nada" three or four times, and they will be released on high cash bail paid by their superiors, or they will be picked up immediately by US marshals to appear later today in federal court or both. There, they will be treated as distinguished personages by the US Attorney in the hopes of turning them. They, of course, understand that if that happens, it will shorten their life expectancies to nada.

The clerk calls the cases, and the district attorney, the inestimable Jack Reilly, summarizes each file, saying that the charges are interstate transportation of narcotics, the judge observed that this is a federal case. Reilly and I both note that it may be true, but right now, we'd like to enter pleas and have the court set bail. Not guilty is the flavor of the month, and $500,000 per person is the bail du jour. Ron tells each, in Spanish, he will be held until either released or transferred to federal court by US Marshall.

With that, my work here is done. As we turn, from Reilly's side a suit approaches, somewhat shiny, somewhat worn, somewhat Fed. He intercepts my now former clients as the bailiff is leading them toward the lockup. From my side, another suit appears, not at all wrinkled, quite natty and nicely tailored, covering a vest, with an attaché case that cost considerably more than my Volvo, possibly even when it was brand-new, handing me a card, with the name embossed with which I'm familiar, saying that he would appreciate my investigator explaining to these gentlemen that from here on out he would be their attorney, and would I please confirm. Ron does, and I do.

The Fed figure then introduces himself, speaking Spanish, as a US Marshall, explaining they will now be transported to federal court, where the expensive suit will meet them. That this Mr. Collins will not see them again. The four Guatemalans smile and say "Gracias" to Ron and me.

I reply, "de nada," that being the extent of my Spanish, except for "dos cervezas, por favor," a very useful phrase, but not in the present setting.

As we turn to head for the grand jury at 11:00, I ask Ron, "Did you catch up with Friar Laurence?"

"Yes, indeed, I did."

"And did you find out what happened?" I ask.

"Oh yes, you're going to love this. Absolutely. It's really good. Tomorrow's headline in the *New Haven Register*? WWF (WORLD WRESTLING FEDERATION) SIGNS 400-YEAR-OLD FRIAR ..."

And with that, we are off to the grand jury room.

The grand jury sits in a different building, one with Grecian columns and marble stairs, hallways with brass light fixtures, and an elevator that can actually accommodate a number of people carrying briefcases and laptops. It would never have been called elegant, even in its finest years, but it did aspire to judicial seriousness and a certain sober respect for the law. Much of that has been lost in the time since September 11, when public buildings have been honeycombed and barricaded with security devices, gates, portals, and entries, with a maze of adjoining tables, deputy sheriffs, and the like. Still, it is a notch or three up from the ancient building where my Guatemalans were arraigned just a few minutes ago.

I proceed up the steps, through the swinging doors, put my attaché case on the table and walk through the magnetic security entry; on the other side, pick up the aforesaid case, and look for Ron. He and I connect; we go to the lockup, ask to speak with our client, Friar Laurence. A small smile plays across the deputy sheriff's face, who is working on a wisecrack, and says, "Go to the attorney conference room. I will bring him out."

This is uncommon efficiency. Friar Laurence has already been arraigned and scheduled for trial across the street on stalking and whatever. Those are misdemeanors, which should not be presented to a grand jury. But because of this morning's activity, he is now in court for what arguably could be a related crime. As Ron briefs me on the matter, it is clear that the District Attorney, Edmund Coke, sees the fracas with Tommy Belsky as related to the stalking of Romeo and

Juliet. Indeed, Juliet herself was on scene, as was Romeo. Is the stalking now a felony case linked to this morning's felony assault? It appears one of the "victims," Tommy Belsky, may have been badly hurt ...

If the case is now at the felony level, Edmund Coke can move it from the District Court to Superior Court, bypass a preliminary hearing and delay in the District Court, and try the case himself, increasing the penalty from a misdemeanor maximum of one year in County jail to 10 or 20 years in state prison. Moreover, by bringing witnesses before the grand jury, Coke can assemble his case while insulating it in grand jury records from my motions for disclosure. More, my client and I have no right to appear before the grand jury and argue against an indictment.

Friar Laurence is brought into the counsel conference room and uncuffed, whereupon he slumps into one of the tired, scuffed and filthy oak chairs, looking himself a little tired, scuffed and somewhat filthy, and says, "We have to stop meeting like this."

The deputy sheriff steps outside. Ron and I sit opposite the good Father, a gray steel Formica-topped rectangular table between us, with Ron's notes from the interview with Friar Laurence on a legal pad before me. I say, "Nice dinner last night. From Ron's notes, it looks as though you stayed a while." I smile, Friar Laurence smiles, Ron doesn't smile; he never does. "I was hoping for some leftovers, but this is not what I had in mind," I say.

I continue, "It looks as though Dorothy Arlow dropped you off this morning somewhere near Hillhouse high school on her way over to Yale New Haven Hospital, correct?"

Answer, "Yes. About 7:00 or so. I was going to walk to the Green, enjoy the spring flowers and contemplate the interesting and lovely turn my life has taken."

"And instead," I say, "it looks like destiny has taken a hand."

"It certainly does," replies Friar Laurence.

"Tell me about it," I replied, "and while we're doing this, have you had breakfast or coffee yet?"

"Yes, Mrs. Arlow was the perfect hostess."

I pause, no innuendo, so I continue, "So, she dropped you off in proximity to Hillhouse High School, somewhere near Sherman Avenue, about 7:00. What happened next?"

"I was walking along, following a stream of students as they parked their cars and went toward the high school when I heard voices shouting. I didn't pay much attention, but then as they became more strident, I looked in that direction, and I walked up that way half a block or so. The stream of students had converged around a pocket of four students, three males and one female, who was the center of the argument.

"A couple of the boys had army boots, all three were wearing fatigue pants, each was wearing a T-shirt with a political slogan, I didn't bother to notice what, and they were hassling the girl. As I drew closer, I heard her crying; 'Leave me alone, I don't want anything to do with you, go away; we are done.' At this point, I heard her mention Romeo's name, saying that if Tommy, the one who was bothering her, did not leave her alone, he was going to find himself in a lot of trouble with Romeo.

"It seemed to me that the young lady was Juliet, she was certainly attractive enough for the part, and the person harassing her, Tommy, was a former boyfriend, since he said, 'I am not going to let you break up with me and pick up with that greaseball.' He was older than the high school kids, looked like he might have graduated from college; he then used several ethnic slurs and reached out to grab Juliet's book bag as she turned toward the school. Two of her girlfriends rushed to her aid, one of the other two boys pushed them aside, as Juliet fell, he laughed at her.

"By this time, I was close enough to grab laughing boy, spin him around, and say, 'Seems to me you should be getting your ass up toward school right now, young man.'

"I am twice his size; he took that in and said, 'You may be right, Father.'

"I am always right," I said, turning to the second kid, dressed in Nazi clothes, with a little hank of black hair across his forehead and a smudgy little mustache under his nose, for all the world looking like a Hitler knockoff, and I said, "and that goes for you as well, head on in.' He just stood there.

"At this point, the older one named Tommy turned on me, and said: 'I've seen you in court; you are just another pedophile priest.'

"At this, I said, 'Fortunately for both of us, you're not my type, but if you touch that girl again, you'll find out exactly what kind of damage a pedophile priest can do.'

"He squared off in front of me, said 'Fuck off,' and moved as if to punch me."

I had been following Friar Laurence's account in the notes that Ron had taken earlier, and a question arose, "What were the other kids doing at this point?"

"They had been starting toward school," Friar Laurence said, "but they stopped, obviously interested, and formed a large circle around

Tommy and his juvenile Hitler friend and me. A couple of them said, 'Kick the shit out of them, Father.' I said to Tommy, 'Walk away.'

"He seems a person of limited mentation and only repeated what he had just said, stepping toward me with his right fist cocked and raised.

"I let Tommy throw his punch, stepped back, blocked it up and away with my left hand, and spun him around with my right, grabbed him by his shirt and the seat of his pants, and said, 'Time for you to head to school, sonny,' and I threw him in the direction of the front door, now somewhat obscured by the large group of students who had congregated, entertained, and laughing.

"He spun back toward me, said, 'That ain't my school,' and braced and threw a second punch, this one grazing my chin and becoming entangled in the chain and crucifix which my Order wears, substantial symbols made of hardy materials, and when he pulled back, scratched his wrist, which produced a small amount of blood. I have some here on my shirt. I heard a voice—I'm not sure from where—say, 'blood of Christ.' That produced a chorus of laughter.

"Tommy slipped and fell, rolled away from me, which showed good sense, bent over, and then seemed bewildered as he started to get up; there was blood on his T-shirt and his fatigue pants and a good deal of blood coming down his right arm. He had gone down with a scratch and come up with a sizable blood flow.

"Two campus security police officers had arrived by then, the crowd scattered, Tommy and his Hitler friend loudly informed the officers that I had attacked Tommy, they had asked what I was doing on campus, no religious recruiting allowed. I had pushed Tommy down, hitting or stabbing him with something.

"Juliet started to protest; the two girls who had been standing nearby said to her, 'let's get out of here. You don't need any more trouble with Belsky.' And they left quickly.

"One officer said to me, 'Are you here on campus on any official business?' I had to admit I was not, that I was simply intervening to try to break up an argument. Belsky and his friend claimed that they had observed campus regulations, and they wanted me arrested. The two police officers said that regulations were stringent, Zero Tolerance, or something like that, and required that they take any trespassers into custody, particularly when the trespasser had injured a student.

"At that, Belsky told them I was in court for stalking teenagers and had been ordered by Chief Justice Popham not to go near students, especially those in the high school play. One of the officers said, 'Well, looks like we need to call the New Haven PD.' One officer stayed to talk with the kids; the New Haven PD took me downtown, apologetically, and booked me. And here we are."

I sat back, looked back over Ron's notes; they coincided perfectly. I asked a couple of questions. "Was Romeo there? Did you see anybody named Romeo?"

"Yes, toward the end."

"Did you have a sharp object of any kind, which could have caused the cut?"

Friar Laurence hesitated and then said, "None that I can think of."

I turned to Ron and asked, "Did you look at the desk sergeant's Booking sheet, and what was the charge?"

"I think I put it in that report, Frank, and it was assault with a dangerous weapon. In the section to describe the weapon, there was simply a notation, 'not found.'"

"Well," says I, "there's a lot of that going around. Did they take the crucifix?"

Friar Laurence replied, "Yes, it is sizable, made of wood and metal, and it does have sharp edges. It may well have blood on it."

I turned to Friar Laurence and asked, "Was it in your hand? Did you use it as some form of knife or weapon?"

"No," replied Friar Laurence, perking up for the first time this morning and saying, "No, we leave that for the Baptists and Evangelicals. The crucifix was hanging, and Belsky got entangled with it, pulled away hard, and cut himself."

"So," say I, "a morning stroll becomes a felonious assault, once again with a phantom weapon, in violation of terms of release on a stalking case, now linked to a fracas involving Juliet and her former boyfriend. It doesn't get much weirder than this!

"One thing is clear; Edmund Coke will use this incident to leverage you out of District Court and into Superior Court and to use the grand jury to gather his witnesses and testimony in a manner protected from our defense discovery. He'll go for a felony indictment from the grand jury, which always grants them, and the maximum you face goes from one year county time to ten or more in state prison."

"So, Francis, is there any good news in all of this?" says Friar Laurence.

"Well," I said, "there is this. Our prosecutor friend, Edmund Coke, did the very predictable thing, according to the docket, and charged you with felony assault with a dangerous weapon, with companion counts of stalking and violation of terms of release."

"And the good news is?" asks Friar Laurence.

"Oh, that," I replied, "according to the docket, our assistant DA this morning is Kathleen Chung."

"So?" From Friar Laurence.

"Well," I opine, "The grand jury will hate her. Nobody likes her. I should modify that statement, nobody, except me. She and I get along great. That's good news."

"I had some special plans for tonight," said Friar Laurence.

"Don't give up hope," said Ron, "Francis here has been known to work magic or something close to it."

"I pay Ron to make statements like that," I said, "so he will be the one who gets sued for malpractice, not me. Let's go."

We knock on the door, the deputy sheriff appears and says to Friar Laurence that he "won't need cuffs, just please don't make a break for the altar. Or," and here he grins, "hit me with your crucifix."

We turn to our left, go across the balcony to the doors labeled grand jury. Inside we find our assistant District Attorney, the Dragon Lady, Kathleen Chung. As the name suggests, she is of Asian descent, probably Chinese, but emphatically Chinese-American. The reference to her as a "Dragon Lady" could, of course, be a racist slur, but it is more an appellation of respect and would probably apply even if she were of Irish, Italian, or Brazilian or any other descent, since it more encapsulates her style than her genetic composition. She is bright, quick, relentless, takes no prisoners, and loves leaving a courtroom floor quivering in the flesh of her opponents. In addition, she is tall, slim, dressed to the nines (whatever that means) at all times in fine business suits and heels, told me once that she makes her own clothing, getting up at 5:00 AM and stitching until 7:00, no longer takes continuing legal education courses because she teaches most of them, and is probably headed for a State Supreme Court appointment. Soon. Perhaps tomorrow.

With all of that, going up against her can be fun. Whether she will be fun this morning remains to be seen.

Kathleen smiles when she sees Ron and me; Kathleen always smiles, "Francis and Ron, the Katzenjammer Kids (I never knew where she got that), always a pleasure, particularly when you are representing clergy. How did that happen? Are you doing penance"?

"We got lucky. How does this get before the grand jury?" I ask

"I wondered the same thing," Kathleen answers, "until I saw the amended bill of indictment, revised at about 10:30, only a few minutes ago, and sent over from the office, with a copy for you. Here it is."

"Thanks," I say, "Good of you to give us so much time to prepare," pausing, "there does seem to be a felony count here, assault with a deadly weapon. Is that what you are presenting this morning?"

Kathleen responds, "That, the stalking, and violating terms of release, since it seems the good Friar, or is he a father (oh my, I have made a little funny there) was hanging around the schoolyard and assaulted several students, leaving one in blood.

"Since we have a grand jury readily at hand, and since your client and you have no right to appear, there's no reason not to get it wrapped up right before lunch. The two campus officers are here as well as the victim, Tommy Belsky, who is a Yale grad student and a member of the cast of *Romeo and Juliet*, and his two high school friends."

"Well," I rejoined, "all you need for a winning hand is two more cards since the victim was the aforementioned Juliet, as witnessed by her two friends." Kathleen observes, again with a smile, "I see no need to call them; it would only muddle my case, which otherwise should only take 15 minutes or less. It's a slam dunk. Not that grand jury hearings are ever very difficult."

The last point is well taken. Grand juries are the black hole in the criminal justice system. They consist of 12 to 20 jurors, they only hear the evidence the prosecutor presents, the suspect or defendant is not in the room, nor is the defense attorney nor is a judge. The prosecutor presents an accusation, called a "bill" of indictment, and invariably the grand jury returns a "true bill." Next case.

Throughout American history, grand juries have on occasion run amok and done good things. Sometimes, very rarely, on their own, they bring down corrupt city administrations. Sometimes they take on organized crime. They may even help in investigating foreign interference in American elections.

This is perhaps the most important function; a grand jury is sometimes not used for charging purposes but for investigation. With the prosecutor issuing subpoenas, grand juries can compel witnesses to come in and testify in complex cases, such as conspiracy, organized crime, governmental corruption, and the like. It becomes a tool for laying the groundwork prior to filing charges, building a case, and bringing the indictment.

But most of the time, it is a routine rubber stamp of routine cases, made particularly easy for the prosecutor since only a majority vote is required and rules of evidence are relaxed. Oftentimes, no witnesses are called, and the district attorney simply reads from the police reports.

As I say, this is a black hole in the system, of use to the prosecution, rarely to the defense.

So, I propose to Kathleen a deal. She, at this point, is shuffling today's files on the counsel table; she has 15 cases to present, each a slam dunk, a modest agenda, and expects to be done by lunch or 12:30 (about five minutes to the case) at the latest. In half of these, witnesses will not even appear. The last thing she wants is complication.

Kathleen turns to me and says, "Francis, the last thing I want is complication."

I reply, "I know that. In fact, I just thought that.

I say, "What I propose is that you question the supposed victim, Tommy Belsky; we stipulate the statements of his two friends and only question Juliet Capulet, plus one of the three girls whom the Friar was rescuing. I will do my usual slashing, obtrusive cross-examination."

Here, Kathleen interjects, "You never cross-examine, Francis. It's not your thing. Everybody knows that."

"Well ... (I do not finish the sentence). In return, Friar Laurence will testify, and you can cross-examine, we both get witnesses we could not get otherwise, and the rules of evidence are relaxed. You and I sum up, you get your indictment, and you provide us a copy of the transcript."

Ron is standing off to the side, smiling. He is thinking, "Nobody ever does this."

Kathleen says, "Nobody ever does this. I can get my indictment without any of this."

I reply, "Maybe. But, if you take my offer, you get my client on the record, no Fifth Amendment bar. If not, I'll take an interim appeal, lack of due process, and denial of the right to be present and cross-examine."

Kathleen replies, "You will lose."

"Perhaps," I say, "but it will create a lot of work for you, and you will never examine my client, ever."

Kathleen smiles; it is a winning smile, the kind a shark smiles when passing tuna casserole at a church supper, then says, "Let me shuffle through these 15 dead soldiers, and think about this while getting rubber stamp indictments, and call you during lunch hour. It sounds interesting. What are you hiding? Francis." She smiles. "You're hiding something."

I am hiding something. She smiles. I smile. We both know we are going to do it.

Ron and I go back to get Friar Laurence out of the lockup, taking him into the conference room and recapping the arrangement I have proposed. Friar Laurence appears more buoyant and seems to be wearing well, having heard five confessions, in a hastily segregated filthy corner of the filthy lockup, where he heard some filthy stories, which he does not relate to us. Thank heavens for penitent clergy privilege.

He has also been asked to perform a gay marriage, obviously by a couple unacquainted with the quaint idiosyncrasies of Friar Laurence's particular denomination. He is thinking of doing it.

The Abbot joins us, and after I recap the proposal once again, he asks the same question Ron was thinking, "What is in this for us?"

"It is a gamble," say I, "since we are laying Friar Laurence open to broad cross-examination. The usual limits don't apply in a grand jury proceeding. But we would be getting the Dragon Lady to bring in and let us question witnesses who we would have difficulty running down, such as Juliet and her two friends, plus Tommy and his two friends, whom she probably would not otherwise bring before the grand jury.

So, this is all good stuff, what lawyers call "discovery," not usually available at grand jury for a defense attorney.

And there is the thing that Kathleen accused me of "hiding." It is this. There is an outside chance of defeating the indictment; my hope is that Kathleen's abrasive personality and Belsky's abrasive, diseased persona will alienate the grand jury. Add to this, allowing Friar Laurence to make a statement. I have heard Friar Laurence speak, and I have heard the Dragon lady speak, and the grand jury will love Friar Laurence.

My cell phone rings, it is the Dragon Lady, she says "Francis, it's a deal, 2:00 PM, if you insist, I put on Belsky and Juliet Capulet; we stipulate into the record the other witnesses from their police statements. The Friar testifies, I cross and we both sum up for ten minutes. Incidentally, one of the kids found a steak knife with blood on the ground. The lab is doing printing and matching. If the Forensics Tech and the results are done in time, I will put him on, and you can cross.

"Deal?

"Deal," I confirm.

"You never disappoint," says the Dragon Lady. "I'm going to my favorite Chinese food truck over near the Hospital. I'll bring you back Szechuan ginger beef. Mild, medium, or hot?

"Hot. I like it hot," I say.

I hear her smile on the phone.

The Abbot, Friar Laurence, and Ron have all heard Kathleen. There is concern about the knife. I say, "Not to worry. By now, even if the knife was yours, we know that your prints won't show. We also know that, most likely, the knife is from the high school cafeteria, and I will ask Juliet if she has seen knives like this, where, and are they commonly available in the cafeteria? Conclusion: the knife was picked up by some high school kids and passed off to Belsky. Maybe Juliet can tell the grand jury whether he tried to slash his wrists on other occasions when they were dating."

It is now 12:30. I say to Friar Laurence, "I will prepare an outline of talking points for your opening testimony, but it will not be word for word. We will count on your experience over the decades as a speaker to carry the jury to the proper conclusion. Under cross-examination, be warm, be winning, be upset, but not petty or angry, and the grand jury will absolutely want to cut you loose.

Where are you from, where are you going, what are you doing here? Simply answer truthfully, you don't know.

Does any of us truly know the answers to those questions?

"Folks," I say, "we are about to make history ... One more time. It is déjà vu ...," and here I pause, with practiced assurance, for Ron to say, "All over again!" Which he does, Yogi Berra being his favorite philosopher. The deputy sheriff comes for Friar Laurence, Ron and I head back to the office, I tell him to pull together two pages, no more, of outline bullet points presenting Friar Laurence's testimony for me to review before we go back to the grand jury room.

Jo brings in a Dunkin' coffee and two cannoli, very clearly not from Dunkin', says she's having lunch with Dorothy Arlow. I raise my eyebrows quizzically; she says she never kisses and tells. I raise my eyebrows again ... Well, okay, maybe she tells ... But this time, she doesn't.

Just another lunch break at the office. The cannoli can go in the fridge, I prefer Kathleen's Chinese. Hot. I like it hot.

CHAPTER TWENTY-FIVE
THE DEN OF THE DRAGON LADY
BYE-BYE BELSKY

Ron brings in the talking points for Friar Laurence's testimony, basically referring to his Dominican Order experience, the time he is spending in New Haven, how he happened to be walking past the high school when the fracas broke out, and what he did. If he is asked about some of the stranger aspects of his New Haven experience, he should answer honestly and simply that he does not know. For example, how did you get here? Where do you go from here? What is your purpose here? Who will win tomorrow's Red Sox/Yankees game ...

Ron and I return to the grand jury room, review the talking points with Friar Laurence and the Abbot, gather up our client, and he and I enter the grand jury room for what is my first visit within a grand jury room as a participant, so to speak, in active proceedings. The Dragon Lady greets us, points us to counsel table, and tells us to sit; we sit.

Eighteen jurors, good and true, we hope, are brought in by the deputy sheriff and seat themselves. There is no questioning of them; they are sworn again and reminded that they had been sworn previously; they are familiar with Kathleen since she presented 15 dead soldiers to them this morning. There is no judge to direct the proceedings, to rule on objections, to chastise me. That is a good thing.

The room itself is clearly not a courtroom. There are high, narrow windows, a high ceiling, overhead Victorian lights dropped by cables or chains, the oak paneling and wainscoting of a courtroom, but there is no bench for the judge since there is none presiding. Still, there are oak tables and a witness box, a place for a court reporter, a deputy sheriff.

While Kathleen is assembling herself, looking through her file, sharpening her teeth, I turn to Friar Laurence and say that it is important to relax, to be himself. Certainly, when he makes his initial presentation, that will be easy. He should answer questions in a confident, not dismissive, way.

"Francis," Friar Laurence says, "you saw me on Sunday?"

I nod.

He continues, "Was I good?"

I nod, "You were great."

"I will be great again. And modest." He smiles. He is a performer.

Kathleen Chung smiles. She goes on the attack. She gets quickly and indignantly into her argument, addressing the grand jury, saying, "This is an unusual case, but not difficult. This man is a Catholic Priest and after Sunday's mass, was heard by our chief prosecutor, Edmund Coke, to say that he wasn't sure why he is in New Haven or where he goes from here, but he is afraid that he will commit harm while he is here. His name is identical to the priest in *Romeo and Juliet*, which is in production, as you may know, with opening night set a week from this Saturday. Coincidence? Perhaps.

"Our chief prosecutor Coke approached Friar Laurence after the mass to ask whether he knew that the two actors in the lead roles are from the Montague and Capulet families. The good Friar said he was unaware of the production. Many of you will recognize those family names from two long-standing New Haven businesses, Montague Ferrari And Foreign Auto Dealership and the Capulet Funeral Home And Family Eternal Rest Service. Some of you will also recognize they are the family names in *Romeo and Juliet*."

"Coincidence? Perhaps."

Here, Chung's voice began to drip acid.

"Consider also, this. Friday a week ago, at a local watering hole for prosecutors and defense attorneys, Morrie's, my opponent here, Francis Collins, after having had perhaps a few too many, indiscreetly said to, among others, Edmund Coke, he had been delayed by a potential new client, who appeared from nowhere, had given what seemed bogus addresses, and sought defense services, for homicide, which was as yet uncommitted. That man is Friar Laurence, here before you today. His character by the same name in the play caused deaths ..."

"Coincidence?"

And now the Dragon Lady's fist pounded the table, and her voice rose in indignation as she said, "I don't think so."

"Finally, you will hear testimony that Friar Laurence attacked Tommy Belsky at Hillhouse High School this morning. Tommy was a member of the *Romeo and Juliet* cast, and he was talking with the girl playing Juliet, Juliet Capulet. You will hear Tommy and Juliet and their friends testify this afternoon. They may disagree. But this much is clear: Friar Laurence, in a hearing before Chief Justice Popham two days ago, had been ordered to stay away from the high school and the members of the cast, as condition of bail, an order he willfully violated this morning, and, a further violation, he assaulted Tommy Belsky, leaving him bleeding on the ground.

"And so, ladies and gentlemen of this grand jury, the charges in the bill of indictment are willful violation of a lawful court order, a felony; assault with a dangerous weapon, a second felony; and stalking, ordinarily a misdemeanor, but a felony when done with felonious intent. Frankly, I hope you will be as indignant as I.

"Over the past 10 to 15 years, child abuse and pedophilia by clergy have been endemic and rampant in this nation. Such cases are hard to prove. They require a pattern of seemingly random acts and frightened victims which, all too often, come forward only years after the crime. Here, the pattern has been developing over the past week and through the excellent initiative of our prosecutor's office, we have a chance to intervene before the event. Before this defendant, having come to New Haven because of the unique, highly incriminating set of circumstances developing here, as I say, while he is still stalking these children, you have a chance to indict him and lock him up before he commits whatever crime it is that brought him here ..."

Kathleen Chung's voice rang through the grand jury room; it seemed almost capable of swaying the overhead lamps, of rattling the tall windows. She had been standing in front of the grand jury box, her hands on the rail, now she spun quickly, pointing at Friar Laurence, and added, "which I fear, sadly and strongly, is homicide!"

She paused, then strode in her carefully controlled manner, back to her counsel table, and as I rose to respond, quickly confronted me and said, "I am not done!" Each word hammered and spaced like a nail gun. Again, she paused, then turned back to the grand jury, and said, "Let me close by reminding you of what you already know.

"At this point, we do not need to persuade you to a unanimous vote by proof beyond a reasonable doubt. The nature of this case and your work is such that necessary proof may only emerge later. For right now, all you need to do is find by a majority vote that there is probable cause to return an indictment to hold this defendant for trial, at which time the standard will be proof beyond a reasonable doubt."

Here, she paused, and then in a low, measured, emphatic voice, said, "Which we will prove. For right now, I hope you will agree, what I have summarized will constitute more than enough probable cause to hold this man for trial on the felonies charged. For the sake of the children, of their parents, I pray you, return a True Bill. Thank you."

And with that, Kathleen Chung sat down. Friar Laurence leaned toward me and said, "By the robe of St. Francis, she is awfully good. I'm ready to convict me right now."

I said, "She rarely loses. But she has never met me or you in a grand jury room, so her record is about to be broken. I have set up a trap for her. In case she missed it, I will lead with it in my opening statement." With that, I stood and opened with that very same, brief statement.

"Ladies and gentlemen of the grand jury, this is an unusual moment in an unusual case. My client and I have agreed, which is almost never done, for the defendant to testify to the grand jury. He asked and I agreed, because his story is unusual and it needs to be told, and Friar Laurence himself is best able to tell you that story. But since you will first listen to the prosecution's case, please keep this much in mind." Here I stood centered before the grand jury, some distance from the rail.

"Friar Laurence is here in New Haven as a guest of the Dominican Order, in which he was ordained a long time ago. The Abbot thinks highly enough of him to ask that Friar Laurence hear confessions and deliver sermons, one of which he delivered this past Sunday, ironically castigating the Catholic Church for its failure to protect children from the clergy, the very crime Ms. Chung accuses my client of. If he is the malevolent pedophile she suggests, would the Abbot take him in? Have him do confessions? Deliver sermons? Consider the Abbot's trust before you mistrust Friar Laurence." Here, I move to the right-hand side, in close, speaking to one-third.

"Next, this past Sunday, after the mass, standing on the lawn outside the church, in conversation, what Ms. Chung reports as being overheard was, in fact, said by Friar Laurence. He is afraid that he will do harm at some point, what, he does not know. Similarly, when he came to me, it was for defense services for charges as yet not filed, possibly homicide. He does not know. He found himself at the Abbey here in New Haven a week or so ago, unclear as to how he got here; again, he does not know." Now I moved to my left, to the middle section of the grand jury, and address them.

"Is this the pattern of a man stalking children? The web of lies of an evil man? Or is it, as you will hear, the truth of a man seeking his purpose and meaning in life? If he were evil, it would be easy to lie. Instead, the truth is, he is what the Abbot calls, a seeker, a traveler, frequently guests at the Abbey. He does not know the endpoint. That is what he seeks."

And now it was to the left third of the grand jury, and my movement and varying delivery kept them all involved.

"What Friar Laurence does know is that this morning he was on his way to the Abbey, walking and enjoying a fine spring day when he heard voices raised in heated argument. He went to see if he could help, found he was at Hill House High School, saw a boy strike a girl, knock her down, and intervened. There were three young men against him, and he prevailed. In the process, one of them, Tommy Belsky, cut himself on the Friar's heavy wood and metal crucifix, but Belsky later claimed that he was cut by a steak knife." I stepped back some eight to ten feet from the rail, centered myself for the closing.

301

"That is, it, in a nutshell." And here I paused, took a drink of water, raising my voice to make sure all of the jurors were awake and heard me. "We deny that Friar Laurence willingly violated a court restraining order, deny that he assaulted Tommy Belsky, and deny that Friar Laurence is here stalking anyone. He did not even know that the play was in rehearsal, to be performed in a week." And here, I attempted to match Kathleen Chung's oratorical skills, but probably failed, "What you will hear is from a man seeking the world over, for meaning and a resolution of his life. Such a person does not belong in a jail cell; he belongs at liberty to continue his search.

"Thank you." And with that, I sat down and turned to Friar Laurence and said, "Well?"

He replied, "Francis, me lad, let's just say if this is a relay race, you kept us in contention. Well done. Now it is up to me."

"That, and maybe a little skillful cross-examination on my part and, and, maybe, just maybe, they are tired of being a rubber stamp for the prosecution."

Having overheard that last part, Kathleen leaned over, smiling, and said, "Not with me entertaining them, Francis."

With that, the Dragon lady stood, rising to her full five-foot-ten with three-inch spike heels, and said, "We will call our first witness, Tommy Belsky, to the stand, and I will ask the clerk to swear him in as a witness."

As this was happening, I turned to Friar Laurence and said, "She is taking a chance. One of Belsky's friends might have been a better choice. You only get one chance to make a first impression. The jury will hate this kid. This is the trap."

The rules of evidence and interrogation are relaxed in a grand jury, so Kathleen Chung said, "Mr. Belsky, please tell the jury in your own words, what happened between you and Friar Laurence this morning, and start with where you were."

"Well, I'm usually called Tommy, if that's okay with you. I was talking with my girlfriend, Juliet Capulet, just before classes were to start at about 7:45. A couple of my friends and a couple of her friends were there, and we got into an argument about what happened the night before." He paused.

"Tell us about that," said Kathleen Chung.

"Glad to. We are in the cast of Romeo and Juliet at the Yale Drama School, where I am a grad student, and the Director, Professor Burbage, had what he calls a 'Director's Overview,' where the director tells anyone interested what he thinks he's doing.

"So, this guy Burbage ..."

Kathleen Chung interrupted and said, "Do you mean Professor Burbage, who is on the faculty of the Yale Drama School?"

"Yeah, that's him," said Belsky, "I am in my second year for the Master of Fine Arts, and him and me have had a number of classes and a number of arguments."

"Go on," said Kathleen Chung. She turned and made eye contact with me. I raised my eyebrows, doing my best imitation of the Abbot. I am not sure what she wanted.

"Yeah, well, he's talking along and saying; basically, he's going to scrap most of what Shakespeare wrote and substitute his own ideas." Kathleen Chung sees that she has made a mistake, turning Belsky loose instead of keeping him on a short leash and talking about the incident this morning.

She says, "I wonder if you could get back to the point, Mr. Belsky; what happened this morning?"

"Well," Belsky says, clearly pissed, "this is the point. This is what it's all about. Juliet and me were arguing this morning because last night she took Burbage's side, where he's going to make sure that these kids live, Romeo and Juliet, when Shakespeare decided 400 years ago that they should die. That's why it's called a tragedy; do you get it?" And with that, he leans forward toward Kathleen Chung.

Friar Laurence leans toward me, and murmurs, "This is very interesting. I see the trap."

Kathleen Chung is now trying to get her witness back on track and take back control of her case, but the kid keeps going, saying, "So when he said this, I just said no way! Shakespeare wrote the play, and we have to perform it his way. Romeo is responsible for killing half a dozen people and lying to Juliet's parents and marrying an underage kid, and he deserves to die. I may have called Burbage an effing idiot. At this, he blew up."

"One last bit on this, and then it's back to what happened this morning, so wrap it up," says Kathleen Chung. She is not a person to be crossed, but Belsky does not understand this.

Belsky says, "I don't know what you mean by wrap it up, but I can tell you that what happened was I told Burbage that Romeo must die, and Burbage told me to get off the set, that I was out of the cast, and when I tried to walk out with Juliet afterward, since we had been, you know, a couple, she told me it was over. She said that she's in love with Romeo. Which is just plain fucking nuts; I mean, he's just a high school jerk-off."

I have seen runaway witnesses highjack a case, but at this point, only if Kathleen Chung had been Mother Teresa would I have thrown her a life preserver. The Dragon Lady drew herself to her full height, and apologized to the grand jury for her witness's choice of language, and then turned to Belsky and said in as direct and flat voice as possible, "Return to this morning. You were having an exchange with Juliet Capulet."

"Well, that's what it was. I wanted to make up to her this morning. I thought she owed me an apology. She refused to talk or apologize and turned away, walking toward the school. I reached out to grab her, got her by the purse, and she fell."

Clearly, Kathleen had not had a chance to interview this witness or review his statement. It would have been best to get him offstage as quickly as possible, but instead, she asked, "Did you push or shove her or cause her to fall in any way? Was it intentional?"

Ooooops!

"Well, since I'm under oath, I guess you might say, yeah, I didn't want her to turn away from me, she had basically kicked me to the curb last night, and she was doing it again this morning, and so yeah I kind of shoved her and she fell. But you know stuff happens." And Belsky shrugged his shoulders, opened his hands, looked to the grand jury as though they would understand, even if this dense district attorney did not.

I turned to Friar Laurence and said, whispering, "Okay. She has a choice. Get this clown off the stand and come in with one of his two friends to patch it up, or go on and have him testify about the confrontation with you. Without that, there's no assault with a dangerous weapon. Personally, I would get him off the stand."

Friar Laurence replied softly, "This is very interesting. It's like you are writing a play as you're performing it."

At this point, Kathleen does the opposite of what I would've done and says to Belsky, "Tell us what happened concerning Friar Laurence."

"Yeah, well, okay, I was wondering if you were ever going to get to that." Belsky is all righteous attitude now, "He comes heaving up the school lawn, old guy badly out of shape, grabs one of my lieutenants, spins him on toward the school, sends him on his way, tries the same with the second kid, Otto Schmidt, and is about to do that with me, when I squared off on him, and he saw that he had his hands full. We exchanged words, I told him to fuck off, and then I took a swing at him cause he blocked my way. My hand caught the chain with his crucifix, heavy wood and metal, cut badly, as you can see," and here Belsky held up his left arm wrapped at the wrist with a heavy bandage, "the doctor had to stitch and wrap me up.

"A couple of the campus policemen came up, asked what was going on, my lieutenants and I said this priest had attacked us, we were just asking whether he was trying to evangelize on the campus, against the rules, when he took a swing at me. When they got his name, they connected it to the case where he was told to stay away from the high school and the cast, so they called the New Haven PD who took him downtown. That's it."

Kathleen Chung asked, "Who swung first?" Mistake.

"Well, I guess maybe I did," said Belsky, "but it was because he blocked my way and shoved me. He's a pretty big guy, but I'm not so small myself either, and I had to defend myself."

"So, you were acting in self-defense?"

"Yeah, I guess you could kinda say that I don't know what else I could of done. After my hand hung up on the chain, he grabbed me, and we tangled, and I could feel a knife cut my wrist, and that's when the campus police came up."

"I couldn't believe it; they apologized to him."

"Mr. Collins, I have no further questions. Do you wish to inquire?"

I was so delighted with Belsky's performance, I thought, as usual, to ask no questions. I turned to Friar Laurence and said, "I think this guy just imploded and maybe blew up her case. We have the knife thing covered later, so I'm inclined to ask no questions."

Friar Laurence said, "I think we are way ahead of the game. But maybe you could put a ribbon on this present."

I paused, then said, in response to Kathleen Chung's invitation, "Maybe one or two."

I rose, said to the grand jury, "Ladies and gentlemen, as Ms. Chung is aware, I am renowned for asking almost no questions on cross-examination. But I do have one or two of Mr. Belsky.

"You refer to your two friends as 'lieutenants,' do they help you in some organization or group?"

"Yeah, they're sort of junior members in a patriotic group I lead. We put America first. We are originalists, like with our flag and immigration and that Shakespeare stuff."

"Without too much detail, is it fair to say that you believe in defending Second Amendment rights and the Constitution against minorities and left-wing radicals?"

"Yeah, that, and keeping our population pure, plus a lot more."

I looked at the interracial grand jury, and Kathleen Chung, and turned back to Belsky, and ask, "So, let's suppose that the forelady of the jury over here, or Ms. Chung, the Prosecutor, wore a Muslim burka or a Sikh turban would she qualify as a twofer?"

Belsky got angry, pretending not to understand, and said, "What are you getting at?"

At this point, Kathleen Chung rose and said, in measured tones, "Mr. Collins, I hope you're not going to explore this too much."

"No, thank you, Ms. Chung; I believe that is enough."

I then asked, "Prior to last night's exchange with Juliette Capulet, had you and she had a falling out?

"Depends upon what you mean," said Belsky.

"Had she said the two of you were done, she didn't want to see you?"

"Oh yeah, but she had said that lots of times, and she never meant it."

"And then last night, after the walk-through and Burbage had kicked you off the cast, did she tell you again, that you and she are through?"

Here, Belsky, getting clearly and visibly agitated, replied, "Yeah, but as I just told you, I mean you're a little slow on this Mr. Collins, she didn't mean it. She's just a kid."

I could see Kathleen Chung becoming nervous, and I decided to wrap it up, "And so you went after her again this morning? I mean, Mr. Belsky, how many times must a young woman tell you to get lost before it finally registers that she really, really has ended it and does not want to see you again?"

Belsky leaned forward and said, "I guess I know her mind better than she does."

With that, I turned to make certain that the grand jury was following this, and took a drink of water, looked at Friar Laurence, who gave me a slight nod, and I went in for the kill.

"So, tell me, Mr. Belsky, when you went to Hillhouse High School this morning, how could you be sure that Juliet Capulet would be there? Did you go by her house first?"

"Yeah, I did. I didn't want to waste my time," retorted Belsky.

"And then followed her?"

"Yeah, in my car, slowly." he laughed.

"You are not a student at the high school, are you?"

"Not in ten years," Belsky laughed again, "I went to the University of Southern Connecticut majoring in theater, and I'm in my second year at the Yale Drama school. I have a successful career going, and it doesn't involve being a high school student."

"So, you are maybe ten years older than Juliet Capulet?" And here I turned and directed the rest of my questions facing the grand jury, "You followed her to school knowing that she didn't want to see you and had made that plain several times over the preceding days, and you grabbed her and knocked her to the ground, wouldn't you say, isn't it fair to say," and here I turned back directly to Belsky and accused him, "that it is you who was stalking Juliet Capulet and not Friar Laurence and this morning he stopped you from committing a crime?"

Here Belsky got out of the witness chair, confronting me, and shouted, "Crime? She loves me, I love her, and that ain't stalking. Lovers pursue each other. Stalking is what that priest over there did," pointing at Friar Laurence.

And with that, I turned my back toward the witness, facing the grand jury, and said, low and slow, "Oh yes. That's right. Friar Laurence was stalking Juliet Capulet this morning when he sent your two high school flunkies off to school and prevented you from hurting her further. No, Mr. Belsky, it is you who should be charged here with stalking, not Friar Laurence."

With that, Belsky slumped back in the witness chair, and I said to Kathleen Chung, "I have no further questions, but would like to thank Mr. Belsky for his time. He has been very generous."

He caught the irony that I hadn't tried to suppress and turned to the district attorney and said, "That's it? This pedophile knifes me at the high school, and this is all I get?"

"No," said Kathleen Chung, "there is one other thing you get; you get the door. Will the bailiff please show Mr. Belsky to the hallway? Thank you."

CHAPTER TWENTY-SIX

SAYONARA DRAGON LADY

NO TRUE BILL

As Belsky exited the grand jury, furious, bent on vengeance, District Attorney Chung desperately maintained her renowned calm, seeking to regain control of her case, and told the grand jury that she proposed to call Mr. Belsky's two friends, to corroborate his story from this morning. I stood and said to the grand jury that counsel frequently stipulate, when possible, to what testimony would say, and so, "If Ms. Chung is agreeable, we will stipulate that she may simply provide you the lieutenants' testimony by their police statements." This, of course, had been our agreement, and I did not want Kathleen to weasel out of it.

I could see the wheels turning in Kathleen's head; if these were strong character witnesses, she would lose their benefit, but what was the likelihood any friend of Belsky's would have any character at all? And she hadn't prepped them but knew they were two junior grade Nazis. And so, Kathleen Chung agreed to stipulate and provide the grand jury with the written statements.

With that, as her next witness, she called Juliet Capulet, who was ushered into the grand jury room and quickly sworn.

Juliette Capulet was everything Central Casting could have hoped for. Pretty, perhaps beautiful, in a dark Italian sort of way. Only a junior in high school, so still developing, but she already had the sweeter attributes of Al Pacino's love in Italy in the Godfather or of Olivia Hussey, perhaps the first teenager cast as Juliet, in the film by Franco Zeffirelli. It was clear that this Juliet already had the presence of an accomplished actress, say Cher in *Moonstruck*, and one could understand why she had been cast for a performance at the Yale Drama School.

Kathleen Chung knew that if this witness turned out well, the indictment was easily within reach. She began by saying to Juliet that we had just finished hearing from Tommy Belsky, to the effect that last night they had a falling out and that this morning, at the high school, he had pursued this subject and her further, and he had then had a fight with Friar Laurence, the Defendant, sitting over here. Was all this true? Yes, she answered. Would she please elaborate?

Juliet was happy to do so. She said that this morning at Hillhouse High School, she and her two friends were on their way to class when Tommy Belsky approached her. He, of course, had no business being there since he was not a student and was there simply to speak with her. He said he was still upset about last night's encounter with Professor Burbage at the Directors Overview and by her refusal to leave with him, although she had broken off their relationship at least a week ago. She had refused to apologize this morning and turned to leave when he grabbed her by the arm, then the strap of her purse, and had forced her to the ground. She cannot quite recall whether she slipped or he pushed or both, but she went down, and one of his two friends began laughing at her.

Kathleen Chung attempted to minimize the amount of force, but it was clear that Juliet was upset and hurt. She then attempted to have Juliet describe the encounter with Friar Laurence coming on the scene quickly and with force, Juliet confirmed Belsky's description that Friar Laurence had sent one friend on to classes and had told Belsky to do the same. Belsky, of course, was not a student, but Friar Laurence did not know that. And so Belsky had resisted, throwing a punch at Friar Laurence. And then a second.

At any time had Juliet seen blood? The answer was yes; after the second punch, Belsky had pulled his arm back and with it a crucifix on a chain, which seemed to cut Belsky's wrist as he fell. When he got up, there was more blood, by which time two campus policemen were on the scene. After an exchange of comments, Friar Laurence was arrested, which seemed unfair. Juliet added, "I mean, the priest was just trying to help and protect us."

The testimony was direct, full, and winning. It seemed Kathleen Chung had made her case, that the defendant had come on the scene contrary to the restrictions upon bail release, encountered and injured a member of the cast, had done so pursuing at least one member of the cast, and an indictment was in order.

Kathleen Chung turned to me and said, "Your witness Mr. Collins."

Friar Laurence leaned over and said, "Is this the part where I say to you, K.I.S.S.?"

This was unexpected, and I smiled, "You must mean, keep it simple, sweetie? Yes."

"Just a few questions, Ms. Capulet," I began. "First, Ms. Chung seems to be implying that Friar Laurence was forbidden to "stalk," whatever that means, Mr. Belsky, as a member of the Romeo and Juliet cast or as a student at Hillhouse high school. Was he either of those things?"

Answer: "No."

"So, the terms of his release, relating only to members of the cast or students at Hillhouse high school, were not violated this morning?" I asked, facing the grand jury.

"Well ..." Juliet began to answer.

Kathleen Chung cut her off, saying, "Counselor, you know full well that calls for a legal conclusion and is what the grand jury itself is to decide. Let's wait until Juliet finishes law school before asking her legal opinion."

With that, I moved on and asked, "Now, Ms. Capulet, were you frightened this morning?"

Answer: "Totally."

"By whom, Friar Laurence or Mr. Belsky?"

The answer seemed so obvious that Juliet smiled and said, "By my old boyfriend. I had never seen the defendant before, but it was clear he was a priest and was doing his best to help me, in response to my cries."

"So, you felt threatened by Mr. Belsky; had he ever caused you to be afraid previously?" I asked.

Answer: "Yes, several times, when we argued about his politics. But also, when he wanted to go too far physically."

At this point, Kathleen Chung intervened, saying, "I don't think we should pursue Mr. Belsky's politics any further, Mr. Collins."

To which I replied, "I agree, counselor, so only one last question along these lines, Ms. Capulet, at any time this morning were you afraid of Friar Laurence?"

Answer: "No, I was totally glad he was there."

With this, I said, "I want to end my questioning by referring to Mr. Belsky's being cut, with resulting blood. Did you see him throw the punch that got entangled in the chain and crucifix?"

Answer: "Yes."

"Do you recall whether it was thrown with his right hand or his left?"

Answer: "I was standing to Tommy's right, I could see that he threw the punch with his right hand, and I might add that I know from personal, intimate experience he is right-handed."

At this point, Kathleen Chung became intensely focused on where I was going and rose to object even before I began the following question, which was: "Then, Juliet, can you explain why the bandaged cut which he just showed the grand jury was on his left wrist if it was his right hand that became entangled with the crucifix?"

"Do not answer that," said Kathleen Chung, turning to me she added, "you know perfectly well this witness is not qualified to give medical opinions any more than legal opinions."

"One last question then, Ms. Chung, if I may see the knife which the forensic technician has with her this afternoon," walking to the clerk and reaching for the Ziploc plastic bag which held the knife, "and show it to Ms. Capulet, my final question would be whether she is able to identify where one might find such silverware in common use, if she knows."

Again, Juliet Capulet smiled her radiant smile, because the answer was so obvious, and said, "Hillhouse High School cafeteria; The initials on the handle are HHS. And they are on all the handles of the silverware. I will leave to your imagination what the students say they stand for ... Most of us have taken a number home over the years as souvenirs."

I said, "Thank you, Ms. Capulet. I wish you luck with your production of *Romeo and Juliet*, a production in which it may well be that the young teenagers do not die. Do you think, with Mr. Burbage, that Romeo should live?"

And, here, young Juliet Capulet lit up the grand jury room with her smile, and her answer, as they say, came straight from the heart.

"Oh, yes. He should totally live. I love Romeo. Oh, my yes!" And, then, turning from me to the grand jury, "You should all come tomorrow night. You too, Ms. Chung."

In such a moment, you could hear a pin drop, the way she said it, the way she meant it, the grand jury was breathless, and after a long, silent pause, all I could say was, "Thank you, Ms. Capulet. If this witness is excused, Ms. Chung, I will now call Friar Laurence."

"You are a bit premature," Mr. Collins, Ms. Chung said, "I have three questions of Juliet. This morning, when Friar Laurence came on the scene, were you and your friends, and Mr. Belsky and his friends, on the high school grounds?"

Answer: "Yes."

"Did the fight between Friar Laurence and Tommy Belsky take place on the school grounds?"

Answer: "Yes."

Chung pursued, "You are absolutely certain?"

"Yes, totally."

With that, Kathleen Chung turned to me and asked, "Any questions?"

To which I replied, "No."

The district attorney said to the witness, "You may be excused, with our thanks and best wishes for your performance."

And with that, Juliet Capulet, a young woman radiant in love, exited the stage of the grand jury room, having turned in an absolutely scintillating performance and destined to turn in one of the finest performances in the centuries-long history of her role.

Ms. Chung turned to the grand jury and said, "We are about to hear from the defendant, an unusual event in my experience in grand jury inquiries, but first, we have one other witness, a forensics technician, who has examined the knife used against Tommy Belsky."

I stood and said, "Allegedly. Allegedly used against Tommy Belsky."

"Yes," said Kathleen Chung, "and now, will Maria Mercutio please take the stand?"

Ms. Mercutio came forward from the audience section, occupied the witness chair, and was sworn. In short order, in a most perfunctory way, District Attorney Chung established that she had a bachelor of science degree from Southern Connecticut University, was licensed as a forensics technician, and served as such with the New Haven Police Department for 15 years, and had with her the knife I had earlier shown to Juliet, and she had identified as coming from the Hillhouse High School cafeteria, said knife being in a Ziploc bag, and labeled as State's exhibit A.

Ms. Chung then asked Mercutio whether she had conducted any tests on the knife and with what results? She answered, "Yes. Tested for the presence of blood and had found O+, the most common type. Had also tested for fingerprints, had lifted two or three good specimens, one thumbprint and one index fingerprint on the handle."

Chung then asked, "Were you able to identify the sources of blood and the fingerprints?"

Answer: "Yes. They matched the records of Tommy Belsky in our CSCD files."

"One last question. Any question in your mind that this is the knife that cut Tommy Belsky?" Over my vociferous objection, Chung saying, "Save it for the trial."

The witness said, "None whatsoever."

"Your witness, Mr. Collins."

"Thank you," I said, "Ms. Mercutio, how did this knife come into your possession?"

"It was in the criminal evidence closet at headquarters, where I requisitioned it."

"And, if you know, how did it get there?"

"The records indicate that it was received and signed in this morning around 10:30 by the desk sergeant, William Doyle, who tagged and bagged at that time. Nobody else had signed it out, except me, since that time."

"And," I asked, "did the record made by Sgt. Doyle indicate who he received it from, under what circumstances, and how or why this person said he or she had found it and was turning it in?"

"None," said Mercutio, "the only notation by Sgt. Doyle was that a tall, young man in his 20s, had come in, wearing a trench coat, pulled the knife out of the pocket, put it on the desk, said, 'this is the knife that cut Belsky this morning' and walked out."

"Let me observe," I said to the grand jury and District Attorney Chung, "that this witness has failed to establish chain of custody sufficient to connect this knife to any stabbing this morning, and so it would not come into evidence at trial." Before Chung could state the obvious, I continued, "But assuming it is admissible for our purposes, an issue you ladies and gentlemen may resolve differently, I will ask Ms. Mercutio, whether she found any fingerprints of anyone else on the knife?"

Before Chung could object, Mercutio replied, "None."

I noticed Friar Laurence stirring uncomfortably in his chair. I was watching the jurors' reaction, and it was immediate. There was an obvious question on their faces, and I asked that question, "Wouldn't you normally expect to find prints of three different people: the assailant, the victim, and the person who turned in the knife?"

Chung stood and said emphatically, "Mr. Collins, I don't think I will allow speculation by this witness."

At that point, there occurred one of those moments that lawyers live for, when the grand jury forelady said, "Ms. Chung, I think the other jurors and I would like to hear the answer to that question."

Kathleen Chung turned, glared at her, and said, "I don't think I will allow it."

The forelady, whom I learned later is, among other things, a high school boys soccer referee, said, "If we put it to a vote, Ms. Chung, I'm certain you will lose. If you prevent this witness from answering this question, I can almost certainly guarantee you will not get a true bill from this grand jury. Are you going to allow the question?"

Chung said to me, "Mr. Collins, proceed."

I turned to the witness and said, "Do you recall the question?"

Ms. Mercutio said, "Yes. Ordinarily, there would be three sets of fingerprints by three different handlers. Here there is only one set, which suggests that the same person used the knife, received wounds, and delivered the knife."

"And that would be Mr. Belsky?"

Answer: "Yes."

And could you tell whether the prints were from a right-hand?"

Answer: "Yes. Right. I mean, right-handed"

"One last question, Ms. Mercutio. Friar Laurence has been booked and printed and is 'in the system' as we say. Did your tests find his prints on the knife?" Ordinarily on cross you never ask a question when you don't know the witness' answer. And I hadn't spoken to Ms. Mercutio previously. But I knew this; Friar Laurence left no prints.

Her answer: "No, his prints were not on the knife."

I noted the time as being 3:00 in the afternoon and said that if the State had no further witnesses, we would call Friar Laurence as our only witness.

"It's about time," Kathleen Chung said, "it will be interesting to hear what he has to say."

With that, Friar Valerian Laurence, recently of Verona, London, New Haven, and Hillhouse High School, rose from the counsel table, proceeded to cross the open space to the witness chair, took the oath, and ended it strongly with "so help me God." He gave his address as being New Haven, Connecticut, the Dominican Abbey on the green.

I began the examination by saying, "Friar Laurence, where are you from, and what are you doing here?" At this, the grand jury chuckled; a couple did laugh out loud since the question was succinct and direct and went to the heart of what everybody was wondering. Lawyers aren't supposed to be able to do that.

Friar Laurence began his response by saying, "Simple questions sometimes have complex answers. I found myself at the Dominican Abbey on the green here in New Haven a week or two ago, and the Abbot, Friar Dominic, asked me those same questions. My answer was, I am from Verona, Italy, and London, England some 400 to 600 years ago, an obviously impossible answer, and I'm not sure what I'm doing here. In a narrow sense, I am doing what Dominican priests do, serve the parish, serve parishioners, administer sacraments, deliver sermons ... I have done all of that over the past week or so, as well as over my lifetime, but that does not answer why here, as opposed to London or Verona, 400 to 600 years ago.

"As I have begun to try to answer these questions for myself, it seems that this is a special time and place for my life. As many of you surely know, I am deeply involved in the characters' lives in Shakespeare's *Romeo and Juliet*. Friar Laurence, and I am he, arranged Romeo and Juliet's marriage, deceived their parents, created artifices causing Juliet to seem dead, causing Romeo to kill himself, causing Juliet to do the same, causing enormous heartache and misery for people who had trusted me as a priest, bound by my Holy Orders to do God's work.

"That play is being performed here in New Haven, and the leads are descendants of the original families in Verona, Italy, a number of the figures in this community, including Mr. Collins, my attorney, are either descendants of people in the play or of people in Shakespeare's time. And, so, for example, the lead prosecutor is a certain Edmund Coke, generations ago Edward Coke was the lead prosecutor in Shakespeare's time. Mr. Collins' progenitor was Shakespeare's attorney. Simon Forman, a physician who testified in a case Mr. Collins defended yesterday, has the same name as a physician in Shakespeare's time.

"I could go on to enumerate for you other similarities coming together here in this time, in this community, but I won't. Instead of adding clarity, they would add confusion. I cannot say there is a destiny for me in this maelstrom of gathering identities, But I have to believe there is. Else, why would I be here?

"I can say on a personal level what I am seeking. Contrary to Ms. Chung's heartfelt concern, I am not seeking to harm children. Indeed, until Mr. Coke showed me the article in the *New Haven Register* last Sunday afternoon, I was unaware that the play was being performed and that these wonderful children will have a theatrical chance of a lifetime. And, so may I. For the play as being performed here may save lives, not end them, and in the process save me from the heartbreaking fate I have endured for centuries.

"Some of you may remember that at the end of *Romeo and Juliet*, I confess all that I did to the Prince, who represents both Man's law and God's judgment, and the Prince said he would return later to deal with me. But he has never returned. Judgment has never been imposed on me, I have never had a chance to undertake repentance, I have not been given a chance to seek redemption and earn God's love. My life is in suspension. I cannot even enter purgatory, for one must first die before being able to work out the debts they owe to seek God's love. Some of you may have read the novel *Lincoln in the Bardo*, a place between death and eternity. But I am not even there.

"What is unique about today, this place? It must be that Romeo and Juliet may live, rather than die, and should that happen, should Professor Burbage be successful, the implications for me are clear: the evil which I did all those centuries ago, and repeat in every performance, will not be done here. For the very first time. If so, I may find an ending, and with that, the chance to work for redemption, God's absolution, and the possibility of peace."

He paused here held his hands up before his face; the late afternoon sun shone through the windows into the jury room, and it passed through the Friar's hands and illuminated his uplifted face, in a warm golden aura, Friar Valerian's halo, it seemed. There were tears in his eyes and the eyes of many in the jury box, as he added, "Truly, I say to you, if I seek any death, and I'm not sure I do, it is only my own. What I said last Sunday about fearing I might harm others, was true, but is now past.

322

"It is clear to me that the possibility here in New Haven in this new century is that Romeo and Juliet may live and that I may play a role in bringing that about. It is coming clear to me that I am here now in this time and place, to earn a chance, at long last, to do penance, achieve redemption, and at long, long, last, peace.

There was a long collective sigh, a collective deep breath, as though the very walls of the jury room had been moved to pity. I had a sense that we had all swung back in time and then quickly back again, on a pendulum which settled, lightly and briefly, on this time, Friar Laurence's time, his brief moment. We had a glimpse of what possibilities lay before us. And now we had to gather ourselves.

I got Friar Laurence a glass of water; he collected himself, drinking, and asked, "Shall I go on?"

I looked to Kathleen Chung and saw for the first time inconceivably the Dragon Lady had tears in her eyes, and she said, "Yes there is a voice saying he should." I turned and sat down.

Friar Laurence continued. "Here we are; it is springtime in New Haven. I sit before you in a time of renewal and hope. I only ask for this time, indeed this very moment, that you let my life play out. How could anyone believe I would harm the marvelous Juliet who testified a bit ago? I have a sense that my days in this community and on this Earth are very limited. A true bill would mean they shall be spent in custody. Please let me spend my last days in freedom, tasting liberty, and earning redemption and God's love."

Friar Laurence was leaning forward in the witness chair as he made that appeal, shoulders hunched, his hands wide open, his deep voice shrunk almost to a whisper, but it carried the day, and he carried the room. He returned to the counsel table, sat beside me, and

323

whispered, "I cannot spend tonight in jail. I have to be elsewhere. Please make that happen."

I replied, "I think you just did it. I'll try not to screw it up."

Kathleen Chung rose to deliver her closing argument. It was direct, brief, and lawyerly, having only three points. "Ladies and gentlemen of the grand jury, this has been a remarkable contrast to the 15 cases you heard this morning. But the rules are the same. I have only three points to make.

"First, you do not have to decide guilt or innocence, only whether there is probable cause that later evidence may warrant a trial on stalking, breach of a court order, and assault. You have heard evidence supporting each of these.

"Secondly, you have also heard that there are other witnesses, friends of Mr. Belsky's, friends of Juliet Capulet's, who have not been called but would be called as witnesses if you return a true bill. So, there is more evidence yet to be heard.

"Thirdly, underlying the first two points, is the testimony of the defendant himself, delivered powerfully and compellingly, but when stripped to its basics, it consists of vague, unsubstantial, preposterous tales of time travel, crimes admitted in other places and times, connections to our time and place so weak and tenuous that we must fear, without a reasonable doubt, this delusional man poses a significant danger, and the only remaining question is to whom and how soon?

"A true bill of indictment is the only answer.

I rose, stood in the center of the room where the fading sunlight shone through into a warm circle of amber shade, catching golden dust illuminating the moment, and began by complimenting Kathleen Chung,

"Ladies and gentlemen of the jury, as always, I'm impressed by the lawyerly qualities of opposing counsel. Truly she is excellent. Unfortunately, her argument proves too much. If you embrace her position by returning a true bill against Friar Laurence, it will be because we do not understand him and because we do not understand ourselves.

"Truly, each of us is here without knowing for certain where we came from or where we are going.

"Friar Laurence has told the truth, with all of its uncertainties and, it is said, the truth will make you free. It seems to me we can trust him. He could have lied, developed facile cover stories for all of the uncertainty surrounding him; he is a powerful and experienced speaker, he could have deceived us. Instead, he has trusted us, and we should trust him.

"As for the charges, you should vote to dismiss the bill of indictment. Stalking requires an intentional pattern inflicting fear; Friar Laurence has done that with neither Mr. Belsky nor Juliet Capulet. Assault with a deadly weapon requires proof that Friar Laurence used a weapon, and such proof is lacking, and that he intended to harm Mr. Belsky, when he intervened with the best of motives to prevent a crime. As for violating a court order, he did go on the Hillhouse high school grounds, a technical violation, but as to that, you should consider his motive, and more importantly, that such an issue should not be presented to you but to the court entering the order, Chief Justice Popham.

"Your response should be 'no true bill,' with a directive that Friar Laurence be freed from custody and that his crucifix and chain be returned to him. Thank you for your attention, and please accept my best wishes."

With that, I sat down. Friar Laurence leaned over, said, "Thank you, Francis, much to the point and nicely done. I especially appreciated that you did not argue the absence of my prints on that knife. And that you asked for the return of my crucifix, I feel naked without it."

Kathleen Chung rose, said to the grand jury that they could remain in the room for their deliberations, and counsel and the defendant would be in attendance awaiting their decision. She trusted it would not take very long.

With that, the three of us exited the grand jury room. Kathleen Chung reached into her attaché case and removed a Ziploc bag, marked Evidence: Case 2020-579, and removed a crucifix and chain, handing it to Friar Laurence.

I looked at her and said, "Kathleen, are we receiving goods taken improperly from the evidence room at Headquarters?"

Friar Laurence received the chain and crucifix in his hand like a glass of water for a man lost in the desert and placed the chain around his neck, as she said, "No, Francis, this is not entrapment. Friar Laurence is not the only one with time prescience. That grand jury is about to return no true bill, so why delay returning what should never have been taken in the first place. Turning to Friar Laurence, "You are now free to go. And Friar, please stay out of trouble. My brilliant career cannot take another hit like this one."

We walked into the late afternoon sunshine, and Friar Laurence thanked me profusely. Ron and Data approached, quizzically, hearing the ending, and in unison said, "Unbelievable," which it was and still is.

As we walked back toward the office, we met Jo and her husband, who took Friar Laurence arm in arm, Jo saying to me, "You and Meg have the kids again tonight. We're headed to Arlow's for dinner. I'll bring leftovers tomorrow morning for you and your family." And as they proceeded on their way, they were joined by Dorothy Arlow, the two women in the middle, flanked by two enormous men.

I had the presence of mind to ask, "What's for dinner?"

"Ribs," came the answer. Jo said, "we're going to show this Italian priest and his Northern lady ('His Northern Lady?') "how we do barbeque in North Carolina. Enough of this Northern Italian crap."

And the four walked off, casting long shadows, each man huge against the setting sun, Dorothy and Jo in between, Jo moving the way only she could. Somehow, as incongruous as it seems, as I watched them go along the Green, and I could see only their silhouettes, I was reminded of another Dorothy, walking arm in arm, with the Tin Man, the Scarecrow, and the Lion.

CHAPTER TWENTY-SEVEN
CLOTHES MAKE THE MAN
AND GENDER DYSPHORIA HELPS

It is now Friday morning, and the usual drill is happening. The Chief, RBG, Meg, and I are showering and shaving (that is, one of us, possibly two, too much information, you don't need to know) preparatory to trying on clothes (occasionally met with, "Oh no! THAT'S not going to happen!"), descending to the breakfast table, encountering whatever it is that Meg laid out last night, after our kids and the Arlow kids turned in, homemade oatmeal, Pop-Tarts (for me), chopped fruit mixture of some kind, yogurt, fruit juice, and lunch fixings, the latter in the refrigerator to be laid out on the kitchen counter as we demolish breakfast. Possibly wrapped cheese sticks or cereal bars accompanied by an apple or banana, nothing too heavy, there's always the school cafeteria.

The random breadth of these offerings is greater than usual to accommodate last night's second, successive, successful sleepover of the Arlow children. Meg had picked them up at Dorothy's home, each with appropriately stuffed backpacks, accompanied by excited anticipation from the kids and profuse thanks from the mom. This time, with a bit of advance notice in preparation, clothing, homework and television were all coordinated. Successive and successful. Suffice it to say, that between now, 7:00 and 7:45 AM, all things necessary will be achieved, and our expanded world will be put in proper perspective, and then it is OTD.

Oh, and a few words are exchanged, such as, "And you, what's going on?"

"Preliminary work on CBD and ovarian cancer. It'll be quick. You?"

"Three cross-dressing teenage boy prostitutes, charged with being, well, cross-dressing teenage boy prostitutes, and wrapped in the first, second and fourteenth amendments, at least for this court occasion, in the United States Constitution."

"Oh, them again?" from Meg, immediately followed by piqued interest from the youngsters in the group, the oldest asking, "anyone I know?" Final word, from the physician, "be careful who you touch ... do you have latex gloves?"

We divide children, divide routes, divide lanes of traffic, locate the appropriate schools and drop-off points, call out as they depart the cars, "Who's (book) (lunch) (cell phone) (iPad) is this?" and go on to the lesser important details for which we are paid—saving various aspects of the universe as we know it.

At the usual time, about 8:15, I exit Big John's Little Elevator through the expanding scissors of the accordion door, note that Jo is in place and in sync with her desktop computer and New Haven Green view, pause for the customary machine-gun delivery of the daily staccato bulletin:

"Awesome ribs last night, yours are on your desk, to be shared with your equally awesome bride; our favorite interior decorating firm of Crutcher, Payne, and Hazel have separately checked in and are ready to be met in the courtroom at 9:30; our shrink has checked in and should be available at 2:00 PM if she can escape from the lockup in Middletown (lockup? escape?); one of the Johns called to say that he is suing us for damages inflicted on his wife on learning that he had retained the services of the aforesaid "favorite interior decorating firm;" my man and I are going to be at Burbage's walk-through tonight, despite his protestations to the contrary, as will Charlie Whiting and his bride to be, do we need tickets? Friar Laurence called from the suite they have for him at the city jail, asking that you once again get him out, and, BTW, what's a "bench warrant?" Oh, and sorry about the Grand Jury voting a true bill on Friar Laurence's indictment last night ... there's a call from the Dragon Lady ...

I reply, striding toward my office, "Great on the walk-through. No, On the tickets. Bench warrant? Well, that's a warrant issued to enforce a court order, for example, if Chief Justice Popham got pissed and thought the Dragon Lady had screwed up or Friar Laurence had violated his restrictions." I follow the aroma and vapors of barbecue ribs to my office, trying to ignore what I think I heard Jo say, 'Sorry about the grand jury voting a true bill,' yeah, that part, on the indictment. Wait, I thought we won that. So ... did the Dragon Lady manage to waterboard an indictment out of those people I had hypnotized into submission?! No, she's mean, but not unethical ...

"Oh shit, no! Ron," I call loudly, "go over to the DA's office and find out what happened. Check with the jail and see what they are holding Friar Laurence on, pretext and amount. Ask him how the ribs were."

"I'm on it," he replies.

"Oh," I added, "did you tell our cross-dressing teenaged prostitutes what to wear today?"

"No, I thought you did," (Well, think I, this is going to be interesting) Ron fires back, as he disappears down the staircase, on his way to the jail, to visit our retainer client priest, who by now should be getting a weekly room pass.

With that, I sit behind my desk, throw the ribs in the Ziploc bag into my spare attaché case, and flip through five plea folders for 9:00 AM, and begin, for the umpteenth time, reviewing the 10:00 AM file on Crutcher, Payne, and Hazel for trolling for white, suburban Johns. Ron has done his usual thorough work, pulling together the police reports, interviewing the White adult male victims about how they were drawn to these Black teenage boys, dressed as female prostitutes, drawing the attention of mostly white adult male citizens, striking a financial services arrangement and taking them back to a tired and tawdry room in a tired and tawdry apartment in a tired etc. section of town. Lights were turned out, grabbing and grappling occurred, lights were turned back on, two of my clients were beaten badly, police were called, and complaints were filed by my clients against the victims and by the victims against my clients. The vice squad has no difficulty separating wheat from chaff, and so my clients are no longer victims and are on trial. They are chaff ...

This is not our first rodeo; I have asked previously and stopped asking why Crutcher, Payne, and Hazel work this particular gambit. Every time, it ends with their being beaten up, a local, low-level version of a rigged television WWF free-for-all. They could set this up as a same-sex encounter, possibly turning a handsome profit. To that, their response is simply, "We are what we are, and the police should protect us."

A different level of questioning is simply, is what they do illegal? They dress as women, offer sex, and get beaten up, even though they are willing to have sex, but as guys, usually having to return whatever money has been paid. It is not prostitution as usually so defined. There is no law prohibiting suicide by cross-dressing. And, anyway, prostitution is no longer a crime in Connecticut, downgraded to a civil violation. The vice squad and the prosecutor's office have settled on two ancient, venerable, common-law crimes, "night walking" and "lascivious carriage." Sounds like fun.

Having traced the statutes back some 300 years, our man Data proposes a four-stage defense. One, they didn't do it, that is, they just weren't out there, lasciviously that is. Problem is, to make this argument, we have to concede "lasciviously" has meaning. (See, third argument below.) Anyway, if it means soliciting prostitution, that is no longer a crime; Ergo, if they were doing that, it is no longer lascivious ...

Two, if they were in fact behaving lasciviously, their conduct was a product of gender dysphoria, a syndrome akin to insanity, but insanity has been abolished as a defense. Anyway, they know right from wrong. We checked out diminished capacity, but that only reduces the level of the charge, which in our case is already as low as we can go. We gave up on arguing that our guys are victims, which of course they are, because, in the most childish of senses, our guys "started it." So, we end up with "gender dysphoria," a syndrome and a label for conduct so self-destructive it has to be sick. We expect to lose this.

Third, we will argue, the statutes are unconstitutional, vague, discriminatory, overly broad, denying due process, the right to bare arms, etc. See argument one above. Not exactly the same as ex post facto, but sort of the same idea: you can't tell what is covered until after you do it ...

Fourth, the application and enforcement of these statutes are directed particularly at minority members, mostly African-Americans. (Did I mention my clients are black? 40% of New Haven's population are African-American, but, more importantly, nearly 80%

of New Haven's poor are African-American. And, interestingly, so are the members of the vice squad.). Selective enforcement arguments usually lose unless done intentionally and based upon suspect criteria, like race or religion. Right. Good luck proving it ...

We have experts on the dysphoria point. Ron did the shopping; in the world of criminal trial psychiatrists, there are prosecution experts and defense experts; we have two of the best. They always testify for our side. Sometimes we win.

We did a practice argument, a "moot court," on these four points a week ago, before three other public defenders in our office. It wasn't pretty. Conclusion: In a weird way, the weirdness of our clients makes the dysphoria argument our strongest.

I prepped my youngsters for the probability of a guilty finding. We waived a jury trial, if only because a trial judge might be so pissed off by my clients that he would punish them for wasting his time with a jury. The prosecutor's office, certain of the conviction, agreed to go for probation and community service (There's potential for humor there if you think about it) if we waived a jury trial to save time. So, we did.

Everything about this case is weird, and so, in a weird way, the prosecutor is looking forward to an interesting case, something out of the ordinary. The Assistant DA who caught this case is Larry Levy, himself a bit weird. At one point, I complained to the presiding judge that Larry was carrying a Glock in the courtroom, practicing Quick Draw during court recesses. He was scaring my clients, who themselves are pretty scary. I got half a loaf: Larry continues to pack; he just can't draw. And so it goes.

With five plea files in a slim folder under my left arm and the fat nightwalking folder in my attaché case, Data and I decide to risk life and limb and join Big John in his Little Elevator. As we get in, he comments, "Life on the edge, eh? Everybody exhale altogether now," and he closes the door, carefully scissoring it past us, as we lurch three times to the second floor, and then two more to the first, where the doors open. We occasionally do this when I need applause, which should greet us, but never does. And then, a bit seasick, it is out the door, cross the street, into the old criminal court building.

The criminal courtroom is, as always, filled with noise, bodies, business transactions, injustices, and occasionally, almost randomly, instances of things done right. Since this is a Friday morning, add to all of the above, five solid days, the aroma, perhaps rank stench of overcrowded, tension-laden, rapid-fire, fear-driven human chaos.

Ron stands off to the right, sees Data and me, waves to us, sweeps grandly with his left arm to indicate the five plea bargain defendants seated with him, and gestures to us to come toward him. Easier said than done in the milling crowd, but we achieve proximity, and Ron reintroduces clients I have met previously. We form a brief huddle. I remind each client of the remaining charges, the prosecution's recommendation, the requirement that each must enter his own plea of guilty and truthfully answer that he is pleading guilty because he is guilty, and that he understands the judge is not necessarily bound by the recommendation. If asked whether anyone has made promises, he should answer "yes, Mr. Collins has," and I will then advise of the prosecutor's recommendation to be affirmed by Mr. Levy.

Other lawyers are going through similar exercises, we are simply better at it, and so I get Larry's attention, he calls our five cases, and it is Showtime. Since these are all misdemeanors, and there is nothing hideous about the facts or the clients, there is no presentence report. Larry sums up each case from the prosecutor's file. My presentation is chiefly directed toward the defendant, trying to paint a picture about family, employment, contrition, and the like. The judge asks whether the defendant wants to say anything, usually not a good idea, but sometimes there is.

The recommendation is invariably accepted, although sometimes the victim will speak up from the audience section, possibly with a victims' advocate, and then all bets are off. Not a good idea for efficiency, but some victims are apt to think the point of all this is justice. Go figure. The deals are done, so ...

That leaves our gender dysphoria trio. The case is called, Larry says we're ready for trial, and our cross-dresser kids are transferred to the trial court. Larry Levy is delighted to go with us since he prefers deviant defendants to mass arraignments. Who wouldn't? The remaining arraignments and pleas will be handled by newer district attorneys or student interns from the Law School Clinical Program, an innovation at Yale to ensure that graduates could find the courthouse. It would have helped me early on, especially the men's room.

Ron and I step outside the swinging doors of Courtroom 2, onto the crowded landing, where, if anything, noise and body heat are at a higher pitch than inside. We look for our three clients for the upcoming trial. I do not see them. I ask Ron; he does not see them either. And then it clicks. We had always seen them in their conventional working clothes, on their day jobs. In those settings, as uncomfortable as it may be for them, they are dressed like young men.

Now, appearing in court, they have not only given up their day jobs but their day job attire. And so, I see them. Three striking, African-American females, in short skirts, high heels, low-cut tops, and wigs, Crutcher is blonde, Payne is a brassy red, and Hazel is a deep purple. Would I have advised against this? Well, at least there's no question now about credibility ... Next time (there will be a next time), maybe they should do red, white, and blue.

They see us, they wave, they stroll over in what I take is their sedate move, and they ask, "Are you ready for court"?

I answer, "Absolutely. And I see, very clearly, that you are as well." This generates three brilliant, lipsticked smiles, a bit on the anxious side.

As we enter Courtroom 2, I see that the presiding judge is none other than Chief Justice Popham. It occurs to me that he may know why Friar Laurence is once again residing behind bars on Whaley Avenue. He nods to Larry Levy and me, saying, "Gentlemen, it seems we have something a bit out of the ordinary here. If I am going to have to babysit this court for a week or two, I thought I should at least be able to choose something memorable. I can thank Mr. Collins for that earlier this week. And again, earlier this morning. I hope he won't disappoint now."

Larry opens by giving a brief description of what my clients were doing a few weeks ago on a Saturday night, saying that this seemed an open and shut case. I responded by saying the defense agreed on the facts but felt a conviction would be out of the question because of Data's Four-Point Plan (I didn't mention Data), described earlier and recapped for the Chief as being: they didn't do it, if they did it wasn't their fault, and anyway the statute is bad, and they were being picked on.

"Well," said Popham, "nicely done. The only thing you left out was self-defense, Mr. Collins, which seems as though it would be a bit of a stretch here." (I think, well, maybe next time ...). And then turning to Larry, Popham said, "Who are your witnesses?"

Larry responded that he would call at least one of the arresting officers, Arnold Buffalo, of the Vice Squad, and one of the male victims or customers, who would like to be referred to as Mr. Doe, for obvious reasons.

I then stated that we would call at least one of the defendants, "Probably Crutcher or Mr. Payne and an expert in psychology, Doctor Laura Miyazaki"

Popham said, "Well then, Mr. Levy, can we get your two witnesses on before lunch and wrap up this afternoon? Only four witnesses, after all?"

Larry responded, "I will move with all due deliberate speed, Your Honor."

"Oh no, Larry, don't do that," I groaned," that would take years!"

Larry seemed puzzled, never having understood why he is known as Slow Mo Larry. Larry looked down at his papers, then into his attaché case, speaks with Officer Buffalo (no stranger to my clients or me) ...

"Today, Mr. Levy, today," was the Chief Justice's contribution, "tick tock."

"Yes, sir," was Larry's response. Eye-rolling was mine. Larry states, "our first witness will testify under the name, John Doe."

"State calls John Doe."

A rather unimpressive, undeveloped, balding man in his 40s, looking very much like a failed accountant, or Paul Giamatti, or Bob Newhart, depending upon your generation, rose from the audience section, came through the gate, was sworn by the clerk and sat in the witness chair. Levy then asked whether we would stipulate that John Doe could proceed, although this was not his real name, under the usual oath of telling the truth. We did so stipulate.

Larry posed his first question.

MR. LEVY

"Mr. Doe, on the night of March 5, this year, a Saturday night, were you in the Wooster Square area of New Haven at about 7:30 or 8:00 PM?"

A. "Yes."

Q. "Were you in the company of another White male, a friend, who we shall refer to as John Smith?"

A. "Yes."

Q. "Would you please tell us what happened?"

A. "Smitty and I came out of the Esquire Pub, having had a few, and were talking about where to go next, with a view toward scoring."

Q. "By the term 'scoring,' do you mean obtaining drugs or finding sexual partners and, if so, male or female?"

A. "Yeah, that's what I mean."

Q. "Were you looking for sex with a male or a female?"

A. "A woman, you know, a chick, a broad, a cunt ... whatever."

Q. "A woman?"

A. "Yeah, a woman, what kind of guys do you think we are?"

At this, Walter Payne, sitting immediately to my right, rose and said, "Your Honor, I can answer that."

The Chief said, "Mr. Collins, control your client."

John Doe said, "Good luck with that, I couldn't."

The Chief then turned to him and said, "That applies to you too, sir. Get on with it; what happened?"

MR. LEVY

"Tell us what happened, please."

A. "Smitty and I were standing there, and these three black chicks came swinging by. I mean, they had on short skirts, net hose, high

338

heels, blouses cut down to their navels, pretty much what they're wearing today, though I can't see their navels, plus wigs. Smitty turned to me and said, 'You know what they say.'"

I said, "No. What do they say?"

"Smitty laughs, slaps me on the back, and says, 'Once you've had Black, you never go back.' So, I calls out to the tall one, the one sitting next to Mr. Collins there, who had on a blonde wig. I said, Hey Blondie, you got a place? And she says ..."

At this, Crutcher, on my left, grabs my elbow and says, "Object."

I stand and say, "Objection." Then I turn and say, "Why?" And he says, "Because I ain't no "she," I'm a man," loudly enough so that half the courtroom bursts out laughing.

At this, Chief Justice Popham addresses the audience, telling them to restrain themselves and "curb your enthusiasm," and then turns to John Doe and Larry Levy and says, "you will refer to the defendants in the male gender, as men."

MR. DOE

"Well, at least they looked like women, and they looked hot; they also looked as though they were, you know, like, available. Selling. So, Blondie says, checking in with her partners, ah shit, I mean his partners, 'Right around the corner, if you can pay the rent.' I say, How much? The little one, sitting to Mr. Collins' right, says, 'For the three of us, $350 for an hour.' Smitty says, 'Bullshit. Make it $250.' We settle on $300, and we follow them around the corner and draw a round of applause from people on the sidewalks, it being a warm night for a change, and them being regulars.

Well, we get there, and go inside, and it's a real dump."

At this, Hazel, to my far right in the purple wig, on the other side of Payne, stood and shouted, "It looked a lot better before you two motherfuckers trashed the place." Larry objects, the Chief orders Hazel to sit down, I am once again instructed to control my clients, and throughout all of this, John Doe is laughing.

MR. LEVY

"Get to the point of what happened."

A. "Well, what happened is, Smitty says, 'Let's get out of here.' Blondie there, says 'Not without paying us our money!' Smitty says, 'Okay, then earn it, bitch. Each of you, strip, and let's see what you got.' And they do. Halters come off. The bras come down, and there's nothing. You know, I mean, NOTHING. Right? The skirts are dropped, the panties are dropped, and now, THERE is something. You know what I mean, I mean, SOMETHING! Each of them is really hung. The full package, the Full Monty, as they say."

"Believe it," says Crutcher.

The courtroom is quiet; you could hear a pin drop or a pair of panties ... maybe a bra.

Larry lets an unconscionable amount of time go by, flipping through notes, turning pages, speaking to Officer Buffalo on his left, and then asks a complex question.

MR. LEVY

"What happened then?"

A. "I said, what the fuck? Smitty says, 'You must be shitting me.' The little one there, sitting to Mr. Collins' right, says, 'Okay, who bends over first, you or me?' Smitty says, 'Bend over this,' and throws a chair at Shorty, who ducks, and the chair hits the tall one with purple hair. She's knocked over, Smitty kicks her, then he gets punched out, I grabbed him, and the two of us run out the door.

"Well, the little one with the red hair stands in the door and hollers, 'Hey, Whitey, come on back, we're just getting started, man. I've got a Johnson just for you' and hangs it out. I turn and punch her in the face, hurting my hand, and we're out of there. Two vice squad cops were standing nearby, obviously waiting for this, and they moved in to arrest the three pervs."

CHIEF JUSTICE

"Wrap it up, Mr. Levy."

MR. LEVY

"That's it?"

A. Well, not quite. I kept a bra and panties as a souvenir. I laundered them if any of those three gentlemen are in need of clean clothing."

I hear Hazel, two seats to my right, say, "Fuck you."

CHIEF JUSTICE

"One more comment like that, Mr. Hazel, and we will not need to finish this trial for me to send you straight to jail. If there's nothing more from Mr. Doe, it's Mr. Collins' turn to examine.

Mr. Collins?"

MR. COLLINS

"Looks like this isn't exactly what you are looking for, is it?"

A. "No."

Q. "What were you looking for?"

A. "Well, you know, we thought maybe a little three on two, the three being women, which they weren't."

Q. "So, when you found they were male, you got upset and angry?"

A. "Absolutely, wouldn't you?"

Q. "You were looking for hetero-sex, heterosexual sex, right?"

A. "Yes. Answer, yes."

Q. "But that isn't what it was, right? So, last question, did you and Smitty get pissed off because they were guys or because you weren't going to get laid?"

A. "Because they were guys. And made us look like fools. And they were creepy."

MISTER COLLINS

"I have nothing further of Mr. Doe, except to say I'm filled with admiration for his social tolerance and good taste."

CHIEF JUSTICE

"We don't need sarcasm here, Mr. Collins. Mr. Doe, if there are no further questions from counsel, you are excused with the pity and disgust of the court. Mr. Levy, do I understand you have a second witness before we break for lunch? And to help you move along faster, am I correct that it is a vice squad officer, sitting next to you, at counsel table, and I will now call him to the stand and ask the clerk to swear him."

This is done with great expedition, and Officer Arnold Buffalo is sworn in. Slim, tall, a receding hairline, tense, in plain clothes. He settles himself, opens a buff file folder, appears to glance at it, and then looks up at Larry Levy, who asks, after a long Larry Levy-style pause,

MR. LEVY

"Officer Buffalo, were you one of the two vice squad officers whom Mr. Doe has just described?"

A. "Yes."

Q. "Have you been in the courtroom throughout Mr. Doe's testimony, and to the best of your recollection and belief, is Mr. Doe's testimony true and correct?"

A. "Yes. On both scores. Answer, yes."

Q. "And would your testimony be identical to his in almost all material respects?"

A. "Yes, we have discussed this thoroughly beforehand and before our testimony today."

"I have nothing further of this witness," says Larry to the Chief Justice, and then turning to me, says, "How's that for speed?"

"Not bad, Larry," I say, No mo, So lo Mo, for you, bro ..." And then I stand to address Arnold Buffalo, a pleasure I have had on multiple occasions.

MR. COLLINS

"Officer Buffalo, how did it happen that you and the other officer, was it Big Bob Gifford, were already present at the defendants' apartment when they arrived with Mr. Smith and Mr. Doe?"

A. "Well, counselor, we have a long-standing relationship with your three fine young men, and a visit on a Saturday night to their environs is always entertaining and often productive. On this particular occasion, we saw the three defendants approach two white males, your clients being in full regalia, I might say, as they are now, and we waited for the inevitable to happen. It usually does, and it did that night."

Q. "I take it, by 'the inevitable,' you mean that all of the individuals entered the apartment, and shortly after, violence occurred, as described by Mr. Doe, and you observed the white men exit in haste?"

A. "Yes."

Q. "Now, Officer Buffalo, how many times in the past have you observed the defendants in similar situations, where would-be customers inflict physical harm?"

A. "Dozens."

Q. "And how severe is that harm?"

A. "On both sides, there are usually at least bruises, and often cuts and wounds, with blood."

Q. "And, do arrests result?"

A. "Absolutely. Your clients have been arrested at least a dozen perhaps 20 times for such conduct, and are on probation right now for the last time, a month ago."

Q. "Then, have you ever asked them why they keep doing it? I mean, it hardly seems rational; it seems self-destructive."

A. "No one ever said that your clients are rational, Mr. Collins. Early on, I did ask them, and the response from each was, it's what we do, it's the way we are, why aren't you protecting us, instead of arresting us?"

Q. "Well, doesn't that seem like a fair reaction? Do you ever arrest the frustrated, angry, assaultive, white, would-be customers?"

A. "Absolutely not. They are simply men in a downtown section of New Haven, looking for a good time, and responding to assaultive behavior by people like your clients."

Q. "And by people 'like my clients,' you mean these irrational, self-destructive, deviant sicko young men?"

A. "Absolutely, perverts, in my opinion. To protect the public, we arrest them."

Q. "Last question then, is it fair to say that your pattern of arrest, in each instance, ends up with custody being imposed upon teenage African-Americans with some form of emotional or psychological disability? Would you agree with that?"

A. "You know what, you could say that, but you could as easily say that these punks are out there looking for excitement and getting their rocks off at the expense of law-abiding citizens. If they are African-Americans, so be it. As you may have noticed, counselor, so am I, and nobody ever cut me no slack."

Q. "Oh, one other thing, officer, you have seen these young men often enough to know they will repeat their behavior, correct? Have you ever referred them to social service agencies, either within your department or the Department of Human Services?"

A. "Hell no, I'm not a social worker or a nursemaid. They know what they're doing and what they're looking for. And I'm paid for arrests."

Q. "Oh, yes, are the Johns, the victims, always white?"

A. "Yes, even though it's partly a Hispanic part of town, counselor."

Q. "Always white? Why?"

A. "Figure it out yourself."

With that, I turn to the Chief Justice and say, "I have nothing further," and the District Attorney says the same, so the Chief congratulates us on finishing at the noon hour and declares that he will recess until 1:30. Everyone in the courtroom rises, and I am once again struck by the extreme height my clients gain by wearing 3-inch spikes, causing me to reflect how fortunate I am to be surrounded by prostitutes I can look up to, and as I ruminate on that subject, I hear the Chief say that he would like to see Mr. Collins in chambers. I turn to my three clients, asking them to stay out of trouble for at least the next hour and a half, and turn to the door which leads to the judge's chambers in Courtroom 2. I knock, the Chief says enter, and I do.

The conversation is mercifully brief. Chief Justice Popham says, "I assume you have learned that your career criminal client, Friar Laurence, is back in the New Haven jail. The District Attorney who handled the grand jury yesterday, Kathleen Chung, called my chambers and left a message with my clerk to the effect that she had failed to indict him. This, as we well know, both of us, is almost unheard of in the history of Anglo-American jurisprudence and will have predictable consequences for Ms. Chung's career.

345

"Upon learning this, I spoke with her and determined that your client violated my restraining order, as a part of his release, that he not approach members of the cast of *Romeo and Juliet* and that he not go upon the grounds of Hillhouse High School.

"Ms. Chung advised me that he did so. Tell me, is she correct?"

I answered, "Your Honor, you put me in a difficult position, where you are asking me to testify against my client, in effect."

Popham leaned forward and said, "Mr. Collins, if you think this is a difficult position, in a short while, you'll be able to tell me how it compares to sharing a cell with your client. I instruct you, now, to answer, and if I am out of line, you may certainly take an appeal or file a complaint."

I reflect upon the undeniable wisdom of the observation just made, and I answer, "Yes, Your Honor, he did so to prevent bodily harm being inflicted on one of the cast, the young lady who is playing Juliet."

Here, Popham leaned forward across the desk in the shoddy, sparsely furnished chambers and said, "I don't give a shit what his motivation was. He was instructed not to do that, and he violated those instructions. There were police officers on the scene within moments, and they could easily have handled the entire matter.

"Upon learning this, I told Ms. Chung that I was holding your client in contempt and I ordered Ms. Chung, before releasing the grand jury, to have them return to their deliberations and get me a true bill, and separately I ordered her to prepare and execute a bench warrant, whether or not that indictment was returned. Apparently, it was, and the bench warrant was executed this morning. He will remain in jail without bail.

"I intend to see to it that his trial on stalking, assault, violating a court order, and contempt is accelerated and that he remains in custody for at least the time it takes for the play to be performed and completed before he is ever released into the community again.

"One other thing, I also instructed Edmund Coke to involve your client in Operation Net Nanny, as an active candidate for prosecution. I tell you this now to make sure you do not interfere. Under no circumstances are you to advise your client concerning this; if you do, you will be charged with obstructing justice.

"And make no mistake about it, I will be sitting on that case, and this time, unlike the bail hearing and the competency hearing, you and your client will see why I have earned my well-deserved reputation for being a Law-and-Order judge. My only regret is we no longer have drawing and quartering or even hanging. Pity."

"Now, I would appreciate it if you would leave my chambers, and after lunch, we will take care of this freak show you have dumped on my docket."

Freak show? Operation Net Nanny? I say nothing, thank the Chief Justice for his time, and exit with what I hope is at least the appearance of calm composure in the face of a truly extraordinary performance.

On my way back to the office, I call Kathleen Chung on my cell and ask her if what Popham described actually happened. She said it had, with one variance, she had refused to recall the grand jury, and her boss, Edmund Coke, had browbeaten a true bill out of them. Popham and Coke, in a conference call, had told her she was done as a prosecutor.

And then she paused and said, "You know, Francis, I have always had high regard for you, and so perhaps you might consider, although you didn't get this from me, going to the judge who administers court business when Popham is absent from Hartford, as he is now.

"At present, that would be Judge Roderigo Lopez, who has no love for Popham. You could file with Judge Lopez an application for a common-law writ of quo warranto or possibly mandamus to set aside the bench warrant. If you were to subpoena me, of course, I would make myself available on a moment's notice ... Let me add, I am for law and order, but right now, I seem to be the only one on my team who really believes in it."

I quickly decided to revise my prior opinion of the Dragon Lady, and decided as well to risk this following question: "What the Hell is Operation Net Nanny?"

There is a long pause, and Kathleen then says, "I have been forbidden to make any disclosure in this matter. Let me say, tell your client not to cruise the Internet responding to underage ads. It will be a setup, followed by a charge of attempted rape. You did not hear this from me." With that, she hung up.

This weird week was getting weirder each day, in every way. Could it get any weirder? I wondered. The Dragon Lady fired because not tough enough? A trial court judge, on temporary administrative assignment, overriding his boss? A Chief Justice instructing the prosecutor's office to set up a criminal defendant on attempted rape charges? Raping someone's nanny?

Oh, come on! I wished it were tomorrow morning, so I could look back and see how this all played out.

Be careful what you wish for ...

CHAPTER TWENTY-EIGHT

DON'T STEP ON SUPERMAN'S CAPE

I grabbed a Thai box lunch from the food cart in front of City Hall, rode Big John's luxury express to the third floor, was greeted by Jo on her way out to lunch, getting an eye roll from her, and was joined by Data. Data had met with Friar Laurence, who is now being held in isolation, per instructions of the Chief Justice. Friar Laurence is desperate to be at Burbage's walk-through tonight. If, he said, he is in some fashion, somehow, to redeem himself, to make penance, or to atone, it has to be within the framework Burbage is developing. He is unclear how that will play out, but any opportunity seems fraught from a jail cell.

Data had inquired of the district attorney's office, learned of the Chief Justice's intervention, and prosecutor Coke's actions regarding the grand jury and Kathleen Chung. He had already begun research on using common-law writs to spring Friar Laurence and settled on habeas corpus, a time-honored and constitutionally grounded remedy, meaning "have the body before me," the issuing judge; that would be Roderigo Lopez. It operated against the jailer, not the Chief Justice. An end run, sweet.

I am beginning to see why Roderigo Lopez was transported all this way from Shakespeare's time ... He is now in a position to shut down the Chief Justice who had, centuries ago, shut him down. Data said he loved it, would put the writ together with a memo, and travel to Hartford with it, practicing under the Connecticut student practice rule, with me as his Yale Law School approved mentor, ask for an ex parte hearing and go for habeas.

And while this was going on, I would appear before the very Judge we were trying to shut down. As they say on PBS, this would be my "brief but spectacular moment." I said to my team, "Seems to me it's time for Thai."

Data said, "Every condemned man gets his favorite last meal— hope you like Thai. Save some for Friar Laurence."

With that, they repaired to our library to get the paperwork ready for Jo's return. "She's going to love this," said Ron.

"She already does," replied Data, "She's got the forms all filled out. They're on Francis' desk."

We did not pause to wonder whether getting Friar Laurence out was, as they say, A Good Thing. Or whether we may soon join Kathleen Chung on the unemployment line.

I tossed off my Thai, Ron wolfed down his salami and Swiss Sub, and he and I returned to the courthouse, intercepting our three cross-dresser clients along the way. They were not difficult to find.

As we walked, I turned to Ron and asked, "Do you know anything about Operation Net Nanny?"

Ron stepped back, stopped and looked at me, and said, "Why?"

I replied, "The Chief Justice is trying to use it against Friar Laurence."

Ron replied, "It's a sting operation to get men to solicit sex with 13-year-old girls. There are already a dozen men doing ten years for attempted rape."

I was stunned and said, "Looks like our Friar Laurence may be next. I will walk our ladies into the court; you get to jail ASAP and talk to Friar Laurence. He is to talk with nobody, absolutely nobody, male or female, about possible contact, even in the confessional, with a teenage girl. Especially in the confessional!"

"Jesus!" said Ron, "These guys are giving hardball a bad name."

People opened a path for my clients and me along the sidewalk as we went up the front steps and returned to Courtroom 2 to be greeted on time by Chief Justice Popham, who said, "Mr. Collins, I believe it is your turn. Two witnesses?"

"Your Honor, we will have one of the defendants testify, followed by one expert witness. Let me call to the stand Charles Crutcher."

The Chief Justice said, "To be clear, let me inquire of Mr. Payne and Mr. Hazel as to whether they are exercising their right to remain silent?"

The two aforementioned gentlemen nodded and then said "Yes," upon prodding by me.

The Chief continued, "Are you as well, stipulating that your testimony would be identical with that of Mr. Crutcher?"

Answer, nod, yes.

"Well," Popham added, "never let it be said that I do not protect defendant's rights, and so let me advise you, at the end of Mr. Crutcher's testimony, if there is any correction you wish to make or objection, please feel free to call it to my attention at that time."

Both of my gentlemen, being very polite gentlemen, said, "Thank you."

I stood, said, "Thank you, Your Honor. The defense calls Charles Crutcher to the stand." Charles Crutcher stood with great deliberation and dignity, in three-inch heels, she/he was six foot two, towering over me. As I may have said before, a hooker I could look up to.

He/she walked to the witness stand, was sworn by the clerk, sat down, arranged various garments and body parts in a dignified and decorous fashion and turned to the Chief Justice and said, "Good afternoon, sir." He ignored her/whatever.

MR. COLLINS

"Let me begin, Mr. Crutcher, by asking your preferred pronoun."

A. "Thank you for asking, in this setting and my work setting, I prefer 'he.' In the setting described by officer Buffalo and Mr. Doe this morning, I would, of course, go by 'she.' But in all other settings, including my job, and this Court, I speak as a male."

Q. "About that, let me ask, what your work is?"

A. "I work in a laundry, doing cleaning and ironing. I might mention that my codefendants are also regularly employed, Mr. Payne as a manager/accountant at a speedy automobile oil change business and Mr. Hazel in the Yale University food service. Each of us is self-supporting, and we share an apartment."

Q. "Yes, well, we heard a good deal about the apartment this morning from officer Buffalo and Mr. Doe. Was what they described substantially accurate?"

A. "With some minor exceptions and nuances, the answer is yes. We did present ourselves to Mr. Doe and Mr. Smith as they came out of a local pub; there was an exchange of comments which led to our inviting the two gentlemen back to our apartment, on a contractual arrangement totaling, I believe, $300. Once inside, one of them, I believe it was Mr. Smith, essentially said let's get to it, and so we proceeded to disrobe. It was clear they were there for sex and that we would provide it.

"Once we were in a state of dishabille, they saw the variety of sex that we offered, and they became flustered, embarrassed, then angry, and then violent. To try to get past this, which we have encountered before, Mr. Payne asked who wanted to go first, and in what way? Smith said something about faggots and perverts, which we definitely are not. Mr. Hazel said that they were a couple of white, loser creeps, and he wouldn't go down on them for all of the money in the world, but he would fuck them up the ass.

"Smith then punched somebody or, wait, threw a chair, and it broke on our dining table. This pissed off Mr. Payne, who, despite his size, is very capable in the martial arts, and so he went after Smith, Doe jumped on him, I pulled him off, somebody hit me, and Mr. Hazel grabbed Smith and threw him out the door, I did the same with Doe, and that was the end of the fight. Of course, it was not the end of the matter because here we are, courtesy of Officers Buffalo and Gifford."

Q. "Have you had contact with them before, as officer Buffalo described?"

A. "Yes."

Q. "With similar results?"

A. "Yes."

Q. "So if the officers were sitting outside as you all went into the apartment, and they know from prior experience what is going to happen, could they have intervened and prevented the violence?"

A. "Yes. But of course, that would defeat the purpose, wouldn't it? They are vice squad officers, they get paid by the arrest, and so they needed to have an incident happen rather than to protect the public safety by preventing an incident."

Q. "Similarly," I said, "it might have been prevented if you had simply told Doe and Smith, going in, that you all three were male and that the sex you had to offer would be based on that fact. Isn't that true?"

A. "Of course, that is true. We could have avoided a dozen or two dozen similar incidents, leading to violence, by simply not doing what we do, which is to dress in a particular, provocative way, as we are today. But that's not the point, is it?"

Q. "Tell Chief Justice Popham, if you would please, about the way you dress and carry yourselves on occasions such as this."

A. "Well, Your Honor, we dress in short skirts and tops, high heels, fishnet stockings, with bright and brassy wigs, to draw attention to ourselves, then in a particular fashion which says that we are available, if anyone is interested, for purposes of sex trafficking. Of course, it all amounts to nothing if there aren't people like Doe and Smith with similar interests. So, for lascivious carriage or night walking, it requires two people. As we understand the term, it requires sexual activity that is prohibited or deemed immoral, which is no longer true of prostitution in Connecticut. So, we present ourselves as available-for-sale. That's it."

Q. "Let me close out my examination, Mr. Crutcher, by turning to one last area and trying to clear it up. When you knew that Smith and Doe were coming back to the apartment with you, did you also know to a certainty this would lead to violence?"

A. "Absolutely. It always does. That's the point, isn't it? We need the excitement, the thrill, the danger, even the pain and hurt provoked by our tricking and defrauding these straight, white, pathetic males into violence. It's what we are."

Q. "Mr. Crutcher, you say that is what you 'need,' what do you mean by that?"

A. "We have to have it. There's no choice. We are driven to it, and when we first got together, it was part of our sex play, but the edge and urgency of danger is all greater, and better, this way. Do you understand?"

MR. COLLINS

"No, I do not understand, even though I believe what you say is true for you. Let me now turn to Mr. Payne and Mr. Hazel, sitting here, having listened to your testimony, and ask them if their testimony would be substantially identical?

"Gentlemen, I need you to say yes, indicating assent for the court stenographer. She cannot simply enter a nod of the head in the record."

DEFENDANTS PAYNE AND HAZEL

"Yes."

MR. COLLINS

"They both answered 'yes.'" '

The stenographer turned to me and said, "Thank you."

With that, I turned to the Chief Justice and said, "Your Honor, that's all I have of this witness and only one witness more."

He turned to Larry Levy and said, "Mr. Levy, any questions, and if so, please be quick." Larry stood, with his sloth-like agility, rifled through some notes on his counsel table, turned to Arnold Buffalo, mumbled a few words, turned back to his notes, then dived quickly into his attaché case. Chief Justice Popham said, "Now. Today. I am advancing in age and will be retiring soon; I would like to conclude this case before then."

Larry seemed surprised at the acerbic tone and said, "Your Honor, I do have a few questions."

Larry then addressed Charles Crutcher.

MR. LEVY

"Mr. Crutcher, do you consider yourself transgender, homosexual, a sexual deviate, psychotic?"

A. "NO!"

Q. "Is this compelling need you articulate, to dress as a female and entice people into relationships based on that appearance, present in any of your other relationships or situations in your life?"

A. "No."

Q. "True as well for your codefendants?"

A. "Yes."

Q. "So as you three go to work in a food service, or quickie gas oil change place, or whatever else you do, you don't look as you look today, correct?"

A. "Yes, conventional male-appealing dress."

It occurred to me that Larry was running up some points, albeit slowly, but they were pretty good points. I was curious as to what would come next. It was good.

Q. "So, Mr. Crutcher, what moves you is entrapping other people into an uncomfortable situation, abusing them emotionally, placing them and yourself in danger, and experiencing physical pain. Is that a fair statement, the essence of what you're doing? On a Saturday night?"

A. "It is both. I have to dress as a woman, and I have to experience the violence."

Q. "But isn't it the violence and the abusing of the other people? The fake strutting and soliciting has no other point, does it?"

A. "Yes. Correct."

Q. "At home, do you dress as you do in your work settings?"

A. "Yes."

Q. "Are there other ways to get the excitement in the violence, for example, presenting yourselves as male homosexual prostitutes and then provoking arguments and fights?"

A. "Perhaps but ..."

Q. "So, is it fair to say, this female slutty presentation is just one among many possibilities that would get you the same thing, violence and danger?"

A. "Perhaps."

Q. "Do these encounters, like the one with Smith and Doe, cause you to be sexually aroused?"

A. "What do you mean?"

Q. "Oh, come on! You know what I mean! Do you get it up, make wood, get a hard on, are you visited by Mr. Johnson?"

A. "This is very personal, and I refuse to answer. This question is insulting."

MR. COLLINS

"I object. This is very personal; it is not relevant or material. Mr. Levy should apologize."

MR. LEVY

"Oh, nonsense! You don't, do you? You can't get it up, can you? Do you ever? What about your fellow pervs, Payne and Hazel? Don't bother answering; you are all a bunch of pathetic losers. Question withdrawn, Your Honor.

"Only two more questions. First, the sexual persona that you are wearing right now in this courtroom, you don't wear it anywhere else except when you're entrapping men into your apartment, so the need to appear as a certain kind of female just doesn't exist Monday through Friday, on your 9 to 5 daily rounds, or in the evenings when you're hanging out together. Right?"

A. "Yes."

Q. "So you can control this mania, as to time, place, purpose. Then tell me, why are you sitting here, all slutty and cheap, as if for sale, looking like this?"

A. "You won't understand this, Mr. Levy, because nothing you can do could possibly work for you, but I do this because I feel pretty. I like me this way. That's why. And you are the loser."

MR. LEVY

"Well, we shall see at the end of this trial which one of us is a loser. Mr. Chief Justice, I have no further questions of this witness, and I understand we will not hear from the other defendants."

Popham turns to me and says, "Mr. Collins?"

I respond, "I have one more witness, Dr. Laura Miyazaki, who is here in the audience section." I turn to the audience section and call for Dr. Laura Miyazaki. A petite, trim, silver-haired professional lady in dark blue rises, comes through the gate in the bar. As she is being sworn, Jo, my highly visible and supremely confident paralegal/office administrator/all-around hero, comes swinging through the swinging doors of the courtroom, opens a sizable folder while in full stride, steps up to counsel table and fans documents thereon in a single motion, with a manner of utter control, hands me a ballpoint pen pointing to three lines, where I sign my name, she pivots back up the aisle, and out of the courtroom, all in one swell foop (well ...), as I turn toward my witness, and ask her to state her name.

She replies, watching bemused as the swinging doors swing behind Jo, "Counselor, I just did that." And then adds, nodding to the space just vacated by Jo, "I also wish I could do that."

Our expert on gender dysphoria, Dr. Laura Miyazaki, settles herself in the witness chair and greets the judge, Chief Justice Popham, with a smile and a "Good afternoon Your Honor." I ask her name and occupation, and field of specialization within psychiatry, which she identifies as gender neuroses, syndromes, and psychoses. I then ask her to describe her training, both academic and clinical. She begins by saying that she holds posts within the psychology department at Yale University and the psychiatric service at Yale New Haven Hospital.

When I begin to ask her residencies and Board certifications, as well as professional associations and awards, Larry slowly rises and says to the Chief Justice, "Your honor, we will stipulate that Dr. Miyazaki is fully credentialed and highly regarded in her field, such as it is."

Popham turns to me and says, "Counselor, are you willing to accept the stipulation, minus Mr. Levy's damning with faint praise?"

I do and move on.

MR. COLLINS

"Dr. Miyazaki, have you been in the courtroom since the beginning of this trial?"

A. "Yes."

Q. "Did you hear the testimony of officer Buffalo and Mister John Doe?"

A. "Yes."

Q. "Did you hear the testimony of the defendant, Charles Crutcher, and based upon the testimony by the prosecution witnesses and the defendants, were you able to form an opinion, to a professional certainty, as to whether the defendants suffer from a condition or syndrome known as gender dysphoria?"

A. "Yes."

At this point, Larry rises and slowly objects. Popham waits, waits, and then says ...

CHIEF JUSTICE

"Mr. Levy, are you going to provide the grounds for your objection sometime in the near future?"

MR. LEVY

"May I ask a question in aid of an objection, Your Honor?"

CHIEF JUSTICE

"You may, quickly."

MR. LEVY

"Doctor, have you conducted a clinical examination or interview with any of the three defendants? Have you examined any hospital records of any of the three defendants? Do you know whether any of the defendants has seen or sought medical attention for any psychological or psychiatric condition, syndrome, or other affliction?"

A. "The answer is no as to all parts of the question."

With that, Larry turns back to the Chief Justice and asks him to exclude any testimony by Dr. Miyazaki for lack of a foundation. Larry, in his slow-mo fashion, raises his hands to the heavens and adds, "I doubt that anyone in this courtroom would want a diagnosis of cancer or pregnancy or even gender dysphoria, whatever that is, without a clinical examination or some form of medical record review. And both are missing here."

I am quickly on my feet and reply, "I can answer that objection with one or two basic questions to the good doctor. May I?"

"You may," says the Chief.

MR. COLLINS

"Is it possible to form a professionally grounded opinion based upon testimony of conduct and beliefs such as you have heard in court this morning?"

A. "The answer is yes. If I were conducting a psychological or psychiatric examination, my questions would have paralleled much of the questioning which I just heard. And my opinion would have been based on the answers which I just heard."

Q. "Also, may I ask, is it commonplace for people afflicted with psychological and psychiatric disorders not to seek treatment or assistance, so that diagnoses are oftentimes based on interviews or statements taken in settings which are not medical or psychiatric or psychological facilities?"

A. "Yes."

CHIEF JUSTICE

"The objection is overruled. Mr. Levy, you may renew it after the close of this witness' testimony. But I will hear the testimony, and to move this along, let me enter a finding that the witness may render opinions, having been qualified as an expert. Proceed."

MR. COLLINS

"Dr. Miyazaki, is gender dysphoria a form of insanity or psychosis?"

A. "No."

Q. Is it an identifiable mental or psychological condition with standardized symptoms, consequences, and treatments?

A. "Yes."

Q. "Can it affect, even compel, certain forms or patterns of conduct?"

A. "Yes."

Q. "Could you please describe what gender dysphoria is and what it means and what it is not?"

A. "Yes, gender dysphoria involves a conflict between a person's assigned or physical gender and that with which he/she/they identify. They are typically very uncomfortable with their assigned gender, its roles, and even their body. This distress affects the way they feel and think of themselves. It can influence behavior, dress, and self-image. Some people may cross-dress, others may want to transition medically."

Q. "Would you like a glass of water? And would you please proceed?"

A. "Yes. For diagnosis, gender dysphoria must last at least six months and have at least two qualities or characteristics (A) a sharp departure between one's assigned or expressed gender and primary or secondary sex characteristics and (B) a strong desire to be rid of those characteristics and replace them with characteristics of the other gender. A person experiencing gender dysphoria has a strong desire to be of the other gender, to be treated as such, and to be affirmed by having the typical feelings of the other gender."

MR. COLLINS

"Let me get you another glass of water, Doctor, and you may continue as you please."

A. "Of particular importance with respect to your clients, Mr. Collins, gender dysphoria is associated with high levels of stigmatization, discrimination, and victimization, and contributes to a negative self-image and increased rates of other mental disorders. They are at increased rates and risk for suicide or self-inflicted harm. And that would certainly be pertinent to the conduct of these young gentlemen."

"Gender dysphoria would explain a good deal of what these young men are experiencing."

Q. "Please elaborate."

A. "Most significantly, what we have is an extensive pattern of behavior maintained over months, perhaps years, and it is directly built upon a rejection of the defendants' maleness, and it places them directly in harm's way; indeed, it would seem that is the very purpose of what they do."

Q. "Would you say that they are insane?"

A. "I hesitate because insanity is a legal concept. Indeed, as you are aware, a number of states, including Connecticut, have abolished insanity as a defense in criminal proceedings.

"We in psychiatry and psychology speak of disease disorders, such as psychoses and neuroses, and disabilities or disorders which are frequently clustered together to constitute patterns and syndromes, identifiable and often times treatable.

"If by insanity, do you mean can these defendants control their behavior? The answer is within an important range, No. They do, however, plan their activities; they understand what they're doing; they realize the risks. They know the difference between right and wrong.

"But what the defendants are doing is so self-destructive, repetitive, and unnecessary that it can only be characterized as utterly driven and irrational. One way of measuring this is to ask the question, do they learn anything from the self-inflicted harm they experience? Answer, no. By any standard, including theirs, it can only be called crazy. They are sick. And it has to do with gender identity, dysphoria."

"Let me conclude, Dr. Miyazaki," I asked, "by asking this, they are charged with essentially the crime of enticing men to have heterosexual sex with them, knowing it is impossible and most likely will lead to violence. Are they out of touch with reality?"

A. "Yes. In the sense that the reality of their conduct will have the exact opposite of its customary purpose: there will be no sex, only violence and bloodshed. At some level, they cannot appreciate this in the same way you and I can."

Q. "Are they driven by irresistible impulses."

A. "No."

Q. "Do they know the difference between right and wrong?"

A. "Yes."

Q. "Are they culpable in the same way you or I would be if we engaged in such conduct?"

Here, Larry moved with almost lightning-like rapidity, well, at least faster than a snail, to object, "Calls for a legal conclusion and speculation and, and ..."

"Enough," said Chief Justice Popham, "I will allow it. Objection overruled. Proceed, Dr. Miyazaki."

She answered, turning to Larry, "Culpability is a state of mind and morality, as well as a legal term. In the psychological sense, these young men are not culpable. Then, turning to me, she said, "Mr. Collins, you or I could not conceivably engage in such behavior. They can because they are diseased. Legally, they may be culpable, but by any other measure, they are sick."

MR. COLLINS

"Thank you, Doctor. Chief Justice Popham, I have nothing further."

CHIEF JUSTICE

"Mr. Levy, any questions"?

MR. LEVY

"Yes. A few."

CHIEF JUSTICE

"Make it so."

MR. LEVY

"Doctor, the term 'dysphoria' basically means confusion, doesn't it?"

A. "Yes."

Q. "A generalized feeling of unhappiness, or dissatisfaction?

A. "Yes."

Q. "But these defendants, are only, shall we say confused, under limited circumstances: let's say, on a Saturday night, when they dress in a particular way, approach men in a particular way, bring them back to a specific place, and propose activity which they know will lead to violence. Correct?"

A. "Yes."

Q. "And they have it down to a precise science, don't they? They know what they are doing, what they are after, yes?"

A. "Yes."

Q. "So, wouldn't you say this is the opposite of 'confused,' that it's clear, controlled, and effective conduct?"

A. "Yes, but that is their response to the underlying dysphoria."

Q. "And also, isn't dysphoria a feeling of being unhappy, the opposite of euphoria?"

A. "Yes."

Q. "But, I do not recall Mr. Crutcher saying, or Officer Buffalo saying, that these defendants seemed unhappy. Do you recall such testimony?"

A. "No."

Q. "Dressing as women, attracting men, experiencing violence, didn't it all sound exciting to them?"

A. "Yes."

Q. "Oh, and one last question, do I recall correctly, please correct me if I'm wrong, that at the end of his testimony, Mr. Crutcher said that he enjoys dressing as he does because it makes him feel pretty?"

A. "Yes."

MR. LEVY

"So basically, this is a gang of teenagers cross-dressing to get their rocks off on a Saturday night by embarrassing a bunch of pathetic middle-aged white suburban males at a downtown bar. That was not a question, Dr. Miyazaki. I am done."

MR. COLLINS

"With the court's permission, I, however, am not quite done. I would like to have Dr. Miyazaki respond to that last comment by Mr. Levy. Dr. Miyazaki, is that all we have here? Three young cross-dressers perversely having fun at the expense of straight Johns?"

A. "Absolutely not. They engage in cross-dressing, dressing as women, but with a specific style and effect in mind. It is dysphoric because it is a product of generalized unhappiness, and leads only to unhappiness, in that it leads to violence and harm because they are confused basically about their own sexuality."

"I quite agree with Mr. Crutcher, as he sits here today, in a highly stylized fashion he is, in fact, pretty, as a cross-dresser. But on a Saturday night, when he and his friends follow a course of conduct designed for destruction and possibly death, that is pathology. He has not succeeded as a male, or as a female, and his functioning in the persona he presents today is a rejection of both roles, a form of self-destruction, best evidenced on a Saturday night."

"Thank you, Doctor." I conclude, saying to the Chief, "I have nothing further. The defense rests."

Larry rises and says, "The State would like to call, in rebuttal, Mr. John Smith."

"Request denied," responds Chief Justice Popham, "as I understand it, John Doe testified fully as to the events, and his testimony stands uncontradicted. There is nothing to rebut." With that, the Chief thanks Dr. Miyazaki "for your thoughtful and insightful testimony; you have been most helpful. You may step down."

As Dr. Miyazaki passes my table, I thank her and turn my attention back to the Chief Justice, as he is saying, "Gentlemen, I trust that concludes the testimony in this case."

I say, "We would like to be heard in closing."

"As would we, Your Honor," Larry responds.

"That won't be necessary," says Popham, "we will postpone argument for two weeks, with briefs in a week. I am prepared to make three rulings at this time.

First, I find the defendants guilty of engaging in night walking and lascivious carriage by their own testimony, offered through Mr. Crutcher, as well as that of the officer and Mr. Doe. Nothing could be more obvious or pitiful.

Secondly, my conclusion is not affected by the testimony concerning gender dysphoria, as persuasive as Dr. Miyazaki was, because it does not amount either to insanity or diminished capacity. In any event, these are not specific intent crimes. In other words, it is enough that they chose to engage in the conduct and knew what they were doing. The State does not need to prove they intended a specific outcome.

Thirdly, I find the evidence insufficient to suggest discriminatory policing or prosecution, although I find the misallocation of police resources for these purposes appalling. It is true that the police targeted these three youngsters, and the police pattern is almost as dismaying as that of the defendants. But discretion is inherent in police work and must be tolerated unless for unacceptable reasons, such as race or disability. Repetitive stupidity, either by the police or the defendants, is not discriminatory along race or gender lines. I hardly need to add that it serves no public purpose whatsoever.

"You will note," The Chief continued, "that I have reserved one issue, as to which I want briefs within the week, to be followed by oral argument, on the specific question of whether the statutes involved are so vague as to deny due process under the Constitution, in that they give no guidance as to what conduct is included or excluded. In your briefing, gentlemen, I wish that you consider specifically the recent legislation legalizing prostitution, which previously would have been central to defining what is lascivious. With that gone, do the statutes stand? Due process, equal protection?

"Briefs are due within ten days. You may respond and challenge the three rulings that I have made, and I will entertain closing arguments at that time. But I specifically request briefing and argument on the constitutional issue.

"Let me close by addressing Messrs. Crutcher, Payne, and Hazel to say that this Court is impressed with the quality of lawyering in this case. Both Mr. Levy and Mr. Collins have done their work well, both thoughtfully and economically. In my judgment, it is far more than the three of you deserve. You engage in conduct that is a social affront to civil decorum, public discourse, and the community's safety and peace.

"While the law may ultimately acquit you in this case, as to which I reserve judgment, I am clear at this time that you are a blight upon this community and should seek psychiatric assistance immediately. In fairness, I will continue the terms of your release. I will also consider counsel's arguments as fully as possible. But I hereby order you to desist from further misconduct until I render judgment in this case, and you may rely on it if the judgment is one of conviction, any misconduct in the interim will weigh heavily against you."

With that, Chief Justice Popham declared that "this concludes the business before the court this afternoon, with one exception, "Mr. Collins, I would like to see you in chambers immediately."

I turned to my three clients and said to them, "The kind words that the Chief Justice delivered concerning the lawyering here should not deceive you, he's just setting you up to bang you hard on judgment. Stay clean, stay safe, and stay away from trolling for Johns. You understand me?"

The three nodded in assent, and Charles Crutcher said, "We appreciate what you have done, thanks."

"You're welcome," say I, "and, you may count on it, we will win this thing."

As they exited the court through the magical swinging doors, Ron turned to me and said, "Well done, Boss, but now I think you are about to have your ass handed to you. I'm going to guess that Data made it to Hartford with the papers requesting Judge Roderigo Lopez to set aside Chief Justice Popham's order, which, even for you, can only be viewed as a ballsy, edgy move. I assume Lopez called Popham and maybe even scheduled a habeas corpus hearing for today with the jailer.

"Also," Ron continued, "I got to the jail, talked with our client, cautioned him against any contact, direct or indirect, concerning juvenile females. He told me there had been a strange call, supposedly from the Abbey, to see if he could take confessions this afternoon, and if so, he would be released for those purposes this afternoon. He was to call back. He and I agree it sounded like a setup, and he will call nobody."

And with that, totally stunned, I proceeded, once again, into chambers with a Justice whose ancient memory recalled my visage, and how to draw and quarter defendants, possibly attorneys.

Once inside the chambers, with the door closed, I stand unacknowledged, while Chief Justice Popham angrily throws papers into his briefcase, dons a light topcoat, furiously crams a hat upon his head, and then turns to me and says, "What in Christ's name do you think you're doing?" Several flippant responses flipped through my mind, but I remain silent. Popham continues, "I have received a call, with a fax of papers filed by your office, from my assistant, Judge Roderigo Lopez, in Hartford, all done while you and I were playing footsie with those weirdos, to the effect that you have filed a habeas to challenge my intervention in the grand jury and to have your client, Friar Laurence, released."

I start to say, "Not would have, but ..."

Popham leans forward across the desk, towering over me, continues, "Don't say a goddamned word, I am not done." His voice rises, and the room darkens as the sun shifts west. Despite his shouting, a strange silence settles on us.

"You apparently believe I exceeded my authority in directing the district attorney, Mr. Coke, to replace Ms. Chung and have the grand jury reconsider its decision, leading to its ultimately issuing a true bill against your client. He and I have worked on many cases together, and the grand jury is the instrument of his office (I start to say, "No, they are an independent body ...") and he and they may do as they choose. They choose now to charge your client."

Popham comes around the desk; I step back quickly.

"Moreover, I have separately issued a bench warrant assuring your client's present incarceration. There is no question but that he violated the terms of his release. I did not say there would be an exception for his being an intermeddling do-gooder. Too many pedophiles pretend to do exactly that. My order was clear and unequivocal, and he violated it."

And now, Popham pushes past me toward the door, his voice beating on me, "Your proper response is a motion in trial court on Monday, before me. Be there, with or without your client, and be prepared to have counsel defend you against my finding of contempt, which I hereby make. I am referring you to the Board of Bar Examiners. For immediate review."

As he prepares to exit, shouting at the top of his voice, his face florid and hands shaking, fists clenched, Popham adds, "Rest assured that I am not alone in believing Friar Laurence has come to this time and place for reasons known best to him having to do with Burbage's production of *Romeo and Juliet* at the Yale drama school. I do not for one moment believe he is a fictional character traveling across history and continents. I do believe, however, and this is much worse, that he thinks that is what he is. In his diseased pathology, he can do serious harm to those teenagers, and your efforts are designed to help him toward those ends.

"Finally, I told you not to interfere with Operation Net Nanny. Your client was set up for a phone call today, but he didn't make it. I believe you intervened, contrary to my instructions, and I now remove you as Laurence's defense counsel."

And with that, he slams down his briefcase on a nearby table for emphasis and continues, "I will be at Burbage's farcical walk-through tonight at the Drama School, with police escort, just in case Friar Laurence, with your conniving, gets loose. For his own safety, see that he does not."

371

I stood, thunderstruck, appalled at the vehemence, arrogance, and brute force of this man. I start to say, "Mr. Chief Justice ..." but he strode toward me, holding his briefcase chest high, and pushed me down into a chair, and said, "We are done here," and opened the door to leave.

I forced my way back up from the chair and into the doorway, blocking him (has he always been eight feet tall?) and declare, "You may think we are done, but I will not withdraw from this case, and you have no authority to remove me, and moreover, I hereby demand that you recuse yourself immediately, from both cases I have before you. You have prejudged them and shown yourself unfit to sit on the Bench of this State. Your latest move with Operation Net Nanny is an obscene effort to entrap an innocent man.

"And I will see you in Hell before ..."

A sentence I never finished because, strangely, Chief Justice Popham had moved past me in the doorway and into the outside landing, and I followed in his wake, where he silently, quickly disappeared before my very eyes, shades folding into shades. He was gone. I was left calling into an empty building, light failing far sooner than it should this early on a late Spring day.

And all that was left was an odor, was it the ancient odor of dust, musty corridors, sulphur ... Something very old. Does evil have a scent, an aroma, a faint stench? Reality seemed to be slipping away.

I left quickly for my office and my own corner of reality. Down the stairs, out onto the street, passing the cleaning people, come early on a Friday, puzzled that I seemed to be calling into nothingness, into an empty building, arguing with one who wasn't there.

I slowly regain my composure and balance as I walk back to the office, now a late afternoon on a spring day, a time where the staff and I usually do a quick review of the week past and the week coming up. We assembled for those purposes, Jo, Data, Ron and I. Chiefly it turns into a status discussion on Friar Laurence: a report on the confrontation with Chief Justice Popham setting a contempt hearing for Monday, with my responding by insisting he recuse himself, and with my being referred to the Bar Association. Add to that, what appears to be an abortive run at entrapment into Operation Net Nanny, and the Chief ordering me off the case.

Jo, dazzled, comments, "Francis, even for you that is a heavy load in one chambers' conference, it usually takes two or three for you to piss off a judge that much."

Data comments that it is "not too surprising, since Judge Roderigo Lopez had granted an ex parte hearing, and was dismayed by Popham's conduct, as reflected in our papers." He said that Lopez had commented, "The Chief Justice had no authority over the prosecutor or grand jury."

Lopez expected to discuss the matter as soon as Popham had finished with me. We should expect a call from Lopez's office momentarily.

That left us with Friar Laurence and the trial on the merits, which we turned to next. The charges were unclear. Stalking would be one, and there we needed to research admissibility of prior, similar acts, as well as intent with respect to the teenagers in this case. As to intent, it would be our position that, most importantly as it turned out, for the first time, the play was being presented in a radically different form. If this was the force drawing Friar Laurence, and the two teenagers were only incidentally involved, could it be said that he was "stalking" them?

Separately, there had been a suggestion that Friar Laurence had failed to register as a sex offender, based upon his prior acts with respect to Romeo and Juliet. While this seemed a stretch, still, he had been involved in arranging an illegal marriage for two teenagers and for its sexual consummation. Did these qualify as "sex offenses" then? Now? Did it matter, now, that there had never been a trial and conviction?

Then there was violating Popham's restraining order and assaulting Belsky. Defenses seemed clear: he sought to protect Juliet from attack. QED.

And, most recently, the approach to draw our client into Operation Net Nanny, so he could be charged with attempting to rape a thirteen-year-old (whose Internet photo, Ron said, was the Force's youngest policewoman), raised questions of entrapment, impossibility and judicial misconduct. Where to go and what to do about these?

Research on these is for D. Data, investigation, especially on Net Nanny, for Ron. Politics, for me ...

Our consensus was, if Popham were to be the judge, to take the case to the jury. No-brainer. Otherwise, it was a tossup. Postpone decision, and review with client. For the time being, we know where he lives. We think.

It was now getting on toward 5:30, late afternoon. The only thing remaining was a quick review of next week's files where pleas of guilty were going to be entered or cases dismissed by the prosecutor, with a separate category of cases coming up for sentencing where judgment had previously been entered. There were basically 15 total. Data had prepared pretrial memoranda, Ron had located witnesses who would appear in person or by letter, saying good things about our clients. Jo had made certain that the witnesses Ron had located had all been advised of the times and dates and locations for appearance. All was good.

And so it goes, our normal routine being somewhat askew because of Burbage's Director's Walk-Through at 7:00 PM. A number of our personalities from this week would be in attendance:

Jo and her husband, Charles Whiting and his once and future bride, Chief Justice Popham and his police security, I suspected Seamus O'Rourke, and, I had inklings, District Attorney Coke and former Assistant District Attorney Chung, who knows? "Oh," Jo reminded me, "Dorothy Arlow expects to be there, she and your Meg will meet you at the Drama School." Friar Laurence, in short order, had assembled quite a following; I was reminded of Dorothy Arlow's reminiscence from her youth, of swallows gathering, drawn to support the imminent flight of fledglings ...

That would be Friar Laurence. But we had no word as to whether he would be released from jail in time for Burbage's walk-through, or indeed, any time prior to a hearing on Monday morning. Jo said she had called the jail three times, and each time the answer was in the negative, Friar Laurence was unavailable and still in isolation. Per order of Chief Justice Popham. Nothing from Circuit Judge Roderigo Lopez.

As people dispersed, it occurred to me that I was keenly hungry, and I also became keenly aware that, as of this morning, last night's ribs had been stashed safely in my extra attaché case. Perhaps my beginning to salivate gave Jo the cue to say, on her way out the door, "I put them in the microwave, delayed setting, you should be able to smell them now."

I thought, my God, this woman is prescient.

"Yes, I am," she said, as she boarded Big John's Little Elevator to descend from her heavenly perch, "and the amazing part is I care so much for you I didn't eat them myself. Of course, I did pig out last night. So did your client. He may be sick, wherever he is. See you at the D School. The Iseman Theater, Green Hall, don't forget."

I call Meg to confirm that she and Dorothy Arlow will be meeting me at the Iseman, which she confirms, asking, "Shall I bring the kids?" Ordinarily, I would say yes. They're bright, curious, and they traded amniotic fluid at birth for Shakespeare. For reasons I don't understand at the time, I say no, as it later turns out, that is a wise choice. And we agree that we will meet at the Iseman, on Chapel, a half block from The Rep. This will be more intimate, a flexible performance space, seating 200 max, for a Director's Walk-Through, informal, yet in full costume and staging.

"By the way," Meg adds, "I can smell the ribs on your breath. You better save some for me." Another prescient woman.

A few blocks on a fine spring evening, under maple and oak trees, the smell of lilacs and dogwood in the air. The pathways across the bifurcated Green are filled with people, old and young, couples of all configurations, all shades of colors and ethnicities. New Haven has become the better part of humanity, a nice place to be. I checked my cell phone, no call from Friar Laurence, District Attorney Chung, or Judge Roderigo Lopez.

People are assembling at the Iseman entrance to Green Hall, many of them Drama students, as I had once been, many are families and friends of the cast, including the Montagues and the Capulets sitting together, my crowd and I gather in the very first row, which I prefer. I find myself seated between Meg, on my left in an aisle seat on the center aisle, and Jo, to my right with her husband. Dorothy Arlow is far off to my left, at the end of the front row, stage right. Directly behind me are the Abbot and Data. At the end of that second row, on stage left, are Charles Whiting and Michaela (oh my God, in wedding dress, as specified.) The front row is only a few feet below stage level, and less than ten feet from the active portion of it. We have good seats.

This is an informal walk-through, with the formal dress rehearsal a week away, and opening night a week from tomorrow, Saturday, at the Yale Rep, a former Calvary Baptist Church, more than twice as large and more formal. So, if Burbage is going to make his epochal, earth shattering, radical revisions, the schedule could not be tighter. But definitely still possible.

Here, the stage is largely open space, a barren, modern set, no need for the usually requisite structure for the upper window, from which Juliet and Romeo play out their moonlight scene, because we are into the Fifth Act. The lighting is at half strength, focused on the stage, and James Burbage comes out, ten-day beard laced with silver, hair over his ears, tweed jacket, Yale University six-foot scarf wrapped around his neck, wearing Birkenstocks. (I think, Birkenstocks?!) As always, the very epitome and paragon of the Shakespeare Professor, par excellence, with all due modesty ...

Off to the left, a boyish grad student, eagerly applauds Burbage's entrance, then looks around, embarrassed that he is the only one. I laugh, turn and say to Meg, "Boy du jour."

She replies, "You're just jealous."

"Not now, not never," say I.

"Double negative," says she.

The boy du jour glares at me ... He remembers Burbage introducing me a day or two ago, and is thinking, is that what a boy du jour looks like, 20 years out? Oh my God ...

There are three aisles, one down the center and one on each side along the walls, each with a door near the stage and an entry door at the lobby. But for effect, Burbage eschews those (yes, eschews, his word) and enters from the back of the stage, striding toward the footlights, toward the audience, steps from one warm spot light to another and says, dramatically, "Welcome to History ..." And then he moves to a second and then a third and adds, "in the making."

He pauses for a smattering of applause and continues, "In a week we will stage a Romeo and Juliet which is different from any other staging in the last 425 years. We are here in the year 2019; this most popular of Shakespeare's plays was written sometime in the middle 1590s, the only tragedie (how does he make it sound the way it actually was spelled in the First Folio?), with one exception, that Shakespeare wrote during that time. The rest were comedies and romances. And that is the way we remember it, as the romance of Romeo Montague and Juliet Capulet, overtaken by the tragedy of family antagonisms and the fatal, tragic bumblings of an incompetent cleric."

Burbage is warming to his task and his audience. He has a rich voice, and athletic confidence in midlife, piercing eyes, and he brings

378

this all to bear on these lovers whom he clearly loves. "They are not extraordinary, they are not kings and queens, they are very young and very much in love, these lovers. The first half of the play is filled with rich comedy, the second half with accident and calamity, along with deception and despair and death. At the end, order is restored and hatred is banished, but at a huge price, death.

"It is my view," he continues, assured his view is the important one, "that death is too great a price to pay. Romeo and Juliet should live and love. They should soar like eagles on the breath of dawn. And tonight, we shall make it so. Tonight, for the first time, the only time, in centuries, perhaps ever ..." and here he pauses "... they shall not die."

Burbage continues now, drawing on the arcane recesses of his knowledge, to say, "This has been done before, but briefly and barely, in the late 1600s. That version where they did not die alternated with the classical version by Shakespeare, done simply for commercial gain, without our profound reason and commitment. For a long time, the chief variation was to allow Romeo to live until Juliet awakens, and they die together. There has been other minor tweaking, Juliet's age being increased to 18, dancing and music added, scenes cut back to allow for grand sets."

Pacing now, swinging his arms like a bird in flight, Burbage takes off with what he intends to do tonight, "Never before have directors and cast sought the true core and meaning of this play and committed themselves to truth, as Shakespeare intended. We will do that tonight. Tonight, we shall soar in romance. The lovers will live to love. History will never again be the same."

Centered now, on the stage, pounding the rostrum before him, Burbage expounds, "And let me emphasize that this is not because death is always wrong. In others of Shakespeare's tragedies, *Lear*, *Hamlet*, *Macbeth*, *Othello*, the tragic flaw justifying death is in the character of the principal figures. It is not, as they say, in the stars, but in themselves. That is not true with *Romeo and Juliet*. Here, one cannot find flaws with the character of the lovers. The fault then, truly, is not in them but in their stars. Shakespeare himself declares this, referring to them as 'star-crossed lovers.' With that as our cue, we will undertake a small, but heavenly, realignment, and the truly Shakespearean play will emerge for all time."

He continues, "Only a few days ago, I suggested several possibilities for the realignment. Perhaps Friar John would reach Romeo in time for him to find Juliet alive, not dead. Perhaps the poison potion Romeo gets from the apothecary is instead a placebo, so they both survive. Perhaps Friar Laurence will arrive in time, to intercept Romeo and explain that Juliet is not truly dead, but awaits him. Has it ever made sense that Friar Laurence was late to the wedding, so to speak?" Here, Burbage chuckles modestly at his own funny ...

"We will present only the last act in the play, and we have spent most of our time on it. Therefore, we are able tonight to walk-through the action, in full costume, in our appropriate places, blocked out, with lighting, leaving to the next few days doing the same for the rest of the play, so that we hope you will all return in a week, for the dress rehearsal, a week from tonight, and opening night a week from tomorrow.

"Ladies and gentlemen, let us present an informal walk-through of Act Five, the Romance of Romeo and Juliet, by William Shakespeare. Lights please. Players, take your places. Begin." And with this, a last flourish, Burbage concludes, walking slowly out of the spotlight, back into the darker stage, from which his voice echoes forth, and in the air there hangs a melody, and opening lines of 'As Time Goes By.'"

As Burbage from the far recesses of the stage introduces,

ROMEO AND JULIET: A ROMANCE

By SHAKESPEARE and BURBAGE

the lights come up partially the actors speak.

ACT V Scene 1

ROMEO

I dreamt my lady came and found me dead—strange dream that gives a dead man leave to think!—And breathed such life with kisses in my lips that I revived and was an Emperor. Ah me, how sweet is love itself possessed when but love's shadows are so rich in joy.

(Enter Romeo's Man [Balthasar, booted])

News from Verona! How now, Balthasar, how fares my Juliet? That I ask again, for nothing can be ill if she be well.

BALTHASAR

Then she is well, and nothing can be ill. Her body sleeps in Capel's monument, and her immortal part with Angels lives. I saw her laid low in her kindred's vault ... And presently took post tell it you. O, pardon me for bringing these ill news.

ROMEO

Well, Juliet, I will lie with thee tonight. Let's see for means. I do remember an apothecary—and hereabouts he dwells—in tattered weeds. Meager were his looks. Sharp misery had worn him to the bones. As I remember, this should be the house. What, ho! Apothecary! Come hither, man, I see that thou art poor. Hold, there is 40 ducats. A dram of poison, as will disperse itself through all the veins, that the life weary taker may fall dead ...

APOTHECARY

Such mortal drugs I have, but Mantua's law is death to any he that utters them. My poverty but not my will consents.

ROMEO

I pay thy poverty but not thy will. There is thy gold. Farewell. Buy food, and get thyself in flesh. Come cordial and not poison, go with me. To Juliet's grave for there must I use thee.

("Well," I whisper to Meg, "that closes out the first of Burbage's options. Romeo's got the poison."

"Be patient," says the Abbot, who I had forgotten was sitting behind me.

"And be quiet," Says Jo, sitting to my right.)

ACT V Scene 2

FRIAR LAURENCE

Friar John, welcome from Mantua! What says Romeo? Give me his letter.

("He looks more like Woody Allen than our Friar Laurence," Meg whispers.

"We can't all be studs, like your husband," I reply.

"BE QUIET." Jo hisses.)

FRIAR JOHN

The searchers of the town, where the infectious pestilence did reign, sealed up the doors and would not let us forth.

FRIAR LAURENCE

Who bear my letter, then, to Romeo?

FRIAR JOHN

I could not send it—here it is again—nor get a messenger to bring it thee, so were thee of infection.

(He gives a letter.)

FRIAR LAURENCE

Unhappy fortune! Neglecting the letter may do much damage. Now must I to the monument alone. Within this three hours will fair Julia wake, but I will keep her at my cell till Romeo come, poor living corpse, closed in a dead man's tomb.

("And there goes option two, Romeo thinks she's dead," I whisper to Meg.

"Patience," again, from behind me).

ACT V Scene 3

PARIS

Give me thy torch, boy. Under yond yew trees lay thee all along, holding thy ear close to the hollow ground. Whistle then to me as signal that thou hearest something approach.

("Bye-bye, Belsky, as County Paris," I say. "Let's see if Romeo kills the replacement." I am ignored.)

PAGE

I am almost afraid to stand alone, yet I will adventure.

PARIS

Sweet flower, with flowers thy bridal bed I strew, which with sweet water nightly I will dew. The boy gives warning something doth approach. What cursed foot wanders this way tonight? What, with a torch? Muffle me, night, awhile.

(Enter Romeo and Balthasar with a torch, a mattock, and a crowbar.)

ROMEO

Give me that mattock and the wrenching iron. Here take the letter. Early in the morning, see Thou deliver it to my Lord and Father. Give me the light. Do not interrupt me in my course. Why I descend into this bed of death is partly to behold my lady's face, but chiefly to take hence from her dead finger a precious ring. If thou return to pry in what I farther shall intend to do, by heaven, I will tear thee joint by joint and strew this hungry churchyard with thy limbs.

BALTHASAR

I will be gone, sir, and not trouble ye.

ROMEO

Thou detestable maw, thou womb of death, gorged with the dearest morsel of the earth thus I enforce thy rotten jaws to open.

(He begins to open the tomb.)

PARIS

Stop thy unhallowed toil, Montague! Condemned villain. I do apprehend thee. Obey and go with me for thou must die.

ROMEO

Good gentle youth, fly hence and leave me. O, begone! By heaven, I love thee better than myself. Live, and hereafter say a madman's mercy bid thee run away. O, give me thee hand, I'll bury thee in a triumphant grave.

("Wow! Burbage does not have Romeo kill Paris here," I exclaim with a stage whisper heard by everybody.

"Of course not, you fool," says Burbage, behind me and across the aisle to my left. How did he get there?

Meg's elbow is in my ribs, going for my kidneys. "Will you shut up?" adding to the hisses.)

ROMEO

(He opens the tomb.)

O my love, my wife! Death that hath sucked the honey of thy breath hath had no power yet upon thy beauty. Thou art not conquered; beauty's ensign yet is crimson on thy lips and in thy cheeks, and death's pale flag is not advanced there.

Ah, dear Juliet, why art thou yet so fair? Here, here will I remain with worms that are thy chambermaids. O, here will I set up my everlasting rest and shake the yoke of inauspicious stars from this world-wearied flesh. Eyes, look your last! Arms, take your last embrace! And, lips, O you the doors of breath, seal with a righteous kiss a dateless bargain to engrossing death!

FRIAR LAURENCE

(Enters graveyard, approaches tomb.)

How oft tonight have my old feet stumbled at graves! Who's there?

BALTHASAR

Here's one, a friend, and one that knows you well.

FRIAR LAURENCE

Bliss be upon you. Tell me, good my friend, what torch is yond that vainly lends his light to grubs and eyeless skulls? As I discern, it burneth in the Capel's monument.

BALTHAZAR

It doth so, Holy sir, and there's my master. One that you love.

FRIAR LAURENCE

(Advancing to the tomb.)

Romeo! Oh, pale! Who else? What, Paris too? What an unkind hour is guilty of this lamentable chance! The Lady stirs.

ROMEO

What said my man as we rode? I think he told me Paris should have married Juliet. Said he not so? Or did I dream it so? Oh, do give me thy hand, one writ with me in sour misfortune's book. I say again, I'll bury thee in a triumphant grave.

(Juliet wakes.)

FRIAR LAURENCE

Romeo! Paris! Alack, alack, what blood is this which sustains the stony entrance of the sepulcher? What mean these masterless and gory swords to lie discolored by this place of peace? Steeped in blood? Cease your fighting.

(Romeo and Paris stop fighting.)

JULIET

Oh, comfortable Friar, where is my Lord? I do remember well where I should be, and there I am. Where is my Romeo?

FRIAR LAURENCE

I heard some noise. Lady, come from that nest of death, contagion, and unnatural sleep. A greater power than we can contradict hath thwarted our intents. I entered between Romeo and Paris to save them from foul death. Come, Come away.

Thy husband in thy bosom is here, and Paris, too. Both alive would marry you. I hereby annul the marriage between you and Romeo; you were not of age, and it was wrong of me to deceive your parents. I'll dispose of thee among a sisterhood of holy nuns. There you may tarry and linger to make your choice. Stay not to question, for the watch is coming. Go, good Juliet. I dare no longer stay. Get thee to a nunnery."

("Holy shit," I say, "all three are alive! Well done, Burbage!" He blows me a kiss, going back up the aisle in the dark.

"Can he annul the marriage?" Asks Jo.

"At that time," says the Abbot behind us, "yes. Underage and no parental consent. It was already a nullity."

"You people, for Christ's sake, shut up?" hisses the Chief Justice rows back to my left.

"Since you put it that way," the Abbot says, "Okay."

Jo, on my right, says, "Juliet looks pissed!"

Meg leaning across, says, "Wouldn't you be?)

JULIET

Go, get thee hence, for I will not away.

(To Romeo.)

I will kiss thy lips

(Kisses Romeo.)

Thy lips are warm. Oh, happy dagger!

(She seizes Romeo's dagger, bares her breast)

This is thy sheath. There rust and let me die.

(To Friar Laurence.)

God joined my heart and Romeo's, thou our hands, and ere this hand, by thee to Romeo sealed, shall be the label to another deed, or my true heart with treacherous revolt turn to another, this shall slay them both. Be not so long to speak; I long to die if what thou speak'st speak not of remedy.

FRIAR LAURENCE

Hold thy desperate hand!

(He lunges for the knife, slips and falls upon it.)

(Stunned, kneeling, he looks up at Juliet.)

Thou hast amazed me. By my holy order, I thought thy disposition better tempered. Wilt thou slay thyself, and slay thy lady, that in thy life lives, by doing damned hate upon thyself? Fie, fie, thou shamest thy shape, thy love, thy wit and usest none in that true use indeed which should bedeck thy shape, thy love, thy wit. Thou shalt live to blaze your marriage, reconcile your family and friends, beg pardon of the Prince, and all will call thee back with 20 hundred thousand times more joy ... You and Romeo and Paris must live ... And now I must die by this knife. I am the greatest, able to do least, yet most suspected as the time and place doth make against me, and here I fall, both to impeach and purge myself condemned and pray, in this end, myself excused.

(Friar Laurence slumps to the floor and dies.)

("Looks like the Friar paid his dues," says Jo.

"I did not see that coming," I say.

"Neither did Shakespeare," replies Meg.

"Cool," says Jo's husband.

"There is more," the Abbot whispers, "Wait.")

Abbot Dominic is right; there should be more, the closing scene with the Montagues and the Capulets and the Prince, regrets and reconciliation, a long speech by Friar Laurence (which, being dead, he cannot deliver, but see Chapter 3 above, if you were not paying attention earlier) and the closing lines by the Prince:

Go hence to have more talk of these sad things.

Some shall be pardoned and some punished;

For never was a story of more woe

Than this of Juliet and her Romeo.

(Exit Prince, Capulets, Montagues.)

But none of this will happen here in Chapter 29, because at 9:15 on a pleasant Spring evening in The Iseman Theater, Green Hall, 1156 Chapel Street, New Haven, Connecticut, where the house lights are low, and the spots are on the covered, slumped body of Friar Laurence and the standing persons of Juliet and Romeo, the world of the living takes over the world of the stage, all the lights in the theater go out, everything is in total darkness except for the weird and garish red glow of the exit signs, and before anyone can say, "holy shit," or its equivalent, a cell phone rings ...

CHAPTER THIRTY

A CELL PHONE RINGS

FRIAR LAURENCE ANSWERS THE CALL

... A cell phone rings, the only sound in the totally dark theater, multiple rows back above us, and a voice answers, saying, "Popham here," and then says, "Jesus Christ!"

We're still sitting in total darkness, and I am thinking, this is not good.

The Abbot, behind me, says, "Patience, Francis."

The Chief Justice continues in a loud voice, addressing, I am absolutely certain, my old friend the jailer over on Whalley Avenue, "You're telling me that the kid playing Friar Laurence in the Iseman Theater tonight is now in the cell where you had the real Friar Laurence? Where the fuck is the real one? Well, how the hell did he get out, and who is this here on the stage right now?"

With this, the emergency lights dimly illuminate the Iseman Theater, and the Chief Justice slams his cell phone to the floor and turns to Seamus O'Rourke, huge state trooper, and points to the slumped figure in the Monk's robe on the stage, until a nanosecond ago a Drama student who looked like Woody Allen, and says to O'Rourke, "Arrest that man, whoever he is. And I pray you have to shoot him to do it!"

O'Rourke rises slowly, reluctantly steps into the center aisle and moves ponderously down toward the stage, as the assembled cast depart with alacrity, leaving on the stage only Romeo, Juliet, now Burbage (where did he come from?) and the slumped body under Friar Laurence's hooded robe. Moments ago, the robe covered a diminutive D student the size and shape of Woody Allen. Now, whoever he is, he looks much larger ...

I turn, sitting in the front row, and face back to Abbot Dominic, asking, "How the hell did you get Friar Laurence out of the cell a mile away and here in a nanosecond?"

He pauses, somewhat annoyed with me, and says, "Francis, it is all simply a matter of time. Now, please try to pay attention."

To which Meg, Jo and Jo's husband, whose name I can never seem to remember, hiss in unison, "yes."

At that moment, three bright blasts of light burst from the three lobby entryways in the back of the Iseman Theater, blinding the audience and revealing a figure in dark silhouette in each doorway. The figure in the center doorway calls out, "O'Rourke, you fat, dumb, Mick loser, don't you touch him, he's mine. Nobody beats me up at a high school one morning and then takes over my play. They are all going to die. Back off, or you're a dead man too."

"My God, it's Belsky," I whisper to Meg; I start to rise, "I have to do something." I take a step across Meg into the center aisle. She clamps her legs on mine, grabs my belt, and slams me back into my seat.

Belsky continues, "And you, Romeo, rich snotty bastard that you are, what made you think you can take my girl? Oh, no, no, no. You should have died in the play, and you will die here. You and that rich Capulet bitch, neither of you deserves to live, and you won't. And you, Burbage, back off, you're like the priest, you're causing all these deaths in this theater tonight ..."

With that, Burbage moves quietly and quickly out of the spotlight, back upstage, closer to Romeo and Juliet.

I feel hands on my forearms, and I say, "I have to fix this,"

Meg and Jo pinning me in my chair, both saying as one, "The hell you do!"

Two strong hands from behind on my shoulders, the Abbot whispering, "Francis, your part was done long ago. You know that. And your turn will come again. But, for now, we must let these players play their parts. The stage is their world. Sit."

I sat.

Nobody except Trooper O'Rourke had moved. We were a tableau in stone, a film noir image, half-light, half-dark, house lights down, footlights half-up, time had stopped, as our eyes adjusted to see Belsky, now midway into the theater, and his two high school flunkies, Otto Schmidt, the Hitler look-alike, in Lobby Door stage right, possibly with one person behind him, and Shooter Number Three in Lobby Door stage left. Each standing with assault rifles on their hips, attired in trench coats and low brimmed hats, combat boots, and fatigues.

Dark figures were rising in their seats; voices began crying out, shadows stumbled into the aisles, down the stairs, away from the doors, wraiths about to die.

My God, I thought, is this a Shakespearean masque? A farce? Is this how it felt and seemed in those schools, Sandy Hook, Columbine, Virginia Tech? In the theater in Aurora, Colorado, the Gay nightclub in Florida ... nightmarish, impossible, unreal? If this was real, some of the people I cared most about in the world are about to die; it seemed hardly possible, but is this how it felt in those other places, to those people now long dead? My mind was racing. Did they think it couldn't be happening? Do I?

Belsky stood halfway down the center aisle with the assault rifle at his shoulder. O'Rourke turned from the Laurence figure lying on the stage back to face Belsky. All reluctance was gone now from O'Rourke, who saw clearly the danger confronting him, and who reached with practiced stealth into his jacket shoulder holster for his handgun. What had momentarily seemed farce was now tense drama, imminent tragedy.

Burbage's voice rang out, "Tommy, don't do it. Don't be a fool. This isn't a play, it's real. People will die."

Belsky replied, "Shut the fuck up, asshole. That's right; people are gonna die! You caused this mess, you're next."

With this exchange, O'Rourke was granted a momentary opening, and he took it, sliding the 9 mm Glock out of the holster, raising it with an expert two-handed grip, squaring his body toward Belsky, only ten feet away, and saying with incongruous, measured calm, professional equanimity, "Don't make me do this, kid. I've got you."

A foot (not mine) stuck out from an aisle seat on Belsky's left, causing Belsky to cry out, "What the fuck!" as he went falling forward toward the stage. O'Rourke's shot rang out, the bullet missing Belsky and ricocheting toward the back of the theater. Belsky lay stunned, his weapon skittering toward O'Rourke.

Schmidt, standing in the far door stage right, his face dark against the outside setting sun, swung his assault rifle left to right, spraying half a dozen shots in rapid succession, and hitting the state trooper twice, before he could squeeze off another round.

O'Rourke, a large solid man, had been standing in classic police fashion, his face and body in shadow; he was lifted off the steps and driven back and down from the impact of Schmidt's two shots. It was a matter of split seconds. He went down onto an empty aisle seat and then slumped to the floor, between rows two and three, stage right, opposite us, incongruously face to face with Belsky.

"Got him! Jesus Christ, I got him. The rest of you think we're joking? Fooling around? Take a look at that. Yeah, man!" The voice was crazed, frantic, almost hysterical. It was Schmidt. "Got him!" he cried out. "Who's next? Romeo? Juliet? Come on, someone, take a shot at me."

"Shut the fuck up, you Hitler dip shit," Belsky called out, getting up from the floor and picking up his rifle, stepping over O'Rourke, aiming at Schmidt.

Shooter Number Three, still standing high up in the opposite doorway, cried out, "Hey, I want a piece of this. Why are we holding back?"

And as I was thinking, startled, these were just high school crazies; they can't actually be killing people; against the bright backlight of the Iseman lobby, I could see him, Shooter Number Three, raising his assault rifle and firing shots toward the center aisle of the theater, from his position, stage left, closing on some of Romeo and Juliet's family sitting in that area, it was all in slow motion, a nightmare, a dream beyond dreaming, a number of people, a large number of people, about to die, when I heard Jo shout, "Somebody take that son of a bitch out! DO IT! *NOW!*"

And somebody did. It was hard to see, in the darkness, with the dim light weakly intruding into the theater, a figure rise, at stage left, stepping back onto the stage itself, another person, calmly, professionally, with the classic two hand grip, and the spread-legged stance, on the same side of the theater as Shooter Number Three, take careful aim up at Shooter Number Three, and as Number Three saw him and began training his weapon on him, all in terrible slow motion, slowly, the silhouetted figure fired just once.

Shooter Number Three uttered a grunt of surprise, folded and crumpled to the floor, letting light in through the doorway, and I could see, in the flash of the handgun, I could see, dimly but clearly, the short, somewhat pudgy, figure of a man who could have been prime minister of a West African nation, or a King in that part of the world, and who someday might be tried for murder, or in the alternative be married to the woman sitting by his side. Charles Whiting took out Shooter Number Three, with extreme prejudice, as they are wont to say, permanently, as they also said, with a single shot, I thought, much as he must have in Afghanistan with opposing forces, so one day he might meet and marry red-haired Michaela, there by his side tonight ... just nanoseconds before Belsky, firing multiple rounds from his automatic weapon, one knee in the center aisle, put Whiting down.

There was bedlam as people tried full force to flee across the stage to the stage doors, but Schmidt called out from his elevated position, in the center aisle, in the back of the theater, "The next one who moves a fucking inch is the next one to die. Nobody leaves here without our say-so. All of you, get down." And with that, for effect, the Hitler look-alike fired half a dozen rounds into the array of lights used for illuminating the stage. His weapon exploded with the rat-a-tat-tat of Chinese firecrackers on New Year's Eve ...

The entire theater went pitch black. So did the outside hallway. There was no overhead lighting. The small theater was echoing with the sound of gunfire, and the air was heavy with the acrid smoke of discharged weapons, over the cries and coughing of frightened people, and the moans and pleas of those shot and bleeding, and the labored, desperate breathing of those dying, people could be heard crawling quickly, clumsily, toward the back of the stage or toward the lobby through the door now vacated by Shooter Number Three.

On the stage itself, Burbage held Romeo and Juliet to his tall body (when did he get back there? I don't remember ...), and the three stood next to the crumpled mound of the robe of Friar Laurence. All of this tableau was in black, illuminated barely and crazily by the red glare from eight exit signs. Then emergency lights came back on, dimly, revealing figures in outline.

Belsky shot now at random, firing half a dozen shots; there were cries of pain and terror. Someone cried out, "Belsky, I can't believe you'd do this." It was County Paris, moments before Belsky shot him.

"Believe it!" came the reply. "And the next time you go to trip somebody," said Belsky, looking down to his left, "remember this. And this!" I could hear the assault rifle crunching into someone's head nearby, twice, and see a body tumbling slowly down the stairs toward the stage. Strange that I could conceive the paradox: Belsky had just killed the man who tripped him, and saved him from O'Rourke's bullet moments earlier.

"Let me go," I whispered, "I can get Belsky from here. I can practically reach him now!"

The hands on my shoulders pressed me down again, and Friar Abbot whispered, "now watch this. It's almost over. This moment, *his moment*, is coming. It's the moment we've been waiting for, for four hundred years."

By the emergency lights, it was possible to see that most of the small audience had fled. And from the high up row where Chief Justice Popham was seated, came his now too familiar voice, "Jesus Christ. He's here. How did he get out of jail?" Somebody, shoot him, he's a part of this."

And what the Chief Justice meant, what he was referring to, in the dim light and the smoke from the gunfire amid the cries of pain and terror, I could see; indeed, the robed figure on the stage had risen. And he stood now, huge and alone, facing Belsky. This was the real Friar Valerian Laurence, once again released from jail, once again facing Tommy Belsky, but this time it is not on a high school lawn, to protect a young teenage girl from the dangers of a cafeteria knife, this time, it is to protect her and her teenage lover from certain death, at the hands of a crazed killer, a spurned lover, with an automatic assault rifle, backed up by an equally crazed, equally armed, confederate.

Friar Laurence turned on the stage and gathered Romeo and Juliet in his arms, saying, "I will see you through this. You will live, and you will love. That man there and I must have our moment, and this man here will protect you and have his moment, too." And he passed them to Burbage, saying, "Keep them safe, I have work to do here." And he turned to face Belsky, now less than ten feet away, standing in the aisle looking up at Friar Laurence on the stage, who closed the distance quickly.

I sat there, seeing and hearing this and wondering where that came from, Burbage, of all people, keeping anyone safe. But Burbage said, without hesitation, "I have them. They will live."

And at that point, from the lobby door above, stage right, came Otto Schmidt's frantic voice, saying, "And I have you, you faggot son of a bitch." With a kind of sick, high-pitched tone, he added, "And you and those two punks are dead meat."

With this, Belsky turned swiftly, aiming his assault rifle at Schmidt, saying, "I told you they are mine. I told you to stay out of this. You never listen, you fucking Kraut bastard. That is the last time you disobey me," and fired two quick shots into Otto Schmidt, who was dead before he hit the floor. Leaving, still, in the door behind him, a smaller figure in outline, holding an identical assault rifle, who quickly knelt beside Schmidt and cried out, "Tommy, you killed him, you crazy son of a bitch."

This kid, Shooter Number Four, raised his automatic rifle and pointed toward Belsky and Friar Laurence. And I thought, he's going to kill both of them. And I thought, now we truly are talking tragedy, that Friar Laurence should've traveled all this way, all these centuries, to put himself in harm's way, to die in the play and to save Romeo and Juliet in our world only to be shot by another crazed teenager, this one with no name ...

But I saw standing behind the no-name high school kid a tall figure, bony and lean, with what in outline was clearly a Smith & Wesson Model 29, which, if chambered with a 44 magnum, was once the most powerful handgun in the world, in his right hand, and he stepped forward above the kneeling would-be shooter, and clocked him against the side of his head as hard as a blacksmith working an anvil. It was Ron Hoffer, who swore he would never, never in his lifetime, ever, ever, go to a Shakespeare production. Unless it featured Clint Eastwood. Which, in that very moment, it did.

Go ahead. Make my day.

Belsky then turned back to Friar Laurence, but he was too late.

Friar Laurence had moved swiftly from the stage to where Belsky stood in the center aisle, and as Belsky trained the assault rifle on him, Friar Laurence grabbed Belsky by the throat. Belsky had time for one shot into Friar Laurence's chest. The two fell together, Friar Laurence on top, plunging Romeo's knife into Belsky's heart.

This had been Romeo's knife in the play, and then taken by Juliet, and then by Friar Laurence, who died by it in the play, and now, in real life, it had become a real knife, again for Friar Laurence. But Belsky had his turn, too; in real life, the knife became a real knife, and it killed Belsky.

As they both lay dying, Belsky laughed, "I got you again, you miserable shit, it's been a long time, but I got you."

Friar Laurence replied, "It's been 400 years, but I will never forget your face, and this time, death has different meanings. For you, back to The Devil, for me, the road to redemption." And then he added, a bit uncharitably, and somewhat lacking in Christian charity, I thought, Friar Laurence added, "Die you son of a bitch. And may your soul rot in Hell."

The Abbot leaned forward from behind me, saying, "I think we can forgive him that last bit." I started to stand, but the Abbot again leaned down upon me and said ironically, sadly, "Wait. Our revels here are not ended."

Strangely, improbably, a still silence settled on the Iseman Theatre.

Over to the far side of the theater, stage right, last seat of the first row, where we had not seen her, rose Dorothy Arlow. She came around in front of the very first row, over to the very front of the center stage, where Friar Laurence lay. His breath was whistling through the hole in his chest, and he coughed blood. She leaned over him, closely, saying, "I knew it would come to this," and then, "I love you."

He said, "I love you, Dorothy."

Dorothy Arlow held his head in her lap and said, "Hush. Be quiet. I know. I want to kiss you. Again." And she did so. And then, she said, "Thy lips are warm." And kissed him. One long, lingering, last time.

I was reminded then that she was medically trained as a nurse, and Meg, also medically trained as a physician, joined her. They looked at each other, and they knew he was almost, certainly, gone. Meg had a scarf and put it in the wound to stop the blood. Each had a coat, a light one for the spring evening, and each laid her coat over Friar Laurence. There was nothing else to do; Friar Laurence was coughing blood, his breath was fading, his huge hands reached for Dorothy Arlow's hands, and they held each other.

Dorothy then quickly, softly, recited a portion from *Romeo and Juliet*, which I'm certain she had memorized only recently, and I wondered how she knew to do so. It was Juliet's speech, in Act III scene two, a portion, only a portion ...

Come, civil night,

thou sober suited matron all in black,

and learn me how to lose a winning match ...

Come night. Come, Laurence. Come, thou day in night;

Come, gentle night ... loving, black-browed night,

Give me my Laurence, and when I shall die

take him and cut him out in little stars,

and he will make the face of heaven so fine

that all the world will be in love with night

and pay no worship to the garish sun.

When she finished, there were tears in her eyes, in Meg's and mine. I was lost in the moment and startled when the Abbot stood, patted me on the shoulders, and said, "We must talk further sometime, but now I must do my work and end this tale of woe." With that, he stood up, went to the end of his row of seats to the center aisle, and walked to where Dorothy Arlow and Jo were still kneeling with Friar Laurence. And then I realized the work which remained for the Abbot.

Abbot Dominic said to Dorothy and Meg, "I must undertake the last rites for Friar Laurence before he dies, so that he may pass into death with as pure a spirit and soul as is possible. Please excuse us; this must be private. I must begin by hearing his confession, his request for forgiveness, his pledge of repentance, and then I can administer what is our final and most solemn sacrament. If you wish, even if you are not of our faith, you can help by praying for the redemption of this man's soul. He has been lost and wandering these 400 years. It is time now to bring him home."

The three of us, plus Jo's husband, joined by Romeo and Juliet and Burbage, sat in the third row and watched the Abbot at work. Others sat as well, in wonder, and the police and EMTs, now entering the Iseman, paused in respect, and we all watched as the Abbot finished the communion, placing the wafer on Friar Laurence's lips ... How had he known to bring the communion elements with him this night of nights?

And then he was gone. Friar Laurence. Gone.

The Abbot rose and returned to us, and we slowly moved up the aisle through the gathering crowd of first responders, police, news people, among the wounded and dying, and left the theater. We waited outside while the Abbot performed the last rites for two of the people inside. And then he joined us.

Surely, I thought, it would be enough that Friar Laurence had given his life to save others, particularly those whom he had harmed in another world and time. Tonight, he had sacrificed his life twice.

In the play. In the flesh. What more could one do? Surely his repentance and sacrifice would be accepted. But then, I remembered the nuns' Catholic teaching of my youth and understood and recalled that it is not the quantity of regrets which counts, but the quality of contrition, the genuineness of the prayer for forgiveness. Friar Laurence, with the Abbot's help, would have to find his own way home. Tonight, I prayed, was a good start.

Still, much out of practice over the last three decades, when I had heard the Abbot's invitation to pray for Friar Laurence's soul and redemption, I had sat then and recited The Apostles Creed, wondering, all the while, why I chose that, and not The Lord's Prayer, and why I still have to this day, perfect recollection of both. I mentioned this to the Abbot, and he looked up at me and said, "Francis, don't just recite it; think it ... perhaps believe it even."

And I asked, "What about Belsky? Does he have a chance at redemption?"

The Abbot smiled, "Everyone has a chance. I would say, though, he is last in line, behind Hitler and Hannibal Lector."

Outside, before heading home, I spoke with the officer in charge of what had been taped off now as a crime scene. In response to my questions, he said that Seamus O'Rourke and Charles Whiting had been taken directly to Yale New Haven Emergency Department, in critical condition, but with good prospects according to the EMTs. Three of the gunmen were goners, a simple matter of taking out the garbage. The fourth had a severe head injury. It could only be an improvement. Four of the audience had been killed, eight to ten had been wounded, either by bullets or flying debris, six had gone to the hospital, the rest had been bandaged up and sent home.

Just another day at the office.

I commented, this seemed to have gone swiftly from catastrophe to commonplace, a bit like the poem about, "This is the way the world ends, not with a bang but a whimper."

An officer looked at me and said, "Aren't you Francis Collins, the public defender?" I admitted as much. He said, "Well, Francis, I guess you're right." Then he paused in the red flashing lights of the squad cars, looked down at the red-stained sheets covering bodies, and then back, and added, "There has to be an end to this shit."

Meg and I said our goodnights to Dorothy, Jo and husband, Burbage, the Abbot and the actors, Romeo and Juliet, their parents, who gave special thanks to Burbage, and then we went home to our kids, thinking in this most horrific of nights there was at least this: Romeo and Juliet went with their parents this night, in New Haven, Connecticut, a long time and distance from Verona, Italy, where once they had lived and died in a story of even more woe.

CHAPTER THIRTY-ONE

EPILOGUE

BEGINNING OF A BEAUTIFUL FRIENDSHIP

We are here at New Haven Tweed International Jetport (I made the "International Jetport" part up), and it is now Saturday morning, 10:00 AM, an early summer day, a bit warmish, the lilacs and dogwoods gone, but the scent of apple blossoms is now with us in Connecticut. A day otherwise very similar to that of a few weeks ago, when I first went to the Dominican Abbey on the Green in New Haven and met the Abbot and was introduced into the strange and powerful world which he and Friar Laurence and other seekers and travelers inhabit. I have been tempted to go back several times, to see if the Abbey is still there, however, I can see that it is, or really to see if Abbot Dominic still presides, or whether as has been said by Shakespeare in other settings, this play is at its end, all of the actors disappearing.

Somehow, I feel that is possible, and I don't want to know that answer. The Chief Justice, Belsky, Edmund Coke, on and on, what has become of them? Are they still with us? And other questions abound.

Do I want to ask them? Do I want to know the answers?

In the future, will *Romeo and Juliet*, be a simple romance, a wonderfully written, beautifully orchestrated, powerfully moving romance, where even Tybalt and Mercutio do not die? And if so, what role will Friar Laurence be playing in it? Will the messenger get through, the pharmacist deliver, the Friar get there on time? I hear, faintly, music, "Get me to the church (tomb) on time ..." Or possibly, will Friar Laurence be gone altogether, having passed on, and will it be as if he never was, and will future theatergoers never know of him?

403

How sad to think that. I can feel tears begin. I came to know Friar Laurence as a 21st-century man, for whom being a hero ultimately came naturally, and streaming YouTube was his favorite because of the SNL reruns. As I say, tears. (But, of course, I am a guy, and guys don't cry.) Yet ...

Do all of these things matter or any of them? Was this just a play, or was it one of those worlds caught up with other worlds, including our own, so that real people became unreal people in real places, which become unreal? That way lies ... Shakespeare! The man who invented the play within the play ...

Some questions can be answered. Burbage did protect the kids, Romeo Montague and Juliet Capulet, guiding them through the chaos to their parents, to the end of clan warfare. There were counselors, and the two youngsters seemed marvelously free of PTSD. The play did go on, as it must, and it opened in the University Theater, the big one on the Yale campus, last night, to a standing room only crowd, thrilled by the musical intertwinings of the two young lovers. There are rumors of off-Broadway, maybe off-off, in June and July or August, and then it's back to school at Hillhouse High, SATs, and the admissions rat race.

You will notice that I am not telling whether there was a role for Friar Laurence in the play last night, although I can say that the Woody Allen avatar was present. Seamus O'Rourke, Ron Hoffer, and Charles Whiting were given standing ovations during the intermission, wrapped, bandaged and propped up for the standing O. As his lawyer, I cannot say whether Mr. Whiting will face homicide charges, but I can say, if so, his sweetheart will stand by him, as a happily married young bride and mother should.

There were other memorable characters, such as Messrs. Crutcher, Payne, and Hazel, also the archetypal Irish jailer, and Big John and his Little Elevator, and of course D. Data and Ron Hoffer and Jo ... We have all kept doing what we were doing, because of course, what else? True as well of Meg and RBG and The Chief. There are early indications of yet another child, this one with a medical name; Marie Curie? Henrietta Lacks? Jonas Salk? Judge Roderigo Lopez? (he having returned to his former life as physician to Queen Elizabeth).

Some people are gone. The Chief Justice seems to have returned to his own time, and marvelously the incumbent CJ has returned from a week-long fly-fishing trip to the Allagash Wilderness in Maine, with no memory of any of this. District Attorney Coke has suffered a stroke (truth? It doesn't rhyme. His name is pronounced "Cook." Go figure.) and similarly has no memory. A nice consequence of this is that Kathleen Chung, The Dragon Lady, has been reinstated and now replaces Coke. The Defense Bar sent her a Welcome Back and Congratulations card, saying (all 20 of us), "We only want to lose to the best." I understand she smiled on opening it.

But truly, the two people I have been saving for last, you always save the best to last, are Dorothy Arlow and Abbot Dominic. You must surely save the best until last.

And so yesterday afternoon, late, a Friday with Morrie's in the offing, two cold PBR's dripping icy sweat in my contemplation, I was accosted by Jo, as I tried, like The Shadow, to slip past, fast and low. "Not so fast, my fleet-footed liege," says she, "a call awaits from that strange otherworldly device, a cell phone, bearing by magic the words of the Abbot."

"Begone, or a pox on thee, Mistress Jo," I replied, "I am off to Sherwood Forest or Burnam Wood, or perhaps some bifurcated Green in which a medieval battle is to be waged, to wet my whistle thereon." Jo will not be so easily rebuffed, saying, "Did you hear, I said the Abbot, He Who Must Be Obeyed?"

Jo can see that I am conflicted.

And so, she continued, "You don't step on Superman's cape, you don't spit in the wind, you don't tug the mask off the Old Lone Ranger, and you don't mess around with ...," and here words almost failed her, but she struggled on, "Jim." Which may be the first name of the Abbot, who knows? She hands me the cell phone, and I feel certain, without seeing, leaps into the elevator shaft, slides down two levels hanging single-handedly on a cable, and sprints out into late Friday afternoon to the arms of her waiting husband, whose name I cannot recall.

Maybe he's Jim. I would vote for him. Or the Abbot.

Then I hear the voice of the Abbot, over the cell phone, "You know, Francis, I heard all of that, and strangely, I am not offended. Tomorrow, Saturday, at 10:30, Dorothy Arlow and her children are leaving by American Eagle, an airline, for Philadelphia. She called to ask whether I could transport her and her kids and see them off and might I arrange for others of us to be there. I said I was certain that you would agree, along with your bride and your sturdy companions, and quite possibly your children."

"One problem," say I (thinking, where? thinking it must be Bradley, near Hartford.)

"Oh that," responds the Abbot. "That would be the mighty Tweed International Jetport, delicately balanced on the boundary between New Haven and East Haven, a much fought over frontier. American

406

Eagle will transport the Arlow family, and we should rendezvous at about 10:00 AM tomorrow. I know I can count on you." Before I could say, well, yes, of course, you betcha, and the like ... It was a click. Well, metaphorically, a click. Huh. Not sure. I just checked. They don't. Cell phones don't click. You could check it out. Hang up on, say ... not your wife.

Then it was off to Morrie's, the legendary PBR's, the relaxing drive home, and the jubilant response of RBG and Earl W. to the prospect of going to a major American jetport, to see off that wonderful lady with her children. And then to bed, to celebrate. To get started on the next two or so. Whatever. Everything.

And so, as I say, it is 10:00 AM at the New Haven Airport's pathetic flight lounge, virtually empty as always, and off in a private corner, Dorothy Arlow gathers with her children and what she now describes as "a very close circle of very close friends." Meg and Jo and the Abbot and Jo's husband, a random assortment of relevant kids, Ron, and D. Data, (no doughnuts at this moment. Really?), are all here. Dorothy Arlow says, "Thank you all for coming. In a way, you will all be a part of this trip, which Abbot Dominic has made possible." And with that, she turns and gives him a hug.

As I am thinking, Philadelphia? Dorothy continues, "We will connect through Philadelphia to Rome and then to Verona. The Abbot has arranged transportation and a ceremony there. It seems they have found an ancient headstone in the Dominican cemetery there, one with no name on it, from around 1564, and have restored it. Friar Laurence's name will be entered on it, and it awaits him."

And I wonder, because my mind is always chasing irrelevancies, will the dates on the headstone read, "b.1564 d.2019?" Well ...

Abbot Dominic then explained, "We have already placed the ashes of Friar Laurence on this plane. When members of our Order die in faraway places we bring them home accompanied by loved ones. Friar Laurence will be accompanied by Dorothy Arlow and her children. We feel fortunate that Dorothy will perform this role. By such means, we maintain the continuity of our Order over centuries.

And here, Dorothy Arlow spoke to say, "I am the one who is most fortunate. Through those of you who are here, I came to know and love Friar Valerian Laurence." She paused and said, her voice quavering, "We had so little time." Here she started to cry, and Meg and Jo went to her. She continued, "And yet we had centuries. I could not have known this love would come with all of you, that we would find it together. I thank each of you and will carry you to Verona in my heart."

Then Dorothy Arlow continued, "I have a particular indebtedness to Abbot Dominic and Francis Collins." Then, turning to us, she said, "I wonder if the two of you would walk my children and me to that stair ramp they have just moved to that plane?"

I am thinking, and I start to say, that they will never allow us onto the tarmac without tickets, but I look at Abbot Dominic, and even before his eyebrows bounce, I know he is about to say, "Patience, Francis." And I reach into my jacket pocket and find a ticket and boarding pass.

And so, we do. We show our boarding passes at the gate, and then down the stairs to the tarmac, and across to the plane, the Abbot on one side, and I on the other, Dorothy Arlow in the middle, a child in each of our hands and the kids mount the steps to the plane door, carrying heavily laden backpacks. We each give Dorothy Arlow a hug, she kisses each of us on the cheek, mounts the stairs, and we wait for her to appear at a window and wave, and we wave back …

The old-style turboprop engines begin to rev, the exhaust begins to blow back, and we slowly move back toward the airport terminal. The plane begins to turn into position and then moves ponderously down the strip as the late morning fog rolls in across Long Island Sound. Closer to the building, we turn and watch the plane taxi down one of New Haven's two, less than major league, runways, over the encroaching neighborhood of mixed residences and light industry.

As we are standing, I say to the Abbot, "Why, really, did Friar Laurence come here, to this town in this time? And what about all of those other people?

Abbot Dominic looked at me and said, "Francis, you are bright, perhaps brilliant, but sometimes you cannot see the forest for the trees. There were two reasons.

"One was quite simply that it was time. Friar Laurence had done enough penance. Four centuries of wandering and pain, that was the judgment entered. The force which imposed that judgment 400 years ago deemed it was now time to make atonement and redemption possible and simply looked for a proper opportunity. This was it. Friar Laurence would have his chance. That is all any of us ever have.

"Laurence succeeded, giving up his life for others, twice: once in the revised play, with Romeo's knife, to save Juliet, and then again, giving up his life to save both children and, in a way, Burbage as well, from Belsky's attack in the real world, our world."

The Abbot is smiling. The plane has taxied back up the runway heading for takeoff, the Long Island early morning fog lies low across the runway. On that plane, Dorothy Arlow and Friar Laurence, and three young children from New Haven, Connecticut, are on their way to Italy and an ancient abbey in Verona.

"Well, don't leave me guessing," I say, "what is the second reason that drew Friar Laurence?"

And here, Abbot Dominic said, "Because it was here that Burbage was about to undo the trap Marlowe set for Friar Laurence. Surely you know. Marlowe, in the form of Belsky, came to prevent Burbage from changing the play and releasing Friar Laurence. Friar Laurence came for the play, to make it happen, Belsky and Coke and Popham came to prevent it. So, in a way, they all came because of Burbage. It was Burbage's time fully as much as it was Friar Laurence's. Remember it was Burbage who stood by and did nothing all those centuries ago in the pub in Deptford and now it was time for him to stop Marlowe. Here. This time."

It was as if scales had fallen from my eyes, and I could see now clearly who Belsky was. For as Friar Laurence had said, there is only one known likeness of Christopher Marlowe, and as indistinct as it is, I could suddenly see in it the visage of Belsky: slight, arrogant, foppish, evil, brilliant, dying at age 29, the age Christopher Marlowe was when he died, when he entrapped Friar Laurence, in that pub outside London, in Deptford, all those long years ago.

So, Friar Laurence not only sought redemption, he fought against an ancient adversary for release from an evil trap set 400 years ago. I could see all of this, but one piece was missing. "Why me? As a lawyer, I contributed very little. Some will think this title, SAVING FRIAR LAURENCE, is a bit of a cheat.

"Ah, Francis," said the Abbot, "your modesty is exceeded only by Burbage's ego. And that is appropriate. You two were the yin and the yang of this," and here he paused to chuckle a bit, "perhaps I should rather say the Alpha and Omega. Marlowe as Belsky and Friar Laurence came because of Burbage, but Burbage was changing the play because of you."

Here I am truly baffled and said, "Burbage hated me. He drove me out of the Drama School. I mocked Burbage, disliked him when I was a student, disliked him since. I have ridiculed him."

"Yes," Friar Dominic responded, "but why did you dislike him? He was harmless, chased after young male grad students, never chased after you; what was it about him that so upset you? What did you do to upset him?"

And I stood there looking down at this wise old man, in his robes, with his crisp, clear glasses, fringe of hair, and it slowly came back to me. "You must be referring to my thesis proposal, the one that was rejected, blocking me from getting a doctorate and forcing me to leave the Drama School. Yes?"

"Yes," said Abbot Dominic, "because Burbage resented you. He ridiculed you. He had your proposal rejected without anyone— including him—ever reading it.

"And you both put it all behind you. Until over the years, he slowly found his way back to your proposal, sitting on a shelf all these years, which he finally read a few years ago." Abbot Dominic paused and said, "Now, Francis, tell me, what were you going to write about in that doctoral dissertation if you had been accepted?"

I turned, and the pain of that rejection, the ridicule and the humiliation, all of it came back, and while I am a guy, and guys don't cry, especially with family and friends inside the terminal watching our conversation, I started to cry because what I had written 20 or 25 years ago is what brought Burbage to produce his play, and that was what brought Marlowe (as Belsky) and Friar Laurence to New Haven in the year 2019.

My doctoral thesis proposal was entitled, ROMEO AND JULIET; A ROMANCE BEYOND DEATH." And it proposed removing the tragic elements from the play, not exactly as Burbage had done, certainly not with the insight and the experience and professionalism Burbage with all of his years could bring, but still that proposal led to Burbage's walk-through five weeks ago, and the play performed last night and that play brought Marlowe and Friar Laurence to New Haven, where Dorothy Arlow embraced her love and was now flying with him to Verona to say goodbye.

"And so," Abbot Dominic said, "in a way, you are the reason Friar Laurence came to New Haven, to do penance and seek forgiveness and embrace death." Abbot Dominic paused, and with utter gravity and seriousness, said, "I hold you in the utmost respect and awe, Francis, you have surely done God's work, Saving Friar Laurence."

We turned to walk back toward the building. But before we could enter the building, I said to Abbot Dominic, "I have many questions, but one that has puzzled me since I first met Friar Laurence and learned he was a Dominican is this, was Friar Laurence really a Dominican monk? Most Shakespeare commentators have thought he was Franciscan. There are at least four points in the play where Friar Laurence seems to appeal to or invoke the name of St. Francis.

The Abbot laughed and said, "Oh, you mean, why did he pray to St. Francis? Good question, amazing that in all these centuries, no one has asked, and I have been waiting to give the answer, as all good Dominicans and Franciscans would.

"Here it is. Dominic and Francis, not you, but the one who became a saint, although there may be hope for you yet, were colleagues in

412

Italy in the early 1200s, living not far apart, with similar educations, called to the ministry of the poor, insisting that all of the members themselves practice poverty, be mendicants. There was one difference. Francis had a monumental ego, and he wanted to be a saint; he wanted to be prayed to.

"We Dominicans follow a more modest role model, our Dominic never wanted to be prayed to; he thought we should only pray to God, and he knew the difference. Oh yes, oh my; he knew the difference.

"But Dominic thought it would be just fine if we pray to Francis. He needs it; I don't," he said. "God will chalk it up as part of our Good Works." And then he laughed ... "We get good guy points when we thank St. Francis for our good works."

"And now, a more serious question," I turned and said to the Abbot, "what is next for you? Friar Laurence is gone, so are a number of the other figures in this story; are you staying?" For the first time ever, I think, I surprised the Abbot.

He said, "Oh my, yes. Our Order has had a presence on the New Haven Green since the late 1600s, just look at the Grove Street Cemetery, and our function is what you have come to understand. There are seekers in this world, travelers, lost souls, and they must be helped, and we must do it. How could I possibly leave such a responsibility and privilege? No, Francis, I am here to stay."

And with that, he turned to me and said, "Let me ask you the same question? Your service to the poor, seeking justice, will you stay with that? Could you leave it? When we have seekers or lost souls, can we look to you, as we did with Friar Laurence, for assistance?"

"Oh, my yes," I quoted back to the Abbot, "what I do is a calling and privilege, and it could only be more, to share it with you. And I hope it includes the world Shakespeare created, so we can round up the usual suspects, and this can be the beginning of a beautiful friendship."

As we walked back toward the terminal, waving to our friends awaiting us there, the Abbot said, "Under the heading of usual suspects, we have recently had an elderly, Christian gentlemen come to us; he has now been staying with us for several weeks, greatly troubled by his treatment in the criminal courts of another state. He prosecuted a man for commercial fraud and then was deceived by a court official into giving up his property, and lost his daughter and home to a ne'er-do-well, leaving him destitute. At the very end, under duress, the judge compelled him to convert to Christianity.

"Shall I send him over to see you?"

"Of course," I replied. "What is his name, and what was his religion before becoming a Christian?"

"He was, and I suppose, still is," the Abbot replied, "A Jew ... I forgot his last name, the first is Isaiah or maybe Ishmael."

"Oh," I said, "One other thing." And here I leaned in and asked "What is your first name: I should know that."

The Abbot looked up and smiled and said, "It's James, James Dominic."

"May I call you Jim?

ACKNOWLEDGMENTS

Predictably, I owe a considerable debt to a number of people, partly because of the length of my career but more because of the breadth of *Saving Friar Laurence*. The book embraces several disciplines, both in practice and academic terms, as well as several centuries, ranging from Shakespeare's time to our present day. It was and is an ambitious undertaking.

As a debut work of fiction, the process was daunting and the prospect intimidating. I have received heartening encouragement and useful criticism from a number of sources. My wife, Margaret, provided great support, useful commentary, and tolerance for my frustrations and persistence. I may say the same for my sister and brother, Judith Isquith and Edward LaFrance, both teachers and readers of my drafts, with useful, sometimes acerbic, comments. A continuing and encouraging source of insights and support and comparative review has been my writing group here in the Portland area, consisting of dedicated role models in writing and persistence, particularly our talented and mighty leader, Suzanne Jelineo.

I particularly want to thank two fine editors, Carol Claton and Vera Haddan, for their proofing, editorial and marketing wizardry. They were helpmates who became friends.

Last but not least, I have been the fortunate beneficiary of two fine teachers. John Finch taught me Shakespeare and theater at Dartmouth College. Years later, looking back over my career as a student, I had occasion to write him and thank him and to say that he was the best teacher in my long career of being a student, never anticipating that I would be at the point now of attempting a novel based on Shakespeare. Similar praise goes to Jay Kobler, Shakespeare performer and longtime instructor at the Kent School, with whom I have taken multiple courses on Shakespeare's plays and from whom I have borrowed the techniques for my own teaching. As to that, I wish to acknowledge the encouragement and support of my Shakespeare students over the past years.

AUTHOR'S BIOGRAPHICAL NOTE

Saving Friar Laurence is Arthur LaFrance's sixth book, but his first novel. His other writings are part of an academic career teaching law school in Arizona, Maine, and Oregon, embracing criminal law, poverty, civil rights, healthcare, and bioethics. Throughout his career, he has stud-  ied and taught Shakespeare, which provides the context and content for *Saving Friar Laurence*, which proceeds equally through the personalities and processes of the criminal courts and the Yale Drama theater in New Haven, Connecticut in the 21st century.

LaFrance won writing awards at Dartmouth College and Yale Law School and pursued a barely noticed theater career in the former and a prize-winning forensics performance at the latter. He then became an associate with a corporate law firm that encouraged their young attorneys to do pro bono work, LaFrance's practice passion ever since. He has argued for indigent clients in the Supreme Courts and Courts of Appeal of the United States, Pennsylvania, Connecticut, and Hawaii and represented hundreds of criminal defendants in trial courts of several states, chiefly in Connecticut, the setting for *Saving Friar Laurence*.

LaFrance, over the years, has pursued a number of interests—tennis, cycling, and painting. His interest in theater remains chiefly Shakespeare, and he has hundreds of books relating to the man, the place, the theater, and times. He finds particularly intriguing the unfinished characters, such as Friar Laurence. LaFrance is at work on a book concerning Shylock and has begun thinking of a third, possibly concerning Caliban and Ariel or Falstaff.

LaFrance lives in Portland, Oregon, with his wife Margaret. He reads weekly with his granddaughter, Avalon, meeting on Zoom. LaFrance, his wife, and constant companion, Scruffy, travel to see their children and grandchildren on both coasts.

Arthur Birmingham LaFrance

Made in the USA
Monee, IL
07 November 2021

81385321R00256